THE BACK OF THE BEYOND

THE BACK
OF
THE BEYOND

JAMES STODDARD

Ransom Books

Visit www.james-stoddard.com to learn more about the author.

To contact James Stoddard email evenmere@gmail.com

Cover illustration and design by Bryan Burke and Scott Faris www.fariswheel.com

Edited by Betsy Mitchell www.betsymitchelleditorial.com

A Ransom Book
Printed in the United States of America.

First Printing: January 2020

10 9 8 7 6 5 4 3 2 1

FAERIE

ANIMONEA

MORLANE

RUHEEN

Westwall

Dusk River

Meadowlark Road

Great Bend

Derisole

DUNSELL WYNECK

Brythibain

IN MEMORY OF MY MOTHER

WHO ENCOURAGED ME TO DREAM

AUTHOR'S NOTE

The memories Russell Rogers recalls of ranching and World War II are those of my father, E. E. (Ted) Stoddard. Like the children of many veterans, I heard these stories in bits and pieces as my dad chose to tell them, so any factual errors can be attributed to my memory of his recounted recollections. Nonetheless, they are authentic in every detail I can remember. Despite the similarities of their pasts, however, the fictional character is not intended to be a portrayal of my father.

* * *

In recording the speech of the objects and non-human creatures of the Back of the Beyond, I italicize their words when they say only a phrase or two, as in, for example, a bird speaking as it passes overhead. Where their dialogue is more involved, I do not italicize. This may appear somewhat arbitrary to the reader but was done with careful intent for clarity.

* * *

Notes on Pronunciation

Animonea is pronounced: Ah'·nah·mo·nee·uh

The ê in Malimenê is pronounced *eh* and rhymes with *hey*. Mal·uh·men·eh.

Joiwend's horse, Maravilla, is Spanish for Marigold. The double L's can be pronounced as *yah*: Mah·rah·vee·yah. So too is Ninette Argilla's last name: Ar·hey·yah, the *g* being pronounced as an *h*.

The J in Joiwend has a French pronunciation: Zhoy·wind

The final *i* is pronounced in Vigili: Vij·uh·lahy, rhyming with *verify*.

All the elm-trees sought to wound me,
All the aspens tried to cut me,
All the willows tried to seize me,
All the forest tried to slay me.
                                              —*The Kalevala*

. . . the leaves rustled in the woods ever so mournful; and I heard
an owl, away off, who-whooing about somebody that was dead,
and a whippoorwill and a dog crying about somebody that was going to die; and the wind was trying to whisper something to me,
and I couldn't make out what it was . . . —*Huckleberry Finn*

CHAPTER ONE

THE BORDER

They rode, nine humans and an elf, down a winding path, leaving the last rows of indigo trees behind, the soft shimmering music of the vibrating leaves growing ever fainter as horses and riders descended from the Debatable Hills into a barren, shadow-steeped valley. The strange, brilliant constellations of Faerie pulsed red, blue, and gold overhead, casting a faint glow below; the moon had not yet risen. All lay silent save for the horses' hooves on the harsh stones and the distant cries of wyverns hunting through the night.

They were finally leaving Faerie, preparing to cross the border into the Back of the Beyond. The Faerie folk claimed that none might go thither without losing their lives. The travelers hoped they were wrong.

Gray Darien, Prince of the Stallion Lords, rode at the front of the company alongside Koothlin of the Light Elves, who had been their guide throughout their journey. They traveled slowly, exhausted from their combat an hour past, giving encouraging pats to the necks of their weary horses. Dried blood darkened Koothlin's left shoulder, and Gray reached a hand across his saddle to steady the elf. "We should stop to tend your wounds."

"Not yet, lad," Koothlin replied. "Duskell Watch lies ahead, and we dare not rest till we bolt its oaken gates behind us. The manticore gave bitter battle; more than once I thought my life ended. I have no wish to meet its brothers in this broken vale." He took a labored breath. "Ah, Prince, I have been happier!"

"Is the pain worse?"

"The wounds are nothing. But the wounds of the heart pierce deep. I know I promised to bring you to this dread place. I do not regret the struggles fought to win it—the marsh-wolves, the handrigites, the goblins, not even the manticore—enough to glut any warrior's appetite for battle. But I rue leaving you to travel to the Back of the Beyond without me. Ill done are companions parted. Are you still determined? You and I could have much glory in the courts of the Elf King. You would be welcomed there."

"I won't quit until I find Tanabel-Tunia," Gray said. "I know she's alive; I've seen her in my dreams."

Koothlin sighed. "Who can deny the dreams of a dreamer in Faerie? But will they bring you joy in the end? I hope, Prince of Stallions, you have not dreamt yourself a night mare." The elf gave a barking laugh, then groaned in pain. "'Twas a droll turn of phrase, think you?"

"It was," Gray replied gently, knowing his companion feverish; and also knowing that—despite his protests of grief—Koothlin would not mourn their parting overmuch. The emotions of elves are mercurial; sorrow cannot abide in their hearts for long.

Gray looked around at his companions, dim shapes in the starlight. They traveled in a defensive formation, Master Tatters scouting before them, Fox Lodan and Ninette Argilla flanking either side, Soonderkainen, Joiwend, and Jaunter directly behind Gray; Russ Rogers and Corporal Spence bringing up the rear. Together they had tracked Tanabel-Tunia's abductors across the realms of Faerie. They were told she and three men were sighted in a nearby village eight days before, and later seen crossing the Westwall into the Back of the Beyond.

When Gray and Tanabel-Tunia were sixteen years old, they had sat together in the palace gardens of Gray's father. Seen from a distance, the lights of Faerie were especially beautiful that twilit eve. As beautiful as Tana herself.

They thumb-wrestled for a buttercup, their eyes locked. Hers were brown. Her brunette hair was long and straight, her nose, besprinkled with freckles. She nearly had him pinned when he slipped beneath her grasp and caught her thumb in an irresistible grip.

He grinned. "The buttercup is mine."

She feigned a pout. "I wanted it!"

He plucked it and handed it to her. "Then my lady shall have it."

"Thank you, my prince."

She drew a petal from the flower and held it against the horizon. "It's the same yellow as the Faerie torches."

He took his eyes off her. The border of Faerie lay several leagues to the west. Over that magic kingdom the fading glow of the sun always cast bands of yellow, green, and purple, shot-through with sparkling, golden lights.

"I'd like to go there someday," Gray said.

"I wouldn't. It's too dangerous. Those who go in don't come back."

"Some have. Our merchants even conduct trade there."

"They throw their goods over the border and come running home." She crossed her arms over her chest. "What if I met the Elf King? The ruler of Faerie since the beginning of time! He'd turn me into a cat or toad."

"I would protect you." He glanced over his shoulder. For the first time since Tana arrived, Gray's ever-present Greek tutor, Aristides, was nowhere in sight. Moving casually, he put his arm around her shoulders.

She leaned closer, her gaze still on the horizon. "I'm sorry tomorrow is my last day."

A pang ran through his chest. "Do you have to go back? It's only been a month. Surely uncle would let you stay longer if you asked."

"There's a jest! My wishes mean nothing to him. I'd stay all summer if I could. Anything to get out of Mare Castle. No one cares what happens to me there, certainly not my foster father. It's better here, where everyone is kind. I remember the first time I came. How old were we? Ten?"

"Twelve," Gray said. "We were riding and you fell off your horse."

She put her hand to her lips. "Oh, I did! I wish you hadn't remembered that."

"It wasn't your fault. A fox startled the mare." He furrowed his brow. "Why didn't we ever meet before then?"

She frowned, her downturned mouth winsome. "I think there

was some sort of disagreement between the brothers, some feud that lasted for years."

"My father and uncle have always been bullheaded." With his other hand he reached over and took hers. "I'm determined not to inherit the trait."

She turned to him. "In you it is a restlessness. You're seldom still, or even if you are, your mind is always working."

"My brothers call me Stargazer. They mock me for a dreamer."

"They're wrong, Gray. You must never lose that restlessness. It's one of your strengths." She smiled. "Perhaps I *would* go to Faerie, if you promised to be my champion."

"I would try, my lady." Their faces drew closer together.

She parted her lips. "Would you protect me, Gray? If I needed you to?"

"I would, I swear."

They kissed, her lips warm and sweet, her hair fragrant as roses. It was a dream come true, one he had imagined every night since her arrival.

A voice sounded somewhere behind them. Instantly, they parted, their eyes snapping to the horizon, their arms by their sides. Aristides was back. A prince and a duchess were seldom far from a chaperon. But that was the night Gray fell in love with Tanabel-Tunia.

Gray's horse momentarily stumbled, shaking him from his recollections. Prince Fox Lodan, Tanabel-Tunia's betrothed, rode in closer, his red hair the color of blood beneath the starlight. "We're nearly to the border. If Koothlin leads us aright and more manticores don't find us, we should reach the fortress soon."

Gray's voice thickened in rancor. "How would *you* know? You haven't been here before."

"Because I'm not an inexperienced whelp who can't read the signs," Prince Lodan said. "I swear, boy, your ignorance astounds me. You speak like an untutored commoner."

"Unlike you, I speak when I have something of substance to say."

Prince Lodan spat on the ground. "So says our baby-leader." He had been calling Gray that throughout their four-week journey.

"Fox is right; we are close," Jaunter said. With his face shadowed beneath the flaps of his tall, felt cap, the Scythian looked monstrous in the starlight, his hair tumbling wildly down his Eurasian features, his jaw out-thrust like a battering ram, his shoulders wide as those of a bull; but he appeared the most terrifying when the starlight caught his deep-set eyes, sleepy yet perilously cunning above the blue horizontal bars tattooed across his left cheek.

The bard-enchanter, Soonderkainen, trotted to Jaunter's side, his jagged cloak belling behind him, his smooth, handsome face a stark contrast to the Scythian's craggy mien. He brushed aside a golden lock. "But how *do* you know? There's been no sign. Even Koothlin recognizes the way only by description."

Without replying, Fox Lodan rode haughtily back to his position, but Jaunter grinned at the enchanter, revealing the gap left by a missing front tooth. "You should conjure up a better nose. Can't you smell it? There are trees and tall grass ahead."

"I'm a bard, not a hunting hound," Soonderkainen said. "And why are you so happy? Are you actually looking forward to this?"

"It will be a new and glorious adventure. They'll sing songs about it."

"Perhaps they will; perhaps they won't," the bard-enchanter murmured. "Perhaps we'll never be heard from again."

"*Tagimasad!*" Jaunter exclaimed in his native tongue. "I'll not have it. There are no better warriors in any land. If we can't find the girl, no one can."

Soonderkainen said nothing; and despite his irritation at Fox, Gray thought with pride that Jaunter was right. Because Gray's small country—the kingdom of En, the land of the Stallion Lords—bordered Faerie, its people were familiar with the peculiar precepts of that enchanted realm. When the trail of Tanabel-Tunia's kidnappers led into the domains of the Elf King, Gray's father had not dared dispatch ordinary soldiers to follow her. Under the direction of Koothlin, the Elf Who Guides, seven ravens were sent into Faerie, seven birds to find seven heroes. Fox Lodan made the eighth member of the company; Gray, the ninth.

Gray's father had not wanted to send him, but in Faerie only the third son of a king can successfully lead in a quest, all others being doomed to failure. It had irked Gray's older brothers, both better warriors than he; and Fox—oldest son of the ruler of the Faerie kingdom of Jenar—despised him for it, but that was the way of it.

So, having seen but seventeen summers, Gray became leader of this company of his elders. Often he felt a child among them, and had to remind himself he was a prince, especially beneath Fox Lodan's taunts.

Born several years after his siblings, Gray had learned early that he could never compete with those bigger and stronger than he. When faced with confrontation as a child, his natural response had been to run away. Only under Aristides' tutelage had he learned to fight both physically and verbally for himself. As a result, he was an excellent archer and a passable swordsman. But most of all he loved heroic songs and tales of adventuring knights and fair maidens. Apart from his concern for Tana, he had always longed to set out on a real quest. And because her trail had led into Faerie, where mortals often find themselves lost in Story, he had truly become the Questing Hero, his thoughts bent on courage, poetry, and his unceasing love for Tanabel-Tunia.

Seven days after the sending of the ravens, Gray had ridden to the misty borders of Faerie to meet his comrades, allowed to enter that country only because its laws decreed that a quest cannot be hindered. For a month he had journeyed with them, pretending to command, but mostly accepting their counsel. Following Tana's trail had proven easy enough; in Faerie there was always a witch or wise woman, a messenger bird or beast to guide them. They had fought terrible battles, often succeeding against tremendous odds. Gray had learned much from his journey and would never be the same when he returned to his father's mortal kingdom.

Joiwend rode up beside him. Even exhausted as she was, starlight became her dark hair and dark eyes. Born and raised on Earth, of French and Spanish heritage, she still retained a hint of an accent. She spoke so softly only he could hear. "You should quit quarreling with Fox. He's a dangerous man."

"I can be dangerous too, and I'm sick of his bullying."

"*You* do not possess an enchanted sword that makes you invulnerable in combat."

His anger rose, but wilted beneath her earnest presence. He gave a crooked smile. "You're right. As always."

"Only because I've seen his kind before. Don't push him too far."

They passed through a series of scattered standing stones tall as men, and Duskell Watch, the border fortress, suddenly lay before them, squat and black in the shadowed vale. A stone wall thirty spans high snaked away to either side of it, the Westwall separating Faerie from the Back of the Beyond. A single sentry called down from the low parapet, a shade silhouetted against the stars, eyes glowing like cats' orbs. "Stand fast! Who comes?"

"A servant of the day and of the High King of Faerie!" Koothlin called. "Who would you expect in this ghastly murk?"

"Monsters to match the murkiness," the sentry replied. "Or murk-men, at least." He drew a sword of blinding radiance, and though Gray blinked beneath its gleam, Koothlin looked with unshielded eyes.

"Oh, I do love this!" the sentry exclaimed. "To see a brave elf lad guiding such a company, riding where no sojourners ever come."

"But I am no lad," Koothlin replied.

"Because you have not lived so many summers as I, I say you are."

"But in Faerie it is always summer; there is but one," Koothlin said. "And so by summers I count us the same age—each one summer old."

The sentry laughed. "Then we are both babes! So one nursling hails another. But let us say I have seen more of summer than you and be done. Tonight we will dine together and speak of that endless summer—the flowers we picked, the maidens we wooed, the beasts we slew on fiery heaths."

Koothlin shuddered and slipped sideways on the saddle.

"What fool am I!" the sentry cried. "I prattle, not seeing you wounded. A moment, and I'll be at the gate."

As the elf vanished from the parapet, Koothlin, leaning on his horse's neck, said softly, "No hurry, plenty of time, no haste. We'll dine on summer pies and dreams, sip hours brewed to elven taste."

So saying, before Gray could catch him, he gave a toneless chuckle and tumbled to the ground.

* * *

Though Gray Darien agonized over every hour not spent seeking Tanabel-Tunia, the companions were forced to remain two days at

Duskell Watch to recover their strength and rest their horses. On the final evening the elves prepared a dinner of roast chimera served to the travelers at a table built around a fire-pit on the rampart overlooking the Back of the Beyond. Unlike the barren valley they had ridden through to reach the fortress, a wood stretched across the vale below them, crowding against the high wall, a forest bedecked more brightly than any troop of soldiers, with flowers for medals and broad leaves for braids, brigade upon brigade of briars and blossoms and brown-barked boles storming the walls with the creeping charge of slow tendrils and roots, patient with the sure knowledge of coming victory, as all wild things are against civilized construction.

Still weak from his wounds, Koothlin the elf sat wrapped in a white robe on a wicker chair. Malimenê, the sentry of the first night, one of six occupants of the citadel, reclined on a stone bench beside him, basking in the rays of the setting sun. As they finished their meal the orb dipped below the treeline; the first stars came out. A cheery flame blazed in the fire-pit, warming the travelers' feet.

"You should convince your friends," Malimenê said, stroking his chin and continuing his conversation with Koothlin, "or call yourself no friend at all."

"I brought them this far as promised," Koothlin replied. "Who am I to dissuade any adventurer from the path of the True Quest? Yet, I have tried. Perhaps Gray might listen to you. You have a way of foreboding about you that could frighten him well enough."

"And you a way of annoying," Malimenê said with a grin. "Had I not a way of forbearing, I'd send you on your forlorn way."

"I consider myself forewarned," Koothlin said, "and thus forestall my fate, for—"

"We didn't come this far to turn back," Gray interrupted, knowing elves could play with words until all thread of meaning was lost. "We've been through too much."

Without warning, Jaunter slammed his fist against the wooden table, causing everyone except the elves to flinch. The Scythian grinned broadly and raised his arms expansively to include the entire company. "Enough of such talk! A feast, that's what this should be!" He lifted a pewter cup, revealing the ram tattoo on his forearm. "A feast to the dangers we've come through to reach this stronghold."

"For you, everything is a reason to celebrate," Fox Lodan said grimly, looking down his aquiline nose. His red hair, cut to his shoulders, flamed in the firelight, heightening the prince's glistening blue eyes and feral features. He was tall, not as broad-shouldered as some, but well-muscled. "You should take a lesson from our glum baby-leader. The boy sulks better than a caged kitten."

Seated beside Gray, Joiwend gave his elbow a warning touch. He bit back an acrid reply.

Jaunter laughed. "You'll be the same as I am when you've seen enough years on the road. An old campaigner takes what he can when he can. Not like you young bulls."

Gray Darien couldn't help but smile. Jaunter's enthusiasm was contagious. "You're not that old."

"Thirty-six next month, near as I know," Jaunter said. "On the steppes, that's ancient. Surviving another day is a cause for rejoicing."

Joiwend laughed, her voice pleasantly low for a woman's. "Only you would find a reason to celebrate reaching the Back of the Beyond."

"I have never understood mortals' longing for peril when their lives are so short," Malimenê said.

"None of that," Jaunter commanded. "I'll not have it."

Russ Rogers pushed his black-framed spectacles against the bridge of his nose. "I've had enough of fighting, myself. I'd welcome a little peace."

"I'll second that one and shake your hand, Sarge." Corporal Spence stuffed a piece of cabbage into his mouth, leaving a scrap on his cheek. Beneath the brim of his American army helmet, his shrewd eyes flickered in the firelight. Only Soonderkainen, Ninette Argilla, and Fox Lodan were natives of Faerie. The rest had been born on Earth, though not all in the same century, and had stumbled into Faerie by various means.

"If you want peace, better you should remain here when your companions depart," Koothlin said.

"I've lived with the screwball Faerie laws for six months, and that's long enough," Russ said. "I aim to see what's out there."

"Me too, Sarge," Corporal Spence said.

"Less talk, more wine!" Jaunter called.

"None of us will turn back," Master Tatters said.

"Why not?" Malimenê asked.

"Because what drove us here must drive us on."

"And what might that be?" Malimenê replied.

"For me the moon, I reckon," Tatters said. "Her dark eyes, her dark brow. She leads me."

"Don't pay any attention to him," Spence said. "He's nuts some-times."

"Enough of that, Corporal," Russ ordered.

"Sorry, Sarge, but you know it's true."

Malimenê rose and looked deep into Master Tatters' ever-wandering eyes. Tanned to a nut-brown, barrel-chested and still powerful despite being easily past fifty, his disheveled hair and constantly moving hands gave him the appearance of a lunatic. He shrugged his shoulders, sending his frayed cloak flapping.

"You are moonstruck, 'tis true," Malimenê said. "I see it within you, yet you have wandered far and learned much." The elf gave a low bow. "The peace of my people upon you, my lord."

Master Tatters gazed at him blankly.

"Tatters, blessed by an elf?" Jaunter bellowed. "Wonders above and below the earth! This is a high day! I'll drink to that!"

Corporal Spence raised his goblet. "I'll drink to anything."

"You'd drink poison if it were poured in a stein," Soonderkainen said.

"That's hard, sir," Spence said, glowering. He tugged at his army helmet with both hands, as if to climb inside it.

Gray Darien looked at the bard-enchanter in surprise. Though Spence clearly disliked the gibe, such barbs from one given little to mirth meant Soonderkainen was actually enjoying himself. Gray looked around the table, studying the others. Save perhaps for Ninette Argilla, they were all elated to be here. Despite his anxiety about their search being delayed these two days, even he felt cheerful, for in the morning they would be on their way to find Tana. Turning to Joiwend, he gestured toward the waiting forest, murmuring, "It's strange, isn't it, being happy when we don't know what we'll face out there?"

"Today is the day we live in," Joiwend said, brushing a dark curl from her brown eyes. "It's enough that we're leaving Faerie." She was a voluptuous woman, fifty years old, though the powers given her by her magic ring kept her body closer to thirty. She had confided the source of her vitality and her true age to Gray alone, the world being filled with those willing to steal or kill to preserve their youth. "For all of us to have lived through so many hardships to reach Duskell Watch—we know the dangers we leave behind. That's reason enough to rejoice. You especially are one step closer to what you most desire."

He blushed, afraid she would say more and the others hear, but she winked and gave his shoulder a reassuring squeeze. He turned his attention to the company and found Fox Lodan addressing Malimenê. "Since we won't be turning back, tell us what to expect. You've watched the Back of the Beyond, but said little concerning it."

"I would rather not, but will for friendship's sake," Malimenê said. "Let me begin by saying that because Faerie lies on the border of mortal lands, a human may sometimes catch a glimpse of its glory: the luster of magic on the hills, a passing flowered scent, a memory from the days of childhood. When mortals see this, they stand awestruck, for we dwell in a reality deeper than their own. Their world is but a shadow compared to ours."

"A passing shade," Koothlin added. "A raindrop falling on Faerie's unceasing stream. We are more real than those enslaved to Time, who die like grass fresh-cut in the field, withering in a moment, soon to the flames."

"Poor tinder, indeed," Malimenê said. "The winking of fireflies, scarce stoking the eternal fires. But Duskell Watch lies deeper within Faerie than any mortal can discern, though poets sometimes journey here in their slumbers, half-mad, never dreaming where they walk, but only walking where they dream. When Faerie first was, the Elf King himself passed through this valley into the Back of the Beyond and returned with a face pale as frightened spooks. He raised fortresses along the western border and forbade our people entrance into that country.

"So we know little, but I have watched and listened, and oft-whiles cunning creatures creep from that forest, rapping upon the door, inviting themselves to dine. I host them in the small gate-house on their side of the wall. I suspect I have entertained mon-sters and saints, and which take one lump in their tea, and which two, I could not say. But this I believe, that even as mortals are less than shades to us, so are we to those beyond the boundary. It is closer to reality; its inhabitants are filled with forces of life greater than our own, and we are hand-puppets, dangling limp by our necks in comparison."

"I little knew when I called you foreboding," Koothlin said. "This talk is too fierce. I will not dwell upon it."

"I am ruined by that country." Malimenê looked grim and drawn in the growing twilight, his eyes dead orbs. His voice quavered as he spoke, so Gray knew his jesting had been bravado. "Sometimes from the ramparts I catch a glimpse—oh but a flash!—and I know how mortals feel dreaming of Paradise. And I, an elf of Faerie, who know not time, nor age, nor insufficiency, am filled with such long-ings as can scarce be borne. And someday I fear I will descend the stone steps leading into the forest and open the little wooden gate at the back of Duskell Watch and run capering against the edict of my king into that land. It fills me with dread, for once I have tasted the fruit of that country, the wine of Faerie may parch my throat. I tell you, did the Elf King's law not prevent me from interfering in a quest, I would deny you passage."

He fell silent while Gray gazed over the forest. A sweet scent, re-pellent and inviting, wafted from the uncanny wood, permeating the fortress. A shiver ran through him.

Jaunter growled in annoyance and Joiwend said, "A song, Soonderkainen, in honor of the occasion."

The bard-enchanter rose to his feet, unslung his harp, and began "The Song of Dirold," his beautiful baritone echoing around the parapets. Joiwend joined in, her voice pure and sweet as spring water. Jaunter added his graveled tones, never in tune, and Corporal Spence, already too full of wine, followed along, missing most of the words. Even Russ Rogers sang. Master Tatters stood and danced, waving his hands in time to the music, moving his arms up and down like a drifting cloud. Fox Lodan sat silent, beating one palm in rhythm against his chair.

Only Ninette Argilla remained unmoved, her face and body

hidden behind the mask and bronze armor she never removed, slipping what little food she ate between its mouth-slit. Gray had noticed that Malimenê treated her almost as if she weren't there, sometimes acting startled to see her, as if she had suddenly appeared before him. Soonderkainen hinted he knew something of her origins, but would answer no questions. She never spoke of herself; she scarcely spoke at all.

Gray dismissed her from his mind and sang along. Joiwend was right. He was happy; they were all happy, regardless what tomorrow might bring. They were leaving Faerie. Anything was possible. They would soon find Tanabel-Tunia. He sighed, picturing her face.

In the year following their kiss, the king had decided Gray should focus on diplomacy, and Aristides had kept him busy studying, practicing logic and rhetoric, and meeting with minor officials from various villages. He and Tana wrote often, but when she did not come to the palace for Summerfest as usual, and ceased writing back, Gray began to despair. Then the news came of her upcoming betrothal to a Prince of Faerie, stunning the entire court.

By the decree of the Elf King, the denizens of Faerie could not enter mortal lands, so the official engagement was to be celebrated at the border between the two kingdoms. Since the palace of En lay close to the boundary, Tana and her foster father, the First Duke of Mare Castle, would stay there a time.

When she arrived, Gray finally got the chance to talk to her alone on the ballroom terrace at a feast held in her honor. The lights of Faerie shone in the distance, steady and unwavering; the torches of the palace cast their glow over the Royal Gardens. Somewhere in the night, two cats argued.

Far enough from watching eyes, Gray placed his hand over hers on the balcony rail. "I've missed you. Why didn't you tell me?"

She glanced over her shoulder, assuring herself of their privacy. "I wanted to write, but I couldn't find the words."

A lump rose in his throat. "Do you love this prince?"

Tears sprang to her eyes. "I've never even met Fox Lodan. The duke arranged it all."

Momentary relief swept over him, replaced by a vast emptiness. "How could he do that to you? It's insane. You'll be—"

"I know." Her hand trembled beneath his. "I'll have to live there after I'm married, following the course of whatever tale I find myself in, trapped in a role, stripped of choice. The duke says it doesn't matter if I live my life in a Story, so long as it's a good one. He calls knowing exactly how my life will go a gift. He says marrying a prince is a blessing for a girl of unknown parentage." She squeezed his hand, her voice growing bitter. "Your uncle never said why he adopted me, but I've always known he didn't love me. He sold me like a prize cow."

They stood silent, Gray's mind churning. "I had planned to ask him for your hand when you came this summer." He hurried on, his voice hoarse. "Only if you love me, of course. I've loved you since we were children."

She studied his face. "I do love you, Gray. Of course I do."

Impassioned, he drew her into the shadows and kissed her. For an instant, she responded, then pulled away. "We mustn't. We can't disobey the duke's wishes."

"We can. We'll run away together, leave En, find a place of our own."

"You would do that for me?"

"For both of us. We'll travel east to Charovia, seek sanctuary there." Gray's heart pounded in his chest. "It won't be easy, but we'll have each other. We'll go as soon as we can slip away. I'll arrange everything."

Her voice came breathless. "All right." She glanced into the ballroom. "Someone's coming." She hurriedly kissed his cheek. "You've always been my protector."

Gray's reverie was broken by the ending of the song. Other tunes followed from the companions' respective homelands. Russ sang a favorite of his called "The Red River Valley," his voice rough but mostly on pitch. Gray always liked that one, though he preferred ballads of brave warriors. Malimenê crooned an elven tune, sad and sweet, wistful as only their melodies can be. Joiwend sang a song in French; Tatters contributed a lay about a woman named Clementine. The moon rose full and golden; the fire crackled; the susurration of unknown insects drifted from the Back of the Beyond. It was a peace Gray would often recall with longing.

"Gentlemen and gentle ladies," Russ Rogers said, pushing his glasses back against the bridge of his nose and catching each of their eyes. "I propose a toast. We've fought together, brothers and sisters in arms. We've been through the fire and now stand at the edge of a great mystery. As Master Tatters said, we've each come for our own reasons, some of us because we were compelled, others voluntarily, but we've made the journey together. May we continue to be a chain against our enemies, each link upholding the others." He lifted his goblet higher, his tanned face unaccustomedly flushed. "May we never separate in strife, but only in friendship. I give you the Company of the Far Riders."

"The Company of the Far Riders," the others intoned, some rising to their feet as they raised their goblets. Jaunter downed his; Ninette Argilla scarcely tasted her own. The rest drank heartily while the elves looked on.

"Hear, hear, Sarge!" Corporal Spence said, his speech slurred. "Good words, sir. Good words."

* * *

They retired early in anticipation of the next day's journey. The others were soon asleep, but Gray remained restless. After throwing himself back and forth among the covers, he finally rose, drew on his clothes, and went to stand again on the rampart overlooking the Back of the Beyond. The night was cool; the forest lay black in the darkness, the starlight of Faerie dying at the border.

"A lovely evening," a voice behind him said.

Gray turned, startled, automatically reaching for the sword he had left in his room.

Koothlin's eyes shone golden in the moonlight. He smoked a briar pipe. "What brings you out so late, lad?"

"I couldn't sleep."

"Come sit beside me, then. We'll watch the stars make their great pivot overhead."

Gray took a nearby chair, and the two sat in momentary silence.

"Are you troubled about tomorrow?" Koothlin asked.

"I just want to get there and be done with it, and I . . . I'm sorry you're not riding with us."

"You've been fine company."

"It's not just that," Gray said. "You're the only one who treats me as the leader."

"By the rules of Faerie, you are."

"That doesn't mean much. Fox Lodan is the real commander. Or Soonderkainen; everyone is a little afraid of his magic, even Jaunter, I think."

"You misunderstand Fox. In Faerie, the eldest son often likes lording it over others. It's a cruel streak in an otherwise valiant man. Jealousy."

Gray snorted. "Fox, jealous of me? There's a jest."

"You are the third son, who must always prevail."

Gray looked into his friend's eyes. "So I've been told, but is it true? More than once I thought I was about to die, just as I might in En."

Koothlin blew a smoke ring toward the moon. "No one said your trials would be effortless, only that you will win through at the last. By his magic, the Elf King, the High King of Faerie, made it so. Everyone in Faerie is subject to his laws, even the elves themselves and the strangers who enter its borders. Because of those laws, lad, whatever you turn your hand to must ultimately prevail, not only because of your order of birth. Your eyes, one blue and one gray — such a difference marks you as the Victorious Prince. So long as you lead this quest, you can be wounded but never slain, defied but never defeated."

"It didn't feel that way beneath the manticore's jaws."

Koothlin chuckled. "Nonetheless, you are alive today as proof of it. You are invincible and must succeed. That includes winning Tanabel-Tunia."

"Tana and I are cousins. I'm —"

Koothlin raised his hand to silence Gray's protest. "Only by her adoption into your uncle's family. Even an elf can see where love lies. Fox sees it too. He may be betrothed to her, but you'll win her in the end. He knows the truth of it, and it gnaws him." The elf frowned and lowered his voice to a mutter. "But I speak amiss, giving poor counsel. What a wretch I am to babble so vainly! All certainty will vanish once you cross the border. The magic of Faerie does not hold there, and even the third son of a king might perish in the Back of the Beyond."

"Then I'm no worse off than I was in En." Gray spoke carelessly, but the elf's words shook him. His reputed invincibility had given him more confidence than he realized. Everything was now uncertain. His thoughts grew dark, his voice, bitter. "Fox doesn't even know her. She doesn't love him."

"That is what makes him so envious."

"He doesn't love her, either. It's all politics. He thinks being connected to a mortal house will give him some advantage."

Koothlin drew a deep draft from his pipe. "Have you considered what the people of the village of Nysa said about her, when she and the three men passed through? Though they lingered half a day there, the villagers sensed no fear in her. Can she have accompanied them willingly, perhaps even arranged it to avoid the marriage?"

Gray's temper rose. "That's impossible." He met the elf's skeptical gaze. "Don't look at me like that. If you knew her, you'd understand. She is perfect, the best of women, beautiful and wise, filled with kindness, good beyond belief. When she walks into a room, it's as if everything stops. When I look into her eyes, it's like . . . it's like—"

"Seeing a reflection of yourself?"

Gray frowned, uncertain of his friend's meaning. "No, it's . . ." He hesitated. "Or perhaps in a way it is, because she seems so much a part of me. We were meant to be together. We have to be! I know it in my heart. I've written poetry about it." He hesitated. "I've told no one, but when she learned her father intended to betroth her to Fox, we vowed to run away together."

"A delightful contrivance. What kept you from doing so?"

"We planned to escape during our journey to the engagement feast, but weren't able to, so I decided it would have to be afterward. But everything went wrong."

That had been the strangest night of Gray's life. The royal company, led by the king and queen, had sat facing Prince Lodan's party at a table set so the border between Faerie and En ran precisely down its middle. No one's hands crossed that line, the Faerie folk because it was forbidden, the mortals, due to fear.

"You're a lovely prize, Tanabel-Tunia." Prince Lodan's voice was deep. "I am not displeased."

A wave of jealousy had run through Gray.

"You surely do me mere courtesy," Tana replied. "It is said mortal women cannot compare to the ladies of Faerie."

"True, if you mean those born to be a Beautiful Princess or Comely Maiden. There are none more fair in all our land."

"So you truly know the course of your destiny?" Tana's voice quavered slightly. "May I ask what your fate will be?"

"I am the Unjust Prince. My second oldest brother is the Prince Who Always Fails. Like every third son, our youngest brother is the Good Prince. Though I am the successor to the throne, I will reign, if at all, for but a short season. In any solitary quest, I will fail and my brother will later succeed. I will strive against him and win for a time, but ultimately he will be victorious over me. I'll die either imprisoned, executed, or in combat against him."

Tanabel-Tunia paled, but her foster father remained impassive. Gray wondered how he could be so detached.

"Is there no way to avoid such a doom?" the queen asked.

A puzzled look crossed Fox Lodan's brow. "I am the Unjust Prince." He raised a utensil above the table. "Would you ask if the knife can keep itself aloft?" He let it drop clattering.

Tana was nearly in tears. "When we are wed, what will happen to me?"

Fox grinned the grin of his namesake. "That is the question on which I pin my hopes! Your normal fate is to become the Long-Suffering Wife, subject to my disregard, never to know happiness; yet, a mortal woman brought into Faerie could perhaps change my course. Who knows?" He eyed her as if she were a found diamond. "Perhaps you will sweep us both into a Story that will make me king."

Tana turned absolutely ashen. Without glancing at her foster father, she said, icily, "So this is my dowry. Gold flows not from the duke's castle, but to it."

"You should be grateful for the chance to wed a prince," the duke murmured.

Gray could not remain silent. "Father, you cannot allow this. It is a prison."

The king did not reply.

"You presume too much, nephew," the duke spat.

"I presume what is honorable."

"What business is it of yours, boy?" Fox demanded.

Gray bristled. Lodan was surely less than five years older than he. "Cicero said 'Not for ourselves alone are we born.'"

Fox Lodan looked Gray over, smirking. "Mortal nonsense. You remind me of a visiting prince who mocked me when I was your age. I invited him to spar in the courtyard with wooden swords. Instead of halting when I scored the first point, I beat him raw. He was lame in one leg thereafter."

Lodan's men laughed; Gray's people sat in stony silence.

"Too bad you and I can't test our mettle against one another, eh boy?" Fox continued. "Perhaps I could win against a third son from mortal realms."

"Peace!" the king commanded, cutting off Gray's reply with a look that could not be denied. "This is not the hour for dissension."

Gray clenched his fists beneath the table.

Ceremonial words were spoken, affirming the engagement. At the speaking of the pledge, made not by Tana, but by the duke, cold sweat broke across Gray's brow. Music played, but he scarcely heard it.

When the evening ended and the royal party withdrew into the palisade prepared for them, Gray determined not to wait another night before spiriting Tana away. As the royals veered off to their individual pavilions, he ushered her away from the torchlight. Her handmaids and a guard started to follow, but he ordered them back.

Hurrying her to the paddock, he retrieved the supplies he had previously secreted there. He wished he could have secured her some rough riding clothes, but there was no time. He helped her to her horse; she turned to slip her foot into the stirrup.

Something struck him a blow to the head. He fell to his knees and was hit again, driven to the ground. His vision went black; he fought to clear it, tried to rise to his knees, fell back down. Through a haze he saw two men grasping Tana, one with his hand over her mouth.

Fighting to rise, struggling to cry out, his voice little more than a moan, Gray saw the abductors throw aside a railing and bolt out of the paddock, Tana bound in front of the leader's saddle. They vanished into the darkness, leaving Gray crawling toward the distant guards . . .

The soft flutter of wings woke him from that terrible memory. A great horned owl landed on the parapet, much larger than any other of its kind, its eyes golden as Koothlin's own. Gray looked at it in surprise, but the elf smiled.

"Fine birds make fine feathers," Koothlin said. "How lovely you look, my lady."

The owl grew before their eyes, its shape changing. Joiwend stood before them, precarious on the parapet, one finger touching the magic ring that allowed her to shift her form. She glanced unconcerned over her shoulder at the long drop, then hopped gracefully down beside her companions.

"A lovely night for an evening's flight," Koothlin said.

She rotated her head toward the elf, her eyes a vacant, unblinking stare, her whole body motionless, still owlish for a time after taking its form. "Whoo . . ." She cleared her throat. "How odd you looked sitting there; but I knew you for friends." Her voice dropped to a whisper. "I flew for leagues along the border. I dared not cross, not without the others. I fear that land. The magic within it is not the enchantment of Faerie. Everything is different. Its dwellers are shrewd and terrible hunters; we will be their prey, mice beneath their claws. We must turn back. Tanabel-Tunia is lost."

Gray recoiled as if struck. "How do you know?"

She stared at him again before abruptly dropping her head, her hand to her brow. "I'm sorry, my friend. I know nothing for certain. That was the owl speaking."

Gray blew out a relieved breath, but Koothlin murmured, "Best to heed an owl's wisdom."

Gradually, Joiwend's eyes became smaller, more human. She took Gray's hand in both of her own. "Owls are cruel, Gray. They know only the hunter and the hunt. We will find Tanabel-Tunia. Whatever I sensed out there, we will face it as we have done all else."

He squeezed her hand, grateful for her comfort, wondering if she really believed it.

"I'm famished," she said.

"I'll have a mouse sent to your chamber," Koothlin said. "Or would you fancy it here?"

She stuck out her tongue. "I only eat when I'm human, as you well know. I'm off to my room; my wings are tired."

She departed, her back bent forward, striding stiff-legged as a bird.

"Not much of a night-owl," Koothlin said.

But Gray did not laugh, and the morning found him still sleep-less, having spent the night mentally composing and discarding, one by one, poems of longing for his magnificent Tanabel-Tunia.

CHAPTER TWO

THE BACK OF THE BEYOND

When the sun peeked above the elven hills the next morning, the travelers said their farewells to Koothlin and Malimenê, and departed by the little back gate, passing along a narrow deer path into the Back of the Beyond.

They had scarcely gone fifty paces before throwing their hands over their eyes, dazzled by a light emanating not from any single source, but from the entire land, a brilliance so intense the whole forest seemed aflame. Blind, squinting in pain, Gray struggled to control his horse. To his left, Corporal Spence shouted, "My eyes! It's burned my eyes!"

Gray nearly panicked, thinking Spence right, but his sight gradually adjusted, leaving him blinking stupidly against the radiance. The sky shone diamond blue; the clouds rose overhead, cliffs in the heavens. The land had appeared vivid from Duskell Watch; now its loveliness overwhelmed him. Words such as *green* and *blue* were inadequate, as if he had never seen color before. He glanced back at the fortress, drear and gray in comparison, wavering and thin as a mirage.

Beyond the path the branches of the forest formed a thick canopy of breathtaking beauty. Tendrils covered the trunks, displaying velvet flowers shimmering in rainbow hues. Thorns, serrated as knives, glistened with dew, each drop a thing of wonder.

Gray glanced at his companions and drew an astonished breath. In the light of the Back of the Beyond they seemed as gods, their every trait accentuated: Jaunter the Scythian, Lord of the Plains, massive as iron, his eyes — distinctly Asian — aflame with wrath and joy; Soonderkainen, Bard and Enchanter, his handsome, beardless face star-glistening as the sun; Russ Rogers, tanned as tempered clay, lean of frame but steady as his name, his cropped, thick hair standing upright like black smoke; Corporal Spence, short and squat as an ape, eyes ever searching beneath his army helmet; Prince Fox Lodan, red hair streaming like lava, his expression cunning as that of his namesake; Joiwend, dark-haired, dark-eyed, constant as the sky, filled with glowing serenity; Master Tatters, cloak flapping, hair entangled, his face swimming in chaotic colors; Ninette Argilla, so faint she was nearly invisible in her bronze armor. Even the horses were transformed — the sleekness of their coats, the massive power of their flanks, their noble brows, the chocolate depths of their eyes.

Gray looked down at his own form. Silver swirls swept over his body, elusive and ever-changing. Around his heart his chest shone golden. He felt powerful, confident, filled with unspeakable joy. Throwing back his head he whooped in pleasure. He was alive!

Caught in that ecstasy, the horses reared, nearly tumbling their riders, hooves flailing to shatter the sky, their wild, joyful whinnies filling the forest. Gray's mare bucked three times like a colt and broke into a dead run through the woods, heedless of caution, the other steeds with her. In his exaltation, Gray did not care. Bellowing like children, the companions sped away.

For long minutes they ran, heedless of the danger, traveling farther than any horse could go without dropping from exhaustion; but when at last their joy was spent and they slowed to a trot, no foam flecked the animals' lips; the beasts were scarcely winded.

Gradually, the intoxication ebbed, the splendor fading from Gray and his companions. They drew to a halt. The forest surrounded them; Duskell Watch was lost behind the trees.

"What just happened?" Corporal Spence asked.

"I don't know, but it was magnificent!" Joiwend exhaled the words, breathless.

"Plumb lovely," Master Tatters rasped. "Loveliest."

"That was a powerful enchantment." Soonderkainen said, dismayed. "I didn't think anything could compel me to act so blindly."

"I felt like a kid again," Russ said. "It's like Malimenê told us; everything here is more alive."

"I could have slain giants," Jaunter growled. "Would there had been some to fight!"

"Well spoken!" Fox Lodan grinned, tapping one hand against his sword.

"Why did you let the horses run so hard?" Ninette Argilla asked, though her mount had galloped as fast as any. "They could have been lamed."

The others looked at her in surprise.

"Did you feel nothing, woman?" Fox Lodan asked.

"I'm sorry. I don't understand . . ." Her voice trailed away, her eyes, seen only through the slits of her armored mask, puzzled as those of a pup.

From the inside of his cloak Soonderkainen drew his small harp, the focus of much of the bard-enchanter's might. A darkness passed over his visage, the shadow that covered the left half of his face when he summoned his magic. His left eye, usually golden-brown, went cold and hard as black amber. The others stiffened, fearing him a little when he donned the mantle of his power. He dismounted and walked a slow circle, but his features soon returned to normal, leaving him shaking his head. "I do not sense any sorcery. I don't know what we experienced."

His words sobered the company, their euphoria fading into embarrassment and apprehension. The wizard's skills had saved their lives more than once; it disquieted them to hear him baffled. Gray drew a deep breath, inhaling rare, earthy scents savoring of the unknown. A humming filled the forest, so near the brink of hearing he half thought it his imagination. Birdsong pervaded the woods, the cries like echoes of voices. A crow sailed past, looped back, and landed on a nearby boulder. It studied them, turning its head from side to side. Gray instinctively reached for his bow, then wondered why he did so. The crow flapped away, leaving its mocking *caw* drifting behind.

"Let's get about our business," Fox Lodan said. "I'll take the point."

The company stirred, the mood broken by the call to the familiar.

"But in what direction should we go?" Soonderkainen asked.

"Outside of Faerie, we can't expect our usual guides. There won't be any sages or dwarves to show us the way, no scrying pools or auguries."

"Why not?" Fox Lodan asked.

"Because that's not the way the normal world works," Russ said.

Fox Lodan shook his head, clearly bewildered. "How does anyone find their way anywhere?"

"We know we have to travel away from the border," Joiwend said. "If we can reach a village, perhaps we can learn where the girl was taken."

They fell into place, red-haired Fox scouting a few paces ahead as he often did, a habit allowing the prince to remain aloof. Gray came next, leading the others, and Jaunter took up the rear, his short, curved bow in hand, his half-moon battle-axe, a *sagaris*, hanging by his side. As was his wont, Master Tatters drifted in and out of the company, constantly searching the ground for tracks. They kept alert, their hands at their swords. And still that soft humming rose all around.

"It's spring in these here parts," Master Tatters drawled. "The endless summer of Faerie lies behind us now."

An hour passed, then two. Corporal Spence said, "Does anybody else feel different, like the fog is lifting?"

Gray looked around. "There isn't any mist."

"He means the enchantment," Russ said. "You're right. My thoughts are clearer; I'm not thinking of myself as some fairy-tale knight."

"As are mine." Joiwend laughed in delight. "We're no longer in the Tale of the Quest. We've been set free!"

"It's what we've hoped for," Russ said. "The Laws of Faerie *don't* operate in the Back of the Beyond. We're finally clear of their influence."

"It's like waking from a dream," Joiwend said. "Not that we weren't aware of it. We've often spoken of it. We've been ourselves but not ourselves, consumed by our mission. And before that, before we met, by the other Stories we chanced upon."

Gray searched his mind. It was true. From the moment he left En and entered Faerie, he had fallen under the realm's enchantment. In that land ruled by the magic of the Elf King, he had become . . .

what had he become? He shook his head, trying to comprehend. He had gone there intent on rescuing Tanabel-Tunia, but once within its borders, had turned into a shadow of himself, at times more shell than man. He now saw that the others had been the same, their purposes and personalities channeled into set roles, like characters in a balladeer's song.

His Greek tutor had warned him this would occur, but thought Gray might be safe enough as long as he was seeking Tana. "Because you are already on a quest, the Story should take you where you wish to go," Aristides had said. "May it also bring both of you back safely."

A shiver ran along Gray's spine. It was like escaping from a dungeon. Terrible were the sorceries of the Elf King that could control the very thoughts of his subjects. Gray wondered how it would be, now that they were their true selves.

"You've all gone mad," Fox Lodan said. "I don't know what you're talking about."

"Nor I, at least not entirely," Soonderkainen said. "But being born in Faerie, we two know we are destined to live our lives following a single path, foreordained to be only what we are and nothing more. In other lands it's different."

"Grotesque and unnatural is what it is," Fox said.

"Not to me, it ain't," Corporal Spence said. "Nuts to the laws of Faerie! It feels good not to be the squire of Russell the Valiant. No offense, Sarge."

"None taken," Russ said.

"It matters naught to me," Jaunter said. "I am what I am in any country."

They soon intersected a stream and followed its banks thereafter, its waters babbling by, an unfathomable choir.

Soonderkainen turned to Joiwend. "I thought we would surely have met someone by now. Why were there no border guards? Try flying above the trees and see if you can spot a village or farm."

"I wish I could," Joiwend replied, softly. "In the last few minutes my powers have failed."

Gray glanced back in consternation. Joiwend's usually tranquil face was drawn. If what she said was true, it would leave her vulnerable in more ways than in battle. Despite her beauty, Gray saw her only as a friend given to motherly advice, but early in their journey Jaunter had made overtures toward her. She had responded by taking the form of a bear, and no one had troubled her again. Through their common dangers, Gray hoped even the Scythian had learned to respect her; but if he had to defend her, Gray would do so with his life.

Soonderkainen slowed his horse and peered at her. "When did you first know? What did you feel?"

"The change was sudden. I can't describe it. It just *is*. Have you noticed anything?"

"Nothing. My magic lies within me; I doubt I will be affected. It is possible yours might return, but that depends on its source." The bard glanced at her magic ring, perhaps guessing her secret.

* * *

The morning passed, cool beneath the forest canopy, chilled further by the babbling stream. Life teemed in the forest—hares and foxes in abundance, wild deer, multitudes of birds. Corporal Spence and Master Tatters went hunting and were gone only moments before the travelers heard the twang of bows and the pitiful squeals of dying rabbits. The two returned with three hares.

"There's hundreds of 'em, Sarge," Spence told Russ, grinning and wiping blood from his hands onto his pants. "Tatters got these before I could even take a shot. We won't starve, that's for sure."

"Perhaps the Back of the Beyond isn't as bad as the elves thought," Gray said, but catching Joiwend's troubled demeanor, wished he hadn't spoken.

"Make no assumptions," Soonderkainen said. "The place is uncanny. There's a feeling in the air. I don't like it."

"This *is* a lively country," Master Tatters said, rolling his eyes around the forest, "filled with beasts and wings and bumfuzzled things. We mustn't let nary a one of 'em gobble us up."

Soonderkainen chuckled. "We'll watch for that, Thomas."

They were used to Master Tatters' quirks. His true surname was Ragsdale, but he had earned his title long before the travelers knew him, doubtless due to his worn clothes and scattered mind. An extraordinary tracker, a skill learned from a people called the

Comanches, he carried some tragedy concerning the loss of his wife and daughters. Despite his homespun ways, he knew smatterings of other languages and had read extensively. His demeanor fluctuated from cheerful humor to a pensive despondency sometimes lasting for days.

Just before noon they descended over rough shale into a valley filled with a mist shot through with rainbow hues of green, orange, and yellow. They rode in a close *V* formation, weapons ready. No sooner did they enter the vapors than Gray felt a tingling up and down his arms. The colors drifted serpentine through the mist, always just out of reach. The horses blew uneasily.

Joiwend clutched her saddle horn. "I feel faint."

Gray dropped back and reached out a hand to steady her. "Do you want to dismount?"

"Not in this fog. I think I'll be all right." Eyes closed, she leaned on the neck of her mare, Maravilla.

They rode out of the mist, back into the sunlight, and the tingling in Gray's arms subsided. Joiwend sat upright and gave him a determined smile.

"That was witchy," Master Tatters said. "The Greeks called such a place the Underworld."

"*Ato!*" Jaunter barked. "Speak not of the land of the dead. You and I have both seen worse, my friend."

"It was another boundary," Soonderkainen said, "perhaps a more important one. I sensed arcane energies within it. We have ridden deeper into the Back of the Beyond. Keep alert, my friends. I do not know what to expect, but we must remain wary."

Before they had gone another fifty paces, Ninette Argilla tumbled from her horse, her armor clattering as she struck the ground. Russ leapt from his mount and hurried to her side, Joiwend following after. Master Tatters and Corporal Spence drew their bows and scanned the forest for assassins. While Fox Lodan hurried back from his position at the point, Gray and Jaunter dismounted and stood guard over their fallen companion, their weapons in their hands.

Soonderkainen left his saddle slowly, his expression thoughtful.

"I can't see her eyes," Joiwend said. "We need to remove her faceplate."

Russ struggled to do so, peering through his black-framed spectacles, his tanned brow furrowed in concentration. Using the blade of his knife, he pried away a pair of rivets and pulled off the mask.

"*Tagimasad!*" Jaunter swore.

An exhalation ran round the circle.

A head of clay lay beneath the faceplate, the eyes mere gouges, the mouth a slit.

"What deviltry is this?" Fox Lodan demanded.

Soonderkainen knelt beside the armor and shook his head. "From the moment I met her, I perceived she was a creation of earth and stone. Only a great Lord of Faerie could have given her life. Though such black magic is abhorrent to me, her body and her armor made her nearly indestructible, and I knew she could be useful. For that reason, I was glad she accompanied us."

"But she had eyes," Joiwend said. "We all saw them. She ate with us."

"Or feigned doing so," the bard-enchanter said. "Whether she required sustenance, I do not know. Hers was no more than a semblance of life."

"So that's why she was so quiet," Corporal Spence said.

"Why didn't you tell us?" Fox Lodan asked.

"Constructs have certain weaknesses," Soonderkainen said. "The fewer who knew, the better."

Master Tatters returned the faceplate, covering the clay features. "Here today and gone today. Maybe fetched back tomorrow?"

"I don't believe so," Soonderkainen said. "The spells that gave her life failed as we moved away from Faerie."

"We should bury her," Russ said.

"Would we bury a broken carriage?" Soonderkainen asked.

"That's right," Fox Lodan replied. "Leave her and move on, I say."

"She wasn't much of a person," Corporal Spence said. "She hardly ever talked and never laughed. You couldn't joke with her or find out anything about her. There's nothing to say over her grave."

Joiwend's eyes welled with tears. "She was a strong warrior. Some of us might have died without her. We could at least admit that."

"Let it be her epitaph, then," the enchanter said, not unkindly.

Joiwend looked at Gray. "The decision is yours."

Gray spoke reluctantly, feeling everyone's eyes upon him. "We don't know what dangers are out here. It's best to keep moving."

"Our baby-leader has spoken," Fox said.

Gray flushed but ignored the jibe. Apparently, leaving Faerie hadn't changed Fox's attitude.

"What about her sword?" Corporal Spence asked. "It's pretty valuable."

"We've lost a comrade and you speak of ducats," Joiwend retorted. "Leave her the dignity of her weapon."

Spence tugged his army helmet tight around his brow. "I was just asking, but if you want to chuck it for the next bum to pick up, it's okay with me."

Gray remounted in silence. Russ tied the bridle of Ninette's horse to his saddle horn and led the animal away. Gray looked back only once at the bronze armor lying among the ivy, dully reflecting the sunlight. Spence was right; Ninette Argilla had always been a puzzle. They hadn't known her because there was no one in the armor to know, yet he felt both loss and shame at leaving her unburied. He should have insisted instead of choosing the easy way.

They stopped shortly thereafter to rest beside the stream in a small clearing surrounded by hoary willows. They refrained from building a fire, eating cold rations while their horses champed tall grass. Low clouds covered and uncovered the sun, sailing in winds unfelt below.

"The clouds have faces," Master Tatters said.

Corporal Spence snorted. "All clouds do, you dunce."

Gray glanced up and was startled by the sight. Each of the clouds wore a long face with watery, watchful eyes expressive as those of a portrait. They seemed to stare down at the company, unsmiling judges in fleeced robes.

Soonderkainen rose to his feet, brow furrowed. The formations drifted toward the southwest, changing and reforming, yet the faces remained, some dissipating only to return, some combining to create other, larger visages.

"It's a trick of the wind," Fox Lodan said. "Isn't it?"

"I wish I knew, Prince," Soonderkainen replied. "This country baffles me. If it's a result of sorcery, it's a kind I can't fathom."

"Then we'll face it with our blades when the time comes," Jaunter said. "I'm no crone to stare at vapors. Let's eat and go on. I'd like to find a village and sleep in a soft bed tonight."

"I'm for that," Russ said, studying his army compass. He showed its needle to Gray. "Look! It's finally working. In Faerie it just spun in circles. We've been traveling mostly northwest."

"Anyone with a sense of direction can tell as much," Fox said.

"I can too," Russ replied, "but this is more accurate."

They fell silent, tight-lipped beneath the watching clouds. Finishing their meal, they plunged once more beneath the shadows of the trees, leaving the glade behind.

The afternoon passed, and the land grew more uneven, rising until they rode among low hills. Gray found himself increasingly anxious. Though the sky remained hidden by the foliage, he had the impression they were still being watched. He kept glancing behind him, fancying faces in the rocks, in the patterns of the leaves on the forest floor, in the earth itself. Nor was he the only one. Fox Lodan kept leaving his place, trotting his horse far ahead, returning with a perplexed gaze. Master Tatters rode incessantly back and forth, scratching his head as he searched for signs of tracks. Jaunter had his sagaris in hand, and Soonderkainen, his harp.

By the time the sunlight angled through the western trees, the companions' vigilance had left them exhausted, and still they found no sign of a settlement. Gray grew despondent, wondering if anyone lived in the Back of the Beyond at all. The country might be vast. Without someone to tell them which way Tana had gone, how could they ever find her?

Russ echoed the prince's thoughts. "Is it completely deserted?"

"Oh, no," Master Tatters replied. "They're here, sure as rain. We've been passing through them all along."

"Who?" Gray asked.

"Whoever they are," Tatters said. "Haunts or spooks, fairies or trolls. Legions we can't see. Legions of legions. They smell like leaves and green grass and seeds."

Corporal Spence sneered. "It's a forest. Everything smells like that."

"Yet Master Tatters is right," Soonderkainen said. "The deeper we travel, the more I sense some uncanny, unknown force. Whatever it is, it grows stronger with every step we take."

"Leaves and Greensleeves," Tatters sang. "Leaves and Greensleeves, leave some Greensleeves for me and mine."

"A bit softer, if you please," Joiwend said.

"Sorry, mademoiselle." Tatters bowed at the waist from his horse's back, his cloak flapping with the motion.

Fox Lodan returned from scouting ahead. "We might as well call a halt. There's nothing before us but more woods, and there's room to camp just ahead."

Following the stream, they soon came from under the trees. A fire had passed through this part of the forest some time before, sweeping along the sides of the tall hills, leaving charred logs half-hidden by new growth. Gray took a deep breath, relieved to be free of the confining foliage, a feeling extinguished when he saw the watching faces of the clouds again, gnarled and heavy-browed as hoary ancients.

They made their camp as the shadows grew long, at the bottom of a sloping hill a hundred paces from the treeline, sheltered on one side by a stand of brambles.

"I say we dare a fire," Jaunter said. "Tatters says there's people about, but I wager there's none around for leagues. It will keep wolves away."

"Prometheus' gift, a lovely rose that cost him dear," Master Tatters said.

"Let's gather some wood, Corporal," Russ said.

"Sure thing, Sarge." Spence tugged his army helmet down and adjusted its strap.

They unsaddled and cared for the horses, tethering them in tall grass beside the stream. Crickets began their night-song as Russ and Spence laid the wood for the fire. With a word and a strum of his harp, Soonderkainen lit the flames.

A soft keening arose, as of distant voices. The travelers froze in place, eyes darting, hands to their weapons. Jaunter grabbed his sagaris and stepped into the growing shadows surrounding the camp, but turned quickly back. "The hubbub is here. It fades beyond the firelight."

Gray walked a tight circle, his blade in his hand, but could not find the source. It seemed to come from the fire itself, and as the moments passed it dwindled into silence.

"More mysteries," Soonderkainen said. "I'll sing some wards tonight to keep us safe, but we must post a watch."

"I'll take the first turn," Gray said, "Spence, the second, Russ, the third." For the first time he missed Ninette Argilla, who had often served as sentry for the entire night. He now understood why she had never needed sleep.

As darkness fell, they clustered close to the fire and dined on the rabbits, their mood subdued. Gray sat beside Joiwend.

"How are you?" he asked softly.

"Like someone who has lost an arm." Her voice trembled as she spoke.

"It will come back."

She gave him a brave smile. "Perhaps you're right. I've had a strange feeling ever since we passed through the mist, as if some-thing *were* coming." She lowered her eyes, her lashes spider-shadows in the dusk. "It may be nothing at all, or perhaps it means something else." Her voice grew even quieter, almost a whisper. "Gray, do I look any different?"

The question surprised him. "Not that I've noticed. Why?"

"Not any older?"

"Ah." He chuckled and looked more closely. "There aren't any crows-feet around your eyes."

She blushed and gave him a ruffled smile. "It's silly of me. Forgive my vanity."

"I wasn't laughing at you." But this was a new thought, that Joiwend, so confident, could be worried that the failing of her magic ring could mean the loss of her beauty. It was a fact about women he should remember.

"This forest is akin to the one in Faerie, angry as Talos against the Argonauts," Master Tatters said. "I druther be out on the plains, where we could espy what was about us."

"Which forest?" Soonderkainen asked. "We traveled through two."

"He means the Velitar Timber," Joiwend said. "That *was* an angry wood."

"But this one wasn't so when we crossed the border," Tatters said.

"It's grown plumb furious since."

Jaunter slapped Fox Lodan on the shoulder. "We were glorious in the Velitar. That battle in the twilight, you and me and Gray; we showed the wicker-cats our mettle! I slew five, and you killed what? Four?"

"Six," Fox said. "I would have taken more if our baby-leader hadn't gotten in my way."

"*Ato!* You wrong him. He did his share. I wouldn't have a left arm today if he hadn't been there. We won honor that night."

Gray looked away. That had been early in their journey. He had stumbled in the fight, causing Fox to trip over him and drop Forlamard, his enchanted sword. Gray had nearly gotten them both killed. But he had deflected a scything claw away from the Scythian, and Jaunter had treated him with respect ever since.

"You may have had a wonderful time, Jaunter, but you weren't under a wicker-cat's withy paws." Joiwend gave a sudden, violent shiver. "I can still feel them at my throat. It's a wonder we survived."

"It was a grim battle, true," Jaunter said, "but I have fought in worse places. When I first left the steppes, scarcely more than a boy, I enlisted as a mercenary for Mithridates against Rome. Those were terrible campaigns."

"Why'd you leave home?" Corporal Spence asked. "Your old man kick you out?"

"You will laugh at me," Jaunter said. "It was because of the horses. I was so much bigger than the other men of my tribe that our mounts, sturdy but little larger than ponies, could not long bear my weight. I left to find a horse to match my size and never went back. I decided I liked traveling."

Gray smiled, doubting that was the whole story.

"I never thought to ask you before," Russ said. "Is Jaunter your real name? It sounds English."

The Scythian ran a rough hand over the blue tattoos on his cheek. "My real name is Idanthirsos. A comrade-in-arms who could not pronounce it called me Jaunter and the others took it up."

"If I had a moniker like that, I'd change it too," Corporal Spence said.

Jaunter frowned. "I kept it in honor of him. He died in battle long ago."

The travelers fell silent, listening to the crickets and the low hum of the forest.

"Was that lightning?" Russ asked.

The travelers glanced around. Brief flashes played behind the southern treeline.

"May be a wet night," Russ said.

Corporal Spence tugged his helmet down with both hands. "Terrific."

With harp and chant Soonderkainen set his wards, his face half-shadow, half-light, terrible to behold. The travelers took to their bedrolls, leaving Gray to contemplate the twilight. He grew increasingly uneasy with the onset of full dark, pacing the periphery of the camp, peering blindly into the night.

The sounds disturbed him the most. The humming remained incessant, and the chirruping insects seemed to speak with voices of their own, a drone of words incomprehensible in their multitude. "*Who, who, whom,*" an owl hooted, drifting by; "*Hunting. Hunting,*" a distant wolf cried; "*Watch!*" a night bird called. Gray ran his hands over his ears, astonished at his own imagination. The day had been wearing, his nerves were frayed. He fed the fire, making it blaze, but it lent him no comfort.

He shook his head. This wouldn't do. In his travels he had grown accustomed to the silence of a resting camp; he knew it could awaken deep fears. At the beginning of their journey, he might have roused one of the others, Soonderkainen perhaps, because of his power, Russ Rogers for his cool sense of command; but he had learned to master those apprehensions and would not be unmanned. He sat down, his back to the flames, watching the night.

A long hour passed. A cool, whispering wind arose, bringing the scent of rain. The clouds had increased and covered half the sky, great thunderheads lit by inner lightning, heavy with moisture. The wind struck, the edge of the storm, a wave of dirt and leaves that made the fire dance. Gray bowed his head against the blast, drawing his cloak around him. Jaunter sat up and rose to his feet, his mass of hair billowing down his back.

The first rumbles reached them. Looking up into the shifting masses, a horror stole upon Gray, for this was no ordinary tempest.

The clouds roiled, creating rolling titans startling in their clarity, vast, angry shapes forming and dissolving into great-jawed beasts, winged monsters, hags' faces, all with sharp, distinct, staring eyes. Gray scrambled up beside Jaunter.

"Targitai's hammer!" the Scythian cried. "The Thunderer is surely in that!"

The others awoke, sitting sleepy-eyed in their bedrolls or rising to their feet.

The lightning flashes came more quickly, forks running rivulets across the sky. A spattering of rain fell. The clouds drew closer, black shot with blue, swarming overhead.

From out of the many forms crossing the canvas of the heavens, the clouds coalesced, sculpting themselves into a single, bearded face painted in stark lines, washed in rain, gigantic, heavy with malice, its features wavering at the edges but firm at the center. It fastened its eyes upon the travelers.

The storm spoke, its voice the howling wind. "Behold! I am Ondoroon, descended from the Upper Air! Glorious Ondoroon! I shall live forever and none can stand before me!"

Lightning ran jagged through the sky, a bolt with a face and eyes at its tines, flashing and gone in an instant. The thunder roared with a voice of its own. The horses stamped and whinnied in fright.

"Soonderkainen! What is it?" Fox Lodan shouted.

If the enchanter answered, it was lost in the crash of a lightning bolt, searing the ground where the campfire had burned, a deafening explosion, a wave pounding against Gray's chest. He threw himself to the earth, scampering away on all fours, instinct responding quicker than reason. When he halted and looked back, he saw the ground broken where the bolt had struck, the firewood and flames scattered to cinders.

Another bolt landed at the edge of the clearing, sending the travelers scrambling again.

"Soonderkainen!" Russ cried. "Do something!"

But the bard-enchanter already had his harp in his hand. He sang his magic, transforming his body to half-darkness, half-light. He grew, unfolding, expanding, his height doubling, tripling, doubling again, extending until he towered into the sky. His jagged cloak swelled at his back; his right eye burned sun-bright; his left eye dulled to smoldering blackness. None of the companions had ever seen him revealed in his full might, and it was almost as terrifying as the storm itself.

He strummed his harp, then released it to dangle from his neck by its strap. Raising his arms, he gestured at Ondoroon, and a blast tore from his fingers, pure ebony from one hand, pure light from the other. It struck the face, tearing it asunder, pushing it back into the depths of the clouds. But almost at once, the eyes reformed, and Ondoroon returned, sending lightning flashing toward the enchanter.

Soonderkainen blocked it with a hand, the bolt quivering in his palm. Shouting in pain and rage, he cast it away, sending it crackling over the companions' heads. With his other hand he drove the clouds farther back, fighting the wind with a barrage of solid darkness. In answer, Ondoroon arched higher, streaming upward to escape the pummeling.

Chanting a song of wind and power, Soonderkainen struck another chord on his harp, forming a golden aura. He gestured, weaving the nimbus into lines of force thrusting toward the heart of the storm. Exultant in his strength, the bard-enchanter's laughter came riding on the wind. He strode forward, driving the enemy back, keeping himself between the companions and his foe.

The wind around the travelers died into preternatural silence.

"He's winning!" Spence shouted. "Look at him go!"

Back, ever back, irresistible in his magic, Soonderkainen drove the storm. The trunks of the trees bent against the force of his might.

Is it any wonder we fear him? Gray thought.

Soonderkainen halted. "You will come no farther!"

The clouds rolled over and over, Ondoroon's face rising and disappearing. Suddenly, it grew again, twice as large. The lightning within it blazed, so brilliant Gray could scarcely look upon it.

"Can you do no better?" Ondoroon roared.

Scores of lightning bolts poured from the clouds, each with eyes and a face, shouting as they flew. Furious lances from the heavens, they scalded the air, splintered the trees, scorched the ground. Soonderkainen spread his fingers wide, seeking to form a shield, but the bolts broke through, striking him everywhere—his ankles, his knees, his chest, his head. The air shook and the earth with it, convulsing the clouds and the enchanter.

Soonderkainen shrieked. He vanished, dissipating, shattered, defeated, wisping into nothingness. His harp tumbled to the ground, melted and burning.

Joiwend screamed. The companions stood frozen in disbelief.

"I . . . am . . . Ondoroon!" the storm cried.

The wind hit Gray full in the face once more.

"Run!" Fox Lodan bellowed.

Gray sprinted to Joiwend and took her arm. "Get to the horses!"

The two of them broke into a run, Masters Tatters and Russ behind them, but when they reached the place where the animals had been, their steeds had broken their tethers and fled.

A bolt of lightning crashed to their left, turning them aside. They scrambled into a grove of cedars, seeking shelter beneath the limbs. The lightning rained down on every side, the glistening, yellow eyes of the tines shearing trunks, incinerating branches. The shock waves knocked the companions again and again from their feet. A nearby tree burst into flames.

They broke from the grove, sprinting up a hillside, instinctively keeping several paces apart lest a single searing shaft take them all. Ondoroon's shrieking laughter boomed down upon them.

Massive boulders, tall as men, lay scattered on the hillside, and Gray sped toward them, Joiwend at his side. Small stones rolled beneath their feet, tumbling down the slope, making the way treacherous. Nearly there, Joiwend stumbled, falling hard on the uneven earth. Gray wheeled and helped her up, practically lifting her off the ground, his strength grown great in his terror.

They reached the boulder and scurried behind it, dropping to their knees, hiding from the gaze of the storm. Bolts struck before and behind them. Gray's hair stood on end; the bitter smell of ozone filled his nostrils.

He looked for the others. Russ and Master Tatters had found sanctuary beneath two standing stones leaning against one another. He heard Tatters shouting, the words indecipherable in the tumult. Where Fox Lodan, Spence, and Jaunter had gone, Gray did not know.

A slow hissing arose, the march of the rain. With a gust of wind, a cold, hard torrent fell. By the light of the lightning blasts, Gray saw and heard a tiny face and voice in every drop, millions of voices together, speaking a single sizzling word. *"Down!"*

With the coming of the obscuring rain, the lightning lessened to single bolts, but these were carefully aimed. A boulder exploded not far from where Gray and Joiwend crouched, a chip striking Gray's face. He touched the wound, his fingers coming away wet with water and blood.

Master Tatters shouted again. To Gray's astonishment, the old pioneer left his shelter and ran in a circle, dancing in the rain, a song upon his lips.

"What is he doing?" Joiwend shouted above the cacophony.

A bolt struck close to Tatters, bowling him over. He rolled to his feet, sticking out his tongue and shaking his fist at the storm, even as he darted toward Gray and Joiwend.

Lightning popped at the old pioneer's heels; he dove headlong and landed at Joiwend's feet. "I'll show him what for, that's what I'll do!"

"Stay down!" Gray ordered, pulling the man close against the boulder.

Tatters pointed. "There's a cave up yonder! Russ spotted it. I'll waltz with the storm. You go!"

"Wait!" Gray shouted.

But Tatters plunged away, calling to Ondoroon, singing snatches of nonsense songs.

There was no time for hesitation. More than once a member of the party had served as a distraction to save the others. Such a sacrifice was not to be wasted. Russ was already running up the slope. Joiwend grabbed Gray's arm, pulling him up.

They splashed through flowing water, scarcely able to see in the downpour. Gray hoped it would make it harder for Ondoroon to strike them.

He tripped, stumbled, and nearly fell, but Joiwend gripped his arm, keeping him upright; then they were both slipping, struggling to remain on their feet on the steepening slope. They seemed to move with impossible slowness. Gray dared a backward glance, glimpsing through the sheets of rain the searching eyes of Ondoroon.

The cave mouth beckoned, a gaping maw. Russ vanished inside.

Seeing its prey about to escape, Ondoroon threw cascades of bolts, the tines striking all around, blinding, deafening, the fireworks of death. Gray pulled Joiwend up the hill and under the sheltering arch into the darkness of the cavern.

"Russ!" Gray called.

"I'm here," the sergeant's voice came from beside him.

Together they crouched at the cave's mouth, far enough back to avoid the eyes of the storm. The barrage had ended; only single bolts struck now.

"Do you see him?" Gray asked between the flashes.

"I can't," Joiwend said. "Foolish Tatters!"

They scanned the slope, straining to find their comrade. Nothing moved along the hillside save the rain. Gray thought he saw a body not far from their former shelter. His heart sank. Ninette Argilla, Soonderkainen, now Thomas Tatters. Half-mad, always unpredictable, the man had been nonetheless endearing.

A form swept into the cave, sending the startled travelers stumbling backward.

"Tatters!" Joiwend cried.

"A lark in the rain, a polka through the puddles," Master Tatters laughed. "I've counted lightning coup."

"You maniac!" Russ grinned, clapping him on the back. "You old maniac."

"What about the others?" Gray asked. "Did anyone see where they went?"

"Spence ran the other direction," Russ said. "I don't know about Fox or Jaunter."

From where they sat the camp was invisible, hidden by the rain.

A click sounded, followed by the flickering flame of Russ' lighter, the wonder torch he had brought with him from his homeland. The cave was mostly gray stone mixed with earth. It smelled clean and dry, and showed no sign of beasts.

"Let's move farther back so that thing can't take more potshots at us," Russ ordered.

The grotto ended at a dozen paces. Along one wall, a centipede fled from the light. Gray ground a scorpion into the earth with his heel, its death-cry an odd scratching noise. They rearranged large stones to use for seats. Russ extinguished his lighter to save its fuel, and they sat in the dark, watching the flashes of lightning beyond the cave mouth, listening to the thunder and the falling rain.

"I didn't think anything could kill him," Joiwend said. "He was so powerful."

"Up into the sky he flew," Master Tatters mourned. "Gone like a hot-air balloon."

Russ dried his glasses on his shirt. "What are we up against out here? Monsters in the storm! Living lightning!"

"And drops of rain with faces," Tatters said. "A whole passel of 'em."

"The elves tried to warn us," Russ said. "If Soonderkainen couldn't survive, what chance do we have?"

Gray reddened, wondering if they blamed him. If he had ordered them to turn back at Duskell Watch, he could have justified it to his father, but he would never have deserted Tanabel-Tunia. Trying not to think of the loss of Soonderkainen, he remembered instead his beloved's bright eyes, her smile, the cascade of her hair, his whole inspiration and the reason for their quest.

Gradually, the rain slowed and ceased; the thunder grew distant. Gray crept to the entrance and peered out.

Ondoroon had moved west, riding its cloud chariot, its gargantuan face turning from side to side, its voice reverberating in the thunder. A glow shone from below the eastern horizon, the first signs of moonrise. Raindrops dripped from the lip of the cave, speaking words too soft to comprehend.

Feeling his way, Gray returned to the others. "Should we look for them?"

"We'd never find them in the dark without shouting," Russ said. "There's no telling what might show up if we do."

"He's right," Joiwend said. "We'll have to wait until morning. We should get some rest."

"Reeesst," a deep voice said. "What enters me to rest without permission?"

Gray's stomach tightened; he dared not breathe.

"It's the cave," Master Tatters whispered. "We're in the innards of the earth."

The voice rumbled, the growl of clay and stone. The entire grotto shuddered, its rocks grinding.

"The entrance!" Russ hissed. "It's closing! Get out!"

Gray, closest to the threshold, reached it first and passed through. Already it was half its former size. Grasping its upper lip, he pushed against it, trying to hold it back. Dirt and splintering stones fell on his head and shoulders, ejected by the cave's efforts. The opening continued inexorably down.

Joiwend sprang out, stooping to clear the entrance. Master Tatters followed.

"Russ!" Joiwend called. "Where are you? Hurry!"

All three thrust against the rock, vainly attempting to slow its descent.

When the gap was scarcely large enough for a man to crawl through, Russ' head appeared. Master Tatters grasped his hand and pulled; Gray seized an arm to help. Russ' foot caught, wedged between the narrowing way. For an eternal moment they struggled. Joiwend reached in and turned his boot, and he was out.

Tatters and Gray pulled him to his feet, dragging him away from the cave. They scrambled down the slope, stumbling and sliding in the mud, putting distance between themselves and this new horror. Reaching their former camp, they stood in a circle where the fire had been, facing outward, weapons drawn. Gray trembled, thoroughly drenched, shaken to the core.

"What should we do?" Joiwend asked.

"Keep your places," Russ commanded. "When the moon rises, we'll find somewhere to hide."

Hardened by their battles in Faerie, they obeyed, holding their ground, their breath coming in gasps. Gradually, Gray felt the pounding of his heart subside. They waited, hopeful for the light to guide their way.

Slowly, the moon's edge appeared, enormous on the horizon. Some trick of the ether made it seem many times its natural size. Gray watched, expecting it to shrink as it rose, but it did not. Despite that, it lit the earth and sky no more than usual, its surface less bright than the moon he knew. It slipped upward, moment by moment, before the awed travelers. When half of it was clear, Russ gave a ragged exclamation.

It was full, but this was not the familiar face of the mountains of the moon, seen for centuries by mortals and elves. The travelers watched its ascent, transfixed. Two half-circles, spaced apart, rested on its top third. Toward its bottom ran a frowning line and out-thrust chin.

The half-circles opened, revealing misty eyes, deep and thoughtful. The curve of the sphere's rugged terrain formed a slender nose and lines upon forehead and cheeks.

Tatters shrieked. Joiwend muffled a scream.

The moon raised its eyebrows. Its voice boomed down from the sky. "Now am I come, glorious beyond hope, arising out of the abyss from which I fell. Rejoice! Rejoice! I shine my light on all the world!"

Looking down, those eyes focused on the companions. "But who are these, these mortal mites, new strangers come to scout the land? What do you here? I like it not!"

Their courage spent, the travelers bolted, fleeing and hiding until dawn from the eyes of the moon.

CHAPTER THREE

THE LIVING LAND

When Richard Spence, former corporal in the 28th Infantry of the United States Army, became separated from his fellows during the storm, his first instinct had been to retreat to Duskell Watch and Faerie. If the others had any sense, he assumed they would do the same. He had spent the night hiding under the sheltering boughs of a weeping willow and now sat on a flat boulder in a clearing, stripped to his white t-shirt and boxer shorts, but still wearing his army helmet and boots while his clothes lay drying on rocks under the morning sun.

One thing he knew for sure, he'd had enough of this nonsense. He never would have come in the first place if the magic of Faerie hadn't forced them to become Adventuring Heroes from the time they entered that country. When the ravens came croaking to summon them to find Tanabel-Tunia, he and the sarge had just killed the giant, Smote. With that Story finished, their minds had been clear enough for them to decide to make a break for the border. But as soon as the birds appeared, they had dropped into the new Quest Story.

He licked his lips, wishing he had a drink. Five foot six, balding in front, he was small but athletic, and quick with his disproportionately large hands. He had a bullet-shaped head, with something of the ape about his flaring nostrils and heavy brow. As a child, his classmates had taunted him, calling him *Flapper* because of his large ears. When he let his long arms hang by his sides, it gave him an even more marked resemblance to the simian, and he had learned to keep them high, often crossed, as if hugging himself.

A flight of grackles landed in the clearing, their garish cries echoing through the forest. Spence grinned, watching one of the males caper before a female, dark wings outspread, tail comically fanning. "A ladies' man, are you?" His smile faded when he recognized words in its abrasive croaking. "*See me! See me! Look here!*"

Snarling, he rushed toward the birds in his boots and skivvies. "Shut up, you! Shut up! If I had my gun, I'd show you." The startled birds flapped away, crying their indignation. He shook his fist at their retreating forms.

"I've had enough of you!" he shouted at the forest. "Enough of all of you!" Striding back to his still-damp clothes, he pulled them on and tightened the strap on his helmet. He had to escape from this nut-farm, even if it meant returning to Faerie.

He had wasted too many hours already; he wanted to avoid meeting Sergeant Rogers, who might order him to stay. They had been through a lot together: the invasion of Normandy, when so many of the 29th Infantry had died that they'd been reassigned to the 28th; the horrors of the Hürtgen forest; the frantic retreat from the Germans during the Breakthrough. Through it all the sarge had kept Spence safe while others died around them. He was the corporal's good luck charm, his four-leaf clover, and Spence watched Russ' back in turn, doing everything he could to keep that rabbit's foot alive; but he was tired of being told what to do, of playing soldier in an army a lifetime away. It was time to move on.

He headed east. The day grew warmer; his clothes grew dry. Coming across the stream they had followed on their way in, he drank deep and filled his canteen. He was getting hungry. He had lost his sword in the storm, but still had his bow and knives, and there was plenty of game, but he didn't want to stop long enough to hunt. He could eat at Duskell Watch.

Hours later, pushing his way through a tumble of branches, he happened on the abandoned armor that had been Ninette Argilla. He sat on a fallen log beside it to rest.

"Hello, hunk of tin," he said. "How's the old girl?" He studied the armor, trying to decide if any of it was worth having. Some of it might fit him, but the added weight would be a burden. He could certainly nab her sword, now that Joiwend wasn't there to argue about it; and it occurred to him he actually *could* take it—in Faerie, where everything had consequences, swiping anything not freely given always ended badly.

The thought made him question his decision to return. At least in the Back of the Beyond, he could do what he wanted, unhindered by the Laws of Faerie. He hugged himself. Freedom didn't mean much if it got him killed. He suddenly felt hopeless, caught between two lousy choices.

He wouldn't be in this fix if sniper fire hadn't driven him and eight other soldiers into that German bunker six months ago. Spence could still picture it—a long, underground blockhouse filled with treasures stolen from France: boxes of jewelry, centuries-old paintings, crates of loot, all stored there for safekeeping. They had found a case of twenty-year-old champagne and shared a couple bottles of it. Spence licked his lips, still tasting it, smooth and sweet, a celebration in the middle of the misery of war.

But there had been something else in that bunker, mystical ornaments unearthed by the SS, occult objects collected by a regime obsessed with acquiring any form of power. The men had laughed at the stuff, passing it from hand to hand, muttering mumbo-jumbo over it while Sergeant Rogers looked on, letting the soldiers have their fun. It was a big joke, until it opened a trapdoor from Earth to Faerie.

If they had known the Faerie Laws, his buddies might still be alive. Spence snorted, remembering it, a bunch of American soldiers thrown into a world of elves, knights, and magic. They couldn't adapt fast enough. They had their guns, but soon ran out of bullets; they were trained, but the training was all wrong. And the Faerie laws forced them to take on heroic roles, making them believe they could accomplish noble, dangerous deeds. Spence would be dead too, except for his gift in acrobatics and weaponry. When he was a boy in Illinois, an uncle who had traveled with the circus taught him knife-throwing and tumbling. He had taken to it naturally and could handle a sword like a professional within a week of entering Faerie.

He thrust his hands across his apish face, wiping away the sweat from beneath his helmet. Were there rules to the Back of the Beyond too? If he could learn them, would he be better off staying? He caressed the bronze armor with his fingers. It might be worth something in trade for a new horse.

A low moan issued from the slit in the faceplate. Spence jumped backward from his sitting position, dexterous as an orangutan, landing on his feet with his knife drawn. He crept closer, studying the armor.

Eyes of the palest watery gray peered from the faceplate. Had they been that color back in Faerie? More green, Spence decided. "Ninette?"

She moaned again, sat up on her elbows, and gave a gasping breath. Struggling for air, she removed her mask.

Her nose was pert, her lips, full. A strand of golden hair peeked from around her helmet.

"What happened? Where is everyone?"

He grinned. "Looks to me like you've come into your own."

She tried to rise and he helped her to her feet. "I feel so strange. Oh, my mask!" She shielded her face with one hand, bending to grope for her covering.

Spence reached down and plucked it up. "I don't think you're going to need this anymore. This place has made you a living doll."

She hesitated, feeling her face with her armored fingers. Removing one glove, she stared at her hand, warm flesh, pink and new. She raised her forearm, inspecting her reflection in the polished surface of her armor, touched her chin, her cheeks, ran her bare hand over her delicate nose and forehead.

"I'm alive! I'm really alive!" She covered her face with her hands and wept.

"There, there, girl!" Spence moved to put his arm around her shoulder. "It's all right. Sit back down awhile. You've had a shock."

She cried while he stroked her hand and murmured encouragement. When at last her tears subsided, she looked at him, a frank gaze. "I never knew there could be so many feelings! Those I had before were faint as ghosts. It's like a shroud fell off me. I can feel *so* much! I can feel my own skin! I can smell the forest! It wasn't like this before." Her expression grew wistful. "There was nothing but longing, like standing on a rocky shore, the only land in miles, looking out to sea."

"Soonderkainen said a magician made you."

"He did! At least, that's what I was told. An elven wizard cast me from clay, but he abandoned me. I was only a diversion to him. A village couple took me in and taught me all kinds of things. They thought I was terribly disfigured because I wouldn't let them remove my mask. I pretended to eat and sleep, but when they finally saw my face, it scared them and they sent me away. Being made of clay, I was nearly impossible to kill, so I joined a company of soldiers and learned to fight."

"You're definitely not clay now."

She raised her hand and examined it again. "When we crossed into the Back of the Beyond, I was afraid the enchantment that made me would fail. It must have, but something here gave me life again." Her eyes grew wide with wonder. "Isn't it exciting? I *have* to ask Soonderkainen what I should do. I don't want to go back to what I was."

"Soonderkainen's dead," Spence said.

Her brow furrowed, her expression collapsing into new grief. She burst into tears once more, a tearing, sobbing sorrow. "Oh no! Not him! He was *so* kind to me!"

She wept until she started to hyperventilate. Spence made her hold her breath until she calmed down.

"What about the others?" she asked. "Did they die too?"

"I don't know." Spence told her of the living storm, and of his intention to return to Duskell Watch.

She hugged herself and shivered. "The lightning must have been terrible; but I'll never go back to Faerie! I don't want to live half a life. I want to be free. I'll look for the others, but if I don't find them I'll go by myself. I can survive alone; I learned that early. And I have my armor." She looked at her hand again. "But it may not protect this soft flesh so well."

She removed her helmet, unfurling golden curls like sunflower petals in the morning light. Her untamed locks were short, her chin, sharp and dimpled—had it been sharper still she would have looked like a witch; instead, it gave her a striking beauty.

Spence considered. It wouldn't be so bad, traveling with such a lovely innocent; and her words made him think. He hated returning to the regimented world of Faerie. Only his fear of the Back of the Beyond had made him consider it. But was the living storm any worse than fighting the cockatrice or hiding from the one-eyed balor? Beneath the sunshine the woods seemed cheerful enough.

He squeezed her arm. "I can't let you go alone. It wouldn't be right—not right at all. No way to treat a friend. We'll go together. We are friends, aren't we?"

She grinned, the smile of a happy child. "That's *so* nice of you, Spence! Thank you! Of course, I'm your friend. Maybe we'll find the others."

"Call me Rick." He had no intention of rejoining the company if it meant continuing the quest. If he met them, he would tell them so. Not even the sarge had a hold on him now. "I'll hunt us up some lunch."

When he returned with a pair of doves, he discovered her skipping and jumping in a circle, barefoot in the grass, her boots and armored gloves lying beside her faceplate in the center of her dance. She twirled and turned cartwheels, laughing like a child. He watched, entranced.

She noticed him and halted, eyes wide, her hands over her mouth to hold her laughter. "Oh, Ricky, this is so much fun! The grass holds me up like springs! But the armor chafes now. I'll need clothes underneath. Do you think Joiwend can loan me something? I'm sure she would. She's *so* sweet!"

While Spence lit a fire and roasted the doves, she strolled around, humming and touching bushes and tree trunks, flowers and leaves. "Doesn't everything smell wonderful? It's *so* nice. Look, there's a bird! I wonder what it feels like to fly? I almost think I could." She lifted her arms and flapped her hands, standing otherwise quite still, watching her fingers move, her expression alight with awe. Seeing his amused glance, she blushed and dropped her arms.

"You think me silly, don't you? I know you do. But you can't know what it's like to be locked inside yourself and then be set free. I don't think I'll ever be unhappy again."

He laughed. "Maybe I won't be either, if you stay around."

"That's nice to say, though I don't know exactly what you mean."

When the doves were done, he made her sit and handed her a slice of meat on his knife. "It's hot. Be careful."

She grew abruptly wistful. "I'm sorry, little doves, that you had to die for us. It's sad." She cooled the fare with her breath and took a dainty bite, then threw her head back, eyes closed. "Ohhh, this is *sooo* good! Does everything taste like this? I didn't know! Nothing tasted like anything before. How do people stand it? I'm going to be eating all the time."

"You'll get fat," he said.

"Then I'll have more skin to feel with."

She rocked and grinned and licked her lips with every bite. Kneeling beside the stream, she cupped the water, took a sip, and gasped. "This is even better! It's *so* cold. Thank you, stream." She splashed water on her face, letting it run down her neck into her armor. "Thank you!"

She turned to Spence, her eyes wide. "Did you hear it whisper? It said, *'You're welcome.'*"

Spence stood, suddenly chilled, remembering the lightning and the grackles. "I didn't hear anything."

"It was very clear."

"We better go." He threw dirt on the fire to douse it and offered her his hand. She took it and they set out, following the stream.

"You feel so warm," she said. "Your fingers almost burn me."

"Lower your voice and try not to talk so much," Spence said. "This place is dangerous."

She put her hand over her mouth. "I am *so* sorry. I haven't been thinking very well, have I? I'll try to do better, Ricky."

"Just Rick, if you don't mind."

"Rick, then. I feel so warm inside toward our friends, as warm as your hand. I can't wait to see them! We've gone through awful dangers together. I never thought about it before, how it makes us close, but I couldn't feel it then. Any one of them might have died for me." Sudden tears sprang to her eyes. "They're all terribly brave."

To avoid another bout of crying, he said, "Do you hear that low humming? I don't think it ever stops."

"It's like forever bees, but I don't mind. I think it's soothing. It's easy to forget it's there."

"I wish I knew what it was."

After traveling another hour, they discovered an orange boat tied beside the banks of the stream.

"This is luck," Spence said. "We'll go in style."

"Oh, but it must belong to someone," Ninette said.

He glanced up and down the banks and began untying the rope. "They're not here now."

"Not yours," a voice said.

Spence whirled around, his long-knife drawn, but there was no one there.

"Not yours," the voice spoke behind him.

He turned back to the boat. "Who's there?"

"Not yours."

"Is that you, boat?" Ninette asked.

"I'm not for the taking." The sound, a wooden resonance, came from the painted eyes and mouth on the prow.

"It talks!" Ninette said.

"Maybe everything here does," Spence said. "Look, you, what do you call yourself?"

"I am Boat."

"Well, Boat, I've just had a powwow with your boss, the one who tied you here."

"But that's—" Ninette began.

"Hsst!" he warned. He raised his voice. "He said we could use you if we needed to."

"Oh," Boat said. "All right."

Spence finished untying the craft. It might be able to speak, but it was gullible. A grin broke on his simian features. The Back of the Beyond might not be such a bad place after all. With luck they'd sail right past the others.

He climbed in, offering Ninette his hand. "My lady."

Smiling, she allowed him to help her into the craft. He seated her in front and took the oars.

"Downstream," Boat murmured, as the current caught them. "Downstream."

* * *

Sergeant Russell "Russ" Rogers peered through his binoculars from around a stand of heavy boulders, hoping the rocks wouldn't start chattering at him. The night's storm had been as bad as any German shelling, but at least with the Nazis he knew what he was fighting.

He glanced at his companions, finally getting some sleep since the moon had set and the country had quieted down. There had been voices in the wind all night and the threat of further storms, but the sky was cloudless and pale in the rising sun. They would soon have to find their horses and the others, if they were still alive.

He chewed dried venison from his pack, thinking himself lucky to have been carrying it when the lightning hit. He wished he were back in Kansas, where he could have a cup of coffee at a drug store. He wondered if the war was over and if they had won. He wondered if Paulette still waited for him. He shook his head. He must have been declared Missing in Action months ago. She'd probably moved on and married some Air Force pilot. But he still dared to hope. He washed the venison down with water from the army canteen he kept buckled at his waist.

He looked at the sunrise and gave a double-take, pushing his glasses against the bridge of his nose and shielding his eyes with one hand.

Lying close by his feet, Gray yawned and asked, "Is there anything out there?"

"Nothing much. The sun has a face."

Gray sat up and looked. The sun was fully above the horizon, ordinary enough in appearance, except it had slits for eyes, a pug-nose, and pursed lips.

"Looks like a cartoon drawing," Russ said.

"Will it attack us too?" Gray asked dully.

Russ blinked and looked away. "I don't know. It seems pretty unconcerned. Maybe if you're the sun, you've got bigger things to worry about." He laughed mirthlessly. "And I thought I'd gone crazy when I wound up in Faerie."

He had never been able to pinpoint what century Gray was from. The lad's attitudes were medieval, but his knowledge of warfare seemed from an earlier time; and whatever dating system his people used bore little resemblance to a modern calendar. Russ assumed he was from somewhere in Europe, but if so, his country of En must be fairly isolated, forgotten in the histories of the rest of the world. Perhaps that came from its lying so close to the borders of Faerie.

They roused Joiwend and Master Tatters, and Russ gave them the rest of his venison. Weapons drawn, they began searching for their companions, following Master Tatters' lead. The old pioneer moved outward in a spiraling circle, squinting his eyes, rubbing his nose, nodding and humming, tuneless as a washboard, bending down to study the rough ground, spinning around with a jolt to snatch up a branch or leaf. His tracking ability was uncanny, and the others watched him expectantly. More than once he had followed Tanabel-Tunia's trail when no one else could.

"The rain washed away most of the signs," Tatters said, "but . . ." He lifted his head and sniffed the breeze. "This way, lady and gents."

He broke into a trot and the other three fanned out, keeping alert. Russ grimaced at Joiwend, who would normally have shifted to wolf shape to add her nose to the hunt. Instead she struggled to keep her balance, a voluptuous woman running uneasily over the rough ground. Gray was looking out for her, giving her an occasional hand. She would need protection in a fight, something they had never worried about before.

They hurried past a copse of trees, traveling back toward denser woods. Tatters grinned, slowed to a halt, and pointed at a rise, where a horse's head could be seen. The animal nickered in greeting.

"Maravilla!" Joiwend softly clapped her hands.

Miraculously, the animals had stayed together and suffered no harm during their flight. Russ grinned when he saw his blond gelding, Flapjack. The two of them had ridden many miles together. Only Gray received his mount less enthusiastically, his horse having been killed in a melee with the handrigites, leaving the Prince of Stallions riding a mare named Nutmeg. Russ felt some sympathy for the lad, but not enough to part with his own mount. A man and his horse got to know each other's ways. It could make a difference in a battle.

During the storm the companions had left their gear at their camp. Leading their horses by the manes, they made their way back. Though not as proficient with a sword as Corporal Spence, Russ had become competent enough, and he held his at the ready. Apart from the face of the sun, scarcely noticeable in its brilliance, the surrounding country looked harmless, yet he had an impression of movement and awareness.

As if reading his thoughts, Joiwend said, "Can you feel it? The land rejoices at the rain."

Something in her voice made Russ turn. A white nimbus hung above her head; an ebullience suffused her features. Even through the worst of their trials, she had always been an attractive woman, but here was beauty beyond the physical, joy radiating from the depths of her brown eyes. It left him breathless. "Joiwend?"

The others looked at her. Gray gasped. Master Tatters threw up his hands and danced a jig, his cloak whirling behind him, shying the horses. "She's glorious! Glorious as the dew!"

"What's wrong?" Joiwend asked.

"There's a halo above your head," Gray said.

"Like a Renaissance angel," Tatters said.

Joiwend raised her eyes. "I can't see it."

"Do you feel anything?" Russ asked.

"Only gratitude for the rain. It touches my animal attributes."

"Are your powers returning?" Gray asked.

She hesitated. "No . . . I don't know. It's more like the delight of a child, of being happy just to be part of nature. Oh, I want to bask in it, not study it! Leave me alone!" But already the glow was fading.

They found their equipment where they had abandoned it, muddy and wet but mostly unscathed. It took a while to sort it out and saddle the animals.

"Some of us should stay," Gray said, as Russ tightened Flapjack's cinch strap. "If the others survived, they'll try to make their way back."

Russell Rogers had been twenty-eight when he joined the army after Pearl Harbor; Gray was a little younger than the men he had led, and as idealistic as any of them, but he showed more common sense. The lad carried himself well and kept a clear head in dangerous situations. Russ supposed it was a result of being raised a prince. He was too intense at times, but that was expected; bloodshed turned boys into men. If the two of them had been back in Germany, Russ would have made him his second-in-command.

"You're right," Russ said. "We'll work from here, then; but I don't want to camp close to that cave again tonight."

"One place may be as dangerous as another," Joiwend said. "And Soonderkainen gone when we need him most!" Her eyes grew misty, but she straightened her back. "Where shall we look for them?"

"I'd like to scout ahead first," Russ said, "see what's in front of us, try to avoid any more surprises."

"You and Tatters go," Gray said, glancing at Joiwend.

The pair mounted their horses and set out, passing around a tall hill, moving northwest. They kept silent and alert, remaining apart as they rode among the trees. Master Tatters strung his bow; Russ gripped his sword. Birds sang in the branches; a bee floated past the sergeant's head. Everything looked normal enough.

When they had gone half a mile Russ drew rein, making a sign for Tatters to halt. Russ dismounted and approached a tall oak. A face seemed to peer out of the trunk at about man-height. He approached it, trying to decide if it was carved. It appeared untouched by any knife. Apparently, it had grown that way, its lines of bark flowing to resemble hollow, gaping eyes, a triangular nose, a scowling mouth. He touched its rugged lips, half-expecting it to bite him. It was solid. The leaves looked strange too, etched with lines suggesting closed eyelids.

"The forest sees us," Master Tatters murmured. "A most uncommon country."

Russ remounted. Flapjack blew uneasily; Master Tatters' horse, Jingles, stamped the earth.

They had gone only a short distance before Tatters abruptly drew his bow and fired toward the ground. The shaft struck a cottontail rabbit hidden among the foliage. Impaled through its neck, the animal bounced and writhed, its pathetic screams filling the air.

Master Tatters slipped off his horse, knife drawn, to end the creature's misery. By the time he reached it, it had grown still, its brown eyes glazing. As he reached down to cut its throat, it said in a high voice. "I . . . die."

Tatters froze, gaping as it took its last breath. He removed the arrow, stroked the animal's furry head and returned to his horse, leaving the body where it lay.

Russ stared at the corpse. "Aren't you going to get it?"

"I'll not eat anything that jaws at me. We've seen magic a'plenty in Faerie, Russ, but nothing like this. We've dropped anchor at Circe's island, and it's my fondest wish not to be turned into a talking pig."

Stunned and thoughtful, Russ led the way. They saw no signs of men, but more and more of the trees had sullen, scowling faces. Beneath their seeming disapproval the pair hunkered low in their saddles and soon turned back, intimidated by their staring eyes. Along the way Russ reached to pick a berry off a bush. A flurry of soft voices arose. He couldn't catch the words at first, but then they grew clear. "*Ask. Ask.*"

He jerked his hand back as if burned, gave Tatters a meaningful glance, and prodded Flapjack's flanks, sending the horse trotting toward the camp.

When they arrived, Gray was cooking quail. Russ wanted to ask if they said anything before they died, but kept quiet, trying to work through what was happening. In Faerie he had been forced to learn a new way of thinking. He would have to do the same here.

"Did you see anything?" Joiwend asked.

"Commanding berries and cottontail confessions." Master Tatters said. Joiwend turned to Russ, who told them the story. It left them pensive, and they finished their meal in silence.

Gray rose. "I'll ride out to look for Jaunter and Fox."

"I'll go with you," Joiwend said.

"Tatters is the better tracker," Gray returned.

"He's right," Russ said.

Joiwend laughed. "I'm a damsel to be protected now? How chivalrous. I can still fight."

"You lack a gunfighter's swagger," Tatters said.

She stared at him in surprise, then stiffened. "I will have you know when I was fifteen, before being taken from the Earth, long before I could change forms, I was inducted into *Les Rangs des Femmes*. I can shoot a bow as accurately as a man and am proficient with both short sword and spear. At flintlocks I was fair. I can hold my own."

As Jaunter had been transported to Faerie from the first century B.C., and Master Tatters from the Old West, Joiwend had come from the seventeen-hundreds, from a tiny country between France and Spain which Russ had never heard of. From her description,

Aquitanita had been a bit magical itself. Perhaps, like Gray's kingdom of En, it lay on the nebulous borders near Faerie.

"We're not questioning your ability," Russ said, "but you're probably rusty at regular combat."

Her brown eyes flashed in exasperation. "What does rust have to do with it?"

"It's an expression. Out of practice, I mean."

She glowered, then softened. She could never stay angry long. "Oh, very well! Tatters *is* a better tracker. But if I'm to be treated like a countess, I expect nicer quarters."

Tatters bowed low at the waist. "We'll see what we can grub up, mademoiselle."

The horses snorted in anticipation as Gray and Tatters approached them.

"Easy, girl," Gray said.

Nutmeg rumbled from deep in her throat. "Weee . . . go?"

Both men stared at her.

"Let us go now," she said, a long nicker.

Russ and Joiwend hurried to them.

"Nutmeg?" Russ said.

She shifted her head to see him better with her brown eyes. "Yes?"

Russ faltered, pressing his glasses against the bridge of his nose. "You're a . . . fine horse."

"I am," she said. "Do we go?"

Gray and Master Tatters rode away, leaving Russ staring thoughtfully after them.

* * *

The prince and the old pioneer kept together, unwilling to separate in this strange land, moving at right angles to the direction of Faerie. Crows flapped among the trees, silently watching. Through breaks in the branches, Gray spied vultures floating on the upper winds, seeking the dying and the dead. Various birds chirruped and squawked throughout the woods; Gray sighted deer by the dozens, scores of rabbits, myriads of gray squirrels.

The horses trotted, ears forward, unusually alert. Jingles spoke for the first time, his voice lower than Nutmeg's. "Where do we go?"

Gray's stomach tightened. What kind of country was this? In Faerie a bird or beast might give a prophecy or a warning, but it always happened for a reason. He cleared his throat. "We're looking for Jaunter and Fox Lodan."

"Their horses have lost them," Nutmeg said. "We will search."

"Yes," Jingles said.

Tatters grinned. "My Jingles has a pretty voice, don't you reckon?"

"You're taking this well," Gray said.

"I've ridden many a mile in solitude on the prairie with only Jingles for company. I'd read him a page or two from "Plutarch's Lives" by the evening fire, he preferring it over the Tragedies. He's a dandy conversationalist when you're lonesome."

"So he's spoken to you before?" Though both men were from Earth, Gray knew Tatters came from a strange and distant country, filled with iron monsters riding on rails and boats propelled by steam.

The old pioneer fluttered his hands. "He's more of a listener. But the Comanches tell tales of jawing with their horses."

Jingles snuffled the air. "I smell water."

"Water," Nutmeg echoed. "Water and men."

"Lead on, lead on," Master Tatters said merrily, fitting an arrow to his bow. Gray drew his sword and loosened the reins, letting the mare have her head.

They passed down a draw. At its bottom lay a clearing surrounding a small pond. Gray and Tatters halted, searching for danger through the hanging branches until Gray spied Fox Lodan standing hands on hips, watching Jaunter butcher a stag.

"Hallo!" Tatters called. "We've come to fetch you darlings to the dance. Have you donned your bells and pink bows?"

They rode down, Gray's feelings mixed, glad to see the Scythian, thinking it better if Fox had stayed lost.

Jaunter waved, unusually silent, and turned back to his work. Fox watched them approach, his eyes imperious. "The baby-leader and the lunatic. Not surprising they should survive in this mad country."

Gray ignored the affront. "Joiwend and Russ are back at the

camp."

"Water," Nutmeg said, dropping her head to drink.

"You must ask," a voice soft as a plashing fountain spoke from the pool.

Nutmeg looked thoughtfully at the pond. "May we?"

For an instant Gray saw a mouth and swirling eyes in the water's depths. "You may."

"The stag also spoke as it died," Fox said. "We've heard noises from spiders and butterflies. The whole forest is haunted. That dull humming ever since we arrived is the voice of the earth and everything in it. I'd give oath to it." He looked haggard. They had all had a bad night of it.

"We shouldn't have killed it," Jaunter said, his hands bloody from his work. "It may have been a god. But we didn't know. I asked its pardon. Maybe it won't return to haunt us."

"Give me your horse," Fox ordered Master Tatters. "A prince should ride."

"Aye aye, Your Majestness." Tatters gave a fluttering salute and started to dismount.

"Tatters will need him," Gray said, glad for an excuse to nettle Fox. "We still have to find Corporal Spence. You and Jaunter can carry the meat back to our original camp. If you know the way."

Fox glared at him. "We can find it."

Gray turned Nutmeg back up the draw, Master Tatters following, leaving the pool behind.

"East, methinks," Tatters said. "Spence is a canny man. I wager he scurried back the way we came. He'd figure it was safest that direction."

Gray was less certain, but he trusted Tatters' instincts, if not always his reasoning. They spent the rest of the morning seeking the corporal without success, until at last the old pioneer dismounted and strode back and forth, peering this way and that, his cape billowing in the breeze, his arms flapping to unheard music. He knelt, touched the ground with a finger, tasted it on his tongue, looked up at Gray and winked. "Come along, you horses and man. He came through here. We've caught his scent." He walked ahead, half-crouched, searching for signs.

Two hours later, after much tracking and backtracking, Tatters halted. "Here's news: the puppet has fled. 'Twas here her tomb, above the earth."

Gray did not understand at first. "Ninette! Did Spence take her body? Why would he do so?"

Tatters spun in a circle, gesturing broadly all around. "Her prints but not her prince has come. See here. Unless he moved her one step at a time, she ambled along herself. She lives, a woman resurrected, and not a wooden one either. She was barefoot for awhile. Her tracks are flesh and bone." His face grew bleak. "We left her to die, just like my dear Jennie and my girls."

"We didn't know," Gray said, appalled.

Tatters grew abruptly sullen. "The winds of time and change will punish us for it, blow it all back on us."

"Can you tell where they went?"

"Toward yonder."

They followed the trail to the banks of the stream. After some time Tatters declared, "They found a boat. You can see its ruts here, where the trail ends." He put his hand on his brow and peered along the waters. Tears welled in his eyes. "They're gone. Long gone."

* * *

Riding back, Gray noticed that the deeper they went into the Back of the Beyond, the more alive everything seemed. The trees looked ordinary enough when they left the stream, but as they approached the camp several bore the faces Tatters and Russ had seen earlier. The horses, who had fallen silent shortly after leaving the pool, began speaking again.

They found Fox Lodan and Jaunter already at the camp. Gray explained about Spence and Ninette, expecting the news to distress Russ, since he and the corporal had been together for so long, but the sergeant only pushed his glasses against the bridge of his nose. "That worries me about Ninette."

"Spence can surely protect her," Gray said. "He's deadly with any weapon."

"That isn't what I meant. She can fight with the best of them, and there's no one more agile than Rick. In France, I once saw him race across a beam, twenty feet in the air, to escape a collapsing building hit by a German shell, the way anyone else would sprint down a football field; but he's always been a man of less than rigorous character—he can't hold his liquor and he wants it too much." Russ shook his head. "I'm not completely surprised he left, but he doesn't need to be in charge of anyone else. He requires looking after." He picked up his faded, olive backpack. "Let's get out of here."

The horses stood champing the grass, murmuring among themselves.

"They all converse now." Joiwend held Maravilla's mane to slip on her bridle.

The mare turned her head to avoid the bit. "This grass is good."

"I'm sure it is, but we need to go," Joiwend said.

"I don't want to."

Jaunter threw back his head and laughed. "We'll see if Joiwend Kindheart can win an argument with her horse."

Russ frowned. "I've argued with horses plenty on ranches, but if they're arguing back, there's trouble ahead."

"We must go," Nutmeg said, nudging Maravilla with her nose.

Maravilla bit at Nutmeg, but allowed Joiwend to put on the bridle.

The animals acted like children, full of opinions, concerned only with what was happening at the moment, and it took longer than usual to get them ready; but at last the companions were on their way, Russ and Tatters leading.

"Can you hear it?" Joiwend asked Gray an hour later, as they passed along a grassy slope. "A whispering. I can't tell where it comes from."

Gray listened. The incessant low humming was now accompanied by a dull buzz.

"They're waking, one by one," Master Tatters said.

A flock of sparrows swept by, tweeting, "*Men, men, men, men, men.*"

More and more of the trees showed scowling faces, until the whole forest glowered at them, hatred etched on every bark, but the worst was yet to come, when a green, staring eye, penetrating in its malevolence, opened on each leaf. The horses halted; Joiwend shrieked; Jaunter cursed in his Scythian tongue. Everyone drew their weapons. They sat astride their mounts, confused and uncertain, expecting an assault. When none came, Gray marshaled his courage and rode close to one of the branches. He studied the unblinking scrutiny of the leaves. A shiver ran through him. Bad enough, if the eyes had been like painted pictures, but these held depth, intelligence, and most of all, contempt.

"We mean you no harm. Only let us pass," Gray said, and not even Fox Lodan made light of his words.

They rode on.

Never before had Gray encountered the oppression of being continually watched, the disquiet rendered by the glare of thousands of eyes. It might have been bearable if not for the unmistakable hostility. The trees loomed over them; he could almost feel them scheming. He hunched down in his saddle under the weight of it. The horses too were uneasy, rumbling their discontent, their ears perked, one or another often saying, "Watch!"

For almost an hour they rode, their faces strained, their fingers twitching on their swords. Gray drew several deep breaths, fighting a growing panic. Just when he thought he could bear it no longer, Master Tatters suddenly nocked an arrow and fired it straight into the face of a chestnut tree. "Leave me be! Quit gawking at me!"

"Easy, man!" Fox Lodan said.

Russ bent down from Flapjack to retrieve Tatters' shaft, which still quivered in the trunk, but hesitated and dropped his hand. The scowls on every surrounding tree had deepened, though no one had seen them move.

"Take it out!" Joiwend cried. "Oh, take it out before they grow more furious!"

Russ struggled a moment with the arrow before pulling it free. He handed it back to Master Tatters.

"The nymphs of the woods," Tatters said. "I shouldn't have done it!"

* * *

By the time they made camp that evening, nearly everything had a voice. The green kindling muttered as the travelers gathered it and moaned when the fire consumed it. The flames cackled softly, like a witch stirring her cauldron. *"Eat them all. Eat them all."* The stream beside their camp murmured on and on. *"To the sea! To the sea!"* A bed of ants at Gray's feet clicked and clattered, their words too soft to comprehend. Even the grass whispered with the slow wind, and the wind fluttered in answer.

The night fell, leaving the companions with their backs to the fire, eating without tasting their dinner, staring into the darkness.

"Tagimasad!" Jaunter said. "I understand why the horses speak. At least they're alive. But sticks and stones! They shouldn't talk."

"At least the meat isn't yapping," Russ said. "Not yet, anyway." He took a notebook from his pack. On many evenings, Gray had watched him writing in it. Turning to a certain page, he tore it out and threw it into the flames. *"Burning,"* the page whispered as it curled.

"What was that?" Gray asked.

"The Laws of Faerie," Russ said. "They don't apply here."

Throughout their journey, Russ' notes on the laws had proven indispensable to Gray. He had them memorized, and they ran through his mind as he watched the page turn to ash. *Only the third son or daughter can succeed in a quest. The third try cannot fail, the first two always must. To disobey a warning is always disastrous. Good deeds are always rewarded. Evil, foolishness, lying, being rude, and failing to keep a promise are always punished. Every magical instrument has a purpose. There are no coincidences or chance meetings . . .* It had taken time to learn to live under those unbreakable rules. Now that they no longer held, his whole way of thinking must change again.

Fox cast his eyes on Gray. "If that's so, we don't need the third son for our quest to succeed. Our baby-leader has lost his value."

Gray returned Fox's glare.

"He's proven worthy as any of us," Jaunter said.

"The real question," Fox replied, "is why we don't leave this madness and return home."

"Are you so frightened you're willing to desert your intended?" Gray asked.

Fox Lodan's eyes hardened beneath his scoffing smile. "Nothing about the Back of the Beyond scares you, does it, boy? You didn't run from the lightning, eh? No, it's a matter of cutting our losses.

This place is wicked, unpredictable. In Faerie, we understood the dangers."

"I won't go back," Russ said. "I won't be under Faerie's laws anymore. Besides, the Back of the Beyond may be closer to my finding a way home."

"Or farther from it," Fox said.

"I'll take my chances."

"I won't return, either, Fox," said Jaunter. "Faerie isn't my country. The Back of the Beyond holds no more fear for me than . . ." His eyes grew bleak; his voice fell away. A look of sheer terror consumed him, an expression Gray had seen him make before, always in the quiet hours of the night.

"Nor will I reverse my course," Joiwend said. "I may never find the path to Aquitanita or see the coasts of France again, but like Russ, I'll live free. Perhaps it was fine for you, Fox, who grew up in Faerie, but the rest of us know what it is to make our own choices."

"What of you, Tatters?" Fox asked. "Does the madman have more sense than these sane ones?"

"If I could go back to my Jennie, find the girls again . . ." Tatters licked his lips, his eyes rolling in his head. "Like Odysseus from the sea. Would even an old dog welcome me home?"

Fox snorted. "Always the nonsense. I should have known."

"He speaks more clearly than you think." Gray thought of his Greek tutor. A stern teacher when the Prince of Stallions was a child, over the years Aristides had become both mentor and friend, teaching Gray history, mathematics, philosophy, art, and government. He wistfully recalled sitting at the old man's feet, hearing his mellifluous recitations of ancient wars and venerable myths.

Master Tatters fixed his gaze on Gray. "That's right. I read the old tales when I could, just like you. But the Tonkawas have my girls and Jennie. They're dead or worse—I know how the Indians treat their captives. I lived with them a time. I got to go on, not back. I got to find what I'm looking for."

"What's that, Tatters?" Joiwend asked gently.

His eyes filled with tears. "A shady tree and quiet water. Peace like a river, flowin' down to the sea."

"*To the sea,*" the stream echoed, its voice louder than usual, causing the companions to glance its way. "*To the sea.*"

"Thagimasida, Lord of Waters, hears us," Jaunter said. "We should make a sacrifice."

"I'd rather not see any blood tonight, especially yours," Joiwend replied. When not using animals, Scythians sometimes cut themselves to offer a bowl of blood to their gods.

"You talk of remaining without mentioning Tanabel-Tunia," Gray said. "We all vowed to find her."

"We had no say in it," Russ said. "The ravens called and we had to answer. I'm tired of fighting. Tatters' shade tree sounds pretty darn good. I might join you, old fellow."

"Gray and Russ are both right," Joiwend said. "We did promise, though under compulsion. I'll keep my vow if I can."

"Without your changeling powers, how long will you last?" Fox asked. "A woman and a boy? Good luck to you."

Joiwend's color rose. "This is the second time today my skills have been questioned. It grows annoying."

Gray controlled his own mounting temper. "Russ, you taught me the expression, 'A man is only as good as his word.' Will you turn back on that now?"

Russ looked down. "What I need in my life is another idealistic kid." He dug his foot into the grass. "All right, I'll stay with you awhile. We'll look for your cousin, but I won't take her back through Faerie—that's on you."

"There's glory in it for certain," Jaunter said. "Alive or dead, we'll find her, or avenge her if she's slain."

"Jaunter, please," Joiwend said. "A little tact."

The Scythian growled deep in his throat.

"So what will it be, Fox?" Russ asked. "She's your sweetheart. You're a good man to have in a fight, but I can't blame you if you want to go home."

For a moment Gray's spirits soared, hope blooming like roses before him. If Fox turned back, he was practically renouncing his engagement. Gray could find Tana and they could be together in the Back of the Beyond.

Fox noticed his expression. "You'd like that, wouldn't you, baby-leader, my going home to our fathers, admitting I'd deserted your precious cousin while the rest of you remained behind. Look at this country, all of you! Remember the lightning. If she came through here, she's dead and rotting in some ditch."

"She's not!" Gray said. "I'd know it if she were."

"Yes, you know her, or think you do. I'm weary of your mooning over her, pining for what's mine. It's a wonder you haven't stuck a knife between my shoulders while I slept."

"That's hardly fair!" Joiwend protested. "Gray—"

"Gray hides behind your skirts so you can dab his tears. Tanabel-Tunia belongs to me, and I say she's not worth finding. If she is alive, she's a harlot in some dirty village by now."

Gray drew his sword without thinking. "You'll not speak of her like that!"

"Put it down, Gray!" Russ ordered.

Fox Lodan rose, eyes glistening, a half-smile on his face. "So the worm finally turns, eh boy?" He drew his black blade, Forlamard, from its sheath.

"Fox, don't!" Joiwend pleaded. "It would be murder."

Through his anger, Gray saw the calculation in his enemy's eyes. So long as Fox wielded his enchanted sword, he could be neither wounded nor slain. No longer under the protection the Laws of Faerie granted the third son, Gray had fallen prey to his taunting and was about to die for it.

CHAPTER FOUR

STRATEGY AND TACTICS

Fox Lodan came at Gray with easy confidence, a half-smile on his lips, his imperious gaze steady, his eyes fixed on Gray's chest. The Prince of Stallions' rash fury died within him. Even without his enchanted sword, Forlamard, Fox was the better swordsman; with it, he was unbeatable. Though lean of frame, he was half-a-head taller than Gray and had a longer reach. Able to move with the speed of his animal namesake, he possessed a great gift for killing. For an instant Gray's courage deserted him. He stepped back, holding his sword in an uneasy grip.

Seeing his hesitation, Fox looked down his aquiline nose at him and smirked, clearly knowing that Gray understood he had been intentionally maneuvered into the fight. Fox swept his red hair back from his forehead and made two flourishing cuts through the air. "I'm going to slaughter you like a pig, boy, and I'm going to enjoy every moment of it."

Despite having been through many battles, facing an unconquerable foe nearly made Gray bolt. Only Fox's haughty disdain restrained him. If he ran, the man's scorn would follow him ever after. He steadied his stance and approached his opponent. *If I must die, I will die for Tanabel-Tunia.* The thought strengthened him, and to his own wonder, he laughed, causing Fox to lift his brow in surprise.

Gray made several rapid cuts, then backed away. Since he could neither kill nor wound his opponent, his hope lay in wresting

Forlamard from his grasp. Without his sword Fox would no longer be invulnerable; but it was a difficult stratagem, requiring Gray to press his blade against his enemy's weapon, seize Fox's wrist with his left hand—and in one twisting motion—wind the sword from Fox's grip. Gray risked losing an arm, and the attempt would become doubly dangerous once Fox recognized his intention.

Fox advanced with rapid precision, using controlled strokes, keeping Gray on the defensive, driving him back toward the edge of the firelight, making it difficult for the Prince of Stallions to see to parry. Still, Gray held his own, and Fox abruptly withdrew, returning to the surety of the light. Gray used the moment to catch his breath.

Fox grinned, beckoning with one hand. "Come get your due, baby-leader. I've tested your mettle. It's time to end this."

Cold intent filled Gray. He advanced again, striking quinte, tierce, seconde, prime, quarte, thrust and riposte, seeking the opening he needed, the chance to enmesh their blades.

Their swords met exactly as Gray wished. Grabbing Fox's wrist, he made a quick, circling motion, using leverage to wrench Forlamard from his opponent's hand. But Fox, the stronger of the two, kept his grip and forced Gray away, nearly causing him to lose his own sword instead.

Gray brought his blade back into line and thrust. To his astonishment, he passed Fox's guard and pierced his side. Fox gave a gasp of pain, clutching the wound with his free hand, his nostrils flaring, his face suffused with shock. Blood rilled from beneath his gashed tunic, darkening his fingers. Both men stepped back, equally startled.

Elation swept through Gray. In the Back of the Beyond, Forlamard was no longer enchanted. Taking advantage of Fox's surprise, he rushed in, beating at his foe, aiming for the kill.

Despite his surprise, Fox was far too adroit to be easily defeated. He parried deftly, both men fighting with new intensity. They stood toe to toe, delivering thrusts and ripostes. Gray no longer thought, but fought automatically, attacking and responding, gaining and losing the initiative. Like machines they dueled, precise, determined, their world narrowing to nothing but hands and steel and the dance of death.

A tremendous animal roar erupted from Gray's left. A grizzly bear reared over the combatants, jaws slavering, teeth glistening in the firelight, claws thrashing toward them, seven feet of bestial fury.

Startled from the trance of combat, the men sprang away, their swords held high in defense. They froze, awaiting the grizzly's charge.

The bear bellowed, its whole body shaking with rage, a black mass of anger, and in the roar a single word. "*Stop!*"

It backed up, dropped to all fours, and changed, the fur receding, the nose shortening, the body shrinking. Joiwend sat on hands and knees, staring at them with eyes golden in the firelight.

"You will cease your battle, or I will rend you," she snarled, raising her hands before her as if she still had claws.

They had seen her take many forms during their journey, but none the size of the grizzly. Nor did any dare approach her, knowing she would retain the bear's temperament for a time.

Into the silence, a loud clapping arose, a strident thudding through the darkness. Joiwend peered around, scowling. The others turned toward Jaunter in astonishment.

"Wonders above and below the earth!" he exclaimed, still applauding. "As pretty a swordplay as I've ever witnessed! And then the bear. A spectacle worthy of the Romans!"

"A good show for less than a nickel," Master Tatters added, flapping his cloak like a crow. "I don't reckon we'll fret anymore about Joiwend fending for herself."

Gray and Fox Lodan glared at one another.

"Your luck holds, boy, so long as there's a woman to protect you."

"Which of us is bleeding?" Gray retorted.

Joiwend growled.

Fox laughed. "I've suffered worse in training, but have it your way, baby-leader." He turned and walked back to the fire.

"We need to clean the cut," Russ said.

"I can do it myself," Fox snapped.

Gray remained where he was, regaining his breath. Fox wasn't one to forget an insult. Losing his sword's enchantment may have dismayed him more than he pretended, but he would soon be planning his revenge. Gray would have to be vigilant.

* * *

The full moon rose that night, peering wide-eyed over the horizon, its voice booming across the land. "Victorious once more, again I rise, Giver of Light, master of all, saving the world from the terrors of night; all who see me stand in awe! I am mighty beyond compare!"

Its gaze swept the countryside. "But see. What wonder that! The travelers from far-flung lands, they yet survive." Its glance moved westward. "And over there, another pair, on yonder banks of the flowing Simborime."

The companions had risen from their places around the fire. "How can it see us at all?" Russ half-whispered. "On Earth the moon is thousands of miles away."

"Little chance of secrecy with him spying on us," Jaunter said.

"Can it be referring to Spence and Ninette?" Joiwend asked.

"It sure sounds like it," Russ said. "I guess Tatters was right; she is alive."

"I'm ornery, but honest as rain," Master Tatters said.

Gray looked away. It had been his decision to leave her. But then he realized they would have buried her body if they had stayed.

"The gods walk this land," Jaunter said. "Maybe they brought her back from the Underworld."

"No," Joiwend said, "it's the Back of the Beyond itself, the whole country. My powers began returning when the halo appeared above my head. I can't describe the feeling, like the joy of living poured into me, the life-force that suffuses everything here. It's greater than magic, better and more powerful. It's what magic would like to be. It brought Ninette back."

"I've felt it too," Gray said, "not just when we first entered the Back of the Beyond. It's like poetry given substance. I feel stronger, healthier."

Jaunter grinned fiercely. "Like I could lift mountains."

"By golly, you're right!" Russ said. "I've been more hopeful than I've felt in years. We've all sensed it, but I couldn't put it into words."

"But what should we do about Spence and Ninette?" Joiwend

asked.

"What can we do?" Russ said.

"Nothing," Gray said. "Tracking them might take days. They're alive and together; they can handle themselves. We must continue on. With luck, we'll eventually run into them."

Fox snorted. He had spoken little since binding his wound, but had sat staring at Forlamard's scabbard.

The rising moon spoke again. "Who are these riders passing through the night? What causes their haste? What drives them on?"

"Did you hear that? There are other people here," Joiwend said.

"Assuming by *riders* he means humans," Russ said.

"I thought you said you were hopeful," Joiwend replied.

Russ grinned and pushed his glasses against the bridge of his nose. "After the creatures we saw in Faerie, I'm just being realistic."

Distant howls erupted out of the night. The hairs on the back of Gray's neck stood up. Everyone sat still, frozen in the moment before action took them. It was the horses who broke the silence, rumbling over and over, "Wolves!"

"Joiwend and I will bring the animals closer," Russ said.

"I'll fetch more wood for the fire," Master Tatters said.

Jaunter drew his sagaris. "I'll help you."

"Don't cut any living trees," Gray warned. "The forest doesn't like it." He blushed, thinking it sounded foolish, but not even Fox ridiculed him for it.

"Bad enough listening to dying branches bemoaning their burning, much less the live ones," Jaunter said.

The horses were in fierce debate as Joiwend and Russ brought them nearer to the fire.

"Stand or run?" Maravilla nickered. "Stand or run?"

"Easy, girl," Russ said.

"Stand or run?" Jingles repeated.

"Stand," Nutmeg said. "Stand."

"Run," Jaunter's horse, Ransom, insisted.

"My rider is lost," Soonderkainen's horse, Far Star, said. "Run."

Flapjack agreed with Far Star and tried to pull away. Gray and Joiwend rose to help, patting noses and stroking flanks, speaking words of comfort.

Russ raised his voice above the babble. "Listen, all of you! You need to stay here. We're going to picket you. We'll keep you safe."

"No," several horses protested, blowing out their breath to utter the word.

"Not tied," Maravilla said.

Reasoning with the animals was useless; they were on the verge of stampeding until Fox Lodan's stallion, Dauntless, the mightiest of the beasts, spoke, "We stand with the man-swords."

"Proud stallion," Maravilla nickered.

Dauntless tossed his head, rumbling in a way Gray had never heard a horse do before. Maravilla lowered her neck, almost bowing. The others did the same.

"Hooves and swords are better," the stallion said, and none refuted him.

Russ addressed him as the leader. "We won't picket you. Stay close to the fire, and we'll protect you if the wolves come."

The stallion blew and bobbed his head.

The wolves bayed again. Joiwend walked to the edge of the firelight, pacing back and forth like a trapped tiger. Gray followed her.

"Oh, let them be hunting something else," she murmured. "Don't make me have to change again."

"What's wrong?" Gray asked.

"It was different when I became the bear. *I* was different. I could think more clearly, I could even speak yet my mind was still not wholly human. And I was so large! So much power in my body. It frightens me, the allure of such strength." She tossed her head, and for an instant the bear's eyes looked out from her face.

Jaunter and Master Tatters returned carrying several small logs, which Jaunter chopped down to size. No sooner had they laid out a sizable stack of firewood than the wolves appeared from the darkness, only their eyes visible at first, a dozen pairs glistening at the firelight's edge. The companions drew their bows. Gray nocked an arrow and chose a target.

A single wolf drew closer, its shaggy form a black outline beneath the trees.

"May we parlay?" it growled.

Cold sweat broke across Gray's forehead. Wolves were cunning; talking ones could only be worse.

"Come ahead," Fox Lodan said.

The wolf padded into the moonlight, a massive animal, lithe and powerful, its coat silver-gray. A white streak ran down its muzzle. Its fangs shone ivory against its red tongue. "I am Mholg. Who leads your pack?"

For a moment Gray could not find his voice. "I do."

The wolf turned toward him. "What do they name you?"

The intelligence burning in its eyes made Gray's skin crawl. "I am Gray Darien, Prince of Stallions of the kingdom of En."

The wolf turned its head back and forth in puzzlement. "No manling can be a leader of stallions. You are strangers here. Interlopers. This land is ours."

"We are only passing through," Gray said. "Leave us alone and we will soon depart." Despite his nervousness, he recognized the irony of assuring a wolf that *they* were harmless.

"You trespass. You break the laws of our land. A price must be paid."

"Name it," Gray said.

"The horses for the manlings."

Nutmeg whinnied, a shriek of fear which cut Gray to the heart.

"We need the horses," Gray said. "We have butchered a deer. Take it and be gone."

"It is not enough," Mholg growled.

Jaunter stepped close to Gray. "We should do as he says. Bargain for one or two of the extra animals."

"Not our beautiful horses!" Joiwend said.

"It's best," Master Tatters said. "It's best."

"Any but Dauntless," Fox said softly. "He has saved my life more than once."

"Tish!" Jaunter spat. "I've drank the blood of my favorite horse when I was starving, and ate him in the end. There must be twenty wolves out there, and they can reason. It won't be a fight that we all survive."

The companions had instinctively drawn close together, their attention riveted on the wolves. Dauntless abruptly thrust his head into their midst. The stallion blew and stamped the ground. "Russ said you would keep us safe."

They turned to the stallion, speechless.

"You gave your word," Dauntless said.

The travelers exchanged glances. Jaunter threw back his head and roared with laughter. "Here is a pretty plight!" The blood-lust was coming upon him, as it did before battle. Mholg lifted its ears at the sound.

Jaunter's laughter dwindled to silence. Finally Russ said, "If the horses fight with us, we have a chance. Besides, if we give any of them up, the others won't forgive us." He smiled grimly. "I did make a promise, and I'm fond of Flapjack."

"We will fight," Dauntless said.

"Fight!" Nutmeg whinnied.

"Fight!" the other horses said.

Jaunter lifted his sagaris and grinned. "So be it! Their leader is mine."

"Wait!" Joiwend said. "A moment, please."

She stepped forward, stopping less than ten paces from Mholg. Her form seemed to melt as she changed, shifting until she became a wolf, a head taller than the pack leader. Mholg growled, hackles rising.

Joiwend howled, a long, blood-curdling wail. "I am Joiwend. We will fight, you and I, for leadership of the pack."

Mholg raised its nose, scenting the air, growling uneasily. "You are woman; you are wolf. This is not possible."

"It is for me," Joiwend said.

"You are female," Mholg said. "A female does not lead the pack."

"Is Mholg afraid?"

The pack leader's nose wrinkled in anger, but it dropped its head. "I cannot fight a female. It is . . ." It made a strange whining noise, a semblance of speech meaningless to the companions. "Unlawful. Females fight females; males fight males. It is the way with us."

"Fight me or take the deer carcass," Joiwend said.

The wolf stared at her with its yellow gaze. Gray held his breath and drew back his bow, waiting for the reply.

For several long seconds the wolf stood motionless. The pack encircling the company drew nearer, their forms outlined by the firelight.

"We will take the deer," Mholg growled.

One or two of the other wolves whined in complaint, but Mholg answered them with a commanding growl. Gradually, most of the wolves withdrew. Jaunter and Master Tatters laid the deer meat outside the circle of the campfire. Two wolves took it in their powerful jaws and dragged it away. Within moments, the pack was gone, vanished into the darkness save for Mholg himself.

The pack leader sat staring at Joiwend. "Yours is not a wolf name."

"But it is my name."

"You should be called Owoono Mwarh, She-Wolf of the Deep Eyes."

Joiwend gave a slight bow of her head.

"My mate is dead," Mholg said. "Join my pack. If you fight the other females, perhaps you will win and become she-leader. We will be ours, together. You would like that?"

Joiwend sat silent for a long moment. "I am honored, but I will remain with my own."

Without reply, it turned and was gone.

Gray let himself breathe again. Jaunter gave a barking laugh.

"Do we trust them to keep the bargain?" Gray asked.

"They're wolves," Jaunter said, as if that answered the question.

Master Tatters danced over to Joiwend, who growled and snapped at him. He threw himself on the ground and rolled on his back, hands low, exposing his throat. Joiwend bent over him, her teeth at his jugular. Gray gasped. Gradually, her form shrank, leaving the woman on hands and knees, teeth still bared.

"Don't eat me, mademoiselle," Master Tatters said. "I'm mostly gristle."

"Joiwend?" Gray said.

She turned, remaining on all fours, staring at him with animal eyes.

"It was well done."

She sat back on her haunches, regarding him. Her voice caught as she tried to speak. "I detest this. This country makes me both more and less an animal. Part of me wanted to go with him, to run with the pack in the moonlight."

* * *

They kept a watch again that night. Gray slept fitfully, his rest broken by occasional remarks from the moon. He woke once to find the sphere peering down at them from directly overhead, its face pocked with the shadows of its mountains. "I spy seven owls. Run, mouse, run!"

Gray finally fell into a deep slumber, only to be awakened hours later by the moon's hollow cry as it slipped below the treeline, its face turned sideways, so it cut its eyes to see its way. "Down again into the vexatious pit! And so to sprout my limbs and climb once more, spider-wise, across the underside of the world, to make my furious trek. But I am undaunted! I will fight the grand fight; you will see me yet triumphant, though—"

It descended below the world's rim, its words becoming muffled echoes fading to silence. Its last rays vanished, soon replaced by the pale eastern glow of morning.

Gray sat up. He had dreamt of Tana, and his longing for her filled him with despair. Could she still be alive in this strange country? Would they ever find her? They needed something to guide them, a village or an outpost. With a groan, he rose to face the day.

No one wanted to hunt animals that could talk back, so the companions ate from their dwindling supplies and rode out again, still following the stream. It had widened and cottonwoods lined its banks. Watching for danger proved wearisome when the whole land could speak—clumps of grass, brambles, birds, insects, some but a faint buzzing or high-pitched murmur, some loud as the voices of men. Even the wide leaves of the cottonwoods whispered, vibrating words too soft to understand. The horses talked among themselves.

"*Looking,*" a bumblebee hummed by. "*Looking.*"

"*People!*" a squirrel cried, slipping behind a trunk.

"*Out!*" a woodpecker insisted, hammering at a branch for insects. "*Out!*"

But the crows that hovered around the travelers cawed and spoke no words.

"It's all yak and yammer," Master Tatters complained, holding his hands over his ears.

Gray stared at a particularly malefic, hideously-scowling oak. "Why are they so angry? The wolves said we were trespassers. Do the trees think so too?"

"I have seen eyes more evil on the steppes of my homeland," Jaunter replied. "And in Faerie." The Scythian looked away. His voice fell to a murmur. "But not here. At least, not yet." His expression grew bleak, the haunted look which was never far from him. "I would rather face the hatred of a thousand trees."

They approached a stand of tall rushes growing around the stream. A shout erupted from among its ranks, all the stalks speaking in chorus. *"Keep away! Keep away!"*

Riding closer, Fox Lodan ripped the head off one of the rushes. Its squeal of pain was nearly inaudible. "This is folly! Better we had turned back when I first said it."

Between the thickness of the rushes and the dangling branches of the cottonwoods, the companions were forced to ride farther from the stream. Despite their efforts to keep it in sight, they were diverted toward the south. The trees grew closer together; the way sloped gradually downward over rocky soil. Protruding roots made the horses stumble. As the sun rose higher, warming the morning, the air beneath the dense canopy became oppressive. The travelers spoke little, overwhelmed by the noise, quelled by the incessant aura of hostility.

"I wish Soonderkainen was here," Russ said, wiping the sweat from his glasses. "I swear we're being directed. Look how clear it looks to our left and how dense to our right."

"We could chop our way through." Jaunter hefted his sagaris. Its half-moon blade spoke, its voice metallic. *"Strike them all!"* Jaunter paled and nearly dropped it. "Is everything here a god?"

"Don't!" Everyone turned at Joiwend's uncharacteristic outcry. Her cheeks colored. "I'm sorry. It's only that cutting might antagonize the forest even more."

Master Tatters bobbed his head in vigorous agreement. "She has the right of it."

"Can you change to a bird and see what's ahead?" Gray asked.

Joiwend's color deepened. She lifted her chin to indicate the sky. "You know I'm not a coward, but I won't go up there alone, not through those branches with so many against me. Even an eagle can be taken down by a flock."

As if in answer, a score of crows rose from the trees and swept away, their caws like laughter.

"The whole land is our enemy," Fox Lodan said. "If we want to live, we need to find out more about it."

"Yet you've not scouted ahead as is your wont," Joiwend said. "You've sensed it too, that we can't let them pick us off."

To this Fox said nothing, nor did he seek to ride out alone.

The next two hours were like traveling through a maze. The companions wound back and forth, struggling to find their way, always angling downward. From the corners of his eyes, Gray thought he saw oak trees lowering their branches to block the path and thorn bushes drawing closer together, but when he looked at them directly, they were always motionless. And still the trees glared with their hate-filled eyes.

They were following a stony draw when they heard a crackling overhead. A heavy branch split from a beech tree directly above Master Tatters. The old pioneer only had time to gape, but Jingles reacted more quickly, shying away. The end of the limb struck Tatters on the side of his skull, knocking him to the ground, one foot still caught in the horse's stirrup. Jingles bounded forward in fear, dragging him a dozen yards before Jaunter sprang to a crouch atop his saddle, startlingly agile for one so large. Leaping off his mount he landed on Jingle's back and drew the horse to a halt.

"Run!" Nutmeg nickered.

"Run?" Maravilla neighed.

"Stand!" Dauntless ordered, pawing the ground.

The companions struggled to calm their animals, and it was a long moment before anyone could dismount and see to Tatters, whose head was bleeding. Russ pulled his army First Aid kit from his pack and knelt beside him. "Can you hear me, Thomas?"

"Are the Tonkawas coming?" Tatters babbled, his expression dazed. "Get the women to the hills!"

"As if he wasn't mad before," Fox Lodan said.

It took several minutes for Tatters to realize where he was, and several more to salve and bandage his head and left arm, the latter badly skinned from his being dragged. At last he was able to stand. He glared and shook his fist at the tree. "You did that on purpose, you overgrown thistle!"

The tree creaked in answer, its branches swaying though no breeze stirred them.

"Make no threats," Gray ordered, wondering if it were only a co-incidence that the old pioneer, who had shot an arrow into the chestnut the day before, had been the one attacked.

Toward noon they reached a clearing. To his consternation, Gray saw they had unknowingly entered a narrow rift with tall hills on either side. Pale, spindly clouds drifted above them, their noses long, their placid faces staring forward. Tangled brambles grew against the hills, forming an impenetrable hedge. Gray pulled out the spyglass his father had given him before he left En, but could see nothing down the ravine. "I don't like this. We're too vulnerable. Archers could feather us from hiding. Let's move on."

"Rest," Dauntless said.

"Rest," the other horses echoed.

"It's dangerous," Joiwend said.

"I smell no men," Jingles said. "No wolves, no bears."

Once more the companions exchanged glances, perplexed by their talking mounts.

"I always trust my Jingles," Master Tatters said.

"Very well," Gray conceded. "Long enough to eat, but then we press on."

"Good," Nutmeg said, dropping her head to graze.

"Ask, ask!" the grass cried, a choir of voices.

"Can we?" Nutmeg asked.

"Yes," the grass said.

Russ walked over to where the horses were feeding and knelt on his haunches, studying the grass. He took off his glasses, cleaned them on his shirt, and put them back on. "May I take a blade?"

"Yes," the grass replied.

He plucked the stalk and examined it, holding it briefly close to his ear. "Since Nutmeg asked permission, the grass didn't protest. Even the ones that are being eaten don't seem to mind. Not only that, but there's a group voice when the whole field speaks, apart from the single voices of the individual stalks."

"Always the perpetual observer," Fox said, not without interest. "But what does it mean?"

Russ shrugged. "I'm just trying to figure out the rules."

"I hope there are some," Joiwend said. "I don't relish having a discussion with my eyebrows before I pluck them."

The companions sat sullen and discouraged, chewing strips of dried meat. A murder of crows came to rest in the trees around them. They were said to be intelligent birds, but of all the animals they alone never spoke. Gray threw a scrap of meat toward them. A single crow dropped to the ground, studying the companions suspiciously before plucking it up. Gray wondered at how many of them he had seen since entering the Back of the Beyond.

"The god in my sagaris whispered to me as we rode," Jaunter said.

"What did it say?" Gray asked.

"It wants blood."

"That figures," Russ said. "It's your axe."

Jaunter grinned. "It will soon have it, I wager, if we ever find any men."

"Perhaps there aren't any," Fox said. "Who would want to live here? Or who could?"

"Touchy," Master Tatters said. "Plumb cantankerous without your bedeviled blade."

"Be quiet, you oaf," Fox said. "I'll not be taunted by the likes of you."

"There has to be a village somewhere," Joiwend said.

"Stinker," Dauntless announced. The other horses snorted and blew. The scent of skunk filled the air.

"Puah!" Joiwend exclaimed. "Someone is unhappy."

Gray glanced around without seeing the animal, but a skunk's spray can travel a thousand paces. The reek burned the companions' eyes.

"The end to a lovely lunch," Joiwend said. "We best go."

"The perfume of nature," Master Tatters said. "I used to trap them for their pelts."

"I'm sure your house smelled lovely," Joiwend said.

Tatters smiled. "Jennie and the girls didn't mind."

"We've been here long enough, anyway." Gray's gaze swept the hills above them.

They rose and packed their rations. The horses grumbled and stole last bites of grass. As they were about to mount, a tremendous racket arose, the cries of scores of birds: raucous blue jays, strident grackles, screeching doves, loudest of all the caws and clacking of crows. The horses nickered in distress. The eruption went on and on, a clattering cacophony. The leaves of the trees shook, adding to the pandemonium. The companions stood listening, chilled in the afternoon heat.

After several long minutes, the uproar subsided. Gray's heart pulsed in his chest. "What does it mean?"

"The Roman coliseum sounded like that," Jaunter said, "before the kill."

The odor of the skunk was fading. "I smell men now," Dauntless announced.

A horn blew. From either end of the rift, a score of riders burst from the trees, accompanied by enormous hounds.

The companions fumbled for their weapons. Gray's sword came out of its sheathe crying, "*Fight!*"

The hounds came foremost, rushing in from all sides. A dozen paces from the companions they stopped, crouching low, ready to leap. Gray looked straight into the eyes of an animal larger than a mastiff.

"Surrender," the dog rumbled.

The crows' cries turned to words, a rattling barrage. "Give up! Give up!"

Gray looked around. Archers armed with crossbows, guised in the colors of green leaves and brown earth, rose from behind the wall of brambles. The companions were outnumbered and out-maneuvered.

"Put down your arms!" a man shouted. "You are under arrest in the name of the Republic of Everything."

CHAPTER FIVE

THE REPUBLIC OF EVERYTHING

On the first day of their journey, Rick Spence decided traveling by boat was pretty swell. The stream ran at a steady pace without their rowing. The evening was warm; the sun's complacent face beamed down, making the water glisten; they passed between light and shadow beneath the shade of willows and cottonwoods along the shore. A fish leapt high into the air, proclaiming, *"Men!"* in a garbled voice before returning to the stream with a splash. The orange boat, its painted eyes wide with happiness, floated through swarms of gnats which sang a high-pitched three-note song, their words indecipherable. "On we go," Boat murmured. "On we go."

"Forward, march!" Spence's army helmet responded, causing Rick to cringe. The thing had started talking that afternoon. He had half a mind to throw it away, but hated to let it go; it had shielded him from Normandy to Faerie.

"The sunshine feels *so* good." Ninette Argilla reclined at the front of the vessel, her eyes closed, her face turned upward. "Don't you think so, Ricky?"

Spence had given up trying to get her to call him Rick. "Sure. Everybody likes a little sun." He watched the left bank, searching for the others, hoping he wouldn't find them. They were probably dead, anyway.

He felt a tinge of remorse at the thought. He didn't much care about the rest of them, but he hoped the sarge was okay. And maybe Joiwend; be a shame for a nice-looking woman like that to die, even if she was uppity sometimes. Jaunter was crazy as Tatters, and Gray was just a kid. Fox Lodan was the kind of fellow Spence understood, even if he didn't like him—cruel for the sake of sheer meanness. He had seen plenty of that growing up. But Fox had learned not to bait him with his sly insults after Spence secretly loosened his cinch strap, sending him sprawling when his saddle slipped. Fox hadn't accused him, but he'd known who did it and learned his lesson.

Glancing away from the bank, he found Ninette studying him, a puzzled expression on her face.

"What are you looking at?"

"I was wondering what it must be like to have a past, to grow up in a family."

"You didn't miss much."

She furrowed her brow, her voice wistful. "But I always thought—I heard families were nice. Having people around you, feeling feelings for them. We were kind of a family, weren't we, you and me and Soonderkainen and the others? It aches inside when I think of not finding them. Aren't families like that, everyone working together, protecting each other?"

Spence scowled, afraid she'd start bawling again. "It ain't always so peachy. It was good when I was little. I was the youngest of eight, and we were well-off until the Crash and the Great Depression. You wouldn't know about those. I should have grown up educated like the three oldest. They went to schools in the East, but my old man lost everything. He hung on for awhile, trying to find work, but then started drinking. He used to get drunk and chase us around the house with a tire iron, threatening to kill us. He shot himself when I was ten. I was the one who found him."

She thought about this, her face perplexed. "That is not good." Her eyes grew misty.

"Nothing to get worked up about. It was a relief not to have him around."

She glanced down at the stream. "I thought families were gentle, like Joiwend."

"People aren't always what they seem," Spence said. "Not even them. You need to learn to be careful."

"But they were *so* good to me."

"Sure, to your face. What you need is some guidance, some friendly advice. Stick with me and I'll show you how to handle yourself."

"That's *so* nice of you, Ricky."

"I can be a good friend, but not to anyone who tries to stab me in the back. Friends don't do it. Remember that."

"I'll remember."

She let her hand drift into the water, watching the trail her fingers made. The stream was mirror-clear, filled with white stones at its bottom. "This is *so* beautiful."

"Thank you," a shimmering voice said. A face appeared in the midst of the water, its mouth and eyes gaping swirls.

"Oh!" Ninette recoiled. Spence drew his knife.

"My pardon," the voice said, though the face had vanished. "I didn't intend to startle you."

Ninette looked around. "Where are you?"

"I am many places. You needn't fear me, though in other parts I am dangerous. Here I am neither deep nor swift."

"I *thought* I heard you speak before, when we were on the shore. Can all the rivers here do that?"

"Elsewhere I am a river, but right now I am only a stream. I go and go and go." Its voice dropped at the end of each sentence, as if traveling farther away with every word.

"I don't understand," she said. "How can you be a person when you're only drops of water put together?"

"Out of the many, one," the stream replied. "One voice and one mind flowing over the leagues, always going and going and going, seeing everything at once, all the plants and trees and rocks and animals, making the stones smooth in my passing, crashing down waterfalls and drifting dreamily among the fronds of stagnant pools, with lazy leaves floating on my surface and frogs up to their eyeballs at my banks, snapping water bugs which scream as the tongues take them. I am a tributary, come from the Omnifire, and many branches feed from me and are me."

"That's a pretty speech," Ninette said. "Do you have a name?"

"You may call me Stream, or Channel, or Sea, or Pond, or Pool, depending on where I am. When I leave the mountains, I am named Simborime, but here I am Meandering. My mothers, the mountains, call me Eddy."

Spence kept silent, listening to them talk. The sarge was always worrying about the rules, and Rick wanted to learn those of the Back of the Beyond without making any mistakes. The stream was obviously more intelligent than Boat, but how far could he trust it to speak the truth?

"Can you tell us what's ahead?" he asked.

"Banks and more banks rolling on and on to the sea."

"We are searching for Tanabel-Tunia," Ninette said.

"Is that a place?"

"No, it's a woman."

"Most people look alike to me. There are multitudes of them along my banks, but I scarcely ever become acquainted with any of them. I am too busy seeking the sea. Can you sing? I like to hear people sing."

"I don't know how," Ninette said. "It's because I'm brand new as a person."

"I know some songs," Spence said. "If I sing for you, can you tell us about this country? We want to learn everything."

"I will explain whatever you wish."

"All right." In his graveled, off-key voice Spence began a round of "Row, Row, Row Your Boat." He had to show Ninette when to come in. She had a nice voice, but struggled to keep the rhythm. His helmet hummed wordlessly along.

"I like this song," Boat said.

* * *

Gray and his companions were allowed to ride their horses, but their weapons were taken, and their hands tied to their saddle horns, so their captors had to lead their mounts. Nor were they permitted to stay together, but were scattered among the company. The commander, Marshal Dartmallow, only asked who their leader was, then placed Gray beside him and ordered him to keep quiet. The archers marched in three lines behind the horsemen. The dogs, each the same massive breed, took positions on the outskirts of the party, their ears up, their eyes alert.

Turning north, they struck the stream once more and quickly

reached a wooden bridge.

"May we pass over?" the marshal asked.

"*You may,*" the bridge said, its timbers creaking to form the words. It was narrow, and it took time for the soldiers to cross, but they were soon on their way again.

Gray studied the marshal. A big man with a deep voice and a bulbous nose, he blinked and squinted as if troubled by the sunlight, giving him a sour expression. Like that of his followers, his skin was a deep bronze; his close-cropped hair and short beard, once jet-black, showed patches of silver. He wore a green cloak and was armored like his men with greaves and a breastplate of heavy leather, only foregoing their bronze helmets. As they rode, he addressed the soldier at his other side. "It's a nuisance, Topper. At a time like this; it makes one dubious. Most unlikely and most difficult. Riding from the direction of Duskell Watch! But did they really come from there, or did they circle around? I don't like being drawn from our mission. It's odd, wouldn't you say? Interlopers from the east!"

"It is, sir." Topper was so thin-faced as to be almost skeletal, with deep-set, feverish eyes under his heavy brow and metal skullcap.

Gray spoke up. "We came here looking for—"

The marshal whirled on him. "None of that from you! Silence I ordered, silence I'll have, or you'll be gagged. The questions come from us; the answers come from you. When we ask them, you will have your say."

He turned back to Topper, leaving Gray wondering how far the marshal would go to obtain those answers.

As they rode, Gray noticed the faces of the trees had become placid, almost friendly, the eyes on their leaves half-closed and drowsy. He wondered whether this was because they journeyed through a different part of the woods, or if it had something to do with their capture. Whatever the truth, the forest no longer radiated its previous malice, and Marshal Dartmallow called to plants and animals as they went, greeting warblers and squirrels and berry bushes. At various intervals, in the clipped tones of a sentry tolling the watches of the night, Topper shouted: "Passing through! Only passing through!" When they came to a meadow filled with wildflowers, he bellowed, "Permission to cross!"

The flowers gently waved, their soft chorus rising all around. "*Granted*." Though the sun still shone upon the field, a pendulous cloud directly overhead, blue-eyed and serene, cast a light sprinkle across the meadow as the company rode along, and the flowers sang in unison, bowing and rising in joy, their orange, blue, and yellow pedals furling and unfurling.

The sun, the rain.
The sun, the rain.
The sun, the rain.

"*Magnifique!*" Joiwend breathed, and Gray, entranced, could only agree.

Two of the dogs served as scouts, often vanishing into the vegetation, soon returning to tell in whines and growls what lay ahead. To Gray's alarm, one of them padded up behind Nutmeg and raised itself on its back haunches to sniff his leg, its enormous jaws pressed against his calf. A beautiful animal, with golden eyes and ivory fur touched with black and gold, its great chest reflected sunlight like snow; its white teeth glistened in its long jaws; its lolling tongue lay pink as hollyhocks. Like all the dogs it wore a heavy, spiked collar to protect its throat against wolves.

Nutmeg shied in alarm, causing the hound to drop to all fours. "Go away, bad dog!"

"She is a good dog," the marshal's gelding said. "She does not chase the herd."

"She is a bad dog," Nutmeg insisted.

"She is a dog," the gelding conceded.

The marshal watched the hound. "What do you think of our captive, Sniffdaisy?"

The dog shook her heavy head and padded off, leaving Gray wondering what the gesture meant.

They soon passed between a pair of low hills marked with a wooden post topped by a carving of a woman's face. It spoke, her lips moving. "*Welcome to the Meadowlark Road.*"

The road was narrow, constructed of pale-red paving stones. A low hedge lined its sides, with iron posts marking breaks to allow access. The paving stones hummed, a barely audible music.

"Permission to travel!" Topper bawled.

"Hooves and feet, I will take you home," the road replied.

"We thank you," Topper said.

Dartmallow motioned with his arm and led the way.

From atop one of the posts, a crow watched the men approach. When they were nearly even with its position, it glided toward them and landed on the neck of Dartmallow's horse.

"Hello, Quacaw," the marshal said.

"Greetings, Oldbeard. To Oldbeard I give greetings." The bird turned one eye toward Gray. "He is one of them. One of them he is. Clawklok's murder saw him. They saw him and told me. Clawklok showed the strangers to me. To me he showed them. The strangers he showed."

"We appreciate his vigilance and assistance," Dartmallow said. "And yours as well."

"Clawklok's murder watches the border of the East. The eastern border they watch. I trust Clawklok. Clawklok I trust. He is from a good egg. From a good egg he is."

Quacaw strutted closer to the marshal's saddle horn, eyeing the ring on his left hand. "You are grateful to me. It is good to be grateful. To be grateful is good. Golden. Pretty. Perhaps, perhaps, you will give it to me, the shining ring, the sparkling ring, perhaps, perhaps." The crow cocked his head and shook his wings.

The marshal chuckled. "You can't have the ring, Quacaw. My mother gave it to me."

"Did she steal it? Was she brave? Did she sneak flapping in, *whisk whisk* and away? Perhaps at night, when the moon was dark? When the moon was dark, perhaps? Perhaps, perhaps, did she take it from an eagle's nest, slipped beneath its wicked claws? From its wicked claws she took it? Perhaps, perhaps?"

"She didn't steal it."

"How sad that is. I sorrow for you. For you I sorrow. She didn't steal. Not worth much, not much, so little. Can I have it? I will take it off your hand. Off your hand I will take it. Your hand will be lighter. Perhaps, perhaps?"

"I'm afraid not, but you will have other rewards if you do as you promised."

Quacaw puffed out his chest. "I am a crow of my word. A crow of my word I am. My word I am a crow of. My murder goes with you. We will all go. I have said it. It, I have said."

He gave the ring a final glance and the marshal watched him vanish into the trees. "He's a respectable bird, that one, wouldn't you say, Topper? More dependable than most."

"Quite so, for a crow, sir," Topper said, stolid as the iron posts lining the way.

The company made better time on the road, passing along rolling hills and through wooded valleys. Toward late afternoon they came to a long building made of rough, unpainted boards. As they drew near, a hound, little more than a pup, sprang from the porch to greet the newcomers, barking "Hello, you are home!" to everyone, stumbling over his oversize feet, and fawning and growling around Sniffdaisy. She batted playfully at him, sending him sprawling; the pup rolled, delighted, and circled her twice, tail tucked, before dropping onto his belly before her. Except for his eyes, one of which was blue, the other brown, the two looked so alike Gray thought she must be his mother.

"Riders!" shouted a voice so deep Gray felt it in his chest. "Welcome to all!" He looked around. The entire front door of the building was carved into a face; the whole structure shook when it spoke.

"Topper, that way station is entirely too happy," Dartmallow said. "Someday I'll have it painted gray and quell its enthusiasm."

The company rode to stables at the back of the station, where men in homespun shirts and trousers hurried out to handle the horses. Topper dismounted and released Gray from the saddle horn, but left his hands tied together. Unable to balance himself properly, he nearly fell getting down, but Topper steadied him and made him stand with the other prisoners.

"What is this place?" Dauntless asked, eyeing the stables suspiciously.

"There are oats," a gray mare whinnied to him from the stable doorway.

"I like oats," Flapjack said.

The other horses all began talking at once, voicing their agreement.

"I will get there first and eat Maravilla's share," Nutmeg said.

"You will not," Maravilla neighed. The handlers had to restrain the two mares from racing to the stable.

The pup trotted to Gray and looked up at him. He was lanky and less than half-grown, with a long tail and a fine head. Gray had always liked dogs, and he offered the back of his bound hands for the animal to sniff. Unlike a normal dog, the pup kept his gaze fastened on Gray's face.

"You are a new one," the pup said, tail wagging. "My name is Blunder. Your eyes are different like mine. Why are your hands tied?"

"They are our prisoners," Topper said.

The pup's ears dropped. "Enemy?"

"Perhaps," Topper replied. "Be vigilant."

Blunder barred his teeth and growled at Gray's hands.

"Good boy," Topper said.

"Someone tell me where Vasps is," Marshal Dartmallow commanded. "I need Vasps."

"He's holding court in the grove, sir," a stable-hand answered.

"Excellent. He should be in a terrible mood, don't you think, Topper? He does his best inquiries when he's sullen. Let's have some fun. I want the prisoners kept separated with a guard and a dog on each. No talking among them; no talking from them. We will interview them one at a time." He looked around. "I don't want to start with the leader. We'll question him last." He pointed at Russ. "That one with the pieces of glass over his eyes. We'll begin with him."

A guard wielding a spear led Gray a few paces from the others. Sniffdaisy approached him, her ears up. "You will sit down," she said. "I will tear you if you are bad."

Gray lowered himself to the grass.

"*Ask, ask!*" the grass said.

Faced with the dog and the demands of the vegetation, Gray was momentarily flummoxed, but finally requested and received permission to sit.

Sniffdaisy rested on her haunches, eyeing Gray's throat, and Blunder bounded up to stand beside her. "I am watching," the pup growled.

Gray groaned as Russ was led away, wondering what torments

his companion might face.

* * *

His hands still tied, Russ was led across the greensward by two guards. They struck a path leading to a stand of stately beech trees, the faces on their smooth trunks solemn and thoughtful, their leaf-eyes wary. Plunging beneath their cool shade, the three wound their way between the boles until they came to a man seated at a square table, dressed in green and golden robes and wearing a turban with an emerald at its center. His skin was a deep brown. His right index finger bore a ring clasping a sizable tiger's eye. Across from him, huddled together on the edge of the table, sat a pair of swallows, their angular wings folded. A foot from them stood a male sparrow. The birds shifted their heads constantly, and one of the swallows fluttered its wings at Russ' approach.

"The sparrow took our nest," the other swallow was saying, each word a different, undulating note. Its breast was russet, its mate's, soft-white. "We built it. He took it."

The sparrow puffed himself up and chirruped, "I am Ooo-ooo-too-hoo, a mighty warrior, Killer of Grasshoppers. They were not there and I am stronger. My mate needs the nest."

The man ran one hand across his face. To Russ' surprise, he spoke in a British accent. "What I do not understand is why we must have this discussion every spring." He pointed at the swallows. "Your people do not complain if the blue jays eat your young."

The white-breasted swallow ruffled its wings in alarm. Russet-breast trilled a series of notes and its mate grew still.

"If the great jays come, that is the way of things," Russet said. "Each eats. Some are eaten. But nest stealing is wrong."

"I am stronger," Ooo-ooo-too-hoo said, taking a threatening hop toward the swallows. Both birds chirped and rose off the table, beating their wings at him.

"None of that!" the man said. "I will not have disruption in the court." The swallows returned to the table. He pointed to the sparrow, his eyes narrowing. "This is my judgment. You are the foolish one. You steal the nest of the swallows who build beneath the eaves. Those eaves are too high and what happens? Your young, who must spend a day on the ground before learning to fly, fall to the earth and die. The swallows lose their nest and raise no little ones. No one wins. You will go back and tell your people nest stealing will not be allowed between the swallows and the sparrows. You will give the nest in question back to its rightful owners. Is that understood?"

"We are the stronger," the sparrow said.

"Are you stronger than the crows?" the arbiter asked. "If you do not obey the judgment, I will tell the Overcowls and they will send the Ravagers."

The sparrow hopped across the table, cheeping in anger.

"If you peck me, it will go hard on you," the man said. "You will obey the court's directive."

The sparrow halted and crouched, his head down. "I will tell the others."

"The Overcowls will be watching," the man said. "You may all go."

The sparrow cheeped and flew to a branch where a half-dozen of his kind waited. Apparently, it was felt he had handled the case poorly, for a furious dispute arose among them, forcing Ooo-ooo-too-hoo to defend himself against mob violence. The host departed in a chattering flurry.

The two swallows hopped to the center of the table and gave bobbing bows. "Come, husband," Russet said. "I am heavy with egg." They flew in a wide circle and darted away.

"I do not understand why the Overcowls refuse to handle these cases," the arbiter said to no one in particular. "They clearly fall under their jurisdiction." He turned his eyes toward Russ just as Marshal Dartmallow strode up. "He is one of them?"

"One of six," the marshal said. "I want to be here for the questioning."

The man nodded and had a wooden chair placed across from him. "Be seated, please. I am Vasps Geometer. I will ask you questions and you will answer them truthfully."

It ran through Russ' mind that he should only give his name, rank, and serial number.

"You find this amusing?" Vasps Geometer asked.

"No, I was thinking of something else. You're English, aren't you?"

Surprise flickered across the man's face. "I was born in India, but came to St. Albans as a child. How do you know of England?"

"I'm American, if that means anything to you. What year did you come here?"

"We will ask the questions," Marshal Dartmallow said.

Vasps Geometer raised his hand. "With your permission, Marshal, this interests me. I sailed with Sir John Mandeville in the Year of Our Lord 1321. When our ship foundered off the coasts of the Sumobor, I was washed onto an island and entered a cave that led to Faerie. I eventually escaped to this country, which you know as the Back of the Beyond, though we call it Animonea. I have been here almost thirty years. Now tell me your name and why you are here."

"I'm Russell Rogers. I came to Faerie in 1945 through—"

"Wait!" Vasps Geometer flourished his hands. "That is impossible!"

"You'll find that two other members of our party are from different Earth eras."

"You make an astonishing claim. Go on. You say you are what? An Armenian?"

Russ hesitated. He had been through this with Joiwend and Jaunter. "American. There were two new continents discovered in 1492. The world is actually round, and—"

"Of course the world is round. Geometry shows us that. New continents! Tell me of your history before you came here."

Russ paused again, unsure where to begin. His life flashed before him: leaving home at thirteen when his parents couldn't afford to support him; working as a dollar-a-day cowboy on a ranch in New Mexico; earning money in the WPA during the Great Depression while going to college to study journalism; learning to fly planes there, then trying to enlist in the Air Force when the war broke out, only to be rejected for being color-blind. Later, being drafted into the Army and sent first to England, then France.

Saying none of that, he instead gave a brief sketch of the United States, mentioned being in a war, and told of his arrival in Faerie and the reason for entering the Back of the Beyond. Vasps Geometer listened attentively, occasionally interrupting to ask questions, his eyes glistening with interest.

When he was done, Vasps said, "You are either a madman or the possessor of extraordinary experiences. Your stories remind me of Sir John."

"I find most of what he said suspiciously incomprehensible, a cloak for his true intentions," Dartmallow said.

"He surely came from the same world as my own," Vasps Geometer said. "I can attest to that. The rest . . ." He shrugged. "The worlds are broken, you know, because of zero."

Dartmallow snorted, having apparently heard this before. Russ raised his eyebrows.

"I became a student of geometry shortly before leaving England," Vasps said. "It is a passion of mine. Since no one in Animonea could pronounce my proper name, I even took my new appellation from it. Though the concept of zero, which is nothing, originated in my native India, geometry shows us that it has ruined everything by creating universal asymmetry. When you call nothing something, you present a lie to the world. That lie has spread and we find ourselves in the situation we are in today. The rising of the Wileywood is a direct result—"

"None of that!" Dartmallow commanded. "Your theories are arcane and amusing, but wherever he is from, he may be a spy. Give away nothing."

Geometer closed his eyes and nodded. "You are correct." He looked at Russ. "If your story proves true, we shall speak further. One thing more: may I see your spectacles?"

"My . . . oh." Russ handed over his glasses.

Geometer studied them carefully. "These are well-constructed. They are mostly unknown here. Being somewhat near-sighted, I have made several unsuccessful attempts at grinding my own lenses. Can you tell me how they are made?"

"I don't know. The army issued them to me."

Vasps Geometer grimaced. "A shame."

* * *

When Gray's turn finally came, he found Vasps Geometer a marvel, with his strange clothes and stranger accent. After answering several questions, the prince asked if Geometer was a wizard, causing both his questioners to frown.

"We were told you came here with an enchanter," Vasps said.

"He was killed in a storm."

"Do any of your other followers practice magic?" Dartmallow asked.

The question made Gray wary. His thoughts ran swiftly to Joiwend. "No, they don't." He hoped the others had concealed her shape-changing ability.

The two examiners exchanged glances.

"It is for the best that your wizard perished," the marshal said. "The penalty for practicing sorcery in Animonea is exile or death. That you associated with an enchanter is little to our liking, but we know magic is common in Faerie."

When the examination was done, Vasps poured hot tea into a pewter mug, muttered a few words over it, and offered it to Gray. "You will find this soothing."

"*Drink me*," the tea whispered, its voice so low Gray could scarcely hear it.

He took it reluctantly, hoping it wasn't drugged. "You've heard our story, but you haven't told us why we were arrested. What do you plan to do with us?"

"You will hear the charges tomorrow," Vasps said. "A judgment will be pronounced thereafter. I do not know how it will go. Except for the one who calls himself Jaunter, all your accounts agree. He lied about everything in a passionately convincing manner. What he did not realize was that crows and ravens noticed you as soon as you came to Animonea and followed you every day. They were the ones who alerted us to your trespasses. Still, I admire his audacity, but would not entrust him with my mother's hairpins. Perhaps you can explain him."

"He is a Scythian," Gray said. "Their code of honor differs from our own. Despite that, I've trusted him with my life."

"Yet for a wonder, you remain unscathed," Vasps said. "I will tell you what I have learned. You are a strange company, drawn from many times and many lands. A barbarian, a cultured and beautiful woman, an audacious prince from Faerie, a madman who quotes the ancient Greeks, a soldier from a new continent, and you, their leader, little more than a boy, smitten by love for a comrade's intended."

Gray felt his face burning. Vasps Geometer chuckled. "As you can see, Marshal Dartmallow, unlike the Scythian this one is without guile."

"You will be given supper," the marshal said. "Tell your people to try no tricks tonight. You will be watched. If we have problems, our response will be swift, your punishment, severe."

* * *

The travelers spent the night in a windowless room, their door locked and guarded. All the furniture had been removed, and they were given blankets to cushion the oak floor. The sentries had taken the only lamp with them, leaving them in darkness save for a line of light shining beneath the door. They lay on their makeshift beds, quietly talking. Gray whispered a warning to Joiwend not to shape-shift around the inhabitants. Jaunter suggested several plans of escape, but the others demurred.

"They've not threatened us or caused us harm," Fox Lodan said. "I told them I was a prince. No doubt they will respect my nobility. At worst, they will ransom me to my father."

"Wonderful for you," Jaunter growled.

"I will see that all of you are delivered as well," Fox said. Gray doubted that included him.

"I hope your nobility helps you when we're walking to the gibbet," Jaunter said. "Probably a talking gibbet too. I don't trust them."

"You don't trust anyone," Joiwend said. "They were courteous enough to me. I don't think they know what to do with us. And there is something else. They're in a hurry. Some concern presses upon them."

"How do you know?" Russ asked. "What did they say?"

"A woman can read men sometimes. They are less guarded around us. It was in their voices and casual words." Her voice grew thoughtful. "They are a handsome people, with their bronze skin and dark eyes; we shall see if their goodness matches their beauty."

The companions fell silent. The voice of the moon rumbled

through the walls. "My ordeal done, I rise again. Was ever there such a hero as I?"

In the stillness, Gray's blankets sang, "*Sleep, sleep, I have you covered.*" The floor, cracking and popping with the cooling night air, whispered, "*Settle down, settle down, and I will hold you up.*"

"*I must stand firm,*" the door lock muttered.

Gray dreamed that night he was being smothered.

CHAPTER SIX

THE TRIAL

The next morning the companions were brought to an unadorned dining hall within the way station, floored with oak plank and lined with tables and wooden benches. The guards kept close by, swords drawn, but Vasps Geometer soon appeared and stood at the head of their table, leaving an empty chair on either side between himself and the prisoners. At his word, breakfast was served on wooden plates.

"Your attention, please. I would like your attention." Vasps spoke as if addressing an assembly rather than the six before him. "In the interest of time, I think it best I teach you our eating laws. Ah, none of that!" He pointed at Jaunter, who was about to bite into an apple. "Do not touch the food yet. For your own safety, you must first understand the Mandate of Gratitude. We observed it for you before last night's meal, but you need to learn to avoid any inadvertent violations of our laws. You see before you an apple, oatmeal mash, eggs, and a cup of water. I chose these specifically for you."

"Is there no meat?" Jaunter asked.

Vasps sighed. "Meat is another lesson altogether. We do eat meat, but the Gratitude is given at the killing of the animal. We do not raise livestock to be eaten because it is considered duplicitous to feed a beast only to slay it. As you have discovered, almost everything in Animonea is imbued with life and intelligence. When a thing dies, its life ends, but the result varies according to the object. An apple plucked from a tree still holds the seeds of life and will remain conscious for several days. The oats in this meal have been separated from the plant, and their individual intelligences are fading. The egg was never a chick, and so is like an inanimate object such as a stone—separated from its shell it is only aware at a rudimentary level.

"Fortunately, many of the things of Animonea want to be made use of. Objects given the shape of suitable instruments—cups, bowls, tools—though sometimes made of materials such as dead wood, reanimate when given a new form and usually desire to be of assistance. Their function follows their form. In the same way, the foods before you are agreeable to being devoured, but they require the Gratitude. The rite is simple; various phrases can be used, but I suggest the following words." He addressed his plate. "Thank you for dying that I might live."

"*Be welcome,*" the objects intoned.

"This needs to be done but once before the meal begins," Vasps said.

"What nonsense is this?" Fox Lodan demanded. "I am to beg permission from apples and oats? Treat them as my master? I'll not be made a fool." He raised his cup to his lips.

The guards' swords were instantly at his throat. "*Cut!*" the blades hissed. "*Cut!*"

Vasps' voice rose in anger. "You will not break the laws of Animonea! You are already in trouble; do not compound it with stubbornness."

Fox set the cup down.

Vasps spoke more gently. "Please understand this is no mere custom. If the Mandate of Gratitude is ignored, the inhabitants of Animonea will rebel. It happened once before, long ago, first the animals, then the plants and other objects. It could mean civil war and the end of the Republic of Everything. Is that clear? It must be, if you are to survive here. Are there questions? Very good. Now we will recite the Gratitude together. Please rise."

They stood to their feet and repeated the words. Joiwend smiled, amused, and gave Jaunter a sidelong glance. "It appears we must all learn better table manners. I, for one, approve. Our company could use a touch of refinement."

Jaunter grinned back at her. "You may have taught me the use of a fork, lady, but don't think this will win you the battle. They'll not tame me overmuch. Still . . ." His brow furrowed. "By Tabiti! I understand how gods can dwell in swords and trees, but in eggs? These are surely demons."

"Eat your breakfast and don't be insulting," Joiwend said. "Your oatmeal is listening."

"That is sound advice," Vasps Geometer said.

* * *

After breakfast the guards took the travelers to the beech grove where they had been questioned the day before, and made them sit on wooden stools. Vasps Geometer took his place at the small table, but it was Marshal Dartmallow, standing tall and proud, who addressed them. A flight of ravens landed in the branches of the trees behind him, accompanied by a black and white magpie. A gray parrot appeared, its wings pummeling the air as it came to perch, tall and majestic, in the ravens' midst. Scattered clouds looked down with interest; Sniffdaisy, her pup Blunder, and two other dogs watched from the shade of a bramble bush. The trees glared at the companions, indignant and angry, their leaves open-eyed, rustling in contempt.

"You stand charged with breaking the laws of Animonea, the Republic of Everything," the marshal said. "The crows and the forest have borne witness. Raven Glitter will produce testimony."

The raven flew down and landed on the table. It strutted, warbling, back and forth across its surface, then ruffled its feathers and turned a black eye toward the accused, speaking in a croaking voice. "They came over the border, two claws and one talon in number. One died yet lived again, and the scavengers did not feast on her. She and another ride now down Little River. One vanished in the storm; this the crows did not see for they sleep at night, but they heard the trespassers talking. They took four ear-hoppers and three quail without Gratitude. They traveled without permission. At first their horses ate grass without asking, though later they learned and did better. They assaulted bark and bole and trampled the greenery of the earth."

The surrounding trees began a low chant, their totem mouths

moving in unison. "Kill them. Kill them. Kill them all."

Vasps Geometer rapped the table with the palm of his hand. "There will be order."

"*Silence!*" the table boomed. The noise subsided.

"You are certain they came from over the border?" Dartmallow asked.

"The crows saw it," Glitter said. "If the trespassers are spies, it is for the Elf King."

A murmur ran among the trees; the magpie squawked and whispered something to the parrot.

The marshal turned to the Prince of Stallions. "Gray Darien is the leader of these people and will speak for them. How do you answer the charges?"

Gray swallowed. Reminding himself he was the son of a king, he stood up as he would in the Hall of Judgment in his own land of En. "We aren't spies. We have come, as we told you, to find our kidnapped friend, Tanabel-Tunia, and return her to her rightful place. Our trespasses were done in ignorance. We did not know it was wrong to kill the animals, and we did not understand your Mandate of Gratitude."

The parrot gave several whistling calls, and the magpie answered in sweet, sliding tones.

Glitter pointed a talon at Jaunter. "But when scarred-tallhat hunted the deer, he asked pardon after."

"So you do know our laws," Marshal Dartmallow said.

"I thought him a god!" cried Jaunter.

"Silence!" Dartmallow ordered. "Only your leader will speak."

"Jaunter is right," Gray said. "His people consider elk and deer sacred, and he followed their custom when he heard the dying stag speak. Had we known your decrees, we would not have killed."

"Ignorance is no excuse under the laws of the Republic," the magpie said.

"With all respect to our bird friend, our laws are not quite so black and white as he suggests," Vasps Geometer returned. "As for their being spies, the last time the Elf King sent an agent to Animonea was before I was born, and this man's testimony gives evidence that they are not in his service. Or if they are, they were ill-equipped for their mission." He raised his eyes from the table and looked at Gray.

"All animals understand that each must eat to stay alive. Your affront wasn't that you killed, but that you did not offer the Gratitude. Besides, your story fits other known facts."

"What facts?" the tallest of the beeches asked, its voice woody as a lute.

The marshal turned to the grove. "Six months ago we learned that a small party of soldiers disguised as farmers slipped across our western border from Ruheen, apparently intending to pass through to Faerie. They knew our customs and went unnoticed until too late to detain them, when they were seen scaling the Westwall into Faerie. Last week three of them returned accompanied by a woman. They were captured, but escaped before they could be questioned. They must have assumed disguises again, for we've had no word of them since."

Gray scarcely kept from crying out. That was surely Tana! Yet, who were these soldiers who had sought her from a distant land? How had they even known of her existence when no one journeyed from Faerie to the Back of the Beyond? Or had she been chosen by chance, perhaps by a prince seeking a bride of royal blood? If that was true, she might already have been forced to marry. Gray's chest went hollow at the thought.

"Is there further testimony from the accused, from the fowl, or from the forest?" the marshal asked. He was met by silence. "Very well, we will begin with the verdict of the Overcowls."

The ravens croaked and danced along the branches in furious debate, talking in their own tongue, with occasional sing-song interjections from the magpie. Finally they ceased and the parrot spoke in a throaty squawk. "We will speak for the deer and the hares, who are too timid to answer for themselves. When the egg opens, the hatchling does not know all. So too these strangers. From Duskell Watch they passed through the Quiet Wood, where much of the land is not fully awake, and so only gradually became aware that ours is a country where all things live. They did not know our laws and customs. So we say if they are not spies, this is not a matter for the slaying, either for the humans or the horses. But restitution must be made by service given. That is the word of the Overcowls."

"What does the grove say?" the marshal asked.

If the trees debated among themselves, it was undetectable to the companions. The silence stretched out, the minutes passing. Gray fidgeted. When he thought no answer would come at all, the old beech finally spoke. "The forest says both the horses and men are guilty. The forest demands death!"

Vasps Geometer turned to Marshal Dartmallow.

"As the human representative, I agree with the Overcowls," the marshal said. "No executions, but service must be given."

Vasps Geometer rose and stood with his back to the companions, facing the scowling grove. "The vote is two to one, so we must move to the Conciliation Phase. I will address the grove, who is of the minority opinion."

Vasps rubbed his hands together and cleared his throat. "If a tree falls in the forest and a badger is crushed, is the tree at fault?"

"That is the nature of the world," the old beech said.

"If a high limb falls on a man so he dies, should the tree be cut down?"

"That is not the fault of the tree. It is happenstance." The beech looked uneasy, and Gray wondered if it was remembering the assault on Tatters.

"If seven saplings spring up together, and one grows taller, keeping the others from the sun so they wither and die, does it do so out of malice?" Vasps asked.

"It is the way of trees," the beech said. "The strongest must survive."

"Men must move and hunt to live. Is the hunting wrong?"

"The hunting is not wrong," the old beech said.

"If a man who hunts harms the forest in ignorance by walking through it without permission, is the man more guilty than the sapling that shaded his fellows so they died?"

The grove fell silent, the brows of their barks furrowed in consideration, the eyes of their leaves blank and staring. Five minutes passed, then thirty. Gray grew drowsy in reaction to the tension. Finally, the old tree said, "The strangers are not innocent, yet they should not be made to wither."

Vasps turned to the marshal, who nodded and addressed the travelers. "Very well. It is my judgment, and the judgment of the Overcowls and the Grove that you have committed a crime not unto death in the Republic of Everything. Your lives are spared.

However, a Service of Restitution is required. You will render that service until I or another in authority rule it fulfilled. Normally I would take you to our capitol, Ravenperch, to carry out your sentence, but I am needed elsewhere. I cannot leave you blundering about the countryside. You will go with us. Perhaps your service can be worked out along the way. Disobedience will be punished as treason, requiring the immediate execution of your entire party."

The ravens, the magpie, and the parrot lifted wing and soared away. The faces of the trees melted into their bark; their leaf-eyes closed, leaving little trace of where they had been. The companions rose uncertainly.

Gray turned to Dartmallow. "Marshal, we thank you for your clemency, but our mission is urgent. We have to find Tanabel—"

Dartmallow gave him a piercing glance. "You have no idea what you have cost me. I will have to answer to the All-Council for my decision. If you make me regret it, you will hang by the neck from trees such as these, and they will rejoice as you die."

Dartmallow turned and strode away, leaving Gray staring at his back. But Vasps Geometer smiled and took Gray's arm. "Do not be concerned. The marshal has many responsibilities. Do as he says and all will be well. Now come along."

Side-by-side they left the grove, the other companions following.

"As the Marshal of the North Rond, Dartmallow serves as the Representative of Justice in this part of Animonea," Vasps continued. "As you saw, the grove was easily placated. They are creatures of strong emotion but little intellect, though the outcome would have been different if you had actually cut down a tree. I do not think I could have persuaded them then, and the birds would have voted against you. The Overcowls, however, will not forget this day. When next they require some favor from the marshal, they will remind him that they spared humans from death. It would have been more expedient for him to order your execution."

"Why didn't he, then?" Gray asked. "Why did you defend us? We're grateful, of course, but you scarcely know us."

"The Back of the Beyond, as you call it, is a confederation of living things. In such variety there is always disagreement, for it lacks the order found in the exactitude and symmetry of geometry. The marshal is a fair man. He is also human. Explaining the behavior of humans to trees and birds is difficult. He could have voted to let you die; in the end he sided with your humanity. As for me, I thought it a shame to take your lives because of your inexperience. Not only that, but like myself some of you are from Earth, and I look forward to conversing with you."

"Where will we go now?"

Vasps' brow furrowed. "I suppose I can tell you that. I never believed you were spies, unless extremely untalented ones. We will be traveling north and west to Morlane, the Wileywood. Who knows? Perhaps you will find this woman you seek there."

* * *

Within the hour, the soldiers left the way station, Marshal Dartmallow leading, Gray and his friends, unbound but still weaponless, riding together in the midst of their guards. The foot soldiers marched behind the cavalry; the dogs padded at the fringes. The companions' horses huffed and threw their heads, nickering and talking among themselves, excited to accompany so many of their kind. Both Soonderkainen and Ninette's mounts chose to remain with them, and Gray learned that Animonean horses could be neither bought nor sold, but were given new riders by mutual equine and human consent. Dauntless whinnied, stepping as proudly as if it were he who led.

"Going," Nutmeg blew.

"Going," the other horses echoed.

"Permission to travel?" Topper called to the road.

"*Follow me, follow me,*" the road said cheerfully. The trees were placid; the clouds stared down, their faces thoughtful; the sun beamed smiling and serene in the sky. Insects buzzed around the band, humming their endless songs. Even the travelers' clothing began a sonant murmuring. A field of foxgloves chanted with one silken voice, "*The light! The light! We reach for the light!*" and the bees gave thrumming answer.

"It's like a Walt Disney cartoon at the movie matinee," Russ said. "Gives new meaning to the phrase 'a good day.'"

Riding beside Gray Darien, Vasps Geometer smiled. "I do not understand your reference, but the day *is* a good one. Your trial quelled the indignation of the forest for many leagues. We will ride easier for it."

"There's so much we don't understand about your country," Gray said.

"I sympathize with your confusion, for I experienced it myself when I first came to Animonea. Like Jaunter, I thought it a land of demons. I was fortunate to find guidance early, else I might have made many of your mistakes. You still do not comprehend the depth of your crimes. The trees commune with one another and speak to the birds, who talk to the animals. Word of your misdeeds spread throughout the region. The marshal received protests the day after your arrival. We had to respond swiftly, before the countryside took steps of its own to remove your threat. The wolves you encountered were the beginning of what would have become a sustained assault. They knew you were law-breakers. In their eyes that made you lawful prey."

"How do you live among so many voices?" Joiwend asked.

"You will learn to embrace them. To me, they are like the surety of geometry and the equipoise of mathematics, ever present and beautiful. The levels of intelligence differ and must be dealt with in distinct ways. Each species has a unique nature, varying in independence and compliance. Horses are a good example, a blend of loving docility and fierce stubbornness."

"I am not stubborn," Nutmeg said.

"Of course you're not," Vasps said.

"You are too," Maravilla nickered.

"I am not," Nutmeg tried to bite Maravilla's flank.

Gray jerked Nutmeg's reins. "Stop that!" She laid her ears back and fell silent.

"At the trial the raven mentioned our friends, Corporal Spence and Ninette Argilla," Russ said. "Will you arrest them too?"

"They are being watched, but allowed their freedom," Vasps said. "Fortunately, they chose to travel on the river, Eddy, more widely known as the Simborime. He has explained the Mandate of Gratitude and they have followed our laws."

"But how can your people rule this country?" Joiwend asked. "It seems impossible."

"We are a representative government without a king or royalty.

Laws are passed by a majority vote of the All-Council, whose elected officials represent the various groups of humans, forests, mountain ranges, birds, and those land and aquatic animals wise and caring enough to participate. Since many of our citizens are unable or unwilling to come to the polling places, appointed Couriers must travel to them, which makes the canvassing of the vote demanding and even dangerous work—the mountain ranges, slow and ponderous of thought, often cannot make up their minds, forcing the Couriers to remain in the highlands for weeks; the wolves and other carnivores sometimes mistake them for prey. As a younger man serving as a Courier in the South Rond, I once had some difficulty convincing a pride of lions of my sincerity. It was a memorable hour."

A male blue-jay on a branch beside the road gave a raucous call. *"Hear me, riders who pass! I am Tumbalor the Mighty, Nest Conqueror and Eater of Eggs! I am—"*

A pair of yellow-breasted kingbirds rose from the trees, filling the air with their scolding chatter. *"Bad! Bad! Away!"* The jay held its perch only a moment before gliding to another tree. The pair followed, swooping at the intruder's head. Tumbalor the Mighty darted away, losing himself in the forest.

"Good! Good!" the kingbirds jabbered, returning in triumph to their nest.

"Our avian citizens are not without self-esteem," Vasps Geometer said. "Most care little for human affairs. The wisest of their kind are the ravens, magpies, and parrots; from these are chosen the Overcowls."

"Their rulers?" Fox Lodan asked.

"Birds have no monarchy. The Overcowls are their representatives, having sufficient intelligence to make decisions, but even they are sometimes foolish—the lure of bright objects is a terrible temptation to a raven."

"Birds may not possess sovereigns, but there is a pecking order among them," Fox Lodan said. "Your government is a perversion of nature, a desecration of the Natural Law of the Right of Kings to rule. How else can the peasants be protected, except by their liege lords?"

"Our country had kings once," Vasps said. "In Animonea the

people now protect themselves."

Fox snorted. "Then your government will surely fail. The rabble have no wisdom; mob rule can only result in chaos."

"We are guests here, Fox," Joiwend said.

"Not only that, but you're showing your ignorance," Gray said, recalling his tutor, Aristides. "Both the Greek and Roman Republics lasted for generations."

"I neither know nor care about your paltry earthly provinces," Fox retorted. "The Elf King was sovereign in Faerie when Time began. My people's kingdom, Jenar, has existed for thousands of years there." He grinned at Joiwend. "As for watching my words, I wager even guests are allowed an opinion in a country where every twig has a voice in the government."

"Precisely speaking, you are not guests but prisoners until your Service of Restitution is complete," Vasps said, "but your views do not offend me. Your position is an old one, debated many times in Animonea's early days, and still espoused by a few. I have some wonderful charts at home I would love to show you sometime." His brown eyes lit with enthusiasm. "Using mathematics and geometry, I compare both the symmetry and the irregularity of authoritarian and representative forms of government. It is true that a republic is more chaotic, as clearly revealed by the numbers, yet there is also a surprising measure of order if the inhabitants can establish their own Rule of Law. I can explain some of the geometric formulas as we ride. For instance, knowing that opposite sides of a parallelogram are parallel by using a linear equation—"

"That sounds fascinating, Monsieur Geometer," Joiwend said sweetly, a tone Gray recognized as gently mocking. "I should like to see those charts someday, but you haven't yet explained why everything is so alive."

"True, my lady," Vasps said, visibly charmed. "In the mountains of the North Rond stands the Omnifire, a fountain of flame. It is glorious to see. In the spring the melting snow runs into its valley and through its base. Where those waters flow, throughout all the Back of the Beyond, everything grows in knowledge. So it was when the first men came here long ago from the east." He laughed. "It is we, you see, who are the newcomers."

"This Omnifire must be a great god," Jaunter said. "I should like to see him."

"It is the Fount of Wisdom," Vasps said. "It gave us our laws. For those brave enough to enter its flames, if they do not perish by its fires, it gives discernment. Once, each king was required to enter there before his coronation. At first, when they were men of honor, they came away purified and filled with knowledge. But the flames killed or seared some of the later kings, until they feared it and refused to enter. Corruption grew, resulting in war and revolution. Our republic was formed many generations ago from the ashes of the monarchy. I've often thought it would make an excellent tradition for the royalty of Europe to take such a test."

"Would you walk in the flames, Fox?" Gray taunted.

"The trials of princes are many," Fox Lodan replied. "I have never been found wanting in courage."

"If you had seen the Omnifire you would know it is not a matter of jest," Vasps said. "I have long desired to gain its wisdom, but its flames are not some illusion or trickery. Perhaps when I am old I will be brave enough to enter."

* * *

The soldiers followed the road until noon, when they halted for lunch. After taking their rations from their packs, the cavalry released their horses to graze, not bothering to picket them. Gray and the others followed suit, tying the animals' bridles loosely to their saddle horns so they could reach the grass. Under Vasps' watchful eye, they asked the sward's permission to sit, and offered the Mandate of Gratitude. Two iron entrance-posts stood close by, singing, *"We stand together, we stand as one,"* slightly out of tune from the paving stones' low humming. They had scarcely begun eating, however, before their horses ceased browsing and approached their masters.

"We are unhappy," Dauntless said. "Our bridles are bad. We want bridles like the others."

"No iron," Nutmeg said.

"No iron," Maravilla and Jingles echoed.

Gray grimaced. He had noticed the soldiers' bridles lacked mouthpieces.

Russ chuckled. "I figured it would come to this." Taking a long knife from his belt, he approached Flapjack. "Hold still, boy. I'll cut her off."

"*No cutting!*" the bridle objected.

"Sorry, but it's necessary," Russ said. "With your permission."

"*Be welcome,*" the bridle conceded.

Clasping it to keep Flapjack's head still, he severed the leather holding the bit and drew it from its place behind the horse's teeth.

"Better," Flapjack said, tossing his head.

"Don't get cocky. I can stitch it back on if you act up."

"I won't," Flapjack said.

"I bet." Russ turned to the other horses. "Who's next?"

The animals crowded around and were soon free of their bits. Russ shrugged, grinned, and rejoined the companions. "Democracy at work. Where will it all end?"

While they ate, Vasps pointed out the landmarks surrounding them. "Those distant mountains are the beginning of the Alopean Range. The two highest peaks, over there, are Farsight and Reverie. Between their slopes stands the Omnifire. These foothills where we now journey are called the Middlemounds. During the Revolution, the Battle of the Four was fought near here, when men, wolves, birds, and the forest joined together to oust Nozaron, the last king of Animonea. A few leagues ahead we will cross the Singing Bridge over the Brisk River, a branch of the Simborime."

Gray followed Vasps' directions with his eyes. This early in the spring, the tops of Farsight and Reverie lay mantled in snow. Between the hills to the northeast lay a gleaming ribbon, the contour of the river.

"It's beautiful country," Joiwend said.

"It can be," Vasps said, "but dangerous also."

Throughout the morning Gray had grown despondent. At first, buoyed by Vasps' suggestion that they might find Tana along the way, he had journeyed eagerly, but as the country stretched on, league after league, his spirit had sagged, leaving him anxious and brooding. He needed to be searching for her instead of wandering down this endless road. He had spent the last hour trying to form a plan to either escape or to sway his captors, but it appeared hopeless. Even if he won free, bolting meant leaving his comrades to face the consequences; and the marshal was not a man to be lenient. No one, not even Joiwend, would understand that his was a love like none before, legendary and perfect, the essence of poetry. When he had first entered Faerie, the third son who must always succeed, he had never doubted his winning through. He had pictured their meeting a thousand times, her face aglow with adoration and wonder at his pursuing her through so many dangers. She would fall into his arms and they would ride away, leaving Fox Lodan staring, mouth agape. But there were no guarantees in Animonea. His dreams had fallen into nightmare. Being the third son meant nothing in this land. He chewed his rations without tasting them.

He looked up and found the pup, Blunder, staring intently at him. The Prince of Stallions tossed the last of his dried deer meat to the hound, who tried to catch it in mid-air but missed. Scrambling to retrieve it, he tripped over his own feet and nearly fell before regaining his balance and wolfing it down. He looked at Vasps Geometer, one ear flapped up revealing its pink interior. "Is he still enemy?"

"He is *cobokot*," Vasps replied.

"Cobokot," Blunder repeated.

"What does that mean?" Gray asked.

"It is somewhat complicated," Vasps said. "The actual translation is a reference to scent. It means you are not part of the pack, yet neither enemy nor prey. It is equivalent to saying you are untried and cannot yet be trusted."

Watching Blunder cheered Gray somewhat. Despite his clumsiness, he was a fine-looking animal, his fur thick and white with sparse black spots which also dotted his ears. Whirls of gold and black surrounded his mismatched blue and brown eyes. His teeth were sharp and ivory white.

"You're a handsome one," Gray said. "What did you do to get your name?"

Blunder turned his head back and forth, puzzled. "My mother gaved me my name."

"Like horses, dogs are neither bought nor sold here," Vasps explained. "The relationship between human and canine is based on the concept of the pack. The puppy or its parents choose the man or woman, not the other way around. It is considered an honor to be selected as a pack friend." He reached over and stroked Blunder's head. The pup rolled onto his back and feigned biting at Vasps' hand. Gray was tempted to scratch the hound's belly, but refrained, uncertain whether a cobokot was allowed such familiarity.

Marshal Dartmallow soon ordered everyone back on the road. Inspired by the freedom from her bridle bit, Maravilla tried to lead a mild protest against leaving off grazing, but Dauntless overruled her, and the journey proceeded well thereafter. Within the hour they topped a rise overlooking the long slope of the Brisk Valley, where wound the rushing flow of the Brisk River. The Singing Bridge, a steel frame floored with wood, glistened in the sun above the silver waters. The trees were sparser on the Brisk's far side, where hundreds of pronghorn antelope gathered to drink.

Master Tatters whistled at the sight of them. "Bountiful as the bison before we hunted them out. Glorious!"

"Sound the *bydords*, Topper," the marshal commanded.

"Bydords forwaaard!" Topper bawled. A pair of foot soldiers hurried to the front of the line, carrying short, double-belled brass horns. These they blew in unison. The wide mouths of the bydords sang out, their notes echoing across the valley. "*We hunt not! We hunt not!*" Three times this was repeated before the musicians returned to their places.

"This custom keeps the herd from having to flee as they normally would do," Vasps explained.

"A clever hunter could use those horns to his advantage," Fox said.

"Such a one would be dead by sunset," Vasps replied. "The whole countryside would mark him not only as prey, but as a dangerous animal to be put down."

Long metal cables upheld the bridge, and as the company drew closer, the slow rise and fall of its voice caroled above the torrent of the Brisk, a low resonance shifting in tone, with harping notes above creating a varying glissando. Gray could feel the steady beating of the vibrations against his chest.

"You have come to Animonea at a good time," Vasps said. "The waters are swift this season of the year. The bridge's suspension cables are strong but surprisingly thin, while the supporting pillars are hollow, allowing the force of the river to set up sympathetic vibrations along the structure's length, an excellent example of mathematic resonances applied to architecture."

They reached the foot of the bridge, a span wide enough for twenty men to walk abreast.

"Permission to cross!" Topper shouted.

"*Granted*," the whole framework sang.

As Nutmeg stepped onto the structure, Gray felt the vibrations rise from the oak planks through the mare's body and into his own, a surprisingly rhythmic undulation akin to being rocked on a boat. He drew a deep breath and released it in time to the cadence, feeling the tension in his neck and shoulders flow away. Brooding on Tana had made him even more anxious than he realized.

"This is delicious," Joiwend said. "If only we could spend a night sleeping on the span!" She touched Gray's arm. "Look!"

He followed her gaze to the tumbling river below, where a long face, fierce and intense, appeared and disappeared within the waters. He heard the river's cry, an endless flowing call. "*Hasten to the sea, to the sea, to the sea! Hasten to the sea*!" As the current passed around the support columns, it modulated the bridge's song, so the whole structure rang with its coursing chant. The sun and clouds looked serenely down, the trees quivered and swayed, open-eyed, along the bank. Gray stared in wonder. Sudden tears, unbidden, misted his vision.

"It's like living poetry," he exhaled. Too moved for words, Joiwend reached over and squeezed his hand.

The company began exiting the bridge. As Nutmeg stepped onto solid ground and the vibrations left his body, Gray turned to gaze back at the water, wanting never to forget the moment. Surely in such a wondrous land he would find his beloved.

Blunder, having climbed onto the bridge's flat guardrail, stood leaning over the water, his nose held high. As Gray watched in amusement, the pup pawed at a passing butterfly, only to lose his balance and tumble into the Brisk. The flood carried him downstream, his flailing paws struggling to keep his head above water.

Without thinking, Gray shouted and kicked his mare in the flanks. Trained by their battles in Faerie, Nutmeg responded instantly, shouldering aside the other animals to break free of the crowd. Within moments she was at a full gallop, but Blunder was already several lengths ahead.

They raced along the bank, steep and high above the water, gaining ground on the floundering pup. A deep rut crossed their path. Nutmeg leapt it without losing stride, but had to slow to maneuver between tangled vegetation. They began encountering the pronghorns, sending them scattering to either side, Gray struggling to keep his eyes on both Blunder and their course.

At the water's edge sped Blunder's mother, Sniffdaisy, a little behind him, stretched to her full length, barking as she ran. He kicked Nutmeg's flanks, urging her to greater speed, and she responded with a tremendous burst. He could see Blunder thrusting his head up, trying to stay afloat, furiously paddling toward shore but making little headway.

For long seconds Nutmeg pounded forward, inching her way in front of the pup's position, but the water's edge lay beneath an angling grade several feet below them. With no time for consideration, Gray turned the mare down the bank, pulling up on the reins, keeping her head high to prevent her falling. The ground was precarious, uneven. Gray slid to one side of his saddle, pushed with his leg and righted himself, bounced to the other side. Horse and rider took to the air for an awful instant and all sound seemed to cease.

They landed in the river, their momentum carrying them within a few lengths of Blunder's position. Gray leapt from his saddle and wrapped his arms around the pup. They tumbled through the flood, the current stronger than Gray had expected, a rushing tide. He looked for Nutmeg. She was behind him, treading water; he suddenly realized they might all drown. He could hear the river around him, many voices speaking at once, but the loudest saying, *"I take what comes to me. I sweep it on and on."*

He began stroking with one arm toward shore, kicking his feet as hard as he could, holding Blunder before him. Slowly, they drew closer to the bank. They might make it if his strength could hold and his muscles didn't cramp in the biting-cold water.

Despite his efforts he felt his strokes lessening. Only a few paces more, but he was beginning to lose ground. He tried redoubling his efforts, to no avail. He wasn't going to make it.

Then Sniffdaisy reached them. Grasping his tunic between her teeth, she paddled, adding her powerful limbs to his own. Together they moved toward the bank. Nutmeg swam up beside them and Gray reached, catching her mane. Working together, they came to shore. Gray fell to his knees, holding Blunder. The pup was wild-eyed but breathing. Man, horse, and hounds gasped for breath.

The marshal and several others rode up. Russ and Master Tatters hurried to Gray's aid, helping him sit upright. Even Fox Lodan dismounted and stood watching.

"Courageously done!" Marshal Dartmallow said.

"Brave, but foolish," Fox said. "You could have died for that mongrel."

Sniffdaisy growled at the prince.

Gray could find no reply. For once, Fox was right. He didn't know why he had done it. It had been automatic and stupid. He had nearly lost his horse and his own life. Where would Tana be if he had perished?

Sniffdaisy drew close to Gray. She whined and licked his hand. "You saved my pup. You saved my Blunder."

She looked him in the eyes, a disquieting stare. "You will be his now. You will be Blunder's human. I give you to him to be his pack leader. You are forever pack friends."

*   *   *

Vasps addressed Gray as soon as they reached their evening campsite, a stand of trees sheltered to the east by tall hills. "When a dog honors a human with the gift of a puppy, the rite is normally held as soon as possible. We will do so now."

"Do I have a choice in this?" Gray asked.

Vasps frowned. "You can refuse, but I would not recommend it. It is considered the act of a miscreant, earning you the scorn of the marshal, his men, and the dogs, a black mark that will follow you so long as you remain in Animonea. On the other side of the argument, if you take the oath, you must honor it. To do otherwise could lead to imprisonment or even death."

"You have many rules in your country," Gray said.

Vasps smiled. "Each designed to protect its inhabitants. What do you say, my friend? Your bravery has won the hearts of many. To spoil it now . . ."

Gray shrugged. There was a certain poetry in it, he supposed, like in an heroic ballad, the young prince and the faithful hound. "Lead on."

The ceremony was simple. Gray, Blunder, and Sniffdaisy were made to stand in the center of the camp, surrounded by the entire company. Marshal Dartmallow presided. He made the pup sit and instructed the Prince of Stallions to kneel on his left knee.

"Hand to paw, paw to hand," the marshal said.

Blunder raised his right paw.

"The other paw," Sniffdaisy said. "You will put it on his knee."

Gray covered the pup's paw with his right hand.

"According to the ancient traditions," Dartmallow said, "and by the sacred laws of the Republic of Everything, Sniffdaisy comes to present her pup, Blunder to the man, Gray Darien. Does Sniffdaisy do so willingly?"

"Sniffdaisy does," she said.

"Does Blunder desire to accept Gray Darien as his pack leader, to follow him all his life, to obey his will, to share his prey, to be his nose and his teeth and his scout, to fight for him, to lick his wounds, to die for him if necessary?"

Blunder wagged his tail, panting with excitement. "I will do it."

"Does Gray Darien take Blunder into his pack, to be his leader so long as both live, to share his food, to treat him with listening and understanding, to fight for him, to be his armor and his protector, to bind his wounds, to die for him if necessary?"

With some embarrassment Gray said, "I so swear."

"Then by the laws of Animonea, I declare you one pack, one mouth, one jaw, one nose, one set of eyes. May you always greet one another with wagging tail and a gentle hand. The ceremony is concluded."

Blunder raised himself on Gray's knee and licked his face, his puppy breath warm on Gray's cheek. Gray ruffled the white head.

"Let me be the first to congratulate you," Joiwend said. "I never saw anyone marry a puppy before."

"Very funny." Gray felt his cheeks burning. He avoided looking at the disdainful smirk he knew must mark Fox Lodan's face.

* * *

There was a furtiveness about the soldiers' preparations that night, for they lit no fires, and as the darkness gathered the men grew more circumspect, sitting in small groups, scarcely moving, eating from their rations, making none of the noise one would expect in such an assembly.

The companions had been assigned to Marshal Dartmallow's group, undoubtedly so they could be watched. Gray sat beside Joiwend, Blunder sleeping at his feet. The moon, not yet risen, cast its first light into the sky.

"What am I going to do with a puppy?" Gray whispered to Joiwend. "I don't need a dog to take care of."

"You mustn't receive this lightly," Joiwend said. "You have gained the trust not only of this little one and his mother, but to a certain degree, that of the marshal. These dogs are intelligent, but betrayal is as foreign to them as it is to animals on Earth. They can't comprehend that the hand that feeds might someday slay them. To the canine mind, the importance of the pack is everything. I know, for I have experienced it. It is beyond human loyalty. It is unshakable, incorruptible; if men were steadfast as dogs, the world would be a better place." She reached over to stroke Blunder's head, and he growled in his sleep. "I believe they were given to us as an illustration of the depths of friendship." She smiled. "Besides, he's adorable. He will be useful when he's fully grown."

"I have to take it seriously." Gray kept his voice low. "I've given my word, but you just want someone to play with when you're a wolf."

She laughed and shook her head, her hair rustling in the dimness. "Wolves and dogs will always be enemies, but I'm sure we can get along if I change into a poodle."

Jaunter, already asleep, began to moan. "The eyes!" he whispered. "Keep away!" His voice rose, disrupting the quiet.

Topper, walking by, reached across to him, but Gray grabbed the soldier's wrist. "Don't touch him. He might accidentally kill you."

"He's got to be quiet."

Joiwend gently called the Scythian's name. He woke with a start, fists clenched, flailing at the air. "The eyes!"

"Hush," Joiwend soothed. "It's only a dream. Only a dream."

Jaunter looked wildly about. Realizing where he was, he growled, drew one hand over his brow, and threw himself back onto his bed-roll.

"He has nightmares sometimes," Gray said. "Always about eyes. He won't speak of it. I'm not sure if he remembers them the next morning. We learned to be careful waking him."

The vast rim of the moon appeared above the hilltops, and the soldiers grew even more hushed. Gray watched it rising, slightly less than full. It pursed its lips and opened its eyes. Its voice boomed across the countryside. "I climb once more from the pit unbowed, alive yet not unscathed, this rind of darkness on noble face, a scar received in my deadly race. Still I prevail, Lord of the Heavens! Look upon my works, you mighty, and despair."

"When he's full, he's full of himself." Topper sat down beside them, thin-faced as an axe beneath his metal skull cap. "You'll like him better on the wane. Less haughty then."

Joiwend laughed. "Is he who we're hiding from?"

"We aren't hiding," Topper said. "Being prudent. He's a blab. We don't want him telling the whole world a company of soldiers are traveling toward Morlane."

"Why the secrecy?" Gray asked.

"Because of the enemy."

"What enemy?"

"I shouldn't speak of that, even if you are a pack friend. You'll find out when we reach the Wileywood. Plenty of time to face the invaders then."

CHAPTER SEVEN

DOWNSTREAM

For Ninette Argilla the world was a place of utter wonder. In Faerie, before her Awakening, she had possessed little sense of self, viewing her life as through a distant glass. Given with the best intentions, Soonderkainen's instructions on living had remained interesting but remote. Now she could taste and feel and *be*; now her awareness—her joy and sorrow and anger and selfishness—threatened to overwhelm her. She felt everything, and it was magnificent, but it was hard.

"On we go," Eddy the stream murmured. "On and on to the sea."

"On and on," Boat echoed, its painted eyes gleaming. In its eagerness, it had forgotten its former owner, and no longer asked when it would be returned.

This was their sixth day on the water, traveling at a fair pace through a land of tall hills and low mountains. They had crossed a much wider river four days before, a terrifying torrent Eddy called the Brisk. His voice had changed once they entered it, growing deep and wild; he sent them plunging and spinning, heedless of their safety, and Ricky soon diverted the craft to a narrow stream on the far side. After that, Eddy was gentle and kind again, guiding them each night to the safest spot to camp on his banks. He explained the laws of hunting and eating—the Mandates of Gratitude—and told them wonderful stories about the animals and plants lining his shore. Under his guidance Ninette was growing used to everything being able to talk, even the moon, which sometimes frightened her, and he was good company whenever Ricky became quiet, as he often did; but the corporal was nice to her too. She had wept on learning they must have passed the other companions, and he had shown her card tricks, making her laugh, and rubbed her shoulders to help her relax. She was learning how sad it was to be sad; it made her sad now to think of having *been* sad. But she liked the way Ricky and Eddy tried to cheer her.

The sheer multitude of animals in the Back of the Beyond gave her endless delight. Hordes of birds passed overhead or fluttered through the trees, jabbering and jubilant in their spring migration. Rabbits scampered along Eddy's banks; deer and elk dipped their heads to drink; and once a mountain lion, marvelous and majestic and sly, watched the travelers drift by. Every animal had a voice, some more intelligent than others, but each beautiful in its own way, and their beauty brought Ninette to laughter or tears.

"Ahead are three bends with a beaver fortress at each," Eddy said. "We sometimes war, for they seek to stop me, building their nests to divert me, turning me into ponds and pools and wetlands where tall herons wade and solemn kingfishers call. But I will not be con-tained and must hurry on, though a part of me remains behind, abandoned, bittersweet in the separation."

"Any people?" Spence asked.

"They await us beyond the bends, in the Place of the Spoiling, where they dump ash and molten metal into me, warming me with strange, liquid fire, leaving me murky for many leagues."

Spence looked at Eddy from beneath the shade of his army helmet. The day was warm and sunlight reflected off the water. Sweat dripped from his brow. "Metal, huh? What kind of place are you talking about?"

"It is named the Yarrow, after the spring flowers that blossom there. You will see it soon."

The sun drifted west above the stream, passing from late afternoon to evening, vanishing into a haze of pink, watchful clouds whose faces left Ninette wistful, for their wide eyes reminded her of Soonderkainen. The air grew cool. Seeking solace, she searched the sky for the first star, grinning and clapping her hands when she spied it.

A slapping noise diverted her attention, an alarm from the first of the dams. A pair of beavers stuck their noses out of the water and studied Boat, one of them making a rapid series of *chups*. As the travelers drew closer, Eddy's waters swept whispering around the animals. "*Let me pass; let me pass.*"

One of the beavers swam nearer, but not too close. "Wood-runner, man-hunker, golden-hair!" Its voice resembled the sing-song whimper of a puppy. It slapped its tail three times in the water. "Won't catch us; can't catch us." It *chupped* again.

"You're laughing at us," Ninette exclaimed, delighted.

"Funny funny no-tails," the beaver taunted. It dove beneath the water, only to reappear a few paces away. Others of its kind circled Boat, making various calls, delighted as children at the strangers' arrival.

"Little-man, Little-man!" one cried.

"Aw, nuts to you!" Spence said. "Go away! If I had a rock, I'd crown you."

"*Attack!*" his army helmet ordered.

"Don't be mean, Ricky," Ninette said. "They're *so* adorable."

"Yeah, well, I don't like nobody making fun of my height."

"They don't intend anything by it."

Boat swept on, leaving the jeering beavers behind, but as Eddy had said, another dam waited around the bend. Whether they had heard the calls of their fellows or were simply following their natures, these too took up the jibes, leaving Spence sullen. The stream widened at the third bend, and timbers from the dam crossed it completely, forcing the travelers to climb ashore and carry Boat around it. Spence tripped getting back into the craft, soaking his pants up to his knees, and the beavers filled the air with their barking laughter. Cursing, Spence found a stone and threw it at one of them. The beaver submerged, avoiding a vicious blow to the head. The others vanished, diving deep.

"That'll show 'em," Spence muttered. "They mess with me, I'll have beaver steaks for breakfast."

"*Yeah!*" his helmet said.

By the time they were back in the water, the last rays of the sun had turned Eddy's surface orange and pink.

"Perhaps we should stop for the night, Ricky," Ninette said. "It's getting dark."

"Maybe. I don't want those beavers getting close enough to sneak up on us while we sleep. They're vicious. What do you say, Eddy?"

"I have never seen a beaver attack a sleeping human," the stream said. "There is a place around the next turning where you might seek sanctuary."

As they came around the bend, shafts of the fading sun shone straight down the river. Shading her eyes, Ninette saw a dock extending several feet into the water from a rock outcropping. From out of the shadows, a tall man stepped onto it, carrying a spear and wearing a helmet and long cloak, a shadow himself against the sunlight.

"What's this about, Eddy?" Spence hissed, drawing his long-knife. "You backstabbing us? I thought we were friends."

"It is the beginning of the Yarrow, as I told you."

Ninette unsheathed her sword. She didn't know much about emotions, but she knew about battle. Eddy's waters were deep here; they were at a disadvantage on the unsteady boat and too far away to leap to shore.

The figure on the rock raised a hand, palm outstretched. "Butter and biscuits. We've butter and biscuits and jam."

"Keep an eye on him," Spence told Ninette, grabbing an oar and paddling toward the outcropping, staying several feet from where the man waited. They lurched to a halt and Spence sprang from the boat, landing half-crouched on the dock, his weapon ready. Ninette followed, less agile off the rocking craft. With the sun no longer behind the stranger, she could see he wore leather armor. The silhouette of a man's head was stitched on his white tunic.

"Butter and biscuits," he repeated. "A good hot meal."

"Who are you?" Spence asked. "What do you want?"

"This is Treg Keep," the soldier said. "Hospitality. Butter and biscuits. No need for concern. Come along."

Without another word, he turned and strode away, ascending a rough stair carved out of the rocks, leading toward the upper bank.

"What do we do, Eddy?" Ninette asked. "Can we trust him?"

"I am a river flowing to the sea. I have watched men kill one another crossing me, their blood turning my body red, their bodies sustaining fish and crows, but that was long ago and I do not know the answer to your question. I have brought you where I flow."

Spence pulled his helmet tight on his head. "We wanted to meet some people. I guess we have to start somewhere. But stay alert and be polite. Let me do the talking."

Sheathing their weapons, they dragged their vessel onto the shore, leaving it hidden among tall reeds.

"Where are you going?" Boat asked.

"We'll be back," Spence said. "You just lie quiet."

"I will," Boat said. But as they climbed the stairs, it began softly humming "Row your boat."

"Crime in Italy," Spence muttered under his breath.

"It makes me sad to leave him." Ninette struggled to control her tears.

When they reached the upper bank, she gave a startled exclamation. Two rows of carved stone heads lined a graveled path, their frowning faces, long and square, the color of umber, their eyes, vacancies lost in shadow.

"I don't like them, Ricky."

Spence tapped one with his knife, the top of his head level with its empty eye sockets. "I heard about natives carving things like this on islands back on Earth."

The statue's mouth scarcely moved as it spoke, its voice hollow as wind whispering through rock; and every other carving along the path spoke with it. *"Welcome to Treg Keep."*

With a shout echoed by his helmet, Spence jumped back, retreating to the middle of the lane. "For cryin' out loud! I should've known!"

Their guide stood waiting for them at a turning of the path.

"Maybe we should go back to Boat," Ninette said.

Spence's jaw set with determination. "We're not gonna let it throw us. Let's see what's here."

They passed along the lane between the sentinel carvings. The forest had been cut back from the path, leaving open sky above. The heads reminded Ninette of the quilted faces of the wicker-cats the companions had battled in Faerie. That too had been in twilight. She shivered and gripped her sword.

The path gradually descended, finally coming to an end at the mouth of a cave, its arch replete with carvings of lions and bears. Their guide stood before the black interior, waiting for them to catch up. Two final stone heads watched from either side of the entrance, but it was the cave itself that spoke in a rumbling voice. *"Who comes?"*

The soldier spoke his name. "I've brought others. Permission to enter?"

"Be welcome."

Stepping beneath the arch, Ninette saw the darkness had been an illusion caused by heavy black draperies covering the entrance. The soldier drew these aside, allowing the three to slip into a wide tunnel lit by ensconced torches.

"Where are we going?" Spence asked.

"Butter and biscuits and Treg," the soldier said.

"What's a Treg?"

"He is Treg. He is the sculptor." The man strode forward, leaving the pair to follow.

"That's helpful," Spence murmured.

The tunnel ended in a high chamber dominated by a massive fireplace carved from the gray rock itself, with two huge, identical busts of a man on either side of its wide, high mantel. A tapestry covered one wall, depicting the same person. A heavy stone table stretched across the center of the room. At its head sat a figure in a high-backed chair. Smoke roiled in a haze to the tall ceiling; the room smelled of burning and ashes. Nor was the man an ill fit for the chamber. Tall and thin, his was the face of the busts and the tapestry, elongated features that made Ninette think of a horse's head. His nose was long; his ears tapered to points. His mottled skin gave the appearance of charred beef. His hair wisped upward, gray shot with black like burning coals, and in the firelight, sparks seemed to fly from it. His garments were ashen gray. About his neck he wore a polished citrine, carved into the likeness of a yellow flame.

He turned his head, fixing dark, abnormally large eyes upon them, a penetrating gaze that rested longer on Ninette than Spence. There was a ponderousness about his movements belying his sparse frame. He raised his hands, palms together before his chin, and Ninette saw they were muscled from use, too large for his body. She found him both repellent and fascinating, and wondered which of the two feelings would prevail.

"*Defend*!" Spence's helmet whispered.

"Who have you brought me?" the man asked, his voice deep and thick as his lips.

"They were alone," the soldier said.

"Where do you journey?" he asked them.

"We're part of a larger group," Spence said. "The others made camp a few miles back. They aren't traveling this far, but we wanted to look around a little, see the country. We thought we'd camp tonight and return to our people tomorrow."

Ninette kept silent, understanding the reason for the lie.

Treg rose, stirring the ashen air. He was even taller than Ninette had guessed, surely close to seven feet. She stepped back as he approached, his eyes upon her. Reaching out with his long arms, he touched her cheek with his powerful fingers, making her flinch.

"Hey!" Spence said. "None of that, buddy!"

Ignoring him, the man studied her. "What clay is this from which you were made? What master carver cast these lines?"

Beneath the bewitching scrutiny of his great eyes, she blurted, "How do you know? Can people tell?" The thought frightened her.

"No one but I could recognize it. I must learn everything about you. I am the sculptor, Tregor Rathus Nethodian Dumaud, known as Treg to the masses." He dropped his hand and turned to Spence. "Is she yours? How intelligent is she? Her movements are quite natural."

Irritation swept through her, the emotion turning her voice to ice. "I belong to me. I don't know how smart I am yet."

Treg gave a slow smile, his eyes gleaming. "Incredible. Magnificent! You must stay the night. Do you . . . surely you don't eat?"

"We both do," Spence said.

"Astonishing! We must feast then." He snapped his fingers, and out of the shadows stepped a wooden figure tall as a man, carved in meticulous detail, its legs and arms separate pieces affixed to its body with wooden joints. Despite its lifelike appearance, it moved stiffly.

"Inform the cook, dinner for three. Only our best."

"Yes, Treg."

The servant shuffled back into the darkness.

"He is one of my creations," Treg said. "I am a great artist, the greatest of all time."

"I thought dead wood didn't talk," Spence said.

"Once the life has faded from it, that is true," Treg said, "but the act of applying the knife, of performing deft cuts to make new forms, reanimates the timber. I am Treg and there is none like me."

Seeing no reason for the man to lie, Ninette accepted the statement as fact. "Do the other artists get angry at you for being better? Sometimes when Ricky does something better than me, it makes me angry. I don't know why."

"I have met no other true artists, only dabblers and dilettantes. The opinions of these are inconsequential."

"Mind if I grab a chair?" Spence asked.

"*Take me!*" the unoccupied chairs urged.

Treg stared at him a moment, as if struggling to focus on his words. "Of course. Let us all be seated." His eyes turned back to Ninette. "You must tell me your name and how you were created."

Ninette sat down, happy to introduce them both and tell her story. She related her waking by the wizard's pool, and of her life as a masked automaton. Treg asked several questions about the methods used to fashion her, and though she was unable to give him answers, she enjoyed the attention. "Because I always wore my mask, everyone assumed I was horribly disfigured. I let them believe that, because I was wooden, but I won't wear it now that I'm human. I don't want people to think I'm ugly; I like looking out from my face." Noticing Spence frowning at her, she remembered his instructions to let him do the talking. She reddened and ended, leaving an abrupt silence quickly broken when two of the wooden servants appeared, bearing dinner stacked on trays. Treg kept his eyes fastened on her as the meal was served in three courses, each requiring a separate Mandate of Gratitude.

There was no meat, but the vegetables and fruit were excellent. Soonderkainen had taught Ninette table manners—her eyes grew misty remembering that kindness—but she couldn't resist grinning and bouncing in her chair at the taste of every bite. Her reactions delighted the sculptor, for his eyes glistened in appreciation and he smiled his thick-lipped smile. Having never been inebriated, she took only the barest sips of red wine, fearful of acting the fool under his scrutiny. But Spence drank enough for both of them without noticeable effect.

"So what is this place?" Spence asked. "What do you do here?"

"I perfect my art while serving the wishes of certain patrons fond of my carvings," Treg said. "They desire an almost endless supply of my work."

"Sounds profitable," Spence said.

Treg scowled. "Remuneration allows life's conveniences, but is otherwise unimportant. The unfolding of my vision is the ultimate satisfaction, knowing that from my soul flows beauty and intricacies beyond the fathom of those not endowed with my higher sensitivities. Symmetry and asymmetry, light and shadow, the wonder of wood and stone, endless facets molded into great art; such gifts I give the world. That is the purpose and point of Treg. After dinner, I will show you my workshop."

The meal ended with a chocolate pastry so good Ninette squealed at the first bite. Spence jumped, his hand rushing to his knife. "Criminy! Don't do that!"

"I'm sorry, Ricky. It's just *so* delicious. I could eat it forever."

Treg laughed, a granite rumble. "My chefs are among the finest. These are but a small sampling of the delicacies I offer."

He rose and a pair of wooden guards stepped from the surrounding shadows, better-made than the earlier servants, moving almost as smoothly as men. One of them opened a door previously unnoticed in the dimness, and Treg led the travelers down a hallway hollowed out of the rock, engraved with illustrations depicting Treg from many different angles, tools in hand, carving various figures.

"Welcome to the Corridor of Treg," the walls whispered.

They were moving deeper into the mountain, and Ninette feared a trick to imprison them.

A noise arose from down the passage, a cacophony of grinding and hammering. The air grew warmer, accompanied by orange firelight. They stepped into a chamber lit by many flames, yet so large it remained filled with countless shadows, its high ceiling lost in darkness, its air thick with the smell of wood, rock, and burning ore.

"Feed!" the flames cried, erupting from kilns and great fire pits dotting the floor. Ninette gaped and Spence whistled in surprise.

Scores of workmen labored there, casting human figures in iron
and brass, creating arms and legs and torsos of clay, fashioning
fingers and toes of fiber and stone. Raw materials poured shouting
from overhead chutes, released by men on high overhead gantries
and walkways, landing in deep troughs for washing and in-
spection. One wall was covered with hundreds of bins stretching
into the gloom. Enormous fans, powered by pedaling workers,
sang encouragement as they vainly sought to drive away the
vapors. In another part of the chamber, other craftsmen fitted
bodies together, adding gyroscopes to hollow heads and joints to
elbows and knees. In the center of the vast chamber stood an army
of created creatures, each holding a sword or spear.

"It's a factory!" Spence exclaimed. "Henry Ford himself would
envy this operation."

"Many are jealous of Treg, but this is only the trifling summation
of my art. The volcanic fires beneath the Yarrow fuel my facility.
My people work in iron, brass, granite, ivory, ebony, gold, exotic
woods—every kind of material. I supply the designs, of course;
these others are but minions to perform my will. I employ
modelers, carpenters, stone masons, smiths, dyers, smelters and
molders of silver, workers in relief, ivory painters, embroiderers—
many others. Their labor frees me to create beautiful things, figures
of earth and wood and stone far greater than the utilitarian
creatures you now observe."

"So your customers buy these from you?" Spence asked.

"My patrons, yes."

"What do they do with them?" Ninette asked.

"I do not question their intentions," Treg said. "That is beyond
the purpose of creation. But I am seeking . . ." For the first time he
hesitated. He looked at Ninette, his eyes glistening. "I have long
desired to discover a way to bring my figures, my Vigili, to true life,
to make them such as you. I would like you to stay at Treg Keep for
a time. You will be well-paid; you will eat from my table. I will require no labor from either of you, only let me observe you to try to
discover the secret of your making."

"I don't know—" Ninette began.

"That's an interesting proposition," Spence said. "You've got a
nice place here. We have other commitments, of course, but we

might be able to work something out. I'll tell you what, we'll take you up on your offer to spend the night, and Ninette and I will hash it out."

"Excellent," Treg said. "If you agree, I promise that regardless the outcome you will leave here wealthy. But more than that, you will have the gratitude of Treg."

Following a tour of the sculptor's facilities, which included several more chambers dedicated to his art, Ninette and Spence were escorted by two iron guards along benighted hallways to their chambers, one leading and one following behind. The soldiers' heavy treads echoed through the stone passages; their identical faces, eerie beneath the light of the candles burning in holders on their epaulets, disquieted Ninette, who in her former life had never known fear. Still unused to strong emotions, she struggled to contain a rising panic. A low moan escaped her lips.

"You okay?" Spence asked.

She nodded, too frightened even to speak. He took her hand and a wave of comfort ran through her. She drew in a deep breath, her courage returning.

The guard stopped before a pair of wooden doors painted the same color as the surrounding rock. The soldier spoke through angular lips, its voice the sound of echoing iron. "These chambers are yours. The rooms adjoin."

"We are locked," the doors intoned. "We bar the way."

The soldier withdrew a long key from a metal cup welded to its side and inserted it into one of the locks. The key said something Ninette could not hear.

"In the name of Treg, be opened," the soldier said, turning the lock.

"Come in," the door replied. "Be welcome."

The soldier repeated the process with the other door. "You will enter."

"Thanks, fellows," Spence said. "You going to keep watch out here?"

"I will guard you," the soldier behind them said.

"I'm Spence and this is Ninette. What are your names?"

"I am Doorkeeper," the one with the key said.

"I am Guard."

"Really nice to meet you. You seem like good folks. Good-looking too. You must be pretty strong."

"We are strong as the iron we are made of," Doorkeeper said. "You will enter your rooms now."

"Thanks for the help," Spence said.

"You are welcome."

Ninette found herself in a small room carved out of the rock, lit by oil lamps in wall sconces, with an intricately embellished dresser and a four-poster bed. Like the rest of Treg's facility, there were always more shadows than light, but to her pleasure, a rectangular bathtub stood in the next room, complete with hot and cold faucets. She sat on the wide side of the tub, letting the warm water run over her hands, listening to it sing as it left the pipe. Here was the chance for a new experience! Since her revival, she had had the thrill of washing her hands and face in the stream, but had never bathed. Sweating beneath the warmth of the sun and feeling the coolness brought by the breeze had been refreshing, but for the first time it occurred to her that she might not smell nice. Joiwend had been fastidious about cleanliness during their travels, bathing in cold rivers whenever she could escape the eyes of the men.

She heard a knock and an opening door. Leaving the water running, she went back into the bedroom and found Spence there.

"Nice joint, huh?"

"I like it, Ricky, if only it wasn't so dark. Do you think we should stay? Do you like Treg?"

"He's an oddball. I don't trust him, but he's sure wealthy as Croesus. Did you see the gold stacked in some of those workrooms? Yards of it. I wonder what he uses it for? Probably decorating his wooden soldiers."

"I didn't notice."

"Well I did, and I say if we stay here awhile there's a chance we could be set for life."

"But the things he said about wanting to watch me. What if he wants to pull me in pieces, to see how I'm made?"

"He didn't say *watch*. *Observe* was the word. You're not a toy anymore; you're alive. He can't just take you apart like a truck engine. You don't have to worry about that."

"Was I a toy before, Ricky? Telling my story to Treg, I realized I was. Something for someone's amusement."

Spence shrugged. "All I know is we're beginning a new life, and Treg is giving us the chance to start it in the money."

She suddenly wanted to cry, though she didn't know why.

"Listen," he said, "don't get worked up. It's going to be all right." He took her hand and hugged her close. She relaxed a little in his arms. He was shorter than she, but really strong and it felt good. He released her, leaving his hands on her shoulders. He looked her in the eyes, his simian face, heavy brow, and flaring nostrils so close they seemed strange and alien in the uncertain light. His breath smelled of wine. "We're friends. I'm going to take care of you. I'll make sure Treg doesn't do anything to hurt you. All right?"

She smiled. "All right, Ricky."

He gave her a quick kiss on the lips. "That a girl! I like to see you smile."

The kiss surprised her, but she had never been kissed before and was uncertain how she felt about it.

"I'll tell you what," Spence said, "I don't want you staying in here by yourself. We better share my room tonight."

She hesitated, unsettled by something in his expression. She was aware of the ways of men and women, and though she had never given it any thought before, this felt different than their time together on Boat. She stepped out of his grip. "I'll be fine here, Ricky. I should learn to be on my own sometimes."

"Suit yourself. I just thought you were frightened before."

"I was, and you were nice. Thank you. I'm really tired now."

"Yeah, sure. Me too. I'll see you in the morning. If you get scared in the night, you know where I am."

He left, shutting the door behind him. A little dazed, she went back to the bath and ran the warm water over her hands again, surprised to see how they trembled.

CHAPTER EIGHT

THE BATTLE

For several days Gray and his companions rode with Marshal Dartmallow along the skirts of the mountains of the living land, always following the Meadowlark Road. The marshal kept them at a quick pace, rising at moonset, riding until they dismounted, stiff and aching, before moonrise, only halting long enough to rest the animals and the foot soldiers. The horses had complained at first, but soon fell into a stoic routine, caught up in the marshal's urgency. It helped that Animonea's mysterious life-energy gave both the mounts and humans increased stamina, allowing them to travel farther and longer than would have been possible on Earth.

The forest gradually thinned to scattered groves. The company passed through the villages of Larks, Dovecote, and Great Bend, where the Brisk River veers sharply south before turning back east. Tall, metal poles had been erected at the cardinal points around each village.

"Are those lightning rods?" Russ asked.

"We call them storm attractors," Vasps said, astride his paint pony, Dreamer. "Thunderstorms are monsters filled with malice, who love to strike at targets below; but they cannot resist the lure of metal. The attractors divert their blows from the villagers. Our soldiers carry portable versions for assembly if the skies grow threatening."

"We could have used such the night we lost Soonderkainen," Jaunter grumbled.

Thousands of migratory birds soared above the company or darted from branch to branch, making their way south, emitting various cries of: "*Fly!*" or "*On!*" or "*Travel!*" For two straight days a continuous cloud of starlings passed overhead, an endless cacophony of: "*Going! Going!*" which became an unheeded throbbing marked only by the empty silence when the last bird passed.

To occupy the time and quell his concern for Tana, Gray learned to listen to the sound of the wind in the branches, every tree stirred by the breeze in its own way, every wafting limb and leaf singing with a different voice—the slow rumble of the oaks, the whispering symphony of the pines, the mummy rattle of the cottonwoods, the ocean-swell sigh of the elms—and in every voice there were words. They lulled him when his despair grew unbearable, and if his beloved had been beside him, the journey would have been a magnificent adventure, ripe for ballads and poems.

Master Tatters drew even with him.

"Any trace of her?" Gray asked.

Tatters threw up his hands and swirled them in the air. "Prince Darien, Prince of Princes and Stallions, I can't find a trail unless they give me time to search for it. I cast my gaze roundabout, I ponder the ground and the trees and the hills; I ask the jawing birds when they will listen, but not even a Comanche could find her traveling with this pack of galoots. Maybe you should have the marshal question the ravens. Perhaps Huginn and Muninn, sitting by Odin's side, can tell us somewhat."

"Dartmallow won't listen to me. I even had Vasps intervene, but the marshal ignores my requests. It's unfair of him. If the whole land is connected, something must know where she is." He sighed. He had no way of even knowing if they were riding toward Tana or farther from her. The thought of leaving her in the hands of her captors was unbearable. If they lost her after coming so far, he would surely die of a broken heart. If anything happened to her, he vowed to exact a terrible vengeance on her kidnappers.

But without her, what would he do with his life? There would be nothing left. He nodded his head sadly. He wouldn't return to his father's kingdom in En to face the shame of having failed; he would remain in the Back of the Beyond and become a hermit, dwelling in a cave in the wilderness where he would sit and write poems to the memory of his beloved, growing old and silver-haired. Such verse, revealing the anguish of his heart, would surely be great poetry, but no one else would ever read it. He would recite it to the trees and the hills of Animonea, and they would weep.

But would that be fair, he wondered, to keep her memory only to himself? If it were truly epic verse, wasn't it his duty to share it with the world, so everyone would know the depths of his love? He might even become renowned. How proud his parents would be if "The Song of Tanabel-Tunia" came to rival the ancient epics of En!

He hung his head. He was contriving nonsense. No one really cared if he and Tana were together. What was it Russ had said in his toast at Duskell Watch? The Company of the Far Riders he had called them, spouting something about unwavering friendship. Yet, how many of them even cared about Tana? He glanced back at them, riding complaisantly along. Spence and Ninette had deserted them. If Fox Lodan had his way, he would already be galloping back to his castle in Faerie. It didn't matter to Jaunter where they went, as long as there was adventure. Russ wanted nothing except to return to his homeland. Tatters was addled in the head, and Joiwend . . .

He faltered. Joiwend cared. She cared about everyone. That was her way. He grimaced. He was being unfair. They had their own lives, and they could never love Tana the way he did. He swallowed hard to keep from weeping.

* * *

The moon rose several minutes later each day, and to avoid his inquisitive gaze the troops did the same, so that in the last two marches they left camp at mid-afternoon and traveled by torchlight until nearly midnight. On the seventh day they returned to a normal routine, Vasps explaining that the sphere grew pensive and unobservant when waning toward full dark.

On the eighth day Quacaw the crow landed on Marshal Dartmallow's saddle horn. After a moment's discussion the marshal called Gray to him. "This woman you seek, she is tall, with long, brown hair and freckles on her arms and nose?"

Gray drew a sharp breath. "That's her! It has to be."

"Takquaw is of my murder," Quacaw said. "Of my murder she is. The fox who lives at Ducks Hill spoke to her. To her he spoke. He said he knew something, perhaps, perhaps. Sly are foxes. He tried to lure her close so *snap snap* his jaws could close. Takquaw is clever. Too clever for fox. For fox she is too clever. She would not go. But he told her. To her he told. Fourteen roosts it was—"

"Two weeks ago," Dartmallow interpreted.

Quacaw turned an insistent eye on the marshal. "It was fourteen roosts."

"Go on," Dartmallow said.

"He saw the woman. The woman he saw. He remembered her spots. She has spots like a dog, but tiny, he said. A man was with her. Into the forest she went. She went into the thunder wood. That is what he said."

"He means Morlane, the Wileywood," the marshal said. "The story is plausible. People look alike to most animals, but the fox remembered the freckles."

Gray's voice shook. "Vasps said we are going to Morlane."

"Yes, not far from where she entered the forest, but this isn't necessarily good news. The Wileywood is an outpost of our enemies. Easy for your friend to enter there, perhaps impossible to get her out."

"I will make it possible, sir." Gray's voice broke with gratitude. "Thank you for this kindness, Marshal. I will never forget it."

"Whether you do or don't, remember this, lad: you are under my command." The marshal's hard, squinting eyes softened. "I was once your age and understand you better than you think, but we are riding into danger. My concerns supersede those of any two young lovers. I expect obedience; I will have obedience."

"Yes, Marshal."

"Quacaw helped too," the crow said. "Perhaps, perhaps, there are rewards?"

Thinking a moment, Gray withdrew a copper coin from his pack. "Will this do?"

"There is gold, perhaps, perhaps?"

Gray grinned. "I'm afraid not, but if I had some, I would gladly give it for your service."

"You will get some later? Gratitude is forever. Forever it is."

"Perhaps I will."

Quacaw seized the coin from Gray's hand and flapped cawing away.

"Beware that scamp," Dartmallow said. "If he thinks you an easy mark, he'll make himself a nuisance."

Heart soaring, Gray rode back to tell Joiwend and the others.

Quacaw returned to the marshal several hours later, and within minutes four soldiers on horseback came riding to meet them, one bearing an insignia of rank similar but not identical to Dartmallow's. By their manner, the marshal was clearly the superior officer. Separating themselves ahead of the company, they fell into discussion.

"I mislike this," Fox Lodan said. "I wager we will soon be going to war."

"I would welcome it if they would return my sagaris," Jaunter said.

"We don't even know who we would be fighting," Fox said. "I'm no mercenary."

"It isn't so bad," Jaunter said. "When I fought under Mithridates the pay was in gold."

"I've got no stomach for killing strangers," Russ said. "It's bad enough when you have a reason. I want to find Tanabel-Tunia and finish our Service of Restitution before there's any bloodshed."

"What will you do then?" Joiwend asked.

Russ' expression darkened. "I don't know. I can't go back to Faerie and get caught up in its rules again. At Duskell Watch Soonderkainen suggested I might find magic here that could send me home, but that was before we knew enchantment was against the law."

Gray soon noticed increasing numbers of crows, and shortly thereafter the company passed a line of sentries. Soldiers and supply wagons bivouacked beneath the trees on both sides of the road. Finding level ground, they too encamped under the shelter of the boughs, again avoiding lighting any fires.

The disconsolate, fingernail moon, setting after dark, moaned in a thin voice, "Oh, who am I, most wretched of creatures, the lowliest of the low? Great was my vanity, beyond reason my arrogance! Too late I repent my hubris, this fool undeserving of compassion.

Half-blind through this ebony shroud, I go into greater darkness, deserving my fate, my firefly light extinguished at last. Would I had been kinder! Would I had loved my fellows better. Farewell all! Think not so ill of me, I beg you!" Weeping, it slipped beneath the horizon.

When the arbiter passed by, Russ said, "Listen, Vasps. You need to tell us what this is all about. If we're going into a fight, at least give us back our swords and let us know what we're in for."

Vasps hesitated, then sat down among them. "Marshal Dartmallow no longer thinks you are spies, but is judicious enough not to return your weapons. But perhaps a history lesson *is* in order. To relate the story, I must go back generations, long before the founding of the Republic, in a time when our people grew lax and the kings no longer entered the Omnifire, but longed to possess the same magic as the rulers of Faerie. Some say the Elf King, wanting to cause mischief, gave them a portion of his wizardry; some say they stole it from him. Whatever the case, they soon became enchanters, masters of illusion. With their newfound powers, they grew tyrannical. A war arose, with some of the animals and plants siding with the people, and others, with the magicians.

"The situation grew desperate. The people begged for someone to enter the Omnifire, yet no one dared. Finally, Aria, a young woman scarcely more than a girl, voluntarily passed unharmed through the flames. The Omnifire cleansed her mind, burning away the dross, filling her with wisdom. Through her leadership, we drove the enchanters beyond the mountains to Ruheen and established the Republic.

"The waters of the Omnifire do not pass through Ruheen, and the enchanters soon made themselves rulers of that country. There are only three passes through the mountains between Ruheen and Animonea, and the Wileywood serves as a buffer between the two lands. That worked well for years, for Morlane has always been less friendly to the Republic, keeping to itself and discouraging intruders. It is the oldest forest in Animonea and longs for the days before the coming of men.

"But about ten years ago, one of the enchanters, Duke Nortallion, made a treaty with the woods. There had been pacts before, allowing some trade between the two lands, but this time the Ruheens gained the right to build what they called a trading post inside the Wileywood. The duke named it Ironwood Station and soon fortified it. At first, we paid no heed. When we finally demanded they cease, Nortallion placated our All-Council with empty promises. Last month the watch we had posted outside the woods was wiped out by an assault from the forest, and many of the trees on our side of the valley were cut down and their roots poisoned. The Ruheen ambassador denied responsibility, but the All-Council voted to take military action. We are going to clean out the rats' nest and return Morlane to its natural symmetry."

"So what part are we supposed to play?" Russ asked.

"That remains to be seen. The mathematics of it are fascinating to ponder. The six of you represent the proportions of a hexagon now attached to our company, a powerful geometric form. This bodes well. Gray's alliance with Blunder increased the geometric bond, which can be seen as either expanding the hexagon to a heptagon, or creating a radial line outward, a path of action. I feel some good must come of it."

"Does the marshal place confidence in your mathematical divinations?" Joiwend asked.

"Sadly, the marshal considers geometry useful for nothing more than construction, but I am working to change his mind. He has nonetheless chosen strategies I feel align well with geometric principles." Vasps rose to go. "But of such military secrets, I best not speak."

Twilight fell soon after, and the soldiers' weapons, perhaps sensing the approach of combat, murmured in the darkness; the horses stamped, restless, discontented. Blunder crouched at Gray's feet, a white blotch in the obscurity.

"Momma says there will a fight tomorrow," the pup said. "Will there be, Gray?"

"Your mother knows more than I."

"If there is battle, there will be much biting. We will have to tear our enemies, won't we, Gray?"

Gray could not help smiling. "I suppose we will. Does that frighten you?"

"No. I will fight with the pack beside you." Blunder laid his head on his paws. "Momma is with the marshal's pack. It is not my pack anymore."

"Do you miss being with her?" With a pang Gray thought of his own mother, the Queen of En. Though he had been gone only two months, it seemed a lifetime. He wished he could send a message to assure her he was well.

"Momma is over there beside the marshal." Blunder gave a brief whine. "The marshal is her pack leader. Topper and Vasps and seven more are of his pack. I like Vasps. He gives me fish bites." He whined again and Gray patted his head. The pup was quiet so long Gray thought he had fallen asleep, but at last he asked, "Is our pack small, Gray?"

"With so many soldiers? Surely not."

"Have you scented all of them?"

Gray frowned. "I can't say I've scented any of them."

"They are not of our pack. Are those you rode with of the pack?"

Gray hesitated. Blunder was asking who he could trust with his life, who would never harm him. Coming from a world where a dog might be sacrificed for a dozen reasons, he did not know how to answer. He glanced at Joiwend, who sat on her bedroll a few feet away, a shadow in the darkness. "She is of the pack."

"The others are cobokot?"

"Yes, they are cobokot."

Blunder pressed his nose against Gray's hand. Gray stroked his head.

"Our pack is small," the pup said.

* * *

Gray climbed from his bedroll into the chill spring air. He had been awake for two hours and had spent the time playing with the pup, who gnawed on sticks, pounced on bugs, and tugged on Gray's tunic sleeves. When Vasps approached, Blunder wagged his tail. "Hello, Vasps. Is it time to go?"

"Good morning, Blunderbuss. It is time."

"That is not my name, Vasps. I am Blunder."

Vasps leaned down to tickle the pup's sides. "It is a joke, little one, a play on words." Eyes bright, Blunder nipped at Vasps' fingers.

"The marshal wishes me to ride with you and your friends this morning," Vasps said. "A quick breakfast and we depart. Morlane, the Wileywood, lies directly before us. This is a day of reckoning."

Though Gray suspected Dartmallow wanted Vasps to keep a watchful eye on the companions, he said nothing. The marshal was a prudent man. Gray glanced at the others and chuckled. Master Tatters swung his arms back and forth, rippling his cloak in imitation of a crow; Fox Lodan carried himself with the arrogance of one born to master men; beneath the flaps of his felt cap, Jaunter's craggy face, one cheek tattooed with blue bars, looked wild and monstrous.

Now why wouldn't Dartmallow trust us? Gray wryly thought.

They ate, saddled their horses, and departed. The Meadowlark Road abruptly dwindled to an unpaved, rough path winding through the trees. The army traveled in loose formation, the marshal and several officers leading, more companies of soldiers joining them as they went. Blunder trotted close alongside Nutmeg. Russ rode beside Joiwend to Gray's right, Vasps, to his left; the others trailed behind. Sensing the men's excitement, the horses stepped lively, ears forward, blowing and snorting.

A fluttering arose overhead. A score of birds flew from tree to tree, following the riders: ravens, magpies, and a pair of gray parrots escorted by a murder of crows. Other than the noise of their wings, they remained eerily silent. But the trees began a low humming.

"The Overcowls have arrived," Vasps said. "Everyone is nearly assembled."

They traveled less than half a league, moving between the hills until they came to the mouth of a wide valley. A broad, devastated field lay before them, filled with hundreds of fallen tree trunks surrounded by gray, dead vegetation. A rutted road wound through it, passing into a tangled forest beyond. At sight of the carnage, a low moan arose from the men's ranks.

Vasps put a hand over his eyes. His voice broke. "This is the Neprian Vale, called the Gateway to Morlane. It was once lush and beautiful. Henceforth, it will be known as Poisonwood Valley. When the trees died, every forest in Animonea mourned, a lamentation beyond anything I have ever heard before. Ten days it continued, all the land groaning. There has not been such a disaster since the Fire of Ojenfray, three generations past. Ruheen soldiers did it to create a buffer zone, carrying feigned Animonean banners to incite the woods against us. It caused a political crisis until we were able to prove to the other forests that we were not responsible. Unfortunately, the Wileywood did not believe us."

Marshal Dartmallow raised his arm and a bydord horn blew. Moving awkwardly to circumvent the decaying trees, the army reformed, stretching itself across the valley, the cavalry at the fore, the infantry standing behind long, rectangular shields. The movement brought the companions directly behind the marshal's entourage. Gray was surprised at the size of the force, which surely numbered several thousand.

"What are they doing?" Fox asked. "Horses can't maneuver in this."

"There is a plan," Vasps said.

"*Forwaaard*!" The bydord sang out. A gray parrot landed on Dartmallow's saddle horn, and the other Overcowls perched likewise among the officers. The crows scattered, vanishing in all directions. The company halted within a hundred strides of the woods. From a distance, the forest had appeared strangely black; this close Gray saw its leaves were a deep olive, long and thin like twisted hands, the knobbed ends of their branches making them look like serpents slowly writhing in the breeze. Parasitic vegetation, ebony and fine as lace, covered whole sections of some trunks, leaving their hosts drooping and leafless. The faces and leaf-eyes of every tree glared at the army, furious and malicious.

"The hamadryads are angry, the spirits of the boles," Master Tatters lamented.

"Haunted, I call it," Jaunter said. "I don't like ghosts."

"It's worse than that," Vasps said. "Duke Nortallion has turned the whole forest against us. He controls it now."

Jingling and shrill whistles sounded at Gray's back, and something flew past his head. Before he could focus on it, several others followed, the first wave of hundreds of humming birds moving in a cloud of flickering wings, their bodies shining iridescent in the morning sun. A smaller group broke off from the others and surrounded Marshal Dartmallow. One of the hummingbirds, blue-throated with a gray breast, darted back and forth before the gray parrot, speaking in a sing-song voice.

"We have come," the hummingbird said. "I am Zinglin Zee, First Beak of the Flying."

"It is well," the parrot replied. "We thank the hummers."

"As do we," Dartmallow said, bowing his head. "Are you ready?"

"We are ready," Zinglin Zee said. "The dark flutterers have driven us from the woods. Now, they are coming into Animonea. We will suffer it no longer."

At the marshal's command the bydords sounded three sharp blasts. "*Attack! Attack! Attack!*" The hummingbirds rose in the air, hovering, emitting a throbbing song, their beaks turned toward the forest. In answer, a black fog rose from the leaves of the Wileywood.

"Are they birds?" Joiwend asked.

Gray squinted to see. "They look like bats."

"You are mistaken," Vasps said. "They are witch moths."

Gray drew his spyglass from his pack.

"*Look!*" the spyglass urged.

Gray brought the creatures into focus. Despite the bat-like angularity of their flight, these were indeed moths, ebony black, their wing-spans wide as a man's outstretched hand. But unlike an ordinary moth, each had a long tail with a serrated barb at its end.

Gray handed the spyglass to Joiwend.

She closed one eye to look. "In my country, we have a similar creature, but without a tail. We call it *Maraposa de la Muerta*, the butterfly of death. It is a superstition among our people that if it enters a home, someone will die in three days."

"We have ordinary ones in Animonea too," Vasps said, "but these are different. It isn't just their poisonous stingers, which can kill; they are the spies of Ironwood Station."

"You expect mere birds to fight demons?" Jaunter asked.

"Do not make that mistake," Vasps said. "The enchanters' powers lie mostly in illusion. Duke Nortallion, master of Ironwood Station, spent over a decade breeding the moths. What he crossed them with to create such a creature, we do not know. But if he is using magic, it is in his ability to control them. Moths are far less intelligent than birds. To bend them to his will must take intense concentration."

The hummingbirds rose to meet the moths. Gray looked through his spyglass again. The birds were of different varieties, some with longer beaks, some with blue or red throats, their backs mostly green. At first, the forces on both sides appeared equal, but more and more of the moths flocked from the Wileywood, until they far outnumbered the hummingbird host.

"So many!" Vasps exclaimed.

Undaunted, the hover of hummingbirds darted forward, rising level with their enemies, emitting a fantastic amount of noise for creatures so small, a rising cacophony of clicks, whistles, and hums. Locked in wedge formations, the black moths hurried to meet them, wings churning in velvet silence.

They met in the air, dancing and darting, crashing against one another. Gray kept his spyglass on Zinglin Zee. The bird met the leader of the first formation, nearly running headlong into it, but both veered away at the last second, the moth dropping downward like a bat, Zinglin Zee hovering backward, then darting in pursuit. The black moth's stinger lashed out over its back like the tail of a scorpion; the hummingbird dashed away, moved forward, dashed away again, and struck from above, driving its long beak through the moth's head. Its wings folded; it spiraled toward the earth. Zinglin Zee sped away, seeking a new target, and was soon lost from Gray's sight.

Gray withdrew his glass, dazzled by the sheer number of forms passing in and out of the lens. To the unaided eye the battle rolled in flashes of movement, flowing back and forth, stingers against bills, a furious cloud of desperate destruction. Though the moths were agile, the hummingbirds were quicker, striking and slipping away before the deadly stingers could catch them. For every hummingbird who plummeted to the ground, three dark forms spiraled from the sky; yet the moths were like a thunderhead moving against small clouds; the sheer number of their foes meant the birds might escape one enemy only to meet the poisonous stab of another. And still the moths continued exiting the forest, rising above the hover, seeking to envelope it.

The soldiers began shouting encouragement to their champions. "*Turrah*, small wings! *Turrah*!" Vasps joined them, adding his deep voice to their own.

The hummingbirds rose higher, refusing to be contained, striking upward at their foes where the moths' stingers could not reach, skewering them on their bills, withdrawing their blades by thrusting the bodies away with their claws, clearing the sky above them. Gray used his spyglass again to follow the ever-rising main body of the hover.

"They're almost out of sight," Joiwend said, her face flushed.

Reaching a peak, the hover wheeled, moving as one, diving down upon their enemies, using their claws this time to rake at the moths' eyes. Black bodies fell by the scores, landing in flapping heaps on the bare earth. The men shouted louder, their voices hot with triumph.

Not far from Gray, a moth landed on a foot soldier's shoulder, stinging him as it died. With a cry the man flung it away and clutched at his neck. For a moment he swayed in his saddle, then reeled, toppling into the arms of his fellows. One of them drew a knife, made a cut where the stinger had struck, and began sucking out the poison and spitting it on the ground. But the victim's eyes glazed. He was dead a moment later.

"It must have hit an artery," Vasps said. "He never had a chance."

Gray glanced at Joiwend, wishing he had a shield. Noticing Blunder sniffing toward the body of the moth, Gray warned the pup away. When he looked skyward again, the hummingbirds had reached the bottom of their descent. The moths pressed down upon them, trying to smother them with sheer numbers. Dozens of birds fell from the sky.

The hummers' cries turned to a continuous whistle—surely meant as a signal—for the whole hover abruptly changed course, fleeing away from the Wileywood to escape the pile. The moths pursued, and for a moment the battle raged directly above the army.

Hummingbirds dropped all around. One landed on the mane of Joiwend's horse, a tiny body, small and fragile. Its chest heaved; its blue throat quivered, trying to draw breath. Joiwend cupped it in her hands.

"Brave warrior," she said.

It spasmed. It fluttered its wings once and lay still, its struggle ended. Its feathers shone bright in the morning sun. Tears streamed down Joiwend's cheeks.

Farther the hover fled, passing behind the soldiers' ranks.

"We're beaten!" Vasps moaned in disbelief. A roar of disappointment erupted from the soldiers. A few archers shot arrows at the cloud of moths until the captains restrained them.

A silence fell across the battlefield, the solders' faces stricken. The moths and hummingbirds were distant specks.

A bydord sounded. Gray looked around, trying to see what it meant.

From the south and east came a jabbering flurry. Flocks of birds rose from the distant trees. Gray lifted his spyglass.

"What are they?" Joiwend asked.

"I see crows and hundreds of starlings. They're attacking the moths!"

Fox Lodan laughed. "Dartmallow outmaneuvered them! Well done!"

The clouds of adversaries flowed back and forth across the sky, dancing their pirouette of death. Seeing themselves over-matched, the moths reversed direction, retreating toward the Wileywood while the starlings followed on heavy wings.

The army raised their swords and cheered as the moths passed overhead, the starlings among them giving their brazen squawks and beating them to the earth with their wings. Once more a rain of the victims fell among the men. Jaunter batted a pair away with the back of his hand without being stung. Gray used his cloak to shield himself and Nutmeg.

"*Feast!*" the starlings cried. "*Feast!*"

"*Keep fighting!*" the crows called.

But seeing so many of their prey upon the ground, the starlings began landing by the hundreds, pecking at the moths to cut them to pieces, avoiding their stingers while devouring them, bit by bit. They hopped among the soldiers and around the legs of the horses, wary of the men even as they fed, tilting their heads to watch them with golden, raptorial eyes.

"Why are they stopping?" Russ asked.

"Starlings won't fight except for the lure of food," Vasps said. "These birds are finishing their southern migration and are hungry. The Overcowls must have promised them they would eat well. But they are a stubborn lot, unwilling to follow commands."

Still, the starlings had decimated their prey, and a steady humming arose, growing both nearer and louder. Behind the starlings, the hummingbirds returned, flying just above the soldiers' heads, the rapid beating of their wings throbbing through the air, their bodies flashing past in a train of bright colors. Some men ducked their heads, but everyone, even Gray and his companions, cheered.

"Buzzed by hummingbirds!" Russ exclaimed, grinning. "Go, little fellas!"

No longer pursued by the starlings, the cloud of moths swirled upward and turned to meet the charge. Despite their casualties they still outnumbered their smaller foes, the hover now a third its former size. But galvanized by the starlings' aid, the hummers drove into their opponents' midst, impaling them, tearing their wings away with their claws, beating them backward with their piston-wings.

Deeper and deeper into the dark ranks the birds flew. Once more the moths dropped by the dozens. But hummingbirds died as well, their beautiful bodies crashing silently to the earth, a rain of prismatic color. And when the charge was spent, the gallant warriors hung suspended in the air, surrounded by their enemies. Both sides had lost hundreds; the ground lay littered with fluttering moths and trembling birds, the dead and the dying. No longer massive clouds, the two sides broke into individual battles of two or three. And everywhere the hummingbirds were outnumbered.

"Small hearts but great," Jaunter said. "How will it end, I wonder?"

"Oh, if only we could help them!" Joiwend said.

Gray put a warning hand on her arm. "Remember, you mustn't change shape. The Animoneans despise enchantment."

The fighting grew more frenzied. With his spyglass Gray saw birds striking and moving away, never giving their opponents the chance to sting. But more than once, he saw a single bird, wholly surrounded by black shapes, the trap closing in, the moths so close they covered their quarry with their soft bodies, smothering its movements, their stingers striking until they found their target. Then the brave hummer tumbled away, eyes closed, its battle done.

The minutes dragged on. The fighters grew weary beneath the morning sun. Their wings heavy with fatigue, they gradually drew closer to the ground.

Topper bawled an order. Groups of foot soldiers rushed in from among the horsemen, garbed in gauntlets, chain mail, and heavy garments, their faces covered in leather save for eyes and nose. They sprinted forward in pairs, a net stretched between them. Slowing as they neared the battle lines, they began catching the black moths, working with care to avoid seizing their tiny allies, their armor proof against the moths' stings. No sooner did they capture several of their prey than they cast their nets on the ground, and other soldiers bearing heavy mallets finished their foes. Unable to gain altitude, the moths perished by the scores.

Beneath the twin assault the black moths broke away, attempting to flee into the Wileywood. The hummingbirds instantly altered their tactics, the noise of their voices and wings changing to rapid clicks, a staccato beating of the air. Bravely, they dashed forward, putting their bodies between the moths and the woods, hunting them down without mercy.

Yet one group of the enemy remained, a few score still banding together. These abruptly drew into a tight formation and shot out across the field, heading straight toward Marshal Dartmallow.

Only Fox Lodan realized what was happening in time to react. "To the marshal!" he shouted, kicking Dauntless' flanks. "Hi yah!" The other companions were caught unawares, but Russ followed Fox's lead, their mounts bounding recklessly over the toppled tree trunks. Before they even reached the marshal, Fox had freed his cloak, and the sergeant, his coat. Springing in front of Dartmallow, swirling their garments, they caught the first wave of the moths, clearing a space in the air before the marshal. Topper and the other officers joined in, forming a wall around their commander, placing their bodies between him and death.

Dozens of moths fluttered around, landing on men and animals. A soldier screamed and then a horse. Men fell from their mounts, writhing in pain. Dauntless reared, striking at the moths with his hooves while Fox struggled to stay in his saddle.

A moth landed on Nutmeg. Gray knocked it away with his fist.

The crows swept in, no more than a score, but with beating wings they pummeled the moths, casting them to the ground. Unable to reach their target, the moths retreated, only to be met by the nets and the hummers. A few starlings helped too, urged on by the crows. Few of the black moths reached the sanctuary of Morlane.

Men hurried to aid their fallen comrades. Four horses were down. Wounded moths flopped on the earth, and the soldiers ground them with their heels.

His face pale, the marshal turned to Fox and Russ. "You have my gratitude."

Fox nodded, but Vasps Geometer said, "It seems these newcomers tend toward acts of valor."

"A lord of men should die in battle, not by the ignoble sting of an insect," Fox said. "What happens next?"

Dartmallow bleakly surveyed the multitudes of hummingbirds littering the battlefield. "The casualties are high."

"But it is a great victory," a proud but tiny voice said. Supported on the backs of two of his brothers, Zinglin Zee hung in the air before the marshal, one of his wings twisted at an unnatural angle. "The Overcowls said we should do this for the good of all. Many of us have fallen, nevermore to hum. But the flutterers will not challenge us again. Now you must peck out the duke, the poison of Morlane."

The gray parrot on Dartmallow's saddle spoke. "It *is* a great victory. The ravens, magpies, and parrots will tell of it to our nestlings. The crows will sing of it among their young. All the hatchlings will know. The story of the courage of the hummingbirds will be remembered as long as birds can sing."

"It is good," Zinglin Zee said.

"We are in your debt," Marshal Dartmallow said, bowing his head. "My people will tend to your injured. You have done your part; we will do ours. Your sacrifice will not be in vain." He turned to Topper. "Sound the bydords. We enter the woods."

The army advanced, passing around the fallen trees and the corpses of the hummingbirds covering the field like precious jewels.

"Is there no regard for the deceased?" Joiwend asked.

"Only humans bury their dead," Vasps said. "Thousands of insects will feed off these, and it will give them nourishment and life. It is the way of Animonea, and it is good."

CHAPTER NINE

TREG KEEP

Rick Spence got little sleep the night he and Ninette came to Treg Keep. Though his pillow and blankets tried to comfort him, he tossed in his bed, thinking of the gold he had seen, imagining the things it could buy: power, position, the respect of women. A girl on both arms, that's what rich guys had. And if a woman didn't do what a fellow said, he just found another one, the way he'd trade off a Lincoln Continental or a gold watch.

He didn't take much stock in Treg's promises of reward. Anybody could talk. That wasn't the real opportunity. Wealthy people always needed someone at their right hand, someone they could trust, just like the sarge had needed a corporal to keep the other soldiers in line. Spence knew how to be that person. He didn't like being ordered around, but he knew what it took to do what a boss wanted; and if he worked for Treg, there would be plenty of chances to line his own pockets.

In the early morning hours, when sleep finally took him, he dreamed he sat on a couch in a mansion, running an endless river of coins through his hands.

He was startled awake by the hammering of Guard's iron fist on the oaken door, a clamor sending him scrambling for his long-lost M-1 rifle and shouting for the squad to take cover. Remembering where he was, he rose cursing. Excited by the activity, his helmet repeated, "*Defend! Defend!*" for three minutes before finally calming down. Spence dressed quickly, but ended up waiting in the corridor with Doorkeeper and Guard for almost an hour before Ninette stepped from her room.

"Good morning, Ricky!"

"What took you so long?"

A pretty pout suffused her features. "I'm sorry. The bath was *so* good last night I had to take another one. I wanted to make myself look pretty the way Joiwend does. Do you think I do? Not as pretty as her, but a little pretty?" She made a slow pirouette.

His irritation melted away. In the dim glow of the iron soldiers' epaulet candles, she was even more beautiful—her heart-shaped face, the symmetry of her eyes and lips, her golden hair falling on her bronze armor. "You look like an angel." She put her clasped hands to her chin, beaming and turning red.

They passed along dark corridors which whispered the name and wonder and genius of Treg, before finally entering the sculptor's dining hall. He was seated once more in his high-backed chair at the head of the granite table. A man and woman Spence had never seen before sat to his right.

Treg rose from his seat and beckoned to Ninette with his long hands. "Come in, come in, my little poppet, my lovely mannequin. I want to show you to my guests. I want to see the wonder in their faces."

The stranger stood. He was tall, with a square jaw protruding like the front of a Sherman tank. His black hair, parted in the center, stiffened by oils, curved downward along the sides of his head like rams' horns. His right arm was in a black sling. Though he wore neither uniform nor symbol of rank, Spence knew by his posture he was a soldier. His wide-set eyes swept over Rick, taking his measure, reminding Spence of a cocky second lieutenant who had caught a bullet on Omaha Beach.

Watching the other woman, Treg took and lifted Ninette's hand, his eyes glistening from behind slitted lids. "This is the one I told you about, a miracle on two feet—Ninette Argilla, a handiwork whose manner of creation I will soon discover once she agrees to stay with me. Then you will see my art in full flower."

The woman, who had remained seated, studied Ninette with an appraising eye. "She looks quite animated. What can she do?"

"Anything I want," Ninette said. "I'm alive. I wasn't until we came to the Back of the Beyond, but now I have feelings and everything."

"How wonderful!" the woman said. "So she reacts like a real person?"

"I'm over here," Ninette said, tears springing to the corners of her eyes. "You can ask me."

"I didn't catch your names," the corporal interjected, hoping to keep Ninette from causing a scene. "I'm Richard Spence."

"Ah, I have neglected my duties," Treg said. "May I present Captain Chel Rendan and the Duchess Tanabel-Tunia?"

Ninette's eyes widened. "We've been looking all *over* for you!" She started around the table, arms outstretched to embrace the woman.

The captain's sword, drawn by his good hand, hissed from its scabbard. Nearly as quickly, Spence yanked Ninette back by the shoulder and drew his long knife, poised to throw.

"*Strike!*" both blades cried.

"Peace!" Treg boomed. "No harm must come to her!"

"Who are you?" Rendan demanded. "How do you know the duchess?"

Spence measured the situation. Ninette and her big mouth! If he couldn't get Tanabel-Tunia to realize they didn't mean any harm, he was going to have to kill this guy. "We're friends of Gray Darien."

"Gray?" Tanabel-Tunia put her hand on the captain's arm. "Wait, Chel."

Spence kept a level gaze on the captain, who looked ready to leap over the table. "We were hired by Darien's father to find you, but Ninette and me aren't part of that anymore. We left the others and set off on our own. We want to start a new life away from Faerie. We don't care what you do."

"But Ricky—" Ninette said.

"Just leave it alone," Spence snapped. "What the others think doesn't matter now."

"Was Fox Lodan with you?" Tanabel-Tunia asked.

"Yeah, he was," Spence said, "but we got separated in a storm. We haven't seen them since."

"A glib tale," Rendan said.

"It would be like Fox to pursue me, if only for the sake of his wounded pride," Tanabel-Tunia said. "But for Gray to come all this way . . ." Her voice trembled.

"A truce," Treg said. "Lay your weapons aside. I do not know the truth, but I will brook no bloodshed in my house."

The captain studied the two. "Very well. You have the word of an officer of the Kingdom of Ruheen, so long as you vow the same."

"That's fine by me," Spence said. "I've got no quarrel with any-body."

"Breakfast then," Treg said. "My chef has prepared a feast appro-priate for such eminent guests."

They sat down, Spence facing the captain across the table. He fig-ured Rendan would honor his word, but he'd keep an eye on him just the same. It gave him a chance to finally see the woman they had trailed across half of Faerie. The way Gray had gone on about her, he had expected a motion picture starlet. Not that she wasn't pretty—a slender brunette in a simple green dress, a little pale, with nice eyes, thin lips, and freckles on her arms and nose—she just wasn't as gorgeous as someone like Ninette. But maybe she had a good personality; maybe she was a lot of laughs.

"Our finding you is funny," Ninette said. "We looked everywhere in Faerie, and when we tracked you to Duskell Watch, the elves said it was hopeless to go on. But Gray insisted and—"

"How many were with you?" Rendan asked.

"Well, there was Gray and Fox and—"

Spence laid his hand on Ninette's arm. "We don't mind telling you, because like I said, we aren't part of that anymore. Nine of us crossed the border. One got killed the first night—"

"That was Soonderkainen," Ninette said. "He was always *so* nice to me."

"Only nine? No others?" the captain asked.

"That's all," Spence said. "I swear it."

"But why did you kidnap her?" Ninette asked. "Are you unhappy being a prisoner? You don't look unhappy. Where is he taking you?"

"Such matters are our own concern," Rendan said.

"Oh! That's not fair!" Ninette protested, wide-eyed. "We spent *so* much time looking for you, days and days, and it was dangerous too. I guess I don't *have* to know, now that we've found you, but I'd *like* to know if you need to be rescued. Not that we're going to rescue you, even if you do need to be, because Ricky says we're not, but it's only right you tell us."

Tanabel-Tunia smiled and patted Ninette's hand. "You really are alive, aren't you? So much so I can scarcely believe you were ever otherwise. And so charming!"

Ninette blushed. "But I wasn't always. Ricky can tell you."

"I believe you, dear." Tanabel-Tunia spoke as if to a child. "We too have come through great peril. The captain's men died along the way. By the time we reached Treg's demesne, I was dreadfully sick and Captain Rendan had been injured by a bear. We're only now nearly well enough to travel."

Ninette's brow furrowed. "I'm sorry about the soldiers. I don't think you want to be rescued."

"Let us simply say I'm going where I must, compelled to do so by bonds greater than any soldier's strength."

"I don't understand what you mean," Ninette said.

Tanabel-Tunia smiled, clearly delighted. "The captain wishes me to be discreet, but I've spent the last weeks in only the company of men and long for the conversation of my own sex. If he will accept my vow not to give away any secrets, perhaps you and I can spend time speaking of womanish things."

"As the duchess wishes," Rendan said doubtfully.

"Perhaps she can serve as your Lady's Maid, since I have none to supply that need," Treg suggested.

"I don't know how to do that, but I can try," Ninette said.

"I can dress myself," Tanabel-Tunia said. "We shall be friends instead."

"That's nice of you," Spence said. "That's real nice. Let's all be friends."

* * *

"But all Treg did was watch me," Ninette said. "I didn't like it. He looks at me like . . . I don't know how he looks at me."

"Hold the brush lightly," Tanabel-Tunia said. "You're pulling my hair."

"Oh, I'm *so* sorry. I'm not doing it right? Did I hurt you? I'm better with a sword than a brush."

"No need to pout, dear. You're doing fine."

"*Stroke easy*," the brush suggested.

"*Light me and I will warm you*," the fireplace said.

"*I will protect you*," Ninette's armor assured.

Ninette stamped her foot in frustration "Please be quiet, everyone! How can I concentrate when you're all talking at once?"

The room fell silent.

"It won't last," Tanabel-Tunia said. "They soon forget. It's maddening. I don't know how anyone knows their own mind in this country."

"I like it better outdoors," Ninette said. "When we were on Boat, the river Eddy drowned out the other voices. He was sweet. Gray calls you Tana. Can I call you that too?"

"Of course you may."

They were in Tanabel-Tunia's chambers, a room carved like all of Treg's dwelling from solid stone, but furnished with an ornate brass bed and matching full-length mirror, marble side-tables, and a woven, saffron rug. The alabaster fireplace was gilt in gold; a skylight, cut through the mountain, brought sunshine dancing on the floor and glistening on the glass chandelier. A tapestry covered one wall, depicting Treg at work. Tanabel-Tunia sat before the mirror in a velvet chair, watching Ninette and studying her own reflection. "We should do something about your hair too."

Ninette halted in mid-stroke. "Is it bad?"

"No, it's a beautiful color. It needs to be trimmed and swept back. It would give you a nice look. There's no one here to cut it, but I can try. What's the matter? Why do you look frightened?"

"Will it hurt?" Ninette asked.

Tana rose, laughing, and took Ninette's hand between her own two. "Such innocence! No, it won't hurt, child."

Ninette reddened, hanging her head. She thought she must be older than Tana, who was scarcely seventeen. "I suppose I am like a little girl, but I've never had my hair cut before. I've fought in battles and I've seen things. I just don't know much about being a woman."

"Do you always wear your armor?"

"I always have."

"It will be fun to show you how to dress. Come, cheer up! We're about the same size. You can borrow some of my clothes. I had only what I was wearing when I left En, but Treg found other garments for me. Nothing elaborate, but we'll put you in something lovely. I know just the thing." She opened a wardrobe, studied a moment, and held up a long blue dress and matching cape. "It isn't the best fabric, but it's comfortable."

"*Try us,*" the clothing urged.

"It's like the sky before dawn!" Ninette exclaimed. "It looks so pretty with your ring. Joiwend has one just like it."

Tana moved her right hand behind the dress, concealing the sapphire stone. "It's a family heirloom. My father gave it to me at my birth."

"Ricky said his father was cruel. Are they all that way? Was yours?"

Tana lowered her eyes. "I didn't know my true sire. I was raised by the First Duke of En. I soon learned he preferred his own children to his adopted daughter."

"I don't think I'll ever understand families," Ninette said. "I wish I had one."

Tana smiled, but her eyes were sad. "A royal house isn't the best place to learn what a home is like."

"Don't you want to go back? Gray said you would."

"Dear Gray! For him to come so far to find me! I hope he's safe."

"The king sent him, because he was the third son, but I'm sure he would have come anyway. Everyone says he loves you. Fox hates him for it, I think."

"They say that?" Tana smiled warmly. "Fox would despise anyone who stood in his way. What about the others who came with you?"

Ninette furrowed her brow in concentration. She named the companions one by one, describing how each looked. "But it's hard for me to say how they *were*. I stayed to myself because no one treated me like a person. Some tried—Soonderkainen did; and Gray sometimes. Jaunter joked with me at first, but I never understood what he meant, and Master Tatters spoke in riddles. Thinking about it, I don't believe Russ trusted me, though I didn't know it at the time.

He scarcely talked to me at all. Joiwend tried to, but I never knew how to answer. Without feelings I had nothing to say, and without a past I didn't have a story to tell."

"Why did you choose to ride with them?"

"I was in Faerie. You know how *that* is. The magic makes you be what it wants. I was a girl in armor, nearly impossible to kill. What could I be except a hero? When the quest called, I had to follow it."

"I know!" Tana's eyes sparkled. "All the time we were passing through there, I was lost in the role of the Questing Princess, though I'm not a princess in En. Sometimes, I scarcely knew who I was. And Chel—Captain Rendan—played the Valiant Champion. Crossing the border into Animonea was like waking from a dream."

Ninette laughed, eyes wide. "That's exactly how I felt! Once I came back to life, I mean."

"We are free from that horror." Tana studied Ninette. "It must be exciting, being a woman warrior, knowing your own strength, able to handle yourself physically. My upbringing was dance and weaving, painting and music, learning other languages and the ways of the court."

"Do you think I'm strong?" Ninette asked. "I don't feel like I am."

"Of course you are. Now come to the looking glass."

Tana held the dress in front of Ninette. "See how it brings out the color of your hair? It almost makes your gray eyes blue. Why are you crying?"

A single tear ran down Ninette's cheek. "I don't know. I'd like to look pretty, it's just . . . I don't know if I want Treg seeing me that way. He kept staring at me, making me walk up and down, and kneel, and bend my arms and legs different ways. He kept talking about 'distilling my essence' for his sculptures. I don't know what that means."

"I won't speak of Treg, for every wall in Animonea has ears, but he is an unusual man. He was kind to us, taking us in when we were nearly dead, but he serves Duke Nortallion, Captain Rendan's lord, and otherwise might not have treated us so well. He contacted the duke, who is sending men to bring me to his stronghold." She bit her lip, considering. "I want to take you with us when we go."

"Oh, could you?" Ninette furrowed her brow. "No, you can't. Ricky wants us to work for Treg so he can learn all about me."

"Does Ricky decide your life for you? Are you in love with him?"

Ninette ducked her head in confusion. "I don't know what love is. I like him, but I liked all of them—the ones I came with, I mean."

Tana sighed. "It seems I must play your mother and tell you about men. We can't do without them, of course. They control too much of the world. Making ourselves attractive is part of drawing them to us, so we can get what we need."

"I don't know what you mean."

"It's like a duel between ill-matched opponents. Men are stronger than we are, so we learn to parry and thrust with tears and smiles and sulking. You have to know when to use your weapons and when to make them believe they've won in the midst of their surrender."

"Is it really a battle? That sounds dishonest. How can you use tears? I thought they just *were*."

"What a dear creature you are! I'm glad we shall be friends." Her eyes shone. "I know what we can do!" Returning to the wardrobe, she withdrew an iridescent gown. "I haven't been able to wear this. It has too many buttons in the back, and I can't put it on by myself. You can help me, then I'll cut your hair and we'll see how you look in the blue dress. It will be fun!"

"I'd like that. Will you explain some more about women and men?"

Tana laughed. "That may take more hours than we have."

* * *

Spence paced beside Treg's dining table, waiting for the others to arrive for lunch. Two oaken servants watched him from the shadows cast by the relentless flames of the fireplace, unmoving, unbreathing, no more company than the other objects that murmured and whispered around him; yet he knew they observed him, and it made him fidget. He wished he could have stopped Ninette from going with Tanabel-Tunia, though he had no excuse for doing so. But when women got together and started talking they got ideas, and he didn't want anything ruining his deal with Treg.

Captain Rendan strode in, stiff as any soldier on parade. The two men exchanged nods. Spence was about to ask him about his people and the layout of his country, when Treg stepped through the door.

"Gentlemen." The sculptor nodded to them and strode to the head of the table. "What do you think of my facility so far, Mr. Spence?"

"It's a swell place. Very impressive. I appreciate the brandy in my room."

"Have you considered my offer?"

"We might be interested, though I wouldn't mind a few more details about the reward."

"Would your weight in gold be sufficient?"

Spence kept his expression as wooden as the servants around the table. "That sounds fair enough, so long as the pay comes regular instead of at the end. Say a portion every week?"

"Agreed. It shall be done." The sculptor's eyes blazed with joy.

Ninette and Tanabel-Tunia arrived at that moment. Spence glanced at Ninette and whistled. "Wow. You look like a million bucks."

"Is that good?" Ninette asked.

"You bet. You're even more of an angel now."

Ninette beamed, a praised child. Her eyes widened. "And you know what? Tana gave me the prettiest underthings. They are so comfort—"

"Ninette!" Tanabel-Tunia gasped, her face reddening. "We don't speak of such in the company of men."

Ninette halted, mouth open. She furrowed her brow. "Oh!" She looked from face to face. Spence was grinning. Even the stern captain smiled. Treg stared, always observing. Ninette clasped her hands in front of her face, ducking her head. "I didn't—don't laugh at me!"

"Hold on," Spence said. "Nobody meant anything. It's all right."

Tanabel-Tunia took her arm. "I didn't mean to speak so harshly."

Ninette closed her eyes, rocking back and forth on her heels, not knowing what to do with her embarrassment and anger. She wanted to cry; she wanted to strike someone. She would have drawn her sword, but it lay in Tana's room.

They led her to a chair and calmed her, Spence stroking her hand and back, Tanabel-Tunia soothing her with soft words.

"Such emotion!" Treg said. "Magnificent! But like a flame it can burn its master. I must remember that."

"Do you really think you can make sculptures as alive as she?" Tanabel-Tunia asked. "It seems impossible."

Treg rolled his long head, rolling his eyes with it. "The true artist does the impossible, Duchess, creating out of nothing, forming that which has never been before."

"But how?" Tanabel-Tunia said. "You see the way she acts. She's human, not a creature to be tested and prodded."

"So all true artistic creations appear, if the vision is clear. They take on a life beyond that of their creator. I, Treg, who have never said these words before, admit that the one who formed her was perhaps almost as great an artist as myself. Imagine if the two of us worked together! What wonders could we fashion!"

Spence suspected they would more likely murder each other in the first five minutes. He didn't care for the way the conversation was going. It would get Ninette stirred up again. "Look, it's no big deal, Treg just wants to examine her, to see if he can make more like her."

Tanabel-Tunia shook her head. "It doesn't seem right. When the duke's men come, I want to take her with me. I could teach her so much, and she could be my traveling companion."

"Impossible!" Treg roared, so violently Tanabel-Tunia flinched. "This is the opportunity of a lifetime. She has come to me for a purpose—a greater purpose than any of you can understand. It is fate; it is destiny! How else to explain that she finds the one man who can exploit what she has, who can take it, refine it? You cannot even dream of what Treg will create once he knows her secrets! You cannot have her!"

Spence glanced at Ninette, who watched the sculptor through half-closed lids. Treg wasn't making this easy.

"Are you certain you wish to take her with us, Tana?" Captain Rendan asked.

Her eyes flashed. "I want it even more now."

"Then I remind our sculptor that he is employed by the duke."

Treg turned to Rendan, his face twisted with rage. "Employed? You say Treg is employed? Like a soldier in your army? Like a minion washing your slop buckets? Treg is Treg. I am my own master;

I follow my own vision. No! No! You cannot have her." His eyes swept over Ninette's form. "If Duke Nortallion takes her, I will give him no more of my masterpieces. He cannot make them move; he cannot make them obey."

Treg's passion died; his eyes grew crafty. "Imagine how powerful my Vigili will be when they possess her fluidity of movement. What creatures they will become!" His voice grew smooth. "And besides, after I have made a hundred like Ninette, I will give her to you. It will be a gift, the gift of Treg."

Spence studied Ninette, surprised at her long silence. She looked neither frightened nor angry, but something new glistened in her eyes, something he couldn't read. Her tears had dried; her face was rigid.

Tanabel-Tunia turned away from the sculptor. "Let us speak no more of it for now."

Spence watched Tanabel-Tunia. She was hard to figure out too. He was certain of one thing though; she didn't act like someone being kidnapped against her will.

"Lunch is served," a wooden servant rumbled.

* * *

Spence spent much of the afternoon exploring Treg's facility. Even as a boy he had known that groups of people had a similar way of thinking; the tighter the organization, the more alike everyone thought. During the war, he had seen a company of captured SS soldiers, blond-haired, blue-eyed, every one of them over six feet tall, the cream of Hitler's Master Race. Despite being dirty, wounded, their uniforms torn, their boots falling to pieces, every one of them had looked down on their American captors like they were scum. Every society formed its own personality: the quick, fierce confidence of the Mustang pilots, the calm efficiency of the army nurses, the calculated cruelty of the drill sergeants—the dog-eat-dog pecking order of a gang of boys or a bunch of enlisted men in a barracks. Smaller than most, Spence knew a lot about that last one. But they had learned size wasn't everything when they dealt with him.

The best place to figure out a system was anywhere men and

women gathered to take a break from work. There was usually someone willing to talk to a newcomer, and Spence soon learned that Treg's people were blacksmiths, artisans, woodworkers, and stone masons, some skilled, others less so. Nor did Treg brook incompetence, driving his underlings by demanding perfection. His people knew better than to seek his praise; they labored hoping to avoid his wrath. But the system was less regimented than Spence had expected. As long as the sculptor got the results he wanted, he didn't care how it was done.

In the late afternoon he chanced upon Captain Rendan marching down a wide corridor, accompanying fifty newly-arrived soldiers dressed in gray. He fell in beside the captain, engaging him in conversation until they reached one of Treg's shadowy chambers, another dining hall furnished with a score of long tables. He took a seat at Rendan's table, a third of the way down, not too close to the captain but still among the upper echelons, ignoring Rendan's disapproving frown. He had used this trick before, betting that the officer, uncertain of Spence's status with Treg, wouldn't ask him to move. People were sheep; assumed authority in a military organization could go a long way.

Spence conversed with the soldier across from him, Sergeant Cleaver, while still keeping one ear on the discussion between the company commander and the captain. His eavesdropping proved interesting. The commander's words suggested that Rendan's authority extended much farther than his rank suggested, perhaps even to the ear of the duke himself. Information like that might be useful sometime.

The sergeant was short and bull-chested, with a round face, pale blue eyes, a lopsided smile, and almost no neck. Like the other soldiers, he wore a leather cuirass and a tunic and sandals. For fear of being thought a spy, Spence avoided asking questions about the army and kept his own origins vague, hinting only that he was a seasoned soldier who had seen some action. Remaining a little mysterious sometimes drew people's interest.

Treg's mechanical men served a meal of rice, eggs, and vegetables. A hubbub arose, caused by the stoneware bowls and cups urging the soldiers to eat. With a sneer, Captain Rendan recited the Mandate of Gratitude, and the rest of the company reluctantly followed suite. Cleaver looked at his food with disdain. "Wretched Talkers."

"You don't have them in your country?" Spence asked.

Cleaver snorted. "Ruheen is nothing like Animonea. Beasts bleating about representative government!"

"Your countries don't get along?"

Cleaver snorted. "It's unnatural, talking animals and trees, asking your food for permission before you eat it. They don't sacrifice to the Twelve Gods nor recognize the Divine Right of Kings. It's a land of lunacy."

"So people don't get attacked by thunderstorms in Ruheen?"

Cleaver laughed mirthlessly. "Nor will we ever. Grand Duke Swayval sees to that." He glanced at the soldiers around him and gave the table a solid rap. It shuddered but said nothing. "We may have to put up with it here, but we won't let the Talkers creep into our country, will we, boys?"

Some of the soldiers laughed, but others glanced uneasily at the wooden servants and the murmuring, ensconced torches.

"We're ruled by the Six Dukes, each commanding a region of our country," Cleaver explained. "The Grand Duke is chosen from their number. Duke Nortallion is here because his lands sit against Animonea's northwest border."

"How far are we from Ruheen?" Spence asked.

"Treg Keep lies at the edge of the Wileywood," Cleaver said. "Both were originally part of Animonea, but we hold the forest now, though it's still haunted by the Talkers. Someday, when the duke gives the word, we'll clean it out, burn the trees, and put an end to all of it. But it has its uses now, I suppose. I've never been this far east before. The duke ordered us down to fetch a woman."

"She must be important, to send this many men."

Cleaver shrugged. "I wouldn't know about that. I follow my orders."

Spence was intrigued. Why would Tanabel-Tunia be valuable to the duke? Maybe he should consider hooking himself to her star.

"So, are you needing recruits?" he ventured. "I'm looking for opportunities right now. I took my pension when I left the army, but I'm getting restless, you know? I'm serving with Treg for awhile; he's offered me a sweet deal because of my experience, but I might want to go somewhere else."

Sergeant Cleaver studied him. "We don't take mercenaries."

"I was thinking of a regular position. I know a trick or two about fighting. I think I can prove myself."

Cleaver smiled his lopsided smile. "There might be a place for you, if you're serious. Especially now. I can't say much, but things are stirring. We need brave lads. But Duke Nortallion requires loyalty above all else. A foreigner coming into Ruheen has to show what he's got."

Not wanting to appear too curious, Spence told a ribald joke to change the subject, but even as he spoke his mind churned. He had no love for this country of intelligent beasts. If Ruheen was free of the strange laws of both Animonea and Faerie, it might be a place where he could get along. He didn't want to serve in another army, but could do so awhile to get what he wanted.

To that end, he spent time with the soldiers. A few bottles of wine borrowed from Treg's servants went far toward making friends, though he was careful to stay mostly sober himself. It helped that the men despised the talking food and furniture. He didn't mind saying the Mandate for them, even while echoing their disgust, saving them from having to do it themselves. Nor did he neglect trying to gain the captain's confidence. This last he did with care, not saying too much, selling himself as an obedient soldier. If he ever got to Ruheen, he'd need someone to vouch for him.

Two evenings later, at supper in Treg's private dining chamber, Captain Rendan appeared without his sling and announced the company would depart the following morning. Both women were absent, Tanabel-Tunia excusing herself because of a headache, Ninette remaining behind to ensure her new friend's comfort, leaving Spence, Rendan, and Treg the sole diners.

"Your timing is fortuitous, Captain," Treg said, his long face half in shadow from the flames of the massive fireplace. "The last of the one-hundred Vigili were completed yesterday."

"How will they be transported?" Rendan asked. "Duchess Tanabel-Tunia's safety is paramount. I want to reach Ironwood Station without delay."

Treg chuckled. "The newest versions of my creations no longer need be hauled by wagons. Though they cannot travel as rapidly as your men, their limbs are tireless. While you rest, my warriors will march on. And unlike the others I sent the duke, these are far more coordinated."

Rendan raised an eyebrow.

"You doubt Treg? It is because you have seen the earliest of my creations. I admit they were cumbersome. But these! Would you like to observe them? They will astound you."

"Then they will be miraculous indeed," the captain said. "You are the artist you claim, Treg, yet your mechanical men only simulate life, and cannot function beyond the borders of Animonea. Human soldiers with minds and wills can always outwit your creations."

"Perhaps for a time, but not forever," Treg said. "Each generation is better than the last. I suspect you share your countrymen's fear of living iron and stone."

"It isn't fear. Duke Nortallion says we must use such tools to battle the chaos of Animonea, but I think it better to command men of flesh and blood whose hearts sing for the love of their liege lord."

"Artists do not fear chaos," Treg said. "It is the fire that guides us. From the chaos we build order; to order we bring chaos. It is the reason we should never be completely trusted. Our thoughts are those of the dreamers of dreams, the stuff of wonder and nightmare, the revolutionary railing against the light. Brought to mundane lives, it gives both pleasure and terror. This is especially true for one such as I, for the greater the artist the less the common rules matter. I am beyond mortal considerations."

Rendan raised his wine cup. "I don't claim to understand art, sir, though I think in the end even Treg must give way to mortality."

"My work will make me immortal. It will last a thousand years. But such musings miss the point." He made a sign and one of the wooden servants shuffled forward. "Bring them."

The Vigili departed, returning moments later with three others of its kind, somewhat taller and broader of shoulder, cast or carved in exquisite detail as armored soldiers, each face different. They moved with easy grace, almost as smoothly as men.

"One of iron, one of onyx, one of hardened clay," Treg said, "each representing a third of the one hundred I have fashioned for the duke. Are they not elegant, Captain?"

"They are impressive," Rendan admitted. "But how well do they fight?"

Rick had remained silent throughout the exchange, hoping to find something he could use to his advantage. "Let me test one of them."

"Excellent!" Treg said. "But I cannot guarantee your safety. Once a command to attack is given, they understand neither mercy nor a foe's surrender. Only a new instruction will make them halt."

Spence couldn't think of any reason why Treg would want to keep him alive, and at least one for wanting him dead, since it would allow him to isolate Ninette. He stood. "I lost my sword when we entered the Back of the Beyond."

Treg gave an order, and a blade was brought. Spence gripped it, testing its balance. "Which one should I fight?"

"My clay warriors are the newest innovation," Treg said. "Properly fired, reinforced with certain materials of my own invention, they are remarkably resilient, able to withstand powerful blows. Though not as indestructible as iron or stone, they are faster and more agile."

At Treg's command the Vigili marched to the middle of the room, holding its heavy sword in both hands. Spence appraised it carefully. It was the color of sandstone glazed to a dull shine. Its torso, head, and limbs, fashioned separately, were connected by rings at its joints. Decorative blue swirls covered its face and arms like tattoos; its black eyes glistened. It was a head taller than Spence and probably outweighed him by at least a hundred pounds. It had a longer reach and a larger sword. He would need every inch of room he could get to maneuver.

Treg pointed first at his creation, then at Spence, followed by a circling motion with one hand. The warrior raised its sword above its shoulders and strode forward.

Spence kept his eyes on its torso, studying its movements. It came at him a little slower than a man, with the barest hesitating lurch between each step. When it was nearly upon him, he circled around. It followed him with its eyes, stepping out with one foot and making a wide turn to pursue. It moved to the center of the room and swiped at him. Its blade sliced through the air, singing, "*Blood!*"

"*Protect!*" Rick's helmet shouted.

Spence stepped back, avoiding the stroke. The space where they fought was large enough to allow him to work.

The Vigili swung its sword in a circling motion, scything the air with precise, controlled strokes, repetitive as a machine. Spence thought of a piston doing its work, unaware of any consequences. He continued to retreat, slipping behind the creature when it came too close, testing it, looking for its limitations, avoiding engaging it. Parrying its swings would be like trying to stop a battleship. He needed other weapons.

The warrior pressed closer, making an unexpected sideways shuffle to keep Spence from escaping. Rick rolled, using all his agility to escape the slashing blade. So the brute was capable of reacting to its situation! It was even more dangerous than he thought. He had little time. Tireless, it could advance until his strength failed.

Darting around it again, he took a running leap at its back, striking it with both feet. It fell forward on its face, not catching itself as a man would. Spence landed with apish grace. The Vigili had not dropped its sword as Spence had hoped. He kicked at its hand, trying to dislodge the weapon, but it held it in an unbreakable grip.

Rick backed away while his enemy drew its legs under it and rose. He needed the moment to get his breath. As he did, he glanced around the room, looking for any advantage. There was almost nothing in the chamber save the heavy stone table, the hanging tapestry, and the massive fireplace with the pair of man-sized busts of Treg atop its broad mantle.

Spence was close to the table, and he darted forward, tearing Treg's pewter cup from the sculptor's hand, spilling a little of the wine. The Vigili came at him again, renewing its scything. Spence maneuvered to one side so the table and the fireplace beyond it lay to his left. Before the thing could draw closer, he rushed at it, throwing the wine in its face. He doubted it would irritate its eyes, but hoped it would blind it long enough to make it hesitate.

Without waiting to see the wine's effect, he tore toward the table, running right past his foe. He felt the breath of its sword slicing the air behind his head. Bounding forward, he jumped onto the table, rolled onto his hands, and thrust with all his strength, springing over Treg's head, catapulting himself toward the mantle. For the barest instant, he thought he had misjudged in the gloom and would miss by inches, but he landed feet-first on the high ledge. He wavered, unbalanced, nearly plunging from his perch, but struggled, regained his equilibrium, and stood on the wide mantle, nine feet above the floor.

The warrior shuffled toward him, circling the table to approach. Rendan and Treg rose, moving to avoid its path.

Agile as any simian, Spence ran across the mantle to one of the stone busts, a sculpture easily as tall as himself. He had hoped to use his sword as a lever, but had lost it in his leap. He looked around. Decorative, oversized replicas of carving tools hung on racks above his head. Seizing one, he wedged its sharp end behind the statue.

"*What are you doing*?" the statue demanded.

The warrior had nearly overtaken him, its sword held high, its reach long enough to sever Spence's ankles. One stroke of those massive arms would bring him crashing down. It drew back for the blow. Spence pushed the lever with all his strength, grunting with his effort. It did not give.

"Stop!" Treg cried. "Not my sculpture!"

Hearing the command, not understanding its intent, the warrior froze in mid-strike. But Spence did not hesitate. With another heave, he brought the statue down. The bust roared in delight as it fell upon the Vigili, crushing it beneath its weight.

A wave of triumph rushed over Spence as he stood on the mantle, his hands on his knees, catching his breath.

"What have you done?" Treg shouted, striding to the shattered bust. "How dare you use my self-portrait? Hours of work ruined!"

Even in his exhilaration Spence chose his words carefully, not speaking at first, keeping his temper while the artist railed at him. In boot camp he had learned to ignore being chewed out by his drill sergeant. Finally, facing only silence, Treg fell silent himself.

"I'm sorry," Spence said, pretending sincerity. "I didn't know what else to do. You wanted me to test your warrior. I couldn't have beaten it in fair combat. I had to use tricks, or it would have killed me. It's an amazing machine. You're a genius for sure."

Treg's features cooled. He turned to the captain. "That is true. Each of my creations is at least as deadly."

But the captain was studying Spence. At last he said, "They *are* faster, Treg, as you claimed. The duke will doubtless be pleased. We will take them to Ironwood Station. I should go make preparations for our departure."

Spence leapt down from the fireplace, landing beside the scattered shards of the warrior, which were talking among themselves. Rendan paused before him. "That was a magnificent display. I've never seen such acrobatics."

Spence shrugged. "It's a natural thing, something I learned as a kid. It's saved my life more than once."

When the captain had gone, Treg muttered, "Rendan has seen but has learned nothing. My magnificence is beyond him. It will be different with the duke once I discover Ninette's secrets."

"Can I help you clean this up?" Spence asked.

Treg's voice was cold. "My servants will attend to it. You are an unusual man, Mister Spence."

"That's what they tell me. Listen, I'd like to make this up to you so there's no hard feelings. You don't have much use for me here. I'm just in your way. What say you speak to Captain Rendan, recommend me to him? If he says it's all right, I'll go with him."

Treg's eyes hardened even more. "And take the girl?"

"You convince Rendan and pay me my first month's wages in gold like you mentioned, and I'll give . . . it . . . to you. You've got way more use for a thing like Ninette than I do."

Treg stared at Spence in his strange, distant way, then laughed. "I will impel the captain to take you, even if I must invoke the duke's name."

"Great. It's a deal. I'll start packing."

Spence showed no emotion as he left the room, but grinned once out of sight. That had worked beautifully. He had shown Rendan what he could do, impressing him just as he intended. And besides the pleasure of humiliating the high and mighty sculptor, he had given Treg reason to think he might be too dangerous to keep around. Sure, he hated leaving Ninette, but Treg was too unpredictable. A little gold now was better than being murdered in bed once the artist decided he wanted her to himself.

Spence danced down the corridor, leaping and clicking his heels. *"Happy!"* his helmet exclaimed. He wished he had some liquor. It had been a good day.

CHAPTER TEN

MORLANE

A shudder ran through Russ Rogers as he sat astride Flapjack, studying the twisted branches of Morlane. The soldiers had finished clearing the rotting timber from the rutted road to allow the supply wagons to pass. While the cavalry waited, half the infantry marched in rough columns into the Wileywood's shadows. The woods reminded him of the snow, the lack of sleep—and the death—in the Hürtgen Forest of Germany, some of the bloodiest combat he had ever faced. His best friend had died in a foxhole beside him there, slain by a sniper's bullet. Without thinking, Russ had rushed after the attacker, running pell-mell through the forest, driven by grief and fury. Luckily, he hadn't found him. In his haste he had left his ammo clip behind.

In a forest nothing was certain; the enemy could come at you from anywhere, high or low. You could die without ever seeing who killed you.

He wished he could turn around and ride away. If not for his promise to help Gray find Tanabel-Tunia, he would have asked Dartmallow to let him go. He shook his head. Millions dead in Europe and he had to nursemaid a lovesick kid.

As the infantry advanced, Marshal Dartmallow summoned Fox Lodan and Russ. They reached him just as he finished speaking to the Overcowls, who took wing, flying away from the direction of the forest.

"A shame to see them leave, eh Topper? At least the crows

promised to stay with us."

"No figuring bird brains, Marshal," Topper said.

"Wise birds in this case, intelligent enough to fear the forest. No matter; they did their part. We don't have them; we'll do without them." He turned to Fox and Russ, scrutinizing them before speaking. "When the moths attacked me, you reacted more quickly than my own men. Remarkable behavior for complete strangers. First Prince Darien saves the pup, then you risk your lives for mine. I admire men of courage, but I wonder at your willingness to do so."

"I can't speak for Gray," Fox said, "but you're a nobleman. We are both men of superior bloodlines. It is my duty to aid those of my own class, especially before the rabble."

"People once thought that way in Animonea," Dartmallow said, "but in the Republic we reject the old doctrine of royalty. Everyone is considered equal. Rank is earned, not passed from father to son."

Fox glanced at Russ. "Then your country is much like his, and I don't believe such realms can survive. The Divine Right of Kings is the one true way of the world."

Dartmallow turned to Russ. "What about you?"

Russ shrugged. "It was a reflex action, that's all. You've treated us fair and square. I guess I didn't want your men to lose their commander. I earned my rank through battlefield promotions when my superiors were killed."

Actually, he wondered why he had done it himself. He had once seen thirty B-17s assault a German artillery emplacement. The gunfire had ripped the flying fortresses to pieces, sending them tumbling, fragile as gossamer, from the sky. Something about the hummingbird battle reminded him of watching those planes go down. He didn't know why that had spurred him to help Dartmallow, but it had. War made men do peculiar things.

The marshal studied him. "If I give your weapons back, will you fight for us? We ride into the unknown against an enemy wielding Faerie magic. You have been to that country; you might see what we do not."

"I don't like killing without a cause," Russ said.

"The cause is the survival of the Republic of Everything. If Duke Nortallion is allowed to reinforce his base, he will use it to invade Animonea and establish Ruheen tyranny. We have dallied too long;

we must stop him here."

"Sounds like Hitler."

"I don't recognize the name, but tyrants are the same everywhere. I intend to march to Ironwood Station and drive him from the forest."

"I guess I can't say no to that," Russ reluctantly replied. After what he'd been through, it was easy to sympathize with a people trying to defend their country.

"If we're attacked, I will fight with you," Fox said. "More than that, I cannot promise."

Dartmallow nodded. "Very well. Return to your places."

Fox and Russ rode back into the line, where Vasps Geometer waited with the others. Only Jaunter looked at ease. Russ could see the brooding tension in Gray's face, the uncertainty in Joiwend's normally unruffled expression. Even Master Tatters looked jittery. The return of their weapons, along with round, wooden shields used by the cavalry, did little to lighten their mood, save for the Scythian, who raised his sagaris high and gave a long, happy howl which echoed among the hills.

When the first group of infantry had passed, the marshal led the cavalry in, followed by the rest of the foot soldiers and the supply wagons, the latter built narrow to pass more easily between the trees. Russ felt the shadows of the forest fall upon him, the heavy brooding of the ancient trees, a weight of anger and sorrow as palpable as if the Wileywood had spoken. It startled him, this eerie emanation of dejection and distress. But if the trees had eyes they kept them lidded; if faces, they kept them hidden.

Master Tatters blanched, moaning, "It's lost its affection, like a young lass whose beau has departed."

Russ couldn't help but agree. The Wileywood was in mourning, bitter and broken-hearted as a rejected lover.

"Our reports told us it was thus," Vasps said. "Most of the birds and animals have been driven out, and those that escaped spoke of the trees' malevolence."

The army neither chanted nor sang; they spoke little, keeping their voices low amid the creaking of the carts, the rustling of boots and hooves on dry leaves, the rattling of equipment and armor. The horses kept alert, their ears up. Even the soldiers' implements grew hushed in the forest's unnatural quiet—the weapons, the clothing, the saddles, the gear. Russ listened thoughtfully. In the last few days he had grown accustomed to the constant voices, like a radio always running in the background, his coat boasting it would keep him warm, a strawberry volunteering to be eaten, a knife longing to cut something. It was wearing, yet he dreaded this sudden stillness.

At least Dartmallow was handling the army well. The officers had divided the infantry into groups of one hundred twenty men, each arrayed in three rough ranks of forty foot soldiers, giving them a semblance of order despite the uneven ground and obstructing trees. A space of thirty yards separated the groups, leaving them room to maneuver if attacked. Russ didn't claim any strategic expertise—his job in the army had been to run communication lines to four batteries whenever his outfit moved, an assignment done mostly at night by truck headlights—but the warriors of Faerie had been less organized, and to his mind, less efficient than the marshal's troops.

He judged there were about two-hundred cavalry. So far, the forest floor remained mostly clear of undergrowth, but if that changed the horses would be at a disadvantage.

Based on the number of supply wagons, Dartmallow expected a short campaign. Russ hoped he was right.

A crow glided in, passing over the heads of the men, a black arrow in the forest gloom. It landed on Dartmallow's saddle horn and turned one eye to the marshal. The companions were riding close enough behind the commander to hear the exchange.

"Quacaw," Dartmallow said. How he could tell one bird from another, Russ did not know.

The crow spoke in his wavering caw. "The moths have fled, Oldbeard. Two I have valiantly killed, my spear my beak, my aim most true. Valiantly I have killed them. I have killed them valiantly. My brothers and sisters have slain others. But not so well as I. I am the best. The best I am. Perhaps, perhaps the best of the murder."

"How far to the old road?" Dartmallow asked.

Quacaw strutted closer to the marshal, eyeing his left hand. "You still have the ring. The ring you still have. Golden. Pretty."

"You digress, Quacaw. The road?"

The crow's eye remained on the ring. "We saw no road. No road we saw. The road is not there. There is no road. No road there is."

"What? There has to be!"

The crow cocked his head and shook his wings. "I do not lie. I never lie. I tell the truth, I am no liar. No liar I am."

"Could you be mistaken?"

"Perhaps, perhaps. We have searched; we have not found. No road we found. We found no road."

"It has to be there."

Quacaw marched up the horse's mane to its head, making the animal's ears twitch. "It is not where it was. It is not where the sparrows said. The sparrows said it, but it is not. Perhaps, perhaps they lied."

Dartmallow scowled. "You couldn't find anyone more reliable than sparrows? Why didn't you tell me this earlier?"

"No robins hop the woods anymore, the woods they do not hop. But an owl said it too. We heard the owl. We knew the owl. The owl we knew. Perhaps, perhaps the owl was wrong."

Dartmallow turned to Vasps, who had ridden up during the conversation. "What do you make of that? Hidden by magic?"

"Possibly," Vasps said. "The enchanters' powers are mostly trickery and phantoms, so it might be an illusion cast to fool the crows, but I do not think they can project such a deception on the minds of our entire army. That would take great power indeed. I believe we will soon cross the old road."

"I hope you're right," Dartmallow said.

Russ took his army compass from his coat pocket and brought it to Vasps and the marshal. "This might help. We're traveling two hundred eighty degrees northwest right now."

"*Pointing north,*" the compass said. "*Holding steady.*"

Vasps Geometer took it and grinned. "These are unknown in Animonea. This one is well-made. Further proof of what you have told us." He handed it back. "Please let us know if we drift beyond our present course."

"I'll watch it," Russ said.

The talk of enchanters interested Russ. Soonderkainen and the other wizards he had met in Faerie hadn't known how to return him home, though they thought it must be possible. Perhaps the magicians of Ruheen had the answer. If so, he might be on the wrong side of this war. He shook his head, refusing to give in to despair. He would have to find a way. He glanced at Gray and chuckled. He had been judging the prince for his obsession with Tanabel-Tunia, but all Russ wanted was to get back to Kansas and Paulette.

* * *

Gray kept alert, anxious to reach their destination, hoping to find some sign of his beloved there. If her captors had indeed taken Tana into the Wileywood, they might have carried her on to Ruheen. If so, he would escape from Dartmallow, with or without his companions, and continue the quest. He hated to break his promise to the marshal, but he was under a higher calling.

Blunder bounded up beside Nutmeg. "Hello, Gray."

"Hello. Where have you been?"

"I was with mother and the other dogs. We are searching for scents."

"Did you find anything?"

"The trees smell funny. There are not many animals. Mother sniffed a squirrel. I smelled a skunk."

Gray chuckled. "I'm glad you didn't find it."

"I know, Gray. Mother told me about skunks. The scent was two days past. There is another smell, like wolves but not like wolves."

"A different breed of wolf?"

"Yes. Mother told Marshal Dartmallow. I camed back to see you."

"I'm glad you did. Would you like to ride on my saddle?"

"Yes. My legs are tired." Blunder bounced up and down, thrusting his paws against the horse's side.

"Stop that," Nutmeg said.

Gray leaned down, grabbed Blunder under his front legs, and pulled him up, the pup scrabbling his back feet against the stirrup leathers until he reached the saddle. He sat in front of Gray, one paw on the saddle horn, head erect, nose high, scenting the air. Gray ran his hand over Blunder's thick fur, a double-coat, rough on the outside and soft beneath. The dog leaned back and licked Gray's chin. "It is high here, Gray." He curled up on the saddle, supported between Gray's thighs, and fell fast asleep.

"If only people were as trusting," Joiwend said. "He's like a child."

They fell silent once more, hushed by the silence of the forest.

The morning passed and still they found no sign of the road. Even Sniffdaisy and the other dogs, sent far afield, failed to discover it.

"We've missed it, haven't we, Vasps?" Dartmallow finally said. "We must have passed it somehow."

"I fear you may be right. I've been doing calculations, working out the distances according to our rough map. Even assuming errors on the cartographer's part, we should already be there."

"Very well," Dartmallow said. "We make our decisions; we follow our decisions. It's the way we get things done. Send word to the front, Topper, to turn straight north."

The orders were carried out, the columns making their slow turn. They had traveled only a short distance before they began hearing the cries of crows. Gray saw them circling a spot just ahead. Reaching it, they discovered the birds hopping and fluttering along a low bough. The body of one of their number lay crushed in the grip of a tree branch.

Dartmallow's face grew gray. "Old Krukenaw."

"He is fallen!" Quacaw lamented beside the corpse. "Fallen is he. His wings lift him nevermore. Nevermore they lift him. He will not eat again. He will take no treasure."

Vasps doffed his turban, revealing thick, curly hair.

"I grieve for him," Dartmallow said. "He often guided us truly and well."

"The killing was seen by Nacal," Quacaw said. "Nacal saw it. The tree caught him. The trees hate everything! Everything they hate! We will watch the trees. We will be watching. We will not roost in them. In them we will not roost. We have danced the mourning dance. The honor is yours, Oldbeard. Yours is the honor."

Getting heavily down from his horse, Dartmallow used a knife to cut the thin branch constricting the body. Laying the crow on the ground, he tucked its small head beneath one of its wings. "Sleep well, brave heart."

The crows rose in the air, scattering through the forest.

Dartmallow shook his head. "He was a most dependable bird. I was a young man when I met him, nearly twenty years ago. But it tells us we travel in the right direction. We've struck their defenses."

"The tree killed it?" Gray asked, disquieted.

Vasps wrapped his turban back on his head. "Like the crows, we must be wary."

They continued traveling north, not stopping to eat, chewing on dried meat from their packs as they went. Quacaw soon returned to Dartmallow. "We found a pool, Oldbeard. A pool we found. Ahead it lies. It lies ahead. Its water is good, but its words are bitter. It says there is a lake farther on. Ironwood Station stands near it. Near it stands Ironwood Station. So it says. It says so. Perhaps, perhaps it tells the truth. Perhaps, perhaps it tells a lie. We do not know if we believe its words."

"Pools don't lie," Dartmallow said.

"Perhaps, perhaps, but this pool is not like other pools. It is different. It is not the same. The same it is not. Its stream is cut off; it dries and dies, and it is angry. The forest has turned it angry. It would hardly speak to us at all. To us it would hardly speak."

"Lead us to it," Dartmallow said.

The riders soon came to the half-filled pool, lying in the bed of a dried brook. The marshal and Vasps questioned it, but Gray could not hear what was said. It refused to allow the horses to drink from it.

Blunder woke and looked around, raising his nose to the air. "It smells like rain." Gray stroked his head while he bit playfully at the prince's fingers.

True to the pup's words, scattered drops began to fall, shouting in their tiny voices, bouncing against the leaves and dripping down to sit gleaming on Nutmeg's saddle and hair. It felt good on Gray's face, but he feared a storm like the one they had seen on the first night in the Back of the Beyond. The trees hid the sky, revealing only gray patches of pensive-faced clouds through the branches. Even these soon vanished behind a rising fog, leaving the forest indistinct and witchy.

"What do you make of it, Vasps?" Dartmallow asked.

"I do not know. Despite their claims, the enchanters are not weather-workers. For the duke to raise a mist would require the cooperation of a body of water larger than the pool. If there is a lake nearby as it said, and if that lake chose to obey the duke, it might cause it, but I think it more likely a natural phenomenon."

"Whatever the case, it makes it difficult," Dartmallow said.

The mist thickened and formed into faces which tried to talk, but could utter only choking, death-rattle rasps. Distressed by their inability to speak, they put soft hands to soft throats, eyes bulging, gaping like drowning men before dissolving into larger mists and larger faces, ghosts fading and emerging. Blunder sat upright on the saddle and growled.

"Easy, boy." Gray ran a hand over the dog's back, more to comfort himself than the pup. Hearing an agonized groan, he turned to see Jaunter staring wide-eyed in fright, his trembling hands clutching his sagaris.

"What is it?" Gray asked.

"Demon eyes from the Land of the Dead!" Jaunter croaked, his tortured voice scarcely more than a whisper, his forehead glistening with sweat. "Will they never leave me be?"

Responding to his master's fear, his horse, Ransom, rumbled, "Danger?"

"Danger?" Nutmeg echoed.

The word sped through the cavalry, every horse repeating it, head raised, ears turned forward, an abrupt chorus dying quickly away. Blunder growled again. Another dog barked. The crows clamored. Weapons and armor rattled their yearning for battle. The noise rose and fell to silence.

The marshal spoke in a steady voice. "Stay firm. All is well." His stallion repeated his words, and these too passed through the company, calming the horses.

"It's only mist," Joiwend told Jaunter. "Why does it frighten you?"

The Scythian did not reply, but trembled so violently Gray feared he might go into a battle frenzy.

"We are here, my friend," Joiwend soothed. "You are not alone. We are with you." In such manner, she spoke until his eyes lost their ferocity and his shivering ceased.

"You think me craven," he said.

"You are the last man I would call a coward," Joiwend said. "You have your reasons."

"I do."

"Perhaps you would share them?"

He shook his head violently. "Not beneath the stares of these mist men."

The haze grew so thick it turned the trees to taloned phantoms in a landscape without hint of hue. The world narrowed around Gray until he could scarcely see the rider in front of him. Nearby sounds grew more distinct. He glanced upward, trying to pinpoint the sun, but saw only a diffused glow.

The companions rode closer to the marshal so he and Russ could refer to the compass. At Dartmallow's command the crows flew between the formations to keep them together, the birds calling to one another to maintain their own bearings, their caws harsh in the blanketing stillness. The marshal remained undaunted. "We knew there would be obstacles, didn't we, Topper? We expected resistance; we will resist the resistance. Mist or no, Ironwood Station is before us. We shall seek it; we shall find it; we shall destroy it."

Blunder raised his head, ears up, alert. A heartbeat later Gray heard the sound all warriors fear. "Arrows!" he bellowed, leaning over to cover the pup with his body, pulling his legs up to make himself a smaller target, thrusting his round shield above him.

They came shrieking down through the fog, at a low angle beneath the forest canopy, singing their song of death. *Strike! Strike!* Most fell quivering to the ground, moaning at having missed, but others found targets. Horses and men screamed all around. From behind his shield, Gray saw a shaft embed itself in a soldier's neck. The man gaped, swayed, and tumbled from his saddle. Gray glanced toward Joiwend, relieved to see her unscathed.

"Archers!" Topper bawled. But already lines of bowmen had formed behind the cavalry, though Gray could not see them through the mist. Scores of bowstrings twanged, aimed only by the angle of their enemies' missiles.

Dartmallow quickly led the men forward through the murk, attempting to avoid another volley by changing positions. Unable to see far ahead, the riders barely halted their frightened steeds in time to avoid running into the ranks of the foot soldiers.

"We should be safe enough now," Gray told Vasps, but the arbiter gave him a doubtful look. Moments later, to his astonishment, a second volley screeched down. Nutmeg nickered and danced in fear as arrows landed at her hooves. One clattered off Gray's shield. Jaunter slid to the side of his horse, clinging to Ransom's neck, using it for protection. Master Tatters batted an arrow away with his sword, shouting in Comanche. Once more the archers of Animonea responded.

"How are they finding us?" Joiwend asked.

"The forest is telling them our location," Vasps said. "Only they can do so this quickly."

Another volley ensued, but Dartmallow ordered his archers to stand down. "Let's not give them any more arrows to kill us with."

Quacaw glided to him. "We have found them, Oldbeard! Them we have found. They are not many. Many they are not. Perhaps, perhaps you can catch them."

"Topper," the marshal commanded. Without further instructions, the hatchet-faced adjutant sent a detail rushing into the forest, Quacaw and two other crows gliding before them. The noise of a skirmish soon arose, and Quacaw came sailing back, eyes glittering in triumph, declaring the archers routed.

"Thank you, Quacaw!" Dartmallow said. "We'll show them we too can communicate with speed."

The soldiers attended their wounded and gathered their dead. The horses milled around their injured comrades, conferring with the men. In Animonea, animals are not put out of their misery as quickly as on Earth, yet the horses did not think like humans; and if there was no hope, they kissed their fallen with nibbling lips before a quick thrust ended their lives, then mourned their deaths with nickering sorrow.

"This is a bad place," Nutmeg said. "We must run."

"We stay and fight," Dauntless ordered, snorting and blowing in anger at the losses to the herd.

"Brave and foolish stallion," Nutmeg said. But she dropped her head and spoke no more.

The going was slow in the mist, and despite the crows' vigilance, handfuls of Ruheen archers continued to harass the army, striking and slipping away, leaving the army nervous and watchful.

"It's desperation, wouldn't you say, Topper?" Marshal Dartmallow asked. "It proves what we thought; we outnumber them by scores. The All-Council was right to send us. We'll do our job and be gone before you know it."

"No doubt, sir," Topper said.

By late afternoon the crows reported finding the lake, a mighty reservoir lying behind an earthen dam. For the first time, Gray saw the marshal taken aback. "A reservoir! Why didn't we know about this, Vasps?"

"We understood the Ruheens had diverted the river Widfroth away from the forest to remove the source of Morlane's sentience, but we assumed the waters had been channeled back into Animonea. They must have built a reservoir instead. Most of our information came from migrating geese. They said nothing of a dam, but you know how unreliable they are." The arbiter shook his head. "The old saying is true: 'Never trust a goose to take a gander.' According to our maps the Alopean range intersects Morlane on the north, creating a natural valley between the arms of the mountains, an ideal location for a levee. The Ruheens probably considered that a more permanent solution. But if its waters were ever released, it would flood the woods, a catastrophe for the entire forest."

Dartmallow's expression hardened to steel. "The All-Council should have responded before it came to this. Prompt action is proper action. I don't like it."

Not wishing to be caught between the reservoir and their foes, the marshal turned west. Two hours passed, and still they did not reach Ironwood Station, nor could Quacaw's murder locate it.

The afternoon wore away, bringing another harrowing shower of arrows. When Dartmallow sent out a party of twenty to flush out the attackers, neither they nor the crows with them returned. Alarmed by the loss, with twilight but two hours away, he ordered the men to make camp. After posting a watch, they dug a ditch with admirable efficiency, throwing the dirt outward to form a low rampart. The wagons contained wooden poles, sharpened on both ends, slightly taller than a man, and these were driven behind the ditch and tied to form a palisade.

"*Together, together, we stand together,*" the palings murmured in the mist.

The men lit no fires; they sang no songs. Gray lay in his bedroll between Jaunter and Joiwend, Blunder by his side, unable to sleep, crushed by the weight of uncertainty. In the blanketing darkness of the night and the fog, it seemed impossible that he would ever see Tana again. He wanted to slip out of the camp and go find her, instead of lying there waiting for morning. But he had given his word, the word of a Prince of Stallions of the Kingdom of En. And if he did desert, where would he go, if not to Ironwood Station? From what Vasps had told him, there were no other strongholds or villages anywhere in the Wileywood. If Tana was close, she was likely there. And if she wasn't . . .

He tossed and turned, and was finally drifting off to sleep when the voice of the moon whimpered from the heights. "Against all odds I have returned. But I die! Oh I die! My vision is stricken. I am blind, made to wander in endless darkness. My cause is hopeless, my plight, unbearable. Will any take pity on me? Is there no one to guide my way?"

Gray sat up on his bedroll. Blunder, sleepy-eyed, raised his head. Through the fog and the forest, Gray failed to detect even a diffused shining in the east and remembered it was the dark of the moon. He lay back down, as dejected as the satellite.

Later in the night he woke again, roused by Blunder growling close to his side. "The trees are watching now, Gray."

Gray studied the nearest trunks. In all this time the forest had not shown its faces. Now it did; and they were the most sorrowful he had ever seen, the downturned scowls, the squinting eyes on boles and leaves hollow with pain. Old, crippled men, the trees of Morlane, not joyous growths basking in the sun, but tormented souls, somehow persuaded to serve the wishes of Duke Nortallion. Like any abused child, their agony had made them angry, their sorrow had left them cruel.

The Wileywood began to moan.

It started as a low keening, as if from deep in the earth, but it rose, a score of voices, then a hundred, a thousand, and thousands more. Dissonant, grating, eerie, the funeral dirge of a forest lost. Despite its vast numbers, Morlane had been lonely for so long; but no one had taught it to seek help to ease its despair.

Blunder whined. Everyone in the camp scrambled to their feet, fumbling for their weapons. Gray drew his sword and stood gaping, uncertain. He turned to Joiwend in time to see a twisted tree branch reaching for her head.

He seized her arm, whipping her away. The branch missed, swiping the air, but stretched toward her again. Gray pulled her beyond its reach, and chopped at it with his sword, but succeeded only in chipping away a splinter.

The horses appeared out of the mist, seeking their riders, their brown eyes wide with fright.

"Formations!" Toppers voice bawled. "Defensive positions!"

Another branch came at Gray. He ducked and parried, entangling his sword in its shoots. It thrust its limb to the side, tearing his weapon from his hand, throwing him to the earth.

Jaunter stepped between him and his assailant, chopping the end of the limb off with a stroke of his sagaris. Without pausing, the Scythian rushed to the tree trunk and gave it two blows, notching wood chips from the oaken eyes. The tree screamed, a noise of snapping wood. Its branches shook as if from a gale. But new eyes appeared above where the old ones had been. Both that tree and the one nearest it turned their full wrath upon the barbarian.

Gray fumbled through the darkness and recovered his sword and shield. Rising, he slashed upward, trying to divert the limbs seeking the Scythian. Abandoning conventional swordsmanship, he flailed at the wood, severing branches.

The companions had instinctively drawn together, each fighting in their own way. A limb grasped Jaunter's sagaris. The Scythian snarled, matching his strength against the power of the oak. Master Tatters dropped his sword and grabbed Jaunter's axe handle, lending his own weight to the fight. Joiwend seized the Scythian by the waist, trying to keep him from being pulled off his feet. Fox Lodan, following Jaunter's example, rushed to one of the trunks and slashed at it with Forlamard.

None of this would have helped, had Dauntless not entered the fray. Rearing on his hind legs, rumbling a challenge from his mighty chest, the stallion hammered the branches with his hooves, tearing them down, freeing Jaunter's axe. "Fight!" he bugled. "Fight!"

Nutmeg and the others obeyed, battering the branches, sending twigs and wood chips flying.

A flame appeared. Russ, his cigarette lighter in one hand, a newly-made torch in the other, brought the brand against the pursuing branches.

"*Burn!*" the torch cried gleefully. Facing the thing they feared most, the trees howled and shrank back.

Master Tatters bounded around the others, cape flapping, scouring the forest floor. Within moments, he had a bundle of kindling for Russ to set alight. Gray and the others seized leaves and dried branches, adding to the pile until a steady bonfire blazed.

"*I hunger!*" the flames cackled, stretching upward.

Dartmallow appeared on horseback, sword in hand, an act of courage that brought his head closer to the seeking limbs. He circled the bonfire. "To me! Shields out! Lightmen forward!"

Axe-wielding infantrymen appeared, bearing torches covered in pitch. Others dumped armloads of wood in piles thirty paces apart. Clearly, the army had been prepared for such an attack. The fires blazed in two long lines the length of the camp, glowing dimly through the mist, turning the darkness blood red.

It was impossible to get completely away from the trees, but with the branches of the nearest assailants driven back, Gray had a chance to look around. By the wavering light he saw the oaks and beeches lifting soldiers high off the ground and casting them to the earth, or crushing them between powerful limbs, their armor useless, their screams hollow in the mist. This lasted but a few seconds, however, before torch-bearing cavalrymen rode around the camp, brandishing their flames, forcing the trees to retract their limbs while the foot soldiers, bearing their long, rectangular shields, formed a wall behind the bonfires. The infantry who bore axes surrounded the trees standing within the shield wall, their torches raised while the trees scowled and roared.

With Topper by his side, Dartmallow rode along the lines, his face stern but collected. "We'll show them a thing or two, won't we, Topper? The duke may be an enchanter, but he doesn't know the way trees think."

Gray hesitated, uncertain what to do. It appeared they had reached a stalemate, but only so long as the bonfires burned. How could any army fight a forest?

An arrow struck the ground half a pace from where he stood, its voice masked by the outcries of the trees. He dropped to a crouch beside Blunder, raising his round shield to protect them both. The pup whimpered as more shafts passed over the palisade walls and fell among the soldiers. Most bounced harmlessly off the shield wall, but others found their mark.

The marshal gasped, and Gray turned to see an arrow protruding from his left breast. Topper leapt from his saddle, catching Dartmallow before he fell. Other soldiers helped draw their commander away.

The barrage ended, yielding the dead and the wounded. The trees had fallen silent, leaving the cries of the injured, the moaning of arrows that had missed their targets, the eager shouts of the swords and axes, the cackling delight of the bonfires. Overhead, the voice of the moon boomed. "What battle is this I hear, though my eyes be blind? What goes forth? What evil wights shuffle through the darkness? Fight on, I say, though hope be black as night."

"Great, we have a cheerleader," Russ grumbled.

Horns blared, and a commotion arose at the palisade's edge, the tearing and splintering of wood. Gray peered over the shoulders of the shield men standing in ranks four deep, but could see nothing through the mist. The soldiers in the first line shouted in amazement and fear, followed by the clamor of battle. The line wavered and began to buckle.

"What is it?" a captain shouted. "What word?"

Soldiers fell, the line collapsing, yet still Gray could not discern the enemy. Then an iron-gray form crashed through the shield wall, casting the men aside like puppets. At first Gray thought it a man covered in armor plate, but it was a metal warrior, moving heavily, its blade dripping blood, a juggernaut heedless of the blows of its enemies.

Jaunter rushed at the creature, moving with starting speed for one so large, timing his assault between its strokes, ramming his shoulder into its chest, knocking it off its feet. Soldiers hammered vainly at it with their swords. Slowly, inexorably, it pulled its stiff legs beneath it and rose again.

Russ thrust his torch in its face, attempting to blind it while Gray struck at its neck. Heedless, it cut the torch in half with its sword, barely missing the sergeant's wrist.

More iron warriors burst through the Animonean ranks, followed by others of stone or fired clay.

"Formations!" a commander called. A few men tried to obey, but against the overpowering force of foes who could batter aside shields and turn steel, their efforts failed. The men of iron were few in number, but they rampaged through the lines, forcing panicked warriors to give way or perish.

Horns sounded again, and a mighty shout filled the night. Behind the unnatural warriors the men of Ruheen burst over the broken palisade wall. Short but broad-shouldered, dressed in leather armor, their faces pale in the firelight, they marched in a disciplined phalanx against the shattered Animonean lines.

The charge thrust Gray and his companions back. A soldier came at the Prince of Stallions, and Gray cut him down with a jabbing thrust. To his right, Jaunter sang his battle song, his sagaris tearing through necks and limbs. Where Joiwend had been, an enormous bear reared, claws ripping at her foes. Fox Lodan shouted as he fought, ferocious in battle. Master Tatters, having found a heavy hammer, knocked the head off one of the clay soldiers and drove it from its feet.

Joiwend's ferocious form and the combined assault of the companions scattered their enemies, and for a moment they stood alone, the battle-tide flowing away from them. In that instant, Jaunter, eyes wide with sudden fear, shouted with a voice of sheer animal horror, "*Not him!*" and in a frenzy of terror, brushed past Gray and leapt onto his horse, nearly knocking the prince off his feet. By the time Gray recovered, the Scythian had vanished into the darkness.

Unnerved by the flight of his bravest comrade, Gray looked frantically about, vainly trying to discover the cause. What he saw dismayed him even further. Decimated by the iron warriors, facing an organized foe, the Animonean army was dissolving into chaos, fleeing in every direction.

Fox Lodan swept his eyes over the carnage. "We're finished! We have to get out!" With a whistle, he called Dauntless to him and sprang onto the animal's broad back.

Gray felt something behind him and turned, sword ready, but it was Nutmeg nosing his shoulder. "Run!" she whinnied. "Run!"

"Run!" the other horses echoed.

Gray swung onto Nutmeg. "Joiwend! Come!"

The bear looked at him without recognition, her eyes filled with fury.

"Please! I know you're in there. Joiwend!"

"I will come," Joiwend growled, dropping to all fours and padding toward the horses, causing the animals to shy from her.

A new wave of Ruheen warriors rushed from the darkness, engulfing Gray and Joiwend in a sea of foes. The bear rose to her hind legs, looming large in the firelight, sending the soldiers scuttling backward in fear. Gray cut to right and left, protecting her back as her claws carved a path through their enemies.

An iron warrior lurched toward her, weapon upraised. She met its charge with her mighty limbs, bending its sword-arm back until it broke at the joint, leaving it dangling helpless at its side. With a push of her front paws, she sent it crashing to the ground.

Seeing the iron man fall, the Ruheens lost their courage. Joiwend broke through their lines, and she and Gray were abruptly out of the fray. When they reached the palisade wall, she slashed its binding ropes away and shoved a section aside. Horse and bear crossed the ditch, bounded over the low rampart, and hurried into the darkness. Gray heard the booming voice of the moon, but did not catch the words. He looked back only once. The army of Animonea had melted away. The men of Ruheen surged around the fires, their standards held high.

CHAPTER ELEVEN

THE GHOST

The morning of their departure, Rick Spence, now assigned to the Ruheen company, was ordered to eat in the dining hall with the other soldiers. He had avoided Ninette, knowing she wouldn't understand his leaving. It was better that way. He didn't want her spoiling his plans by making a big scene in front of Treg. The sculptor was too temperamental and might change his mind about letting Spence go.

When he entered the hall, Sergeant Cleaver gave him a wide grin. "I heard the way you beat that mechanical man. You'll make a fine addition if you can follow orders."

Spence grinned, elated. "I'm looking forward to serving." His showing must have impressed Rendan even more than he'd hoped; and the weight of the gold coins in his backpack felt great. It wasn't as much as he would have liked, but any more would've been too hard to conceal. He would need to keep the gold quiet and find someplace to hide it once they reached their destination.

"We'll give you the Oath and get you a regular uniform and proper helmet once we reach Ironwood," Cleaver said.

"*I protect his head,*" Spence's helmet protested.

Spence tugged it low over his brow with both hands. "I hate to let it go. It's saved my life a few times."

"That's a miracle, then," Cleaver said. "It's fine for an overhead stroke, but worthless against cuts from the side."

"It's for protection from. . ." He started to say *shrapnel*, ". . . arrows and stones."

After breakfast the company marched through Treg Keep's wide passages until they reached a pair of tall bronze doors, each displaying half of Treg's etched face. Marble servants spoke to the doors and swung them wide, ushering the soldiers into the morning sunlight. They looked down from a height, and a narrow road ran before them, descending through a ravine toward deep forest. A low mist rose behind mountains to the north. Level ground extended to one side of the doors, occupied by the one-hundred Vigili Treg had manufactured for the duke. Scattered, flat-bottomed clouds gaped in vacuous curiosity at them.

"Where are the horses?" Spence asked the soldier beside him. "I thought we were in a hurry."

"Duke Nortallion forbids their use in Animonea, since they might be spies."

They waited several minutes before Ninette appeared, followed by Treg and two clay Vigili hefting a large trunk.

The soldier who had spoken before groaned. "I helped carry that chest to Treg Keep. I thought we were rid of it."

"What's in it?" Spence asked.

"Gifts from the duke to the duchess. They said it's her wardrobe, but it was heavy as armor."

Captain Rendan left his place beside the company commander and strode to Ninette's side. "Where is the Duchess Tanabel-Tunia?"

"She's almost ready," Ninette said. "She wanted her things placed under the care of your soldiers, rather than in the hands of Treg's creatures, who she fears might handle them roughly."

Treg curled his lip in disdain. "My creations are more than capable of conveying a trunk."

"I'm only repeating what Tana told me."

"As the duchess wishes," Rendan said.

"I'll go help her finish dressing," Ninette said.

"Good fortune to you, Captain Rendan," Treg said. "Have the duke send word when my Vigili arrive."

Spence watched Ninette walk swiftly away, followed by Treg and his clay servants. Rick doubted the sculptor had come to say goodbye; he probably wanted to make sure Ninette stayed behind. But the girl's reaction was surprising. He had expected her to be red-eyed from bawling, and had tried to keep out of sight so she wouldn't make a big scene, but she hadn't even bothered to look for him. After all the time they'd spent together, that hurt his feelings. He thought they were friends. He had done his best to take care of her, and she wasn't even grateful. He shook his head. You couldn't trust anybody, especially a woman.

Tanabel-Tunia soon appeared, her hair pulled severely back, dressed in a hunting suit with a short, dark skirt over riding pants.

"I regret you must walk," Captain Rendan said. "I would have prepared a litter, but it would never survive the journey through the forest."

She smiled. "We tramped through half of Animonea together, Captain. I can manage a few more leagues. My trunk, if you please."

The company commander detailed two men to lift it. As Rendan escorted Tanabel-Tunia to their places, Spence overheard him say, "Are you well? You seem troubled."

"I'm fine, Captain, just anxious to leave Treg's ghastly demesne."

"I'm sorry we couldn't bring Ninette with us. I know you wanted to."

"Let's not speak of her, Chel."

They passed beyond Rick's hearing. A soldier stepped to the top of the road and bawled, "Permission to travel?"

"*Follow me,*" the road said.

Led by the commander, they marched in formation, Captain Rendan and Tanabel-Tunia surrounded by the officers. Spence glanced behind him; Treg's Vigili followed, inhumanly silent.

The men marched through the ravine and halted at the edge of the Wileywood.

"Captain Rendan on the business of Duke Nortallion!" the soldier cried.

An ancient oak studied them with lidded eyes. "You are the duke's men. You may pass."

"Our thanks." Despite his words the soldier's voice was heavy with contempt.

Beneath the boughs of Morlane, the company grew hushed. Spence had been in the great forests of Germany. They had been old; the Wileywood was older. He wondered just how much older. It wasn't anything he could pinpoint; it was the air, the look of the trees, the feel of his boots on the ground. A shiver ran down his spine.

The road narrowed, becoming little more than a trail, forcing the men to break formation and walk in single file. The trees watched, sullen but nonthreatening. The morning passed without incident.

After lunch Spence and another soldier were ordered to take a turn bearing the trunk. They lifted it by its side-handles.

"Criminey! What's in this thing?" Spence exclaimed. "It weighs a ton."

"The duchess' dainties, I suppose," the other man said.

"This ain't that dainty."

"No talk concerning the lady," Sergeant Cleaver ordered.

"Yes, Sergeant," Spence said.

Carrying the trunk was awkward over the rough ground and protruding tree roots, and Spence was glad when the next pair of soldiers took their turn.

They made no fires that night, but ate cold rations. Spence was one of the men given the first watch, Cleaver's way of making him understand he was no better than any other recruit. Spence didn't mind; that was the way armies worked. He could play the good corporal.

The night was clear; the stars peered down between the branches. There was no moon. He heard the slow breathing of his fellows around him. From where he stood guard, he could see the tent erected for Tana. He licked his lips and pulled a flask filled with Treg's whiskey from his pocket. It was fine stuff, nice and smooth; its warmth filled his chest. He wished he could get drunk; it would be a good night for it.

He heard a stirring in Tana's tent, laughter followed by silence. For a moment he suspected someone was with her. If so, it would have to be Rendan. The way she called him Chel—they had spent a lot of time alone in the wilderness—maybe they were more than friends. But through the gloom he could make out the captain's form, lying protectively before her tent entrance. Though he listened a long time, he didn't hear any other voices.

The next day was much like the first until nearly sunset. The duke had ordered Tana brought with all haste, and the commander drove the men so hard they finally stumbled as they went. One of those carrying the trunk tripped over some roots and fell sprawling. The trunk crashed to the earth, turning on its side, spilling its contents, including the armored form of Ninette Argilla, rolling across the ground.

Tana shrieked and hurried to her friend's side, followed by a gaping Rendan. Ninette struggled to rise, but failed and fell and burst into tears. Rendan helped her to her feet and ordered a soldier to bring her water.

Spence drew closer, making a show of righting the trunk. His mind whirled. It could mean trouble if Treg thought he had played a part in this.

"Tana, how did you . . ." Captain Rendan's voice died away.

Spence overhead her whispered answer. "She was in the trunk all along. I took her form to fool Treg."

The captain raised a warning hand to silence her. He glanced around, his eyes meeting Rick's. Spence looked away. Apparently Joiwend wasn't the only one who could change her shape.

Ninette noticed Spence. With tears still running down her cheeks, she shouted, "You stay away from me, Ricky Spence; you just stay away. You . . . deserter! You would have left me there!"

Spence turned aside, unwilling to face her ire before the entire company.

The commander strode up. "Your ladyship, you shouldn't have done this. The duke may take both our heads and the captain's too. He honors Master Treg greatly."

"It isn't her fault," Ninette said. "It was my idea, once I knew she could—"

"No, Ninette!" Tana said sharply. She met the commander's gaze. "It was my decision. I couldn't leave her to that madman."

* * *

When the iron men attacked Dartmallow's camp, Master Tatters leapt astride his horse and followed Jaunter into the darkness. There had been time for neither saddle nor bridle, and through the mist he glimpsed the barbarian just ahead, riding bareback as only a Scythian—or a Comanche—could, darting and weaving between the trees, slipping from side to side of his mount to avoid shattering his legs against a trunk. It puzzled Tatters, this blind, panicked flight, but if the Scythian was so unnerved, there had to be a reason, a danger beyond even the horror of the mechanical men, and the old pioneer wanted no part of it. He urged his horse on, forcing Jingles to keep up with Jaunter's galloping steed. They moved farther from the bonfires, deeper into the fog. His cloak flapping behind him, Master Tatters laughed wildly and called his comrade's name, exultant in the frenzy of retreat.

He lost sight of the Scythian, then almost ran into him where he had abruptly halted, barely visible through the haze. Startled by Jingle's hoof-falls, Jaunter hurled his sagaris. It shot toward the old pioneer, a black streak in the gloom. He ducked, hearing it pass through the air where his head had been. "It's Tatters! Tatters!"

Jaunter had his long-knife drawn before the words sunk in. "Tatters," the Scythian repeated, his voice a strangled sob.

"What spooked you? What was it?"

Jaunter growled from low in his chest, but said nothing. He dismounted only long enough to retrieve his weapon.

"We best get farther away," Master Tatters pointed to the south. "Let's head yonder."

"Aye." Jaunter sounded resigned, defeated.

They rode more slowly, picking their path through the ghostly mist, allowing the horses to choose their way. The noise of the battle diminished with every step, until it sank into a silence broken by the creaking and murmuring of the intolerant trees. A wolf howled in the distance. Tatters shivered. "Might as well stop here. It's safe as any, I reckon."

"Nowhere is safe," Jaunter muttered, sliding from Ransom's back. Master Tatters inspected the animals to see if any branches had cut them. The horses blew foam and pawed the ground, simmering with the excitement of the run.

"Where are the other horses?" Jingles asked. He whinnied, calling to the herd.

"Easy, boy." Tatters stroked his neck. "Shh. We'll not find them tonight."

Ransom rumbled in protest. "We need them."

"It can't be helped," Tatters said. "Hush now, darlings. There's danger yet and safety in quiet."

It took time to soothe the beasts, but at last they calmed. Through it all Jaunter did nothing to help, but stood gripping his sagaris, staring wide-eyed into the mist.

"The trees are moving," Ransom said.

Tatters looked up in time to see a forked branch like a claw gliding toward him. He raised his sword and lopped a piece of it off, and it withdrew, but other arms descended, seeking the horses and men.

"Jaunter!" Master Tatters shouted.

Looking up, the Scythian broke from his stupor with the sudden, pent-up fury of a wildcat. He flailed at the branches, shivering them into small pieces, leaping back and forth to protect himself and the steeds, spinning on his feet to chop at the encircling limbs. The horses reared, striking with their hooves, sending twigs flying. Though Tatters' sword was less powerful than the Scythian's sagaris, he hewed with all his strength, slicing away shoots and stems.

The branches lifted, retreating, leaving a carpet of moaning shards and sprigs at the men's feet.

Tatters looked around, trying to get his bearings. He feared the tree trunks would uproot themselves, crawling like spiders from their holes to assault them. When they did not, he drew a trembling breath. "We hightailed it from the iron men, but the dryads won't leave us be. We got to stand back to back, the horses with us."

Jaunter grunted in reply and took his position. The horses turned side-by-side, facing opposite directions.

"The trees are wicked," Jingles snorted.

"We'll make them show the white feather," Tatters said.

They stood watching. The branches popped and creaked; the trees continued to murmur. The minutes crept by, second by second. Tatters could feel his heartbeat in his throat. But as the time passed and the forest did not attack again, his pulse and breathing slowed. Perhaps the trees were less bold without the Ruheen soldiers to help them.

Tatters felt weariness fall upon him from the day's march and the night's battle. "Tell me a story to keep me awake, Jaunter. My eyes are powerful heavy."

Jaunter remained quiet so long Master Tatters thought he hadn't heard, but the Scythian finally said, "You start first."

"I suppose that'll keep me wakeful as listening, but I ain't no Aesop nor Homer, and you must settle for a plain story." Tatters paused to collect his thoughts.

"In my early years I lived in land liken to this. Woods and mountains. We dwelt with folks called Quakers back then. They're good people, friends to everybody, but my pa stole from them and they sent us away, so we came to the Republic of Texas. It's a big country, but I didn't know the half its vastness until I was grown and saw its northern border, where lay Comancheria. You'd like the Comanches, Jaunter; they're a horse-people dwelling in a country measureless as those steppes you go on about sometimes, and you'd fit in right well with them. A powerful nation, the masters of the Great Plains, white men daren't ride too deep into their territory. To do so is death by terrible torture. But the whites had settlements along their border and were always dabbing their toes over the line. Course, it warn't a real line because the Comanches didn't understand the notion of owning land—they were the land and the land was them, you see."

"It is the same with my kin," Jaunter said.

"Anyways, some of the settlers had moved into Comancheria, and the Comanches decided they'd had their fill and killed a passel of whites, so the new government in Austin sent soldiers to punish the raiders. I had done commerce with the Comanches, a little trading along the border, so I hired on as a scout. We rode over the hills until we met the plains, a sea of grass reaching from horizon to horizon, as big as the ocean Odysseus sailed upon. The *Llano Estacado* the Spanish called it, and we were ordered to find and engage the Comanches. That was afore I met my Jennie, you see, and I warn't so close to their people as I would be later, so I saw nothin' wrong with doing my bit for the government."

Tatters paused, remembering the sight of the vast prairie, the smell of the endless carpet of blue grama grass, the sound of the moving buffalo herds, now long perished.

He resumed, telling how the cavalry found a sizable Comanche settlement in the canyons at the edge of the plains, but were tricked into pursuing a group of braves while the entire village fled with their women, children, and hundreds of horses and cattle. "We picked up their tracks the next morning, and that's when the Comanches did the nearly impossible, taking their entire company, cattle and all it appeared, hundreds of feet up the steep, almost vertical canyon walls. We followed, but it was rough work, climbing the Caprock escarpment only to see their trail go back *down* into the canyon. We knew we were being outfoxed then, led up and down to give the village time to get away. We descended once more, puzzled our way through their criss-cross tracks, and found they had gone up *again*.

"Once we were back at the top, we felt the temperature drop. A blue norther was coming to the plains, but we caught glimpses of the tribe on the distant horizon. We gave chase and they started discarding lodge poles and tools in their haste. Our moment of battle neared, but the Llano Estacado defeated us.

"The skies closed in, heavy as Thor's hammer; the blue norther hit with rain, sleet, and snow mixed together. The wind howled. The soldiers were in their summer uniforms and night fell upon us. Everyone was exhausted, and we were a hundred miles or more from our supply base. We spent a dreadful night, the ice freezing on our clothes. But the Comanches fled through the storm and were gone by morning. They had outsmarted us from the get-go, and we were dunces by compare. We could do naught but shuffle home."

"Theirs was a strategy worthy of my own race," Jaunter said.

"I learned to respect them after that," Tatters said. "Later on I became an honorary member of the tribe, takin' Jennie for my bride. She warn't pretty, you know, but she was a lively girl and a hard worker. She had been stole from the settlers as a child and raised a Comanche, and their ways were all she knew. I loved her and our two girls dearly and true." His voice grew softer. "Their loss was the greatest heartbreak of my life."

"Were they slain?" Jaunter asked.

"The Comanches' enemies, the Tonkawas, took them because I was a Comanche friend. As soon as I came home and saw them gone, I knew what had happened. I started tracking them and made my terrible mistake. It was evening; the sun lapped the clouds on the western horizon when I came to low hills the Indians considered sacred ground. Well, the Tonks had passed a ways around them, and I knew I could make up time if I rode on through. It was full-dark when I arrived, and a fog akin to this one rose round the hills. I should have turned back then, for my heart misgave me, but I didn't; I had to find my Jennie. The mist grew so thick I thought I was in the halls of Hades himself. I heard sounds—devilish music, things I don't like to recollect, and then the fog vanished, and I was riding in Faerie, as far from Comancheria as Olympus is from Missouri, and my Jennie and girls were lost to me. I used to play the fiddle, but after hearing that strange music on the burial ground, my fiddling changed, and what I played chilled folks' bones, so I play no more. I know I'm not right in the head, and it's all because of my lost lovelies and Faerie magic."

Jaunter did not respond for several moments. When he did, he spoke in little more than a whisper. "Your tale smacks of my own woes, Thomas, for I am under a curse."

"A witch's spell? Circe's enchantments?"

"No woman's hex played a part in it." He sighed. "I have told this to no man, and you will tell no other."

"So sworn, honor bright."

"We promise too," Jingles said. "Do you promise, Ransom?"

Ransom lifted his ears. "I was not listening. I was wishing for grass."

Jaunter snorted and ran his hand along Ransom's neck. "Though I spent my childhood on the steppes, I was not as the others of my kin. I am larger and stronger, the mightiest man in my tribe. I wanted to test my strength against the world, and when an opportunity came, I traveled. It took me many places, and I saw wondrous sights. When I was nineteen, I sailed on merchant ships for a time, and was once wrecked off the coast of Gaul. None of the crew survived except myself, and I was half-drowned. A landholder in that country took me in. His family was wary of me at first, but they let me stay and work for them. They were a hard people, but kind enough to me, a stranger.

"When spring came, the master of the house was gone on business, and I and some of the servants were left to guard the place. I was out in the woods one day, chopping firewood, when a band of twelve raiders approached, having come from the sea.

"These were fierce men, and my thought was, 'We cannot stand against them.' Their leader was a powerful warrior, their shaman and wizard, half-troll I deemed. So I pretend friendship, invite them to the house, and treat them as guests. The mistress thinks I have betrayed her family, and I can but play my part. I entertain them, giving them beer until they are drunk, then I beguile them, telling them about the master's treasures lying in a storehouse built of massive logs, detached from the main buildings. A stone staircase leads up to it. I bring them there under the moonlight, open the door, and guide them in beneath the light of my torch. Seeing the gold bracelets, the bags filled with silver coins, and the rich garments, they dash upon the spoil, knocking each other over and quarreling for the goods. I put out the torch, step outside, and bolt the heavy door. Not one of them has his weapons with him.

"I run back to the house, rouse the servants, and grab an axe and a spear. The servants are too terrified to be much help, and just as we return to the bottom of the steps, the raiders break through the door and come out on the platform at the top of the stairs. In the moonlight they seem as demons as they scramble out. The first two rush at me, impaling themselves on the spear I plant in the ground. I finish them with my axe, rush up the stairs, and kill another of them. Then the rest come out, stumbling over each other, but I hew them with my axe or thrust at them with the spear.

"Sobered by their danger, the raiders retreat into the storeroom and rip the planks to make clubs. Two of them come down the stairs, warding off my blows with their cudgels, not attempting to strike. They force me back, allowing space and time for the others to leap to the ground.

"All this while the servants stand trembling behind me, none daring even to use the two bows they have brought. I would have gotten my death then, if the raiders had realized they are fighting only a single man. But they think there must be many, so instead of attacking me from behind, they flee. The two holding the clubs lose heart and try to jump down. One of those I kill.

"They flee into the boat-house, which is covered in darkness, and I go after them. Some try to run their boat into the water, but I have an advantage: the boat-house is open to the air on the side that faces the sea. I am in shadow, but can see them against the silver of the water, allowing me to strike unseen. I flay from side to side, and some fall into the current or the boat. One of them hits me with an oar, numbing my arm, but I recover and slay all but two. One flees past me into the night, but the last is their mighty captain, Vadispur.

"I tell you, if I had faced him first on the stairs, I would have died, for he is the strongest man I have ever fought. In his desperation, he throws himself upon me, forcing me to drop my weapons. I fling my arms around him and drive my head into his breast, trying to bend him backward and break his spine. None before had ever been able to withstand my strength, but my plan fails. His cold hands grasp my arms, breaking my hold. I seize him again, and he wraps his arms around me. We wrestle for what seems an eternity, neither able to overthrow the other. His long nails cut into my side like knives; the stink of his breath fills my nostrils.

"Our struggles send us rolling from the boat-house into the moonlight. We both rise from the ground, and I try to break his neck, placing my forehead against his chin and drawing him to me about the middle, trying to force his head back. Still, I cannot overthrow him, and my strength is failing.

"We tumble to the ground, I on top of him. I lack the power to continue supporting myself, and see I am about to drop flat onto him. Nor do I think I will ever rise again from his awful grip.

"In that moment I spy my axe beside me. I push away from him, grasp its handle and bring the blade down into his chest. I will never forget the way he looks—the shock of the blow, the pocked face, the wolf-gray matted hair, the eyes, cold and staring. Those haunted eyes!

"I spring backward, escaping his weakening grasp. His eyes transfix me. He speaks a curse. 'You have done ill matching yourself against me. You will never be stronger than you are this night, and to your dying day, when you are in the dark, you will see my eyes staring at you and will never dare to be alone.'

"Those were his last words. I beheaded him and we burned his body, but his curse remained. Any time night fell, I saw his eyes staring at me. I slept with them watching me. When I came to Faerie, I hoped they would not follow me, but they did, more dreadful than before. When I entered the Back of the Beyond, I saw them no more, and thought I had finally escaped my woe."

"Until tonight? You saw his eyes?"

Master Tatters heard Jaunter rustle behind him, the shaking of his head. "Worse. I saw *him*. The Back of the Beyond, which gives life to everything, has given him his body back. But the eyes are the same—so cold they burn crimson in torchlight. That is why I fled. I fear no man, but who can battle a ghost?"

Tatters chuckled.

"You find it droll?" Jaunter said.

"Nary a bit of it, my friend. It chills me to the marrow. We're neither one much for telling comforting tales, is all." Tatters looked around warily. "There's not a sign of anyone now."

"If he comes you may not be able to see him. His eyes appeared only to me."

The men fell silent, watching the trees. The forest had grown quieter, its low rumblings having ceased. The minutes dragged by. Seeing they were no longer besieged, Jaunter said, "It's foolish for all of us to keep watch, and I will sleep little this night. Let me stand guard while you others rest."

"I will sleep with my ears up," Ransom said.

"As will I," Master Tatters said. Having lost his bedroll, he lay down at the Scythian's feet, his cloak his only blanket, his weariness falling upon him like a shroud. He fell asleep clutching his sword.

Jaunter peered wide-eyed into forest darkness, terrified of what he might see.

CHAPTER TWELVE

THE VOICE OF MORLANE

Having escaped the battle, Gray and Joiwend found themselves alone in the woods. Still a bear, Joiwend halted and sat down, head raised, growling and scenting the air. Her horse, Maravilla, stood behind Nutmeg, eyeing her mistress uncertainly. There was reason for her wariness, and Gray remained on Nutmeg's back, unwilling to dismount until her blood cooled.

"Joiwend?" He kept his voice low.

"Gray," she rumbled, as if recalling his name. "Friend Gray."

"I don't like bears," Maravilla said.

"Perhaps you should change back," Gray suggested.

Joiwend grumbled and licked the back of one paw. Her form shifted and she was a woman once more, sitting on her bottom, feet splayed, one hand on the ground before her. She looked at Gray, her squinting bear-eyes still too small for her face, growled a feminine susurration, and returned to licking the back of her hand.

After a moment she ceased, staring in puzzlement at her fingers. With a sour expression, she drew her legs under her, lifted her head, and gracefully rose. "I'm glad I can't see myself do that." Maravilla shied as she approached.

"Bear-stink," the horse said.

Joiwend delicately sniffed. "I'm sorry. I always smell dreadful after, until I have a chance to bathe. I promise not to turn into a bear or anything else when I'm on your back."

"That is good," Maravilla conceded, then abruptly turned her head, ears up. Following her gaze, Gray saw an animal bounding toward them, a white form in the mist. He gripped his sword.

"I founded you!" a voice exulted. "I founded you!"

"Blunder!" In the peril of battle Gray had forgotten the pup.

Blunder bounced his front paws against Nutmeg's side, and Gray lifted him onto her back. The dog danced in excitement, nearly falling off, turning round and round, licking Gray's face. "I lost you, but I founded you," he repeated, over and over.

"Calm down, boy." Gray stroked his sides.

"I bited one but it hurt my teeth. This is bad. What do we do, Gray?"

"What, indeed?" Joiwend said. "This is disastrous! How can we stand against those metal monsters, much less the trees? And poor Dartmallow! I pray he survived."

Gray tried to steady himself enough to think, but it was hard after the shock of seeing the soldiers of Animonea so easily vanquished. He drew a deep breath. This was no time for despair. "Blunder, I need you to do something. Can you search for the others? The ones we traveled with when you and I first met? Don't go far and don't be long, but bring them here if you find them. And any of the marshal's men as well. Can you do that?"

"I can do that, Gray."

"You won't get lost?"

"I can see and smell in the dark. I will not get lost." The dog slipped from the saddle and sniffed his way out of sight.

They sat astride their horses, listening to the forest—the distant sounds of battle, the shouts of men being hunted through the night. Filtered through the mist and trees, the fires of their former camp were mere matchstick glows. Gray kept his sword ready, his eyes on the surrounding boughs.

Blunder soon returned. "I founded some. They are behind me."

Vasps and Russ appeared, leading Dreamer and Flapjack by their manes. All the horses rumbled greetings.

"You escaped!" Joiwend exclaimed.

"We were lucky," Russ said.

Vasps clutched his turban in his hand, weeping. "It is cataclysmic. Those iron men! Who could create such monsters? I saw the marshal fall! It is a catastrophe for Animonea! I should not have deserted him. We must go back and try to help."

"There's nothing we can do to fight those things tonight," Russ said. "Our job is to survive until morning."

Hearing a creaking behind him, Gray whirled in his saddle, bringing his sword up to parry a tree branch stretching toward him. Blade and wood met with a solid *thunk*. Nutmeg shied in fear and the tree recoiled, tearing the weapon from his grasp. Joiwend hacked two-handed at the bough, dislodging the sword. Other branches reached out. The horses backed away.

"Go!" Gray cried.

Russ scooped up Gray's blade and helped Vasps mount before swinging himself onto Flapjack. The horses surged through the darkness, ears up.

"Run?" Nutmeg asked.

"Don't gallop, but keep moving!" Gray ordered.

Other branches reached for them, the whole forest astir. The horses veered back and forth, avoiding the grasping limbs. Just ahead, they saw a heavy form dangling from a tree. Their mounts shunned it, but Gray saw an Animonean soldier, neck caught between two forking limbs, eyes wide in death.

They passed into a stand of massive oaks. These stirred, gradually aware of the companions' presence, spreading their branches toward them like the fingers of awakening titans. Though they moved more slowly than the lesser trees, their sheer size gave them a longer reach, with limbs heavy enough to crush a man.

The horses hurried away, traveling down a long hill. Dreamer stumbled and fell, sending Vasps sprawling. Gray gasped as the horse came within a hand's breadth of rolling over the arbiter.

Russ hurried to Vasps' side and helped him up. Dreamer rose, blowing, holding one hoof off the ground.

"Easy, boy!" Russ ran his hand along the horse's neck.

The paint pony tried to put weight on his leg, but lifted it again, snorting in pain. "I will go," he insisted, hobbling forward on three legs.

"He can't travel." Joiwend swung down from Maravilla's back. "I have to try something I've never done before." She lifted her arms above her head and her hands changed, growing gnarled and wooden.

"Joiwend, no!" Gray said. "You always said it was too dangerous. You might forget who you are."

"I've never attempted it before, but trees aren't mindless here. I can shelter us, and I believe I can retain my intelligence."

Before Gray could protest further, she grew taller, her arms reaching toward the sky, her head vanishing into her body, her feet pushing deep into the earth. She sprouted, a Golden Rain tree, her branches growing, her leaves budding. Within seconds, her lowest limbs spread above her companions' heads, covering them in her canopy, her yellow flowers blossoming in strands.

The attacking trees hesitated and withdrew in confusion.

"Ahh," Joiwend sighed. It was both her voice and that of a tree soughing in the wind. Gray stepped close and saw her eyes batting in wonder, enormous rinds in her rugose bark.

"Can you hear me?" Gray asked.

"Yeeessss!" she said. "Oh, it is a wonder to be a tree! Ah, Gray! I can hear the whole forest talking. They are so angry, so unhappy! How can I tell them we mean no harm?"

Gray put his hand on her trunk, feeling a little sick. "Be careful, Joiwend. Please don't lose yourself."

Blunder whined. "Joiwend is a tree now, Gray. I do not like it."

"Nor I." Gray slumped down, his forehead pressed against her bark, stunned to despair by the rout, hoping against hope that Jaunter and Master Tatters had survived.

* * *

Midnight came and went, and still Jaunter kept watch while Master Tatters slept. Once, he heard the cries of dying men; once, the tops of the trees swayed as if from a mighty wind; but the forest lay still now. Perhaps it slept; perhaps it never slept, Jaunter did not know. He had been in forests at night many times before, but never one so silent. The continuous noise of the rest of the Back of the Beyond was absent here. It was spring, too early for crickets or katydids, but he would have expected the slight sounds of passing animals, the clicking of beetles, the fluttering wings of settling birds. In the quiet he could hear only the gentle, even breathing of the horses, sleeping standing, eyes half-open.

The blind moon released a long moan, an awful sound through the gray shroud of mist. Startled, Jaunter gripped his sagaris and shuddered. To his people the world was a place of dread, filled with spirits. Neither the magic of Faerie nor the talking creatures of the Back of the Beyond had surprised him. There were gods and demons everywhere, and the way to survive lay in appeasing or avoiding offending any of them. Throughout his life he had spoken to ravens and hawks, to the rain, to the wind, and had asked the blessings of anything that might be a god. If they had never before answered in words, he believed they had understood. But none had freed him from the curse of Vadispur.

He caught a movement out of the corner of his sight. When he looked directly at it, it appeared vague, indistinct in the mist. He ran his fingers over his eyes, wiping away the weariness. Something was coming.

He stood, hefting his weapon, his heart pounding. The figure was that of a man, hooded and dressed in thick robes.

"Stand clear," Jaunter commanded hoarsely. "There is nothing for you here."

The intruder halted and looked about, as if not having seen Jaunter until he spoke. His face remained hidden by the darkness and his hood. "Do you know the way out of this forest?" His voice had a rasping, breathy quality.

"Of that I can tell you nothing," Jaunter said. "Begone! Come closer and I will kill you."

"Perhaps we can talk from this distance. I am called Fetch. I have traveled a long way to find you." He looked up, and his eyes were the staring gaze of a dead man.

Jaunter sucked in a chill breath. In one continuous motion, he dropped his sagaris, unslung his bow, and sent three arrows flying toward the man's heart. The shafts passed harmlessly through the creature's body.

"Vadispur," Jaunter spat. He feared no living being, but his knees grew weak before this phantom.

"Vadispur," the specter agreed. "No need to run, old enemy. I can do little more than haunt you. I came with you from Faerie, but it is Morlane that gives form to not merely my eyes, but my entire body. The forest is old, you see, its vitality even more wild and ancient than the rest of Animonea. It gives us a chance to reminisce together, to recollect the night we battled, the way you slew me."

Jaunter said nothing, but his hands trembled.

"Or would you rather be free of me, Jaunter? Would you have me lift the curse?"

Jaunter growled like a beast. What torments would he now face from this monster? He glanced at Tatters and the horses. They were still sleeping.

"Don't look for help from them," Vadispur said. "Only you can see and hear me. But do you think I'm merely taunting you?" He threw back his hood, revealing a gray, tangled mass of hair. "Rather, I offer you a chance to make amends, to redeem my life from this ghostly existence so I may walk once more among men. It is possible, in this country where the life force is so strong."

Jaunter studied Vadispur, seeking signs of irony, but the phantom's expression remained unreadable.

"What do you want?" Jaunter asked.

"That man who rests beside you. The life is in the blood. From his shed blood I can live again."

Jaunter glanced at Master Tatters, who slept an almost preternatural slumber. "What deception is this?"

"None," Vadispur said. "Cut his throat; make the sacrifice. His blood will become mine and out of it I will form a new body. I will leave you, haunt you nevermore. Refuse and I follow you for the rest of your wretched life. It will not be merely my eyes in the darkness. I will kneel each night beside your bed and whisper of our terrible struggle, of the way your axe pierced me, of my dying cries, my expiring breaths."

Jaunter had spent years dreading the setting of the sun, the appearance of the creature's ghostly orbs, but at least he had been able to shut his eyes and close out the sight. Now, he would surely go mad, listening to that voice. He would become a lunatic. All men would desert such a cursed comrade; every woman would fear him. He would be alone with only Vadispur for company.

"I will sacrifice an animal," Jaunter said.

"Only a human will suffice."

"An enemy, then." Out of a hundred captured foes, it was the custom of his people to give one to the gods, but in Rome he had learned they abhorred such practices, only offering those found guilty of crimes. He had eventually embraced that more cultured policy.

"No," Vadispur said. "You took *my* life! Your sacrifice must be personal and costly."

The Scythian looked down at Tatters. They had fought together, eaten together, worked together. And the fellow was a little mad — to Jaunter's mind that meant touched by the gods. To sacrifice such a one . . . Could that lead him to an even more terrible fate? Could there *be* a worse one?

He had killed many men in his life. He had wounded one or two friends in drunken fights. Once, he had put a fellow soldier out of his misery, a man dying from an agonizing gut wound, who begged for an end to his suffering. But he had never intentionally sacrificed a brother-in-arms.

He picked up his sagaris and ran his hand along its edge. He could do the deed quickly, a sudden blow, and Tatters would feel almost nothing. He had not known the man long. It was not the same as killing a fellow tribesman. Gray and the others would believe he had died in the battle. The Scythian would need to slay Tatters' horse too, so he would have a mount to ride to the Land of the Dead. There, being a brave warrior, he would surely be received with honor. Jaunter had a few silver coins he could put in Thomas' pockets before burning the body, so he would not come to the gods a pauper. These things Jaunter would do for friendship's sake.

He looked at Vadispur, trying to penetrate the phantom's thoughts, fearing a trick, but the ghost only stared stolidly back.

Ransom spoke, causing the Scythian to flinch. "Who are you talking to? Is someone coming?"

Jaunter groaned beneath his horse's brown eyes. Was it a god speaking through the animal? Nothing was certain in this land! He would have to slay Ransom too to keep his deed secret. He hesitated. Gray would say killing a comrade was wrong, but though he was brave enough in a fight, the prince was scarcely more than a lad. Yet, even Fox Lodan would call it treachery.

Anger rose within him. Their gods were not his. It was time to quit thinking and act.

He hefted his sagaris above Tatters' sleeping form, readying it for the killing stroke, his hands trembling.

Ransom blew, alarmed.

He sighed and lowered the blade. He glared at Vadispur. "I won't do it! You won't unman me in this way. If you want blood, you will take mine."

Vadispur raised his eyebrows. "You would die for me, old enemy?"

"I will not give you my life. I will bleed enough to give you flesh, but no more."

Vadispur grinned a ghastly rictus, laughed a hollow laugh. "It will do, I think. It will do."

* * *

Since receiving her magic ring, Joiwend had become many creatures. As a bird she had known the glory of flight: the lifting of wings, the launching into empty air, the soaring on warm currents, the innate knowledge of predator and prey; as a bear she had ambled on heavy paws, near-sighted, wrapped in curiosity, hungry for hunger's sake, her whole world one of familiar and exotic scents; as a deer she had felt the waiting quiet, the safety of silence, the watchfulness of the hunted; as a wolf she had howled, bittersweet with longing, at the distant moon, her soul afire with love of the pack. These and other animals she had become, and each in turn had changed her; but nothing had prepared her for becoming a tree.

She stood in the night, sheltering Gray, Russ, and Vasps as they slept beneath her branches. The good earth lay under her, solid and warm, hugging her in its arms, resisting her as moment by moment she penetrated its depths, her small roots turning larger, wriggling their way downward, seeking—always seeking—the water that was life, finding the smallest bits of moisture, drawing them in, bringing them upward, nourishing and nurturing. Her leaves, quiescent in the night, waited to bask in the sunlight of the coming day, rejoicing as they drank the wet mist surrounding them. Her trunk, mighty and steady, pulsed with a life so slow, she could scarcely comprehend it, yet alive in every branch and bole. To her wonder, she discovered every leaf possessed a kind of sight, so she saw all around her at once, even seeing herself, as if she stood in a hall of mirrors. She studied her strands of flowers, admiring the way they draped her, like a hundred pairs of matching, dangling earrings. She was Tree and that was good.

Yet Morlane, the Great Forest, was unhappy, and she could not understand why.

For a long while she brooded, for contemplation is the way of trees. She remembered her happy girlhood in the tiny kingdom of Aquitanita, lying between the borders of Spain and France. She had been born to a noble house in the capitol city of Dumon. In such a small kingdom, every citizen was expected to defend against invaders, and her only brother, Rupert, four years older than she, had encouraged her use of arms. Adoring him, she had trained so hard to please him that she was inducted into *Les Rangs des Femmes* at the age of fifteen. She thought of him now with deep love and gratitude. In Faerie, his training had many times saved her life.

Rupert had also introduced her to Cedric du Maurier. She was seventeen and had resisted several suitors, finding none so noble as her own brother, but with Cedric it was love at first sight. They married in a beautiful ceremony in the *Iglesia de Ifgard*. Her fondest memory was of standing before the priest, the light shining down from the crystal chandeliers into her love's green eyes.

The times thereafter had been both happy and sad, joyous because the two of them were together, sorrowful because they were unable to have children. And then the war came. Everyone served who could. Joiwend was in charge of a gun battery for a time. Cedric was killed in the last days, just before the enemy was ultimately driven back.

Her leaves shook with sorrow. The hurt remained, even after so many years.

Cedric had an adopted sister, Angelina du Maurier, a spoiled creature, gossipy and scheming. During Joiwend's days of mourning, the two women often took long walks together, and Joiwend naively thought her a friend. But one day, on the pretense of introducing her to an old acquaintance, Angelina had bid her come to an ancient manor on the outskirts of the city, cautioning her to tell no one—it was to be an adventure—they would slip away like young girls at play. It proved to be a ruse intended to gain Cedric's inheritance, for she had paid men to kidnap and kill her sister-in-law.

The plan misfired, however, for Angelina was herself betrayed. Arriving at the house, a strange and mysterious dwelling, the women were both taken captive and led down endless corridors for what seemed hours. Finally, when their captors—unaware of Joiwend's strength and training—grew careless, she escaped, fleeing down the winding ways. She never saw Angelina again, for Joiwend became hopelessly lost within the mansion, until she finally stepped through a doorway and found herself in Faerie. Nor was she ever able to find that house again, as if it had magically vanished.

She struggled to survive at first, confined by the Laws of Faerie into the role of the Daring Damsel, a warrior and strategist. She received her ring early on, one of three magic devices given her to overcome the guardians imprisoning a Lost Maiden. After that, the battles were easier.

She had never remarried, for the men there were like puppets on a stage, given wholly to the compulsions laid on them by the Elf King, forced into being little more than caricatures: the Kind Shepherd, the Greedy Boy, the Traveling Minstrel. Sometimes she wondered if they were even alive when no one watched them.

Over the years she had met one or two young men who were also from Earth, but nothing had come of it. Part of it was her age. Her ring might make her look twenty-five, but she was no longer a school-girl inside. She recognized flirtation for what it was. As a young woman, it had been all play; one did not watch oneself perform it. Now she was aware of her actions and her effect on men; she understood the temptation to bask in their admiration. It made her cautious. Besides, she had never forgotten her Cedric.

She shook her leaves, rousing herself from her musings. How wonderful it was to stand in endless contemplation, her roots going ever downward, her branches stretching toward the sky. How easily she might wander, forever lost, drawn deep into the cycles of trunk and bark.

I am still Joiwend, she thought. I must remember that.

Her mind turned to the forest sleeping around her, yet never truly sleeping as humans understood it, save perhaps when the coldest frost of winter drew the sap inward. She could sense the slow thoughts of the trees and the larger attitude of the forest as a whole, for Morlane possessed both individual intelligences and a group mind. The trees were not wise, but naturally stoic, fearing nothing save fire, patient with a capacity for boundless endurance, each solitary bole ready to live and die as chance provided. It was the aggregate mood of the woods that emanated an unmistakable discontent.

She sought its source through the connection of her roots to the soil. She could ask no questions. Rather, thought and information emanated from the network of flora, like an underground river of understanding. There was no hidden reasoning, no secret motivations, no unconscious desires as with a human being, only transparent mind and emotion. Not even the animals had thoughts so pure. The beauty of it made her leaves curl. If she had still possessed tear ducts, she would have wept.

But it was a horror as well, for the forest had been corrupted. Duke Nortallion had promised to make it powerful enough to drive away the humans of Animonea, vowing to withdraw his countrymen back to Ruheen thereafter. From the time men first came to the Back of the Beyond, the Wileywood had distrusted them, for it was an old forest, older than any other in the land, and it remembered the long ages when only animals dwelt within it. But trees are slow of understanding; it is difficult for them to recognize deception. The duke had appeared to them in many forms — it surprised Joiwend to discover that he too could change his shape. He came first as a deer, then a horse, a fox, and a man, in every guise arguing the cause of Ruheen. Morlane had listened and been swayed. At first, he did everything he vowed, but then took actions Morlane could not comprehend, breeding the Black Moths as spies and weapons, and damming the Widfroth River, preventing the waters of the Omnifire from flowing through the land. Without its life-giving stream, the forest grew less intelligent, until it lived in a ponderous confusion, angry without remembering why, obeying the duke because it could think of no other course. Finding only unhappiness in itself, it took no joy in any other living thing. It struck out at the forest animals, driving them away. Without them, the cycle of life was further disrupted — gone were the bees and butterflies, banished by the Black Moths and the Wileywood's fury — and neither flowers nor fruit trees blossomed anymore in ancient Morlane. The squirrels no longer buried the nuts to grow new trees. The cottontails fled; and the foxes, unable to find prey, soon followed. Morlane was alive, but no longer a living, thriving wood.

Joiwend felt the forest's despair and nearly despaired herself. She longed for a tongue so she could shout, "Awake!" but she had neither mouth nor lips, so she journeyed, root to root, with the other trees, seeking through the woods to find what she could discover. Everything one tree had seen, the whole forest knew, and she passed through countless memories until she understood the nature of the land. She roamed among cottonwoods standing outside the earthen dam separating them from the Widfroth River, scenting the water with senses unknown to humankind, miserable at being unable to reach it; she stood beside oaks at the forest's edge, overlooking the plain where the hummingbirds had fought; she wandered to the border between Animonea and Ruheen, among withered elms whose dying intelligence was less than a single spark, the trees beyond standing dumb, unthinking, as if a line had been drawn between the two countries.

She communed with a grove of birches facing Ironwood Station, a fort of rough-hewn wood, the home of Duke Nortallion. The duke's banner, a white whirlwind on a background of blue, sang his name as it wafted on a tall pole. A single sentry kept vigil from a tower, yet the station was alive with watchfulness; every post looked out upon the land with etched eyes of swirled gray. The whole structure emanated awareness. Fearing it might sense her presence, she did not tarry.

Fleeing to other parts of the woods, she saw the men of iron and fired clay, standing quiescent, awaiting orders from the duke. She discovered more of their kind following human soldiers traveling in great haste. Among these walked Ninette Argilla and Corporal Spence. Having never seen Ninette's face before, she knew her only by her unmistakable bronze armor, and she gazed at her in wonder.

How is it possible for her to be so changed? Joiwend thought. So alive! See how she laughs! She is very beautiful. How lovely are her eyes and the way her golden hair frames her face. If she were here, I would be envious. But they travel in the company of the duke's soldiers. Who is that handsome officer, and the woman who walks beside him? He has a noble look about him.

Hearing every word spoken beneath its branches, Morlane knew the names of many. *Chel Rendan. Tanabel-Tunia.*

Joiwend gasped inwardly, excitement rushing through her sap, making her leaves tingle. She had to tell Gray. But first she studied this woman who had won her friend's heart. She was pretty, little more than a child, really, but so was Gray. Amusement ran through Joiwend's branches; she was showing her age. When only slightly older than Tanabel-Tunia, she had thought herself wise. Idealism and naivety were only two sides of the same ducat, and sadly, the world had a way of humbling the young. But there was a certain inconstancy about the girl's eyes. She was probably somewhat spoiled. That too was hardly surprising in the ranks of royalty.

Joiwend stirred her branches, bringing her thoughts back to the place where she stood. It would be dawn in two hours. Russ and Vasps lay sleeping, their heads near her trunk. Gray sat with his back against her, keeping watch. She could feel his warmth; she had never realized how much heat living creatures radiated. The three men had a slight aura about them, visible to her senses.

She tried to speak, but it was hard to remember the way of it. She struggled, not wanting to fully awaken. It was so good to be a tree. If she changed back to human form, she would miss the budding, the spring flowering, the dropping of the seeds.

She put it from her mind. She could remain a tree at least until dawn. Besides, she needed to help Morlane. It had forgotten so much about itself; it was her duty to remind it. Once she had done that, she could become a woman again.

"Gray," she whispered, a soft creaking. He stood at once and turned to her.

"Are you well?" he asked.

"Well indeed." She related all she had seen and heard, speaking in a slow cadence, not telling him of finding Tanabel-Tunia until the last, for fear he would remember nothing else. She thought she spoke briefly, but to her wonder a full hour had passed before she was done, and both Russ and Vasps Geometer were awake and listening.

"Where is she?" Gray demanded. Despite his standing a foot away, she could sense his rapidly-beating heart. "Can you lead us there?"

"I can show you with Russ' compass," she said.

Russ drew it from his pocket. "I knew this thing would come in handy." He lit his cigarette lighter. Though she knew the flame was controlled, a shudder ran up and down her branches. They studied the compass until they were certain of Tanabel-Tunia's direction.

"The trees have been quiet since after midnight," Gray said. "I think you can change back."

"I will when the sun returns, when it's warmer. I need to learn more from the forest. I think the Widfroth River could be an ally. He rages against the dam and might protect us if he thought we would help him. In need, we should go there. Get some sleep. We can talk later."

Gray's brow furrowed in concern, but he only nodded.

She drifted back inside herself, returning to her wandering, awed by the marvel and sorrow of Morlane.

* * *

Many nights, Master Tatters dreamed the same dream. A Comanche shaman sat by his bedroll, wrapped in a buffalo hide and a war bonnet, chanting his magic over Tatters' body. Tatters tried to move, but could not. He fought the paralysis, sweat beading his brow. His Jennie and their daughters stood looking at him from across the prairie, their eyes and gestures imploring his help. There were no stars in the night sky and he could do nothing.

He awoke with a start. Jingles had roused him, pressing his soft nose against the old pioneer's face. Still half-asleep, he wrapped one arm around the horse's neck, using it to pull himself to a sitting position.

"A man came out of the air," Jingles said.

Tatters became aware of nearby crooning. Through the mist, he saw two forms, one seated on the ground, the other lying on his back, the seated figure holding the head of the other in his lap.

Tatters sprang to his feet, gripping his sword. In the dimness, their faces looked alike as brothers, and he could only tell which was Jaunter by his garments.

"Who are you?" Tatters demanded.

"Isn't he beautiful?" Tears ran down the stranger's cheeks. He stroked Jaunter's scarred face with one hand. With the other, he stirred the blood that dripped into a wooden bowl from a wound at the Scythian's neck, blood that also ringed the stranger's mouth.

Tatters sometimes saw things that weren't there, and he wondered if he was still asleep, if this was part of the dream. "What are you doing?"

"He wasn't going to give it all," the stranger said, "but he fell senseless. I didn't know it would be like this. We are connected now, true brothers in blood. I know what he has seen and felt, what he has loved and lost. I love him for it, and all those he has ever loved. Those he hates I hate with a terrible hatred."

Tatters pressed the point of his sword against the creature's chest. He didn't understand what was happening and was afraid to kill the intruder, lest doing so somehow cause Jaunter harm. He remembered reading that the ancient Greeks believed ghosts sought human blood. "Get away from him."

"Not yet. Don't make me go yet. I need more of his blood to be whole."

Gooseflesh sprang up along Tatters' arms. He pressed with his sword, pricking the skin, making the stranger wince. "Begone, bogey or whatever you are, or I'll kill you where you sit!"

The creature snarled, crawling backward on his hands. "I will remember this, Thomas Tatters. I won't forget." He pulled himself to his feet. "I'll remember what you cost me." He turned, seized Jaunter's cloak from where it lay, and stumbled into the forest. One of his legs was shorter than the other, and he limped as he went.

Master Tatters kicked the bowl of blood away and put his ear against Jaunter's chest. The Scythian's heart still beat, though weakly. Tatters staunched and bound the wound.

"What was that thing?" he asked the horses.

"He is called Fetch," Jingles said.

"He is called Vadispur," Ransom said. "He was a wind we could not see. Now he is a man."

* * *

When the morning came, Joiwend could not be awakened. Gray

tried whispering to her, then softly calling. Now he tapped her trunk with the hilt of his sword. "We shouldn't have let her stay a tree so long. Joiwend! Please! Come back to us."

"It is a vexatious quandary," Vasps said.

"Maybe if we cut into her trunk," Russ suggested. "That might get her attention."

"And risk her changing back wounded or maimed?" Gray said. "We dare not try."

Russ lit his cigarette lighter and held it close enough to warm part of her bark. She made no response. Blunder whined and scratched at her with one paw.

For a long hour they waited while the morning sun crept up the sky. Scattered mist still lay upon the land. Russ examined Dreamer's injured foot, and after leading him up and down, man and horse agreed he was fit to travel.

"We can't just leave her," the Prince of Stallions said miserably, "but if we wait too long, Tana will surely be carried to the duke's redoubt."

Russ looked thoughtfully at Joiwend's branches. "It's beyond me. We don't know when she'll change back, if ever, or if she can even still hear us. I hate to leave her like this, but I don't think she would want you to miss the chance to find the girl."

Gray swallowed, close to tears. "If we leave, we have to be able to find her again."

"We have seen few Golden Rain trees in Morlane," Vasps said, "but still—"

"Leave it to Joiwend to be the most glamorous tree in the forest," Russ said. "Maybe we could mark her somehow, tie a rope around her."

"Perhaps this will do," Vasps said, unwinding his turban from his head.

Gray wrapped the turban as high as he could reach around Joiwend's trunk. He gently held a strand of her golden flowers between his fingers. "I'll be back for you. I promise I won't let you stay here like this."

Feeling the worst of traitors, he mounted Nutmeg and led the others away.

* * *

Joiwend heard her friends calling to her; she knew when they departed, but she recognized it only dimly through the haze of the endless rhythms of the forest. She had not answered, was unable to answer, because in the last hour she had recognized her mission, and it was too important for even a moment's distraction. The heart of Morlane was sick and needed healing; Duke Nortallion's guile had filled it with confusion, and confusion was often the first step into evil. Through the years, believing a single lie had led the forest to other deceits culminating in hatred and bitterness.

Joiwend knew only one response when evil loomed in her path — to dutifully face it, standing fast on the truths she knew. She would aid Morlane if she could, even if it meant losing her humanity. She did not consider it heroic, for if not her, then who? Her decision was simple.

So she began with the trees surrounding her. She could not speak to the boughs in words; she could only be who she was, revealing her essence, thinking the truths she knew, portraying the sum of her experience, declaring everything that made her Joiwend. From childhood she had struggled within herself, fighting the animal nature every human possesses, her pettiness, her cruelty, her jealousy, striving both to remain herself and give herself to others. In doing so, she had become the best parts of who she was, recognizing her own weaknesses, battling always against them. It was a contest without end, but in time it had forged her — hammer against iron — into a sword whose edge was Love.

Listening to her, the nearby trees fell silent. One by one they drifted into new reverie, remembering how they had once stood tall and proud and happy in the sun, recalling the nights when the wind wafted through their branches, recollecting the times they had lifted their limbs to the tumbling rain, gratefully receiving it. The bitterness fell from them; the eyes of their leaves looked out and wondered how they, the titans of the world, had descended into such a sorry state.

They needed to ponder; they needed to consider.

The spirit of Joiwend moved outward in a circle, ever farther into the Wileywood.

CHAPTER THIRTEEN

ENCOUNTERS IN THE DARK

Gray was nearly sick with desperation.

For hours he had led Russ and Vasps Geometer through the Wileywood, urging the men and horses ever on, disregarding the animals' complaints and Vasps' objections that they were journeying away from Dartmallow's army. Now, at the horses' insistence, they stopped to rest beside a trickling stream. Nutmeg, Flapjack, and Dreamer filled the air with the noise of their drinking; Blunder lapped the water running over the smooth stones; Russ filled the army canteen he kept belted to his side. The ever-present mist had thinned beneath the sun's rays, leaving vestiges of smoky phantoms lingering in the air.

When they had ridden away that morning, the trees surrounding Joiwend had been strangely quiescent, an effect seeming to spread step by step as the day progressed, the malevolence fading from the many-eyed branches, Morlane's malice folding on itself like butterfly wings, leaving the Wileywood hushed, contemplative, the faces on its trunks thoughtful, listening. At first, the men suspected some ruse to lull them off-guard, but as the hours passed they accepted the change, and Gray suspected Joiwend was the cause.

Still, nothing eased his yearning to find his beloved. Even with Russ' compass to ensure their direction, it would be easy to miss Tana's trail. Gray ardently wished Master Tatters were with them, for bereft of his tracking skills they were forced to depend on Blunder's nose and their own observations.

"We should sleep here tonight by the water," Nutmeg said.

"We have carried you far," Dreamer agreed.

Gray bit back an angry retort. More than once he had explained the importance of haste, but the animals possessed a childlike lack of memory.

"Now girl, you know we can't stop yet," Russ said. "You don't want to let Gray down, do you? We have to find Tanabel-Tunia for him."

"We have gone a long way," Nutmeg insisted.

"And we're proud of how well you've done, but I know you've got more in you," Russ said. "You're strong horses. Maybe there's better water and grass ahead."

Nutmeg raised her ears at the suggestion, her brown eyes thoughtful. "We will go on," she said at last.

"That's the spirit."

They mounted again. "Permission to cross?" Vasps asked the stream.

"Wade in my midst, though I am but a trickle," the stream chimed sadly. The steeds muddied their hooves in the passing.

"You have a way with horses," Vasps told Russ.

Russ grinned and pressed his glasses against the bridge of his nose. "I've been around them my whole life. Before joining the army, I worked as a dollar-a-day cowboy in New Mexico. Most days, I rode the fence line, checking for breaks in the barbed wire, me and my horse alone together for a week at a time. You start to understand each other."

Gray did not know what a dollar was, but he considered Russ the equal to his father's horse-master. He had a firm but gentle way with the beasts and remained unruffled by their ability to talk.

Two hours later they ran across multiple sets of bootprints. Blunder scurried back and forth, his nose to the ground, then bounded to Gray.

"There are many smells, Gray."

"How many men?" Gray asked.

Blunder turned his head in puzzlement. "There are more than four."

"Numbers are incomprehensible to most dogs," Vasps said. "The question is, are these the ones who have the woman? They might be an unrelated part of the duke's army."

Vasps' words made Gray feel hollow inside. "Joiwend said we would find them at about this distance. It must be them."

"I hope you are right," Vasps said, "but regardless, we are traveling toward our foes and must be cautious."

"I will lead you," Blunder said, hurrying ahead.

"You horses stay alert," Russ said. "Let us know if you scent other horses, but don't call to them. Their riders are our enemies."

Interested in the pursuit, the mounts perked their ears and quickened their pace to a jog. Blunder often disappeared into the woods, only hurrying back to assure them of their course. A half-hour passed and the equines' enthusiasm waned. Gray gently kicked Nutmeg's flank, forcing her to renew her gait, always surprised that the animals never complained about being prodded, perhaps because that had been the way of horses and humans for centuries.

The time passed; the day faded. Long clouds drifted by, narrow as snakes seen through the branches. With the coming of twilight, the mist increased once more, obscuring the way.

Dreamer's nostrils flared. "There are horses."

"There are horses," Flapjack echoed.

Blunder hurried back, a white specter in the gray dusk. "There are soldiers, Gray. I founded their camp."

"Good boy!" Gray's heart raged against his chest, pounding out the name of Tanabel-Tunia. After so many weeks, he scarcely dared hope of finding her.

The travelers dismounted. For hours Gray had been considering what to do once they reached the duke's men. Now, keeping his voice low, he did not hesitate. "As soon as it is fully dark, Russ and I will move closer to their camp. Vasps will stay with the horses. I'm going to send Blunder in to locate Tana. This far from her home, knowing she has nowhere to go if she escapes, she may not be closely guarded."

They waited in the twilight while the horses champed yellow wildflowers. Gray struggled against his longing to rush to her side, wondering how he could sit, seemingly calm, when his soul cried out not to leave her a moment longer in captivity. He drew a deep breath and waited through the long minutes.

At last, when the final glow of the sun vanished from Morlane,

Gray patted Blunder's head and signaled to Russ, leaving Vasps reciting geometric formulas to allay his apprehension. The horses raised their heads, placidly watching them depart.

Following Gray's instructions, Blunder kept a short distance ahead to warn of sentries. The pup returned often, finally saying, "There is a man keeping watch."

"Do you remember the description of Tanabel-Tunia I gave you?" Gray asked.

"I have forgotted, Gray. I do not know her scent."

"She is brown-haired, with freckles—small dots—around her nose and on her arms. There may be another woman with her, perhaps wearing armor. Her name is Ninette. Her hair is golden. They are the only two you can trust. Tell her that Gray Darien has come to rescue her. If there is any way for her to escape the camp, bring her to me. If not, bring a message from her. You must not be seen. The soldiers will hurt you if they can. If they try to capture you, run back here. Can you remember?"

"I will remember, Gray. She has spots. I will look for her."

Gray touched the pup's head. "Be careful, little friend."

"I will be careful."

Blunder padded into the darkness. The prince felt a wave of affection at his unquestioning obedience, a loyalty he hoped would not end in the pup's death.

* * *

To Blunder's eyes, the difference between night and day was one of degree. He did not fear the darkness, which he saw only as a dimming of sight, nor was vision his primary sense; the world came to him in waves and flutters and eddies of scent. He trotted through the aromas of earth and stone, tree and shrub, moist air and moldering leaves, the background tapestry for hundreds of other swirling smells. New information flooded his black nostrils: a passing beetle, a spider's eggs, the fragrant jolt of a flower's perfume. Most of these he ignored, scarcely realizing he smelled them; others captured his attention: a wolf's spoor (alarming), a sparrow's carcass (interesting), a grub's trail (edible?), so he sometimes halted, turning circles and sniffing before going on.

It was distracting, and only the odor left by the soldiers kept him from forgetting what he was supposed to do. "Tanabel-Tunia," he murmured to himself. "Dark hair and spots."

His usual state being one of happy curiosity, he never dreaded the future; he only reacted to the present. Except in moments of direct peril, he was never afraid, nor was he anxious now. He was doing his pack-leader's bidding; he was being a good dog.

Scenting the sentry he had seen before, he dropped to his belly, causing a faint protest from the weeds beneath him. He knew people could not see in the dark, but did not know how blind they really were. Keeping on his stomach, he crawled behind a rise and circled the guard. Another sentry stood to Blunder's other side, and he kept an ears-down crouch until safely past.

Pleased at his success, he sat on his haunches and sniffed the air, the scent of iron and clay and people-sweat. And meat! He licked his lips. The aroma filled his head and stirred his stomach. He bathed in its goodness, forgetting everything. He wanted to ask for a bite. The men might give him some.

Something bit his ear, and he scratched at it with his hind leg. That taken care of, he paused, trying to remember why he was there. Ah! Tanabel-Tunia, Gray had said. He looked around. The camp lay before him, a single tent at its center, the soldiers sitting in circles beneath half-shrouded lanterns. Seeing how many they were, he growled his unease before remembering to keep quiet. He crept closer.

At the smallest of the circles, he spied two women. He knew they were female; women were rounder with longer fur on their heads. One wore armor. Unable to go to them with so many soldiers about, he propped his head on his paws and waited, watching to see what would happen.

Time passed and he grew sleepy. Before he could doze, he felt the vibrations of heavy footfalls through the ground. Something was coming. One of the sentries gave a sharp whistle. Blunder now heard the approaching steps. Not knowing which way to go, he waited.

From out of the mist came the not-men, treading heavily over the earth, marching in a rough, square formation. Blunder tried to creep aside, but before he could escape they were upon him, staring straight ahead, their iron arms creaking as they swung them.

Blunder dodged to keep from being trampled, avoiding a soldier in the first row, narrowly escaping being stepped on by the one behind it. He dodged and dodged again. An iron foot struck his hindquarters. Terrified by the pain, he yelped and darted desperately, running into a metal leg that sent him sprawling. Before he could rise, another soldier loomed over him, too close to escape. He gave a weak growl, and to his surprise the not-man turned aside. Thinking his warning had frightened it away, he rose and growled at the next one. Again, it avoided him. Seeing they weren't as brave as he was, Blunder kept his place, barring his fierce teeth, letting them know he would stand against them.

The not-men passed, the pup's triumphant growl sounding at their backs. He licked his hip where the warrior had kicked him, nursing it before looking around.

The not-men did not stop at the camp, but continued through Morlane. Someone on the far side of the encampment gave a sharp whistle once they were gone. Pleased with his victory, Blunder sat down to wait again.

Soon, the soldiers extinguished their lamps and climbed into their bedrolls, but the two women entered the tent, taking their lantern with them. Blunder plotted his course and slipped between the tree trunks, choosing a roundabout way, taking several minutes to reach his destination. Drawing close to the tent, he watched from behind a stand of brambles.

Though the soldiers lay all around the tent, there were fewer on this side. Blunder watched. Several had their eyes closed; some breathed the heavy breath of sleep. But one man, the one who had kept closest to the women, still sat up, his elbows on his knees.

Blunder would wait. It was all he could do.

Finally, the man lay down. When his eyes had been closed for several minutes, Blunder crept from his hiding place, silent as only an animal can be. He walked slowly into the camp, mouth closed, careful not to pant, slipping between the heads and feet of the soldiers.

One of them moaned in his sleep, and a sword murmured in its sheathe. Blunder froze, waiting, his stalking instinct lending him patience. The man settled down. Blunder continued on until he reached the tent. Using his head, he pushed the cloth up and squeezed inside. "*Come in,*" the tent murmured.

Rising, he found the women sitting on cots. The one who wore the armor was taking off her boots. She looked up and saw him. He froze. His mother warned him that female humans howl when startled. It was their nature and they could not help it; but this one did not.

"Oh!" she said. Her hair was golden, like Gray said. "We have a visitor."

The other woman turned and stared.

"My name is Blunder. I am sniffing for Tanab Nett."

The women kept silent until at last brown-fur said, "I am Tanabel-Tunia and this is Ninette Argilla."

"Gray sent me. I will lead you to him."

"Gray!" Ninette jumped to her feet, still holding one of her boots.

"Shh!" Tana warned.

Ninette put her hand over her mouth, whispering, "I'm sorry."

"Can it really be Gray?" Tana asked.

"It is Gray," Blunder said. "I have saided so."

"Oh, Ninette, what should I do?"

The women looked at one another. Ninette bounced on her heels. "Oh, this is exciting! You must go see him."

Tana turned back to Blunder. "Describe Gray Darien to me."

"He has a man-scent. His flesh smells goose-dark and earth-hoof and salt and fire-smoke. There is orange rind and beetle too, but only a little."

"We don't understand," Ninette said. "Can you tell us what he looks like?"

Blunder dropped his ears, puzzled. He had been so clear. He thought a moment. How could he describe Gray to someone who did not know his scent? Did they know him at all? He whined in perplexity.

"What color are his eyes?" Ninette asked.

Blunder wagged his tail. "They are two colors, like mine!"

"It must be him!" Tana said.

Ninette reached down and stroked his head. "You are *so* soft." The scent of her hand and breath pleased him. She had eaten deer for dinner.

"Can we go now?" he asked.

Tana looked wide-eyed at Ninette. "Do I dare?"

"You have to! How can you not? He's looked for you for *so* long."

"Shouldn't I tell Chel?"

"If you do, they'll fight," Ninette said. "I just know they will. The captain is always trying to protect you."

Tana bit her lip. "You're right, but—"

"I'll go with you. Oh, Tana, you must see him!"

Blunder whined. Why were they waiting?

"All right," Tana finally said. "We will douse the lantern and wait a few minutes first, then we'll leave. Any who see us will think we go to attend to our needs. The dog can hide under my cloak."

Blunder wagged his tail. "I will take you to Gray. He will be happy to see you."

* * *

Rick Spence seldom slept well unless he had something to drink. The men were given a beer ration every day, but it wasn't enough to even enjoy, so he was still awake when Tana and Ninette left their tent.

Normally, he wouldn't think much about it. Dames traveled in groups like coveys of quail, but something about this struck him as suspicious, maybe how Tana held herself like she was carrying something, or the guilty way Ninette kept looking around. Whatever it was, Spence liked playing his hunches. Before the pair had vanished into the mist, he slipped to his feet and followed them.

The women went to one of the sentries and murmured a few words before passing on. That wasn't unusual—women needed their privacy in a camp full of men, and Rendan had made it clear Tana was above being questioned. But it took longer for Spence to slip by without being seen, and he had to search for several minutes, silently cursing the fog, before catching sight of them again. The vegetation whispered as he passed, a light stirring too soft to reach the women's ears.

As the ladies moved farther from the camp, Tana took some kind of animal, a fox or a dog, from her cloak, and Spence congratulated himself for following them. What was going on? Were they trying to escape? If so, he could score some points with Rendan by leading him to them. He just hoped they wouldn't travel too far tonight.

When they had gone only a couple hundred yards, they met somebody. Spence drew closer, keeping behind the cover of the trees. He was glad for the mist now. This was going to be interesting.

* * *

Waiting for Blunder to return was an agony. Gray paced before Russ, imagining what he would say to Tana, what she would say to him, picturing her throwing herself into his arms, weeping that he had finally found her. He would spirit her away from the forest, away from this conflict of which they knew nothing, to a place where they could build their lives together and be happy at last. But it all depended on Blunder keeping to his task and remembering what to say; and even if he did, and wasn't caught, how could she manage to get away? Doubts assailed him. He should have gone himself instead of trusting a puppy.

His reverie was broken by Blunder bouncing his front paws against Gray's legs. "I founded her, Gray. I brought her here."

He turned and saw her first through the mist, a shadow in the darkness, tall and slender. Ignoring the dog, he hurried forward, arms wide, wrapping them around her in a fierce hug. "Oh, my lady!"

"Oh, Gray, I am *sooo* happy to see you!" She hugged him fiercely and broke into a sob. "I thought we'd never meet again."

Her voice was wrong; she was wearing armor. She clung to him, crying.

Behind her, Tanabel-Tunia said, "Gray?"

For an instant he couldn't think who he was holding. Remembering Ninette, he released her as if her armor scalded him.

"Russ!" Ninette cried, rushing to hug the sergeant. "I'm so glad you're both alive! We've done *so* much since I saw you. I want to tell you everything."

Finding himself holding an armful of woman, Russ stammered something incoherent.

Blunder bounced against Gray's legs again. "I brought her, Gray.

Is she the right one? Are you happy?"

Ninette rushed back to Gray. "First, we took a boat. He was sweet! And Ricky and I—"

"Ninette," Tana said gently. "You must wait."

Ninette stopped, putting her hand over her mouth. "Oh! I've done it again! I don't always know things."

She stepped back and Tana was suddenly before Gray. His mouth went dry. He stood speechless, embarrassed and suddenly shy.

"I'll give you two some privacy," Russ said. "Come on, Blunder, you've done a great job." They vanished into the mist.

Ninette stood by, expectantly watching Gray and Tana.

"Ninette," Tana said, "you must go too."

"But I wanted to—" She hesitated. "Oh. I understand."

When she was gone, Tana put her hand on Gray's shoulder and hugged him. He pulled her close, basking in her warmth, but too soon she withdrew.

"She's like a little girl, you know," she said.

"She was nothing like that before. She barely spoke." Why did it feel so awkward? This wasn't anything like he had imagined. "Tana, I—"

"Gray, for you to come all this way for me—I never expected anyone to follow us. Certainly not Fox. I never thought he—"

"Fox? He would have left you in the hands of these barbarians. *I* came to rescue you. I would have come alone if I had to. Fox is—"

"I'm sorry. I wasn't suggesting anything. I was trying to say I'm grateful. It's just that—"

"You're safe now, that's the important thing." Gray took her hand. "We're going to get out of Morlane. I'll take care of you." He leaned forward and kissed her, pressing his lips ardently against hers, trying to draw her back into his arms. For an instant she responded, then pulled away.

"We need to talk," she said.

"What is it? What's wrong? Tell me and I'll make it right."

"I came here willingly."

For a moment the words made no sense. He struggled to speak. "I don't understand."

"Duke Nortallion is my father."

"The enchanter? The one we've been fighting?" The world

seemed to slow. Gray felt the blood draining from his face. "That's impossible!"

"You know your uncle was my foster father, but he never told me the circumstances of my adoption. I only learned my true history after Captain Rendan and his men spirited me away. I am Duke Nortallion's first-born. My mother died birthing me. The enchanters of Ruheen have often struggled for power and position, and before I was six months old, one of my father's rivals stormed his fortress. My father escaped with me and was forced into hiding. In Ruheen, the first-born—whether male or female—is the heir, and his enemies sought to kill both of us. I was sent away for my own protection. The duke despises both Animonea and Faerie, so I was taken to mortal lands, where my foster father was given a considerable sum to raise me. But something happened to the enchanter who delivered me. He never returned to Ruheen, and my father didn't know where I was. He was forced into hiding for almost fifteen years, but began searching for me when he returned to power. It took two years before he found me and sent for me."

"Surely you can't believe this," Gray said. "What proof did these men offer?"

"They described this." Tana raised her hand. "When I was given to my foster father, this ring was among my things. I've always worn it on a chain hidden beneath my clothes."

Gray studied the ring in the darkness. "Joiwend wears one like it."

"It is a ring of the enchanters, the source of their sorcery, given to them by the Elf King of Faerie when they first desired to learn magic."

"But Duke Nortallion is evil," Gray said. "Look what he's done to this forest! We faced iron warriors made by his hand. You can't go to him!"

"He didn't make the Vigili; I've met the man who did. Animonea is a horrid country. The Vigili are just more of its dreadful, talking creatures. I want to see my real father, to know my heritage."

"But what about us?" His voice grew passionate. "Tana, I've always loved you. You know that. The summers we spent together in En, the things we said to each other."

"I know." Her voice held resignation. "We were younger then,

Gray. Children."

"But when you were betrothed to Fox, we made a promise we would—"

"I remember what I told you, and I shouldn't have. I was desperate not to marry him, and you were so sweet! You were my protector. But it was—it wasn't love. I see that now."

They stood looking at one another, Gray's whole body trembling. "I don't know how you can say that."

"When we were passing through Faerie, Chel—Captain Rendan—and I became close."

Gray swallowed, his face afire. "You can't be in love with him. Are you saying you are?"

"I don't know. I thought I was. You know what it's like to lose yourself in an ancient Story in Faerie. I became the Questing Princess and he, the Valiant Champion. My thoughts cleared once I arrived in Animonea; I don't know if I love him or not."

"Then come away with me, Tana. Please!"

"I can't. I must go to my true father." She kissed him on the cheek. "Return to En, Gray. I'll never forget that you came after me. Tell me we will always be friends. Perhaps someday, you and I might even be more—but now I must do as I must."

"I . . . see."

She called softly to Ninette, who answered at once. "I am returning to camp," Tana told her. "You must decide whether to come with me or stay with your former companions."

"But I just found them," Ninette said.

"We mustn't tarry. We will soon be missed, and it might place their lives in danger."

Ninette ran her hands along her temples. "I can't leave you, Tana. Not now. You've been such a good friend. I'm sorry, Gray. I'm really sorry."

"Do as you like," Gray said, his voice flat.

"I think we can make our way back without your dog," Tana said. "Goodbye, Gray, and good fortune."

"Tana, I . . ." Not knowing what to say, he only stared at her.

The women disappeared into the mist.

Gray sat down on a mound of earth. Blunder came trotting up.

Russ found him moments later, weeping while the pup licked his face.

* * *

Spence mentally cursed a world where animals could talk. The dog kept sniffing around, keeping him too far away from Gray and Tana to hear everything they said. But he had caught enough to learn that it was like he thought; the girl didn't care anything for the prince. It was almost comical, a bad joke, Gray's old man sending them chasing after her for no reason. A tough break for the kid, but Spence wouldn't waste time feeling sorry for him. He'd had his own share of brush-offs.

He weighed his options. If he wanted to rejoin the sarge and the others, this was the time, but he dismissed the idea at once. It was pointless becoming a wandering bum again when he could go to Ruheen and maybe find better prospects. He slipped away after Tana and Ninette, keeping his eye on the dog to make sure it didn't notice him leaving. If he got caught returning to camp, he could say he was following the women to ensure their safety.

Before he was halfway back, he heard a hissed whisper behind him. "Corporal Spence!"

He turned, his long-knife ready.

"Over here," the voice said. "I am a friend."

"Come out where I can see you," Spence ordered, keeping his voice down.

A tall, familiar form rose from the mist, his empty hands raised. "Jaunter?"

"Not Jaunter, though we are related and I know him well. I am called Fetch."

Spence squinted, trying to get a better look. It was hard to tell, but in the gloom the man could pass for the Scythian's brother. Even their voices sounded similar. "What do you want? How do you know me?"

"I have been trying to reach you, but dared not enter the Ruheen camp. Jaunter told me about you and the other members of your company. He and I are quite close, you see. Because of it, and due to certain natural abilities of my own, I can sense when I am near you or your friends."

"Jaunter never said anything about you. If you're from his country, how did you wind up here?"

"Time is short and that story is too long to tell. You must return before you are missed. Are you open to a proposition, Richard Spence, if favorable to us both?"

"What kind of proposition?"

"One that could lead to a fine profit. I am seeking a ring such as Joiwend wears. Are you familiar with it?"

"Yeah, I remember it. It's a sapphire, probably worth a pretty penny. Tanabel-Tunia sports one just like it."

"So too does Duke Nortallion. I am drawn to magic, and those rings have certain properties I would find useful. Get me one of them, and I will reward you well."

Spence laughed. "Sure. Maybe I should just go ask the duke or Tana for theirs. I probably wouldn't lose anything more valuable than my head. If you want one, why don't you find Joiwend? At least she ain't surrounded by fifty soldiers."

"I am seeking her as well, but you make too little of yourself, Richard. Jaunter tells me you are a resourceful man. Look for an opportunity! I know what you want, for we are much the same. I tell you, if you bring me one of those rings, you will receive not only fair payment, but a place of honor among those who serve me."

"Captain Rendan has been pretty square with me so far," Spence said. "Why should I double-cross his boss for you?"

"You are cautious. That is good. You do not know me; perhaps you think I am an agent of the duke, sent to test your loyalty. Give me no answer tonight, only consider my words."

"I'll take them under advisement."

Fetch turned and limped back into the mist.

"Well, what do you make of that?" Spence muttered.

"*I do not know*," his helmet said.

"Yeah, well, you just keep this under your hat." He grimaced at the unintended pun.

"*I will protect you*," the helmet said.

He scowled. He wasn't concerned about that hunk of tin talking. It wasn't smart enough to remember conversations; but he didn't understand the way Fetch said he had found him, or that nonsense about being Jaunter's relative. None of it made sense. If this joker was so wealthy, what was he doing wandering around alone in Morlane?

Still, it never hurt to consider the options. If Fetch wanted a ring so badly, they must be worth owning or selling to the highest bidder. It might be possible to get one. After all, there were three available.

CHAPTER FOURTEEN

NORTALLION

Fox Lodan came to Duke Nortallion's camp a captive, leading Dauntless before his captors as if he were their commander, a single lantern lighting their benighted way through the mist. Passing the Ruheen perimeter guarded by both human soldiers and Vigili, he was brought into the camp and placed under watch. When the stallion refused to be parted from his master, the soldiers picketed him by a tall rowen, treating him gently for fear that Arion, their horse-headed god of war, might be speaking through him. Fox slept the remainder of the night in the open, a short distance from the duke's pavilion.

The mist remained thick the next morning, and he was given a breakfast of rations and presented to the duke, who was seated on a wooden chair outside his tent. Nortallion was not the broad-shouldered warrior Fox had imagined, but lean, with a short, straggling beard, pale-gray eyes, an eagle's beak of a nose, and bone-white skin so thin it appeared transparent. He wore an ebony cloak, black pants, a white tunic, and a black acorn hat. His grating voice made him sound older than he looked. He seemed almost a phan-tom seated there, misty in the mist.

"Your Grace," an officer said, "we found this man unconscious not far from the battle. He claims to be a prince of Faerie."

Inwardly, Fox grimaced. Bad enough to be forced to flee the fight, but Dauntless had stumbled and thrown him, knocking him sense-less. He had awoken to find the stallion standing protectively over him, defying a dozen soldiers.

"Most unlikely," Duke Nortallion said. "What part of Faerie?"

"My father is king of Jenar, in the northeast," Fox said.

The duke leaned forward in his chair. "I know Jenar. A small realm surrounded by more powerful neighbors."

"You have traveled in Faerie, Your Grace?"

Nortallion gave the ghost of a smile. "That is a perilous undertaking better done by my subordinates. Are you the third son?"

"I am the eldest."

"Then either your mission was doomed from the start, or you were accompanied by others. Which was it?"

"A third son from mortal lands came with us."

The duke pondered that statement. "Why are you here? Why do you fight for my enemies?"

Fox met his bleached stare. "Only happenstance has made us foes. I came with my companions to Animonea seeking a kidnapped maiden. When we inadvertently broke the strange laws of this country, we were captured by Marshal Dartmallow, who forced us to accompany him to Morlane. I escaped when your soldiers overran the camp."

"What woman?"

"Tanabel-Tunia, a duchess of En, a land to the east of Faerie. She is my betrothed."

The duke's eyes flickered at the name. "Do you love her?"

The question surprised Fox. He shrugged. "It is a matter of honor."

"So you do not love her," Nortallion said, with apparent satisfaction. He flicked his wrist, dismissing the subject. "I have had dealings with the High King of Faerie. The elf lord is wily, unfathomable, cruel as iron, deadly to his enemies, inconstant to his friends. Your coming here is reasonable, believable, and so, suspect. His cunning is deep; his plans he prepares decades in advance."

"I have never met the Elf King," Fox said. "If he even knows I exist, he cares nothing for me, and I care less for him. I will speak plainly, Your Grace. My journey through Animonea has taught me much. I now realize that growing up in Faerie was akin to being raised in an exquisite dungeon. Like all its inhabitants, I accepted my destiny as the eldest son, compelled by the Elf King's magic to blindly follow a predetermined course. In that country I can plot but never succeed, win battles but lose wars, be consumed with ambition only to see it come to nothing, while my brother, the third son, inevitably rises to the throne. Every just king in Faerie is a third son, every unjust ruler is the elder brother, doomed to destruction. By erasing his subjects' choices, the Elf King insures that none of them can conceive of overthrowing him, thus maintaining his power through the ages. I never want to be in his grasping fist again."

"You came to this conclusion when?" the duke asked.

"Over time, Your Grace, but beginning soon after leaving Faerie. It was as if a cloud lifted from my mind." Fox refrained from admitting he had first doubted the Elf King when his magic sword failed during his duel with Gray. At that moment, he had realized everything in life was not foreordained. He had still not wholly grasped the wonder of being able to choose his own course, and the old patterns of thought remained, sometimes leading to an unfamiliar sense of confusion, a fear of uncertainty.

"You speak truly, Prince. The Elf King fears Animonea because he cannot control the thoughts of its inhabitants, cannot bend them to his will. He did not build the wall to keep the Animoneans out, but to keep his people in. Somewhat, I envy him. What ruler would not wish such power over his subjects?"

"The rabble, yes, that would be useful; but not the royalty. Of what value is the blood of princes if they cannot bend their minds and skills to the kingdom?"

Nortallion laughed, delighted, a hollow echo in the mist. He sat back in his chair, eyeing Fox. "I perceive you are ambitious, Prince Lodan. Here is what I think: this girl, Tanabel-Tunia, was a means to an end, intended to somehow expand your power or prestige. What would have been your next step? Using her to convince your father to invade a neighboring kingdom? Or perhaps to discredit your younger brothers?"

"What glory is there in ruling except to enlarge one's authority?" Fox asked. "It is the only game worth playing. But in Faerie it was futile. I see that now. The world has become so broad for me, so filled with possibilities."

"Will you stay in Animonea?"

Fox frowned. "Only as a last resort. Though I've never felt so healthy, so alive, as when I came here, the Republic of Everything isn't for me."

"There *is* something in the air here," Nortallion said, "but it is indeed not for such as you and I. You speak with great reason; I will soon learn if you speak the truth. Now tell me everything you know about Marshal Dartmallow's forces, their strength, their weapons, the animals that aid them. The trees of the Wileywood do not comprehend numbers, and the mist blinds my spies."

"The marshal suspected your people of creating the mist."

"As in many things, he is wrong."

"I will tell you whatever you wish to know, so long as you understand I am not a traitor," Fox said. "I haven't pledged loyalty to Animonea or its people."

"Agreed," Nortallion said.

Fox smiled. Despite his circumstances, for the first time since coming to the Back of the Beyond, he felt on solid ground, finally dealing with men who understood the place of royalty. Perhaps Ruheen was a country where a prince could find his way.

* * *

When Tana and Ninette passed the sentry and approached the Ruheen camp, they heard the noise of soldiers stirring: the rattling armor, the strident commands, the eager declarations of boots and spears. Tana's heart misgave her, fearing they had been missed. They were unable to see anything until they reached the outer circle of the encampment, where the dim glow of lanterns pierced the mist. Captain Rendan stood before their tent, too busy addressing one of Treg's Vigili to witness their approach.

"Has something happened?" Tana asked.

"I fear your rest must be interrupted," Rendan said. "The duke set several of the Vigili to watch for our arrival. His camp is close by, and he orders us to come at once. He is anxious to see you."

Tana felt her face flush. "And I to see him! Oh, Chel, what will he be like? How often as a child I thought my life would be different if only my father were there. I'm trembling all over!"

"Take heart. You will see him soon."

"I scarcely believe it. It seems I walk in a dream."

Chel gave her an encouraging smile. "We will make that dream a reality."

Tana turned to Ninette. "We must hurry! We mustn't be the cause of delay."

Under Rendan's urging, the soldiers struck camp and were soon on their way. As always, the unsleeping company of Vigili had gone on before them. Tana walked between Ninette and Chel, taking comfort in their presence and protection. If Ninette acted with the emotions of a child, she carried herself with the confidence of a trained warrior. She had told Tana of the battles she had fought, and though she had been little more than a puppet at that time, those skills remained with her. It was that combination of innocence and fortitude that had fascinated Tana when they first met, for she sensed in her friend the strength she herself lacked.

All her life, there had always been someone to obtain the things she wanted: her nanny, the servants, the members of her foster father's court. It was never a matter of *how* to gain her desires, but from *whom* to win them. As a child growing up in a royal house, choosing the right person was usually easy. When she was older, she used her beauty and station to compel the young men. Though her foster father ignored her, she found those who would do her will. If her desires were thwarted, it was only because she had chosen the wrong person to assist her. She required someone to care for her wishes, to protect her. The thought of facing the world without such an intercessor horrified her.

She had not come to Animonea through her own resolve—she had little of that—but had been swayed by Chel's handsome face and the promise of meeting her father. Passing through the Back of the Beyond had been a nightmare—everything talking. Faerie had been dreadful enough; six of Rendan's men had died fighting a dragon, the rest saved only because Chel was the third son. Three others were lured away by the siren-call of a beautiful *huldra*, never to be seen again. Though Animonea had proven less horrible, Chel's two surviving soldiers had been slain by the same bear that had raked the captain's arm. She had been terrified throughout the journey, longing for the imagined comfort of her father's castle.

Yet, when she saw Gray, his devotion so touched her that she had been tempted to go with him. Just thinking of it brought tears to her eyes, and she was glad for the darkness. But Gray could never give her what she wanted; he could never take her to her father. Only Chel and Ninette could do that.

Following the lone Vigili from the duke's camp, the company traveled less than two hours before reaching Nortallion's army.

Iron and clay Vigili surrounded the camp, a wall of relentless sentinels that parted before Chel's men. A sergeant took command of Rendan's soldiers, leaving Chel, Tana, and Ninette following a pair of guards through the incessant fog. A pavilion appeared before them, and Tana felt her pulse quicken. The duke stood waiting there.

When Chel first found Tana, he had given her a small portrait of her sire, so she knew what to expect, but the artist had ennobled his image, and his gauntness and bedraggled beard surprised her, so she halted uncertainly before him. Unable to find her voice, she curtsied.

He studied her in the lamplight, unsmiling. "Captain, are you certain this is she?" His harsh voice, so different from the warm tones she had imagined, disquieted her so she scarcely grasped his words.

"She bears the ring, Your Grace," Rendan said.

"I see her mother in her, but the ring could make her look so," Duke Nortallion said. "She has not changed from when you first saw her?"

"No, Your Grace," Rendan said. "Nor could she have known of our coming. Our inquiries were discreet. Calant surely brought her to the Duke of En as an infant—it could be no other than he. We were able to obtain a clear description of him from a former servant. We tried to trace him without success. A plague ran through the country during that time, and many perished. I suspect he was one of them."

"Come closer, girl," the duke ordered. "Look me in the eyes."

She did so. They stood a foot apart. It surprised her that they were both the same height. His gaze was steady, searching. Was this pale face truly that of her father?

All at once she seemed to fall into his eyes, as if plummeting from a great height. She felt her mind and heart bared before him, her thoughts pouring out of her, mind to mind, the information going only one direction. She gasped and choked, a frightened sob.

The falling ended, leaving her trembling before him. He took her hand. He scrutinized her ring, which matched the one on his own index finger. He touched them together, stone to stone, and a blue glow flamed forth and died. The barest smile touched his lips. He gently squeezed her fingers, his voice thick with emotion. "I have waited long to find you again, an eternity, an eon, an everlasting night. I swore I would not go down to my grave until you were beside me once more. Daughter of Evenor, child of my flesh, one and true heir to all my holdings, I name thee by thy true name. Enter into my kingdom, Tanabel-Tunia Nortallion."

She looked again into his eyes and saw only welcome there.

"Come into my arms," he said.

"Father!" She burst into tears.

His embrace was not warm; it was smoke and ice and an untouchable longing, but to Tana it was a dream she thought could never come true.

They parted and Duke Nortallion turned his gaze to Ninette. "And who is this?"

"My companion and friend, Ninette Argilla," Tana said. "We met at Treg's. She has given me great solace on our journey here."

"What did you do at Treg Keep, girl?" Nortallion asked.

Tana spoke before Ninette could reply. "She arrived there with another who now serves in your army. She is a warrior and my bodyguard."

The duke turned toward his pavilion, dismissing Ninette from his mind. "Come, Daughter, and tell me of your life in En."

Tana followed, leaving Ninette and Rendan behind.

The duke's pavilion was made of dark-green silk matching the color of leaves and earth. When its flap closed behind Tana, she left the misty world of the forest behind. Three lanterns hung on tent poles, softly humming. Ornate carpets covered the floor, save in a circle at the center, where a cheery fire crackled in a brazier, singing its song of devouring flame while the walls whispered safety and sanctuary. Maps lay stretched on a low table. In a corner, a music box played. Low cushions invited Tana to rest.

"You must forgive these modest surroundings," the duke said.

"This wretched country of babbling things! I have taken great pains to find materials that at least speak in pleasant tones. Sit here among the cushions. I prefer chairs, but find their voices annoying." He poured wine in a pewter cup and handed it to her. "Here is a quiet vintage which will not demand permission to be consumed. Now tell me of your life in En and your journey here."

Tana sat back in the cushions, sipping the wine without tasting it. "I scarcely know where to begin, Father. See how my hand trembles! I can hardly hold the cup or muster my thoughts. My heart flutters!"

"No more than mine," Nortallion said, taking her hand. He turned it over, palm upward and touched her fingers with his own. "You have your mother's hands. She was the daughter of Gleddering Isged, and I loved her from the moment I first laid eyes upon her. I killed a rival to win her, and when we married I sacrificed seventy oxen and eight slaves to the gods."

"There are slaves in Ruheen?" Tana asked, shocked.

"We only enslave our enemies or those who cannot pay their debts. It is the same in En; the commoners serve the royalty there too, though they are not called slaves; and in Faerie everyone is an unknowing slave, in thrall to the caprice of the Elf King. But we sacrifice only the best animals and servants to the gods."

Tana nodded thoughtfully. "Though I was taught much about etiquette and music and poetry, politics was not part of my education. Such training was reserved for my foster father's sons."

"It will not be so here," Nortallion said. "You must learn the Way of the Enchanters, how to rule, how to persuade, how to out-maneuver your enemies."

"Will I have enemies, Father? No one in Ruheen knows me."

The duke chuckled. "*I* have enemies, Daughter. That is enough to make them yours. Because you are my heir and successor, there are those who will desire your destruction the instant they learn of your existence. Does that frighten you? Do not be afraid. I will teach you how to hold power, how to use it, how to extend it. Have you wondered why I am in Morlane?"

"Captain Rendan said to end the threat of Animonea."

"Animonea is an abomination to the gods. The Republic of Everything! The Republic of Chaos. They offer no sacrifices, giving credence only to the laws of their Omnifire. They allow worse than mob rule, granting even animals a say. Once I have secured our hold on Morlane, I will gain the full support of the Grand Duke and my fellow dukes in Ruheen. Together, we will amass an army in the Wileywood and overrun this abysmal land."

"Are the other dukes enchanters?" Tana asked.

"Of course, as is the Grand Duke, who is chosen for a term from the dukes' ranks. No others are worthy to rule, to judge, to lead armies. The commoners are willful and ignorant, easily led to rebellion. We guide and guard them, dispensing iron discipline, granting token rewards, holding grand spectacles to keep them content."

"I know so little about magic," Tana said. "Do the rings truly give us so much authority? Until Captain Rendan found me, I didn't know mine was enchanted."

Nortallion chuckled. "Ah, you think the ability to change our shapes merely sleight of hand. A little power is all it takes, a single advantage, a sole superiority to make one rise above other men. I will demonstrate."

He furrowed his brow in concentration, then rose and stepped near one of the pavilion walls. He faded and disappeared. Tana gasped in surprise.

"I am still here," Nortallion said. "Look closer."

She saw he had not vanished at all, but had changed his color like a chameleon, matching the hues of the silk tent. She clapped her hands, laughing in delight.

"This is no parlor trick. To be able to spy on your enemies, to assume the shape of an officer in the army of your foes and issue false orders—many times I have crept in stealth and learned enough to overcome my opposition." He returned to his normal form. "And there is more. The rings give us long life, far beyond the span of ordinary men. We can also cast illusions over the minds of our foes, if their numbers are not too many. That is a tremendous tool for controlling the commoners. I will teach you all you need to know."

"Where did the rings come from, Father?"

"Our people descend from the kings of Animonea. We once ruled there under the oppressive laws of the Omnifire. We knew the power the Elf King held, and we made a treaty with him in exchange for the rings. But a civil war arose when we claimed our sole right to rule Animonea, and we were cast out. We came to Ruheen, used our rings to convince the people that we were emissaries of the gods, and became their rulers."

He studied her expression. "Do not look so, child! We did not deceive our people. For we *are* the emissaries of the gods, if not gods ourselves. It was plain enough to see. That is why the gods brought us to Ruheen, to rule and to end the aberration of Animonea."

He turned and drained his wine glass. "We should have done it long ago, but we enchanters are both allies and rivals, each ruling his own cities, ever contending with one another. That is why I remained in exile so long—I had to destroy my opponents before I could return to power." He paced to the front of the pavilion and looked out. His voice grew low, as if he spoke to himself. "But I will subdue the Wileywood and all of Animonea. Wretched country with its eternal mist!"

He turned back to her, smiling. "I have spoken too much of politics and power. Tell me of your life in En. Tell me everything about it."

They talked for a long hour. When she left him to go to the tent prepared for her, she found Ninette asleep in a wooden chair outside, frowning in discomfort. Tana gently woke her.

"What is it?" Ninette asked, stretching her shoulders and making a face like a little girl.

"You shouldn't have waited for me," Tana said. "Come, let's find a comfortable bed."

Ninette rubbed her eyes. "What time is it? Do you like him? Is he nice? Are you going to stay with him forever?"

"I'll tell you about it in the morning. I need to sleep."

Tana went to bed happy, for she had found her father; and though he was not as she had imagined, she finally had someone who loved her, who would take care of her for her own sake. She and Ninette slept beneath the furs of bears, and she knew her life would be good at last.

* * *

She woke early the next morning, weary from lack of sleep, but too excited to remain in bed. Leaving Ninette to her slumbers, she rose, dressed, and left the tent. The guard escorted her into the duke's pavilion, where her father stood before a low table covered with a map of Morlane. Seeing her, he stood, taking both her hands between his own.

"Daughter." He nodded toward a servant. "Breakfast, and bring the prisoner." The man hurried away. Moments later, wooden stools and a low cart covered with fruit, mutton, and assorted breads were brought in. The bowls, plates, and utensils created a clamor, asking to be used. The duke glowered, refusing to give the Mandate of Gratitude.

"Game is scarce in the forest," he explained. "All of this has to be brought from Ruheen. The plates did not talk until they had been here a month. Though we dammed the Widfroth River to stop the flow from the Omnifire, the resulting lake is too near and still animates the land. When the dishes become too loud, I have them ground to powder."

The vessels clattered in consternation.

While they were eating, two guards appeared bringing Fox Lodan. Tana gasped in astonishment and rose to her feet. Only a slight widening of his eyes revealed his own surprise. He was thinner than she remembered, doubtless made so in his journeying, but still held himself with an assurance that made him more attractive than his red hair and sharp nose might allow.

"Prince Lodan."

He grinned and bowed at the waist, one hand over his heart. "Duchess Tanabel-Tunia. You've brought us through a pretty chase, and all for naught, it seems."

"I regret your discomfort," Tana said.

"So you do know him?" Nortallion asked.

A chill spread through Tana's veins, a fear her father would force her to keep her engagement. "I know him."

"He claims you were betrothed."

She dropped her eyes from Fox's blue gaze, her voice quavering. "We were, in that other country. It seems long ago."

"You can speak freely here, Daughter," the duke said. "You are under no obligation to this man. I want to know only the truth concerning him. He was found among my enemies, but avers no allegiance to them. What do you say of him?"

Tana felt a weight lift from her chest. "We met only once, Father. He is a prince of Jenar, a kingdom of Faerie. The Faerie folk are strange, and it is not customary for the people of En to traffic with them. Our marriage was arranged as a matter of state. My foster father would never have done so with one of his own children. I was to be sacrificed for reasons unknown to me."

"Was I so repulsive to you?" Fox asked. "If so, you gave no sign. You were to be made a princess."

"I don't mean it that way. Of course it was an honor to marry you, but I did not wish to become a figure in a Faerie Story."

"There is reason enough for that," Duke Nortallion said, "but the question is, can I trust him? I depend on your answer, girl."

"I know him mostly by reputation," she said, meeting Fox's eyes. "I'm told he is skilled and courageous in combat, and an excellent strategist. In Faerie, he played the role of the Unjust Prince, but that is the way of things there. During our meeting, he struck me as forthright enough. That is all I know."

The duke stood silent, contemplating. At last he said, "Prince Lodan, if you forfeit your claim to my daughter's hand, if you swear by your royal blood not to aid my enemies, I will set you free. Stay with us or go, so long as you do not return to the marshal's army."

"I thank you, Your Grace, and so swear by the blood of the princes of Jenar. I would like to remain here. My obligation to the duchess is done, since she is safe in your hands, but I think I would prefer Ruheen to Animonea. Perhaps I can be of some service to you."

"If that is your wish, then come with us to Ironwood Station," the duke said. "We leave this morning."

"I would be honored," Fox said. "May I be bold enough to ask what the duke plans?"

Nortallion scowled. "The trees have fallen silent and I do not know why. They no longer report the movements of my foes, leaving me blind in a land where we are outnumbered."

"Surely your mechanical men make up for that," Fox said.

"The Vigili have no ability to reason, but obey the last instructions they receive. Quite useful when my commanders can point at the enemy and order them to slay, but less suitable when my antagonists are scattered. I had hoped to smash Dartmallow's army, but I will starve it instead. The marshal is not prepared for a long siege. In a week, hunger will gnaw his men's bellies, forcing him to withdraw. The news of his retreat will encourage the other dukes of Ruheen to send me more troops."

"Sound strategy," Fox said. "I look forward to seeing your plans come to fruition." He bowed at the neck. "Your Grace. Duchess. By your leave." Turning, he swaggered out.

The duke chuckled mirthlessly.

"What do you find humorous, Father?"

"That one," the duke said. "Having left Faerie, he understands how it constrained him. He is ambitious and thinks perhaps the daughter of a duke no longer sufficient for his glory. He sets his eyes toward higher peaks and grander promontories."

"Then why did you give him his freedom?"

"I do not surround myself with weaklings, child. An ambitious man, brought to the reins, is worth a thousand ordinary soldiers. If his brains match his bearing, that one, I wager, can win battles."

CHAPTER FIFTEEN

FOX IN THE MIST

The morning after their meeting with Tanabel-Tunia, Russ Rogers rose early, having slept poorly. Since being in the war, he never dreamed, or if he did he never remembered it; but on this day he woke to the memory of crawling up the Normandy beach, vainly tapping the boot of the man in front of him to see if he was still alive. Coming up beside him, he found a bullet hole placed directly between the soldier's eyes. The Germans were excellent marksmen.

He cast the recollection aside and watched the shafts of the rising sun glistening through the ever-changing faces of the endless mist. With Tana found, his obligation to Gray was over. He could go wherever he wished, but all he really wanted was to go home to Kansas. If he went to Ruheen, its wizards might be able to help him, though Vasps claimed they worked mostly through illusion. He wished Soonderkainen were still alive. Though the bard-enchanter hadn't known how to send him back to Earth, he had been a true magician, and his advice might have been useful.

One thing he was certain of: he didn't want to be anyone's soldier. The war would surely be over by the time he got back. Before coming to Faerie he had witnessed the Germans surrendering by the hundreds. There were still the Japanese, but even they couldn't withstand a combined Allied assault.

The battle with the Ruheen warriors had shaken him more than he liked to admit. Having no reason to fight them, he had been half-relieved when the Vigili forced him to retreat before he had to spill any blood. When his squad first came to Faerie, they fought many inhuman and mythic creatures—marsh-wights, gorgophanes, handrigites—but never humans or elves. And there had been days of peace and great beauty. Faerie was a wondrous land, filled with sprawling forests, magic devices, flying horses, guileful wood-sprites, beautiful princesses, solemn unicorns on rainbow-hued hills. Early on, he had spent three weeks in the Wolds Ilessia; and in that land of reverie found he could not stop weeping. Even now, he couldn't understand why. He had seen his share of horrors during the war, but had never been one to sit around bawling—not when he had to leave home to go to work at age thirteen, not during the Great Depression, not when his brother had been captured by the Japanese. Embarrassed, he never told anyone of his weakness. But he had no intention of getting involved in another war.

His brooding was interrupted by Gray's waking. The prince sat up and ran a hand over his rumpled hair. Russ looked at him and shook his head. The prince might be from a different era, but a lad smitten by a lass was the same in any century.

There was no figuring love. Gray and Joiwend had become such good friends during the journey Russ once thought they might end up together. She was a real beauty with a sweet spirit. If not for Paulette waiting back home, he might have been interested himself. But he had never been one to take romance lightly. Maybe it was because he was ten years older than a lot of the men, but he couldn't act like the soldiers who went with the French girls when they had sweethearts back in the states. Love was a serious business. People's hearts were fragile and important, worthy of respect.

"We have to find Tana," Gray said.

"You're not awake yet. You saw her yesterday. Remember?"

Gray rose, rubbing his eyes, half-stumbling to his feet. "You don't understand. I thought about it all night. I don't know why I didn't realize it when she was here. The Ruheen enchanters have placed her under a spell. We need to ride to their camp and rescue her. Where's Nutmeg?"

"I am here with my herd," Nutmeg said.

Gray turned around and looked at her. "Oh. We better go. I need my sword."

"Hold on," Russ said. "Let's talk about this. You can't go riding half-cocked into the Ruheen camp. You need to wake up and have breakfast first for one thing, and maybe consider how the three of us are going to trot into the middle of the enemy without getting killed."

Gray slumped dejectedly onto a fallen log. "You're right. We need a plan."

"No, we honestly don't." Russ sat on the log beside Gray. "What makes you think she's enchanted?"

"She must be! Why else would she refuse to come with me?"

"She gave a pretty good reason, wanting to meet her father."

Gray's unusual eyes hardened in anger. "It's an absurd reason! She doesn't even know him."

Russ studied Gray's downcast gaze, sulking expression, resolute jaw. "Did I ever tell you about Private Hodsteddar?"

"Who?" Gray's voice thickened in annoyance.

"You and I talked one time about the Allied invasion of France."

"I remember."

"We crossed the English Channel aboard the *Dominion Monarch*. It had been a passenger liner before the war, but there were four thousand of us packed in the hold. We each had a spot, nearly on top of each other, where we ate and slept. Hodsteddar loved to play cards, and he was pretty good at it. Not much of a gambler myself, I held his winnings for him, and he won a lot—several hundred dollars before we finally disembarked to the transports to hit the beach."

"Did he live through the battle?" Gray asked.

"He survived the invasion and sent his winnings to his girl so they could have a nice start when he got back to the states. But he received a letter from her later. She had married another fellow, and that was the last he heard of her or his money."

Gray looked up at Russ. "Why are you telling me this?"

"Just because we love somebody doesn't mean they love us back, Gray. It doesn't always work out. Sometimes we have to accept it for what it is, not what we want it to be."

Gray shook his head. "But Tana . . . ever since we were young. And then when we were older she said . . ." His voice rose in anguish. "How can she not love me?"

"Maybe she will someday, or maybe she won't, but right now she needs to find her dad. You should try to be happy for her."

"Happy? She's making a terrible mistake." His eyes grew moist. He rose, walked toward Nutmeg, turned back. "I don't know what to do!"

"There's nothing *to* do. She's already told you what she wants. You have to dust yourself off and go on, put one foot in front of the other until the pain goes away."

Vasps Geometer had risen and was fumbling over his rations. "Russ is right. As for my part, if Marshal Dartmallow still lives, my duty lies with him. I must locate him and the army. I advise you to do the same. We can do nothing against Duke Nortallion alone."

Though Russ heard Vasps, his thoughts remained on his words to Gray, wondering if they applied to himself. Was Paulette still waiting for him, or were his hopes as foolish as the prince's?

"I don't care about Duke Nortallion," Gray said.

"You should consider your future," Vasps said. "You are still un- der the Service of Restitution to the marshal. If you intend to remain in Animonea, you must discharge that obligation."

Russ chuckled. "I don't think we owe Dartmallow anything. We did our part when the trees attacked, and we would have held if not for those mechanical monstrosities. What we needed was a tank squadron."

"Your reference is obscure," Vasps said. "Nonetheless, you have only the two choices of remaining in Animonea or entering Ruheen. I do not think you would like that country, where they look on for- eigners with great suspicion."

"*Your* people look on foreigners with great suspicion," Russ said.

"Yes, but unless they commit a crime, we either escort them to our borders or accept them among our ranks. The Ruheens practice slavery, especially on outsiders."

Russ frowned. "I didn't know that."

"This battle is literally for the hearts and minds of our people," Vasps said. "Our enemies have dammed the waters of life here in Morlane; their ultimate goal is to destroy the fountain of the Omnifire." He reached down and patted Blunder's head. "If they succeed, the animals, the plants, the very stones and fields of Animonea will fall silent. This little one and all like him will gradually lose the power of speech."

Blunder whined and ran to Gray, bounding against his legs until Gray picked him up. "I do not want that, Gray. I like to talk to you."

"Shh," Gray stroked Blunder's side. The pup whimpered, then grew limp in his arms, eyes closed, enjoying the petting, his back feet dangling.

Russ wanted nothing to do with slave owners. It put a different perspective on his notion of traveling to Ruheen. "All right, Vasps, I'm willing to go with you. What do you say, Gray?"

"I don't know where my duty lies," Gray admitted. "You say the duke is evil, that his people enslave others, yet what man speaks well of an enemy?"

"I am telling the truth—"

"The truth as you know it, as you've been told, but if Tana goes to serve the duke, shouldn't I do the same for her sake, to be her defender? My old tutor taught me about the Roman republic, and though he spoke otherwise, I thought it a chaotic country. And it was a land where only the *nobles* could vote. The Republic of Everything seems like Russ' America, which as great as he says it is, is filled with a thousand voices demanding their say. A just king rules well, guiding his people. He is prudent when they are foolish, cautious when they are hasty, strong when they are weak. I don't know what to think of your republic."

"Liberty is not an easy concept," Vasps said. "Live here long enough and you will learn to appreciate it."

A wolf's howl pierced the mist, answered by a cry from the opposite direction. Blunder growled; the horses rumbled uneasily; the men froze, listening. More baying arose, the hunting song of the pack.

"I thought wolves traveled at night," Russ said.

"Why are they still in Morlane, when their prey has been driven out?" Vasps asked. "There can scarcely be anything left to eat except . . ." His eyes widened in fright.

Flapjack snorted and trotted back and forth in agitation. "The bad dogs come!" Russ hurried to calm him.

The howls grew nearer, rising from all sides. In unspoken agreement, the men mounted their horses. Gray lifted Blunder onto Nutmeg's bare back.

"Which way?" Vasps asked.

"Toward Tana's camp," Gray said.

"We can't just ride in—" Russ protested.

"The mist will hide us from the soldiers," Gray said. "The wolves won't attack a large encampment. If we get close enough, the scent of so many men may frighten them away."

Russ nodded, seeing the sense of it while doubting Gray's motives. Pulling out his compass, he pointed through the vapors. "The camp is that direction." He had lost his bow and shield during the Ruheen assault, and the men's swords could never turn back an en-tire pack. He longed for hand grenades and an M1 rifle.

The horses trotted through the forest, ears forward, listening for danger. The mist painted the world drab gray; the shifting forms of the leering mist-men obscured the travelers' vision further; they could see less than twenty yards before them. The trees rose out of the fog, eyes closed, sleeping titans. Russ drew a nervous breath; his heartbeat pulsed in his neck.

A wolf yowled immediately to their right, startling both horses and men. "Easy," Russ whispered to Flapjack, patting his neck. "Easy, boy. The camp should be close."

The danger was now two-fold. They could either pass the camp unawares or ride right into it. Gray was pressing forward too fast, driven by his own and the horses' apprehension. Before Russ could tell him to slow down, the Prince of Stallions raised his hand and drew to a halt. Blunder leapt from Nutmeg and trotted forward, nose to the ground, vanishing into the gloom only to quickly return.

"The camp was here," Blunder said. "I smell it."

Riding on, they discovered the signs: discarded arrow-points, a broken lantern, a wide swatch of ground trampled by the heavy treads of the Vigili.

"They lefted after you talked to the woman who made you sad, Gray," Blunder said, sniffing the earth.

Russ looked around, wondering what had caused them to withdraw in such haste. "If we follow their trail, their scent might still discourage the wolves."

They rode ahead, Blunder leading the way, pursuing the tracks west. But wolf cries soon arose from that direction, close and menacing, compelling them to turn north. For an instant, Russ thought he saw feral eyes watching them, but they vanished, leaving him uncertain whether it was a wolf or the constantly changing faces of the mist. "We need to find somewhere to make a stand."

They rode on, huddled together, weapons ready. The minutes turned to an hour, the hour to two, and still the wolves remained close without attacking. The ground grew rocky, but the companions found no place of refuge. Before the war, when he had been a cowboy on the Cross L's Ranch in New Mexico, Russ had watched a pair of coyotes run a jackrabbit to death around a small pond, one keeping abreast of it, trapping it against the shore while the other rested, trading off each time they circled the water until the rabbit dropped in exhaustion. Having seen how intelligent Animonea's wolves were, Russ was sure they were being intentionally driven to some unknown destination. What were they planning? Were they too intending to run their prey to death?

At the top of a low rise, Blunder halted, hackles rising, teeth barred. A fox sat on a flat rock at the base of an oak, its eyes fixed on the dog. Its coat was russet, its breast, white. Rather than flee from the men's approach, it remained where it was, though Russ could see it trembling.

"I am a messenger," the fox said, teeth chattering. "My name is Evening Breath. The red wolves sent me. Please take the dog away."

"Blunder," Vasps said. "Come here."

Blunder growled again. "He is a fox."

"I am a vixen," she said.

"Here, Blunder," Gray ordered.

The pup took one quick step forward, stalking his prey. The vixen tensed, preparing to spring up the tree.

"Blunder!" Gray said. "Come here."

Blunder reluctantly obeyed, looking over his shoulder at Evening Breath while retreating to a position beside Nutmeg.

"The red wolves sent me," she repeated. "They made me come, though I fear your swords. They said I would not frighten you as they do. They want you to follow and see."

"See what?" Gray asked. "Why have they pursued us?"

"They want you to see. They need your help."

Russ flushed, thinking of the coyotes and the jackrabbit.

"I am only a fox, too small to hurt you. The wolves say they have spoken to the trees. They say the trees whispered the name of Gray, who is not a fox, though that is a fox name. Joy Wind told them. They say to tell you it was Joy Wind. You are Gray, yes, of the two-colored eyes? You will come? The wolves will eat me if I do not bring you. They offer me truce if I take you to them."

"Foxes are wily." Nutmeg stamped her foot, causing the fox to crouch in fear.

"They are," Vasps said, "and scarcely to be trusted."

"I am an honest vixen."

"I do not doubt it," Vasps said, "but I don't know what that means." He turned to the others. "What do you counsel?"

"We should not follow the fox," Nutmeg said.

"We should not follow the fox," Dreamer said.

"We should chase the fox." Blunder's tail wagged in excitement.

"Do we have a choice?" Russ asked.

Vasps bit his lip. "Perhaps not. Either she is telling the truth, or we are being driven to where the wolves can kill us without risking their own lives."

Flapjack rumbled. "I do not want to go."

"But if we stay, the wolves may still slay us," Vasps said.

"We should go," Flapjack said. "I do not want to be eaten."

"We should go," Dreamer said.

"We should not go," Nutmeg said.

"We should stay and fight," Blunder growled.

"Man, oh man," Russ exhaled the words. "This is no time for a vote."

"We can't survive if they attack," Gray said. "We might as well follow her."

They fell silent. At last, Nutmeg dropped her head to crop a weed. Still chewing, she studied the others, her brown eyes thoughtful. "I will go with Gray."

"We will go," the other horses echoed.

Evening Breath hopped down from the rock and trotted away. "I will lead you."

Blunder barked, eager to pursue.

"Ride with me, pup," Gray said. "You can watch her from here."

* * *

Despite Gray's words, the longer Evening Breath led the companions, the more anxious he became. They were riding at the mountains' feet, traveling ever farther from Tana, leaving her to the designs of Duke Nortallion, whom he pictured as a slit-eyed necromancer, gleefully rubbing his hands while claiming to be her father. The vixen escorted them onward, her tail nearly straight as she trotted around the boles. Once, she stopped to scratch her ear with her hind paw, then stood staring, head held high, as if seeking her way before turning slightly east and trotting on. Gray kept his eyes on her, trying not to think about the wolves. Now that it no longer served their purpose, the pack had ceased howling, but Gray caught glimpses of them weaving among the trees, cloaked in the mist, keeping pace with the riders. If this was a ruse, if they chose to attack, the men would have little chance. Coerced by the vixen, driven by the wolves, he felt helpless.

"I smell water, Gray," Blunder said.

"The air is full of it," Gray said.

"Not the mist, Gray. This is much water. I think it is a lake."

Nutmeg half-turned her head to look back at them, her nostrils flaring. "It is a lake. I am thirsty."

"Thirsty," the other horses answered.

The ground had been rising for some time, but now they rode down rounded slopes intersecting a dry river bed. Smooth stones lay in former pools at its bottom; enormous cottonwoods girded its forsaken banks.

"The Widfroth!" Vasps said. "I knew it would be this way, but I wish I had never seen it! This is tragedy! This is disaster! His whorling waters, the vast mathematics of his winding banks, his eddies and tides, the geometric perfection of his progress, his carving of earth and stone according to arithmetic certainty. All lost, never to be regained! Even should he flow this way again, it will never be the same! Curse the duke and his henchmen! Curse the enchanters of Ruheen!"

Weeping, the arbiter pulled at his hair and struck his breast. His reaction astonished Gray, who had grown up in a land where trees could be felled, and rivers dammed with impunity. This, more than anything he had yet seen, gave him a glimpse of the bond between humans and the creatures of Animonea, and he struggled to comprehend it. He had been taught that nature was to be conquered, to be placed beneath the hands and whims of man, a thing rather than an ally. Despite everything he had seen, he had failed to realize the depths of affinity among the Animoneans.

They followed the bed a short distance before Evening Breath veered away, ascending once more. The mist grew thicker, forcing the riders to move closer to their guide. The climb steepened, compelling them to dismount. They topped the rise and looked down through the vapors on a lake lying below. Though the air remained still, they could hear the water surging, as if moved by wind and tide. The scent of fish and fetid vegetation reached Gray's nostrils.

Blunder whimpered; Gray looked around and started. The vixen had vanished, but a wolf stood watching a few paces away, smoky in the mist, his red coat blending to black and tan. Slightly smaller than the gray wolves familiar to the prince, his body was so gaunt his ribs protruded, his eyes were hungry, his fangs, sharp around his red tongue.

"I am Loogth. I lead the pack."

Dreamer whinnied in fear; Flapjack stamped his feet in challenge; Gray and Russ raised their swords.

"Peace!" Loogth growled. "Will you have truce?"

"We will have truce," Vasps said hurriedly.

The wolf growled and nodded his head.

"Put away your weapons," Vasps ordered. "They will not harm us."

Gray slid his sword uneasily into its scabbard, the blade grumbling for want of blood. "Why have you brought us here?"

"Joy Wind, the tree woman, said you would aid us." Loogth padded into the mist, his voice drifting back. "Come."

Blunder whined and growled, and Gray stroked his head. "I won't let him harm you."

"We will fight together," Blunder said.

"We will not fight unless we must."

"You are the pack leader. I will obey."

Descending, they paced above the waters' edge. The way grew level and uniform in width, and Gray saw they traveled along an earthen dam. He wished he could see clearly enough to tell how long it was. They followed it only a short distance before returning to sloping, rocky ground.

"It must be as I thought," Vasps said. "Duke Nortallion has constructed the dam between the mountains of the Alopean range."

Tall caves dotted the slope. Loogth led them along a path ending at the mouth of one of these, its floor submerged in the waters of the encroaching lake except on one side, where ran a narrow path. The wolf halted and looked over his shoulder, his eyes baleful in the gloom. "We go in. Not far. You will not need flames to light your way."

They stepped beneath the shadow of the rocks, Gray and Nutmeg leading, Vasps and Dreamer at the back. A blue heron wading in the shallows fled in alarm, crying, "*Away!*" as it flew. Despite Loogth's assurances, the cave soon grew too dark to see, forcing the men to halt. Gray gripped his sword. They were helpless against an attack.

Vasps' voice echoed hollow off the stones "The eyes of men are unlike those of wolves. Unless you wish our horses to lead us, we must have a light."

Loogth's laughter rumbled out of the darkness, a merciless hacking. "Manlings eyes are weaker than I thought. How do you live, who cannot hunt at night? Make your fire, if you must."

A snap sounded and the soft flame of Russ' lighter arose. "Let's do this quick. This thing won't last forever."

The path wound onward until they came to a dry area the lake did not reach. Loogth paused at the water's edge, and Russ lifted his lighter higher; the cave continued beyond its illumination. Rats squeaked and fled from the light.

"Since being imprisoned, the river calls himself Widfroth no more," Loogth said. "Now he is Brythibain, for he is angry. He refused to speak to you unless I brought you here. If he does not like what you say, he will rise and drown you."

"That is bad," Blunder said.

"Is this how you honor truce?" Vasps demanded.

"I risk my own life," Loogth said. "I am a strong swimmer, but I do not know if I can stand against the flood." The wolf lifted his head and howled, his words reverberating against the stones. "*I have done as I said!"*

The lake surged and eddied, slapping the rocks, wetting the men up to their ankles. Hollow eyes and a gaping mouth, ghastly in the dim light, glared from the water. "Where I am ocean, I drown multitudes." A larger wave surged in a long line, slamming against the company, knocking the men off their feet and driving the horses back. Sputtering, Gray clutched Blunder and pushed against the rocks with his legs to avoid being pulled in with the flow. Russ' lighter was extinguished, plunging the cavern into darkness.

"I am Brythibain Everlost!" the lake roared, his voice the thunder of waterfalls. "I am Captured and Unrequited. Men deprive me! I am obstructed from my beloved, the sea! I seek her; I grieve to find her; I boil beneath the sun! Evaporation takes me! I am Brythibain and I hunger for her and her alone. I must move on, I must course! Why do the humans impede me, I who was Lazy and Eddy and Singing and Rushing? What is man that he contains me?"

Gray heard another wave rising. He scrambled backward, deeper into the cave, still holding Blunder. The water slapped against his feet. "Spare us! We are not your foes!" His voice sounded empty in the echoing cave. He steadied himself for the next assault. The current rippled. The sound rose, then died away, leaving the noise of droplets dripping from the grotto walls.

"Is everyone all right?" Gray asked.

"I am here, Gray," the pup in his arms said. To his relief, Vasps, Russ, and the horses also answered.

Brythibain gave a mirthless, watery chuckle. "Humans listen only when they fear me. Which is the one called Gray? Joy Wind said he was important. She said he would give great aid."

"I am," Gray said, "but I don't know what she meant. I've nothing special to offer. Only my own sword."

"They need to hear the tale," Loogth said. "They will not believe the wolves, but they will believe a lake. Tell them, Brythibain."

"Can't they see for themselves?"

"Tell them."

The waters gurgled, an impatient rushing, then calmed once more. "I flow through the Omnifire, giving life to Morlane. But the trees have listened to the words of the duke to their own destruction. He hems me between the arms of the mountains; his metal men stand guard upon the dike, and no animal can withstand them. Because I no longer flow through their land, the trees' minds grow weak and will soon fail altogether. The more foolish they become, the more they drive their own extinction, purging the life-giving animals from beneath their boughs. The beasts have left the woods, many coming here, seeking the sanctuary of my waters: the wild birds, the mice and rats, the raccoons and badgers—all who can survive on insects and fish. When the trees fall asleep for good, the animals may return, but they too will lose the power of speech. Morlane will fall silent. And still, I cannot reach my love, the Great Sea. I shift my waters, hot and cold, creating a mist to blind the duke, but it does no good, and I am helpless to attack him."

"The Red Wolves have nearly despaired," Loogth said. "Many of our brothers and sisters fled east, but I and my pack would not. This land is ours. My people hunted Morlane before humans came to Animonea. Now, we think there is hope. Joy Wind has spoken to the trees. Her spirit is sweet; she speaks of life and beauty. She is like a pack leader—through her strength the whole forest listens. Her words spread from bough to bough. She tells the old oaks the truth, that the duke's words are lies; she makes the hawthorn and the willow remember their sapling youth, when the sun shone and the squirrels and jays romped and flitted among their branches. Morlane has fallen silent, listening to the voice of Joy Wind. The trees no longer speak to the duke, leaving him deaf and blind. If you would overthrow him and destroy the dam, the Red Wolves will fight beside you. Will you do it?"

Brythibain swirled, sending his waves splashing against the rocks. Gray wished he could at least see the lake's face.

"I can speak for myself and for the soldiers of Marshal Dartmallow," Vasps said. "We came to the Wileywood to stop the duke."

A momentary silence fell, finally broken by Russ. "I'm not from around here. I've wanted no part in your wars, but it seems to me this duke is no better than the Nazis, wanting to take what's not his. He starts with trees and rivers and wolves, but sooner or later his kind want to own everybody. So I'm in for now. I'll do what I can."

"What of Gray?" Brythibain demanded. "He is the one. Joy Wind said we could trust him."

Gray set his jaw. "I will decide nothing under the threat of death."

Angry waves slapped against the cave, wetting Gray's feet. When they ceased, Brythibain said. "I will not drown you or your companions in my anger. I will honor your decision."

"A prince does not make a vow lightly," Gray said. "I need a moment to consider. Let me walk outside in the light and think."

"Very well," Brythibain said.

Guided by the distant illumination from the entrance and the lapping of the lake against the shore, Gray stumbled out of the cave and sat down, Blunder beside him.

"What will you do, Gray?" Blunder asked.

Gray wondered that himself. He no longer knew what to believe. Throughout their journey he had thought only of Tana, seeing the talking animals merely as obstacles to finding her, never considering them as beings unto themselves. But was Brythibain's longing for the sea so different from Gray's yearning for his beloved? He had ridden through Animonea as if through a dream, scarcely appreciating its beauty or wonder, and it shamed and surprised him that Joiwend should trust him to help its inhabitants. Did she really believe he could make a difference in this strange war? His heart ached when he thought of her, a tree standing in Morlane. They were friends, but had he truly appreciated her? He had always treated her with courtesy, but she had given him so much more in comfort and counsel. And his other companions—solid Russ Rogers, ferocious Jaunter, even mad Tatters—had he seen them for who they were, or only as a means to reach Tana? Was he cursed to only see the value of what he had after it was gone?

Russ too had tried to give him advice, but Gray had dismissed it. What if he was right? What if Tana wasn't under a spell; what if she really didn't love him? And if she had gone willingly with the duke, could Gray fight against her father? Surely that would be a base betrayal of his love, to seek to wound that which she held dear. The creatures of Animonea were, when all was said, animals, not humans. In En, what man gave a thought to killing a beast?

Yet, the lessons Gray's old Greek tutor, Aristides, had instilled in him were not forgotten. He understood the difference between wise and poor government, whether in the kingship of En or the states of Greece and Rome. A king's duty was to lead and respect his people—to chastise them when necessary, but ultimately to serve them. Animonea, so full of life and joy, was a good country, a noble experiment in the extremes of self-rule. If Duke Nortallion desired its destruction, he was either misguided or a tyrant. But if the latter, how could Tana, who was beauty and truth and nobility itself, so willingly follow him?

Too restless to sit still, the prince walked along the rough slope beside Brythibain. An egret waded around a nearby rock, its head moving back and forth as it peered into the water. "*Fish, fish, fish,*" it whispered.

"It is sad, Gray," Blunder said, giving a low whine. "The animals cannot go into the woods to hunt and play."

"I suppose it is," Gray said.

"It *is*, Gray. It is cruel." Blunder kept his eyes on the egret as he spoke. He dropped into a stalking position, moving forward one slow step at a time. The egret, lost in its searching, seemed not to notice. As the bird drew near the water's edge, Blunder leapt into the lake. The egret veered away, leaving the pup floundering.

"Come back," Gray ordered, uncertain how Brythibain might react to the intrusion.

"*Silly dog!*" the egret taunted, gliding farther away.

Blunder paddled back to shore, and Gray pulled him out. The dog shook himself, splattering water on his master.

"He is fast, Gray," Blunder said, eyes alight with excitement. "I missed him."

Gray laughed. "You were saying you felt sorry for the animals."

"I did? Yes, I remember. It is true. Even the wolves. They are cruel, but skinny. Their ribs stick out. It is not good to be hungry. But I do not want them to eat me."

"Nor I," a voice said.

Gray turned, his hand on his sword hilt. Blunder growled and barked. A man stood above them on the mountain slope, indistinct in the mist.

"Jaunter?" Gray said. His smile faded; this was not his friend. Gray drew his blade.

"One of his relatives. Call me Fetch. See, he loaned me his cloak."

"He is alive?"

"He still lives," Fetch said. "He roams the woods with Master

Tatters. But it is you I came to see."

The man's eerie resemblance to Jaunter chilled Gray. Whatever he was, troll or man, he could not possibly be Jaunter's relation. He was more like a poor forgery. Instead of the Scythian's fierce joy and rough grin, a brooding darkness lay about his sunken eyes; his mouth turned down, a constant scowl.

"How did you know where to find me?"

Fetch grinned. "The friends of Jaunter are dear to me. I have a gift of knowing when I am near you or your companions."

"I do not like him," Blunder growled.

"My dog has good sense," Gray said. "You do well to keep your distance."

Fetch laughed. "The prince does not recognize a well-wisher, but Jaunter told me you love the woman, Tanabel-Tunia. Would you win her?"

"What business is that of yours?"

Fetch drew a glass flask from his cloak. "This is a potion I made from roots and herbs found in Morlane. Give her but a single sip and she will love you forever. I do this on behalf of Jaunter, who once saved my life."

"You are a wizard?"

"I possess some small amount of power. I only ask one favor in return. As I said, I can sense when I am near one of Jaunter's allies, yet I cannot locate Joiwend. My magic informs me she is in danger. Can you tell me where she is? I need to know so I can help her."

Gray studied the man. "So you bring me a bribe?"

Fetch smiled, a hideous grin. "You mistake me, though I admire your caution." He tossed the flask to Gray, who caught it in mid-air. Glancing at it, he recognized it as the one Jaunter always carried.

"You wouldn't want anything to happen to our friend, would you?" Fetch asked. "Let me be of service to her."

"Joiwend is not to be found."

"She is dead?"

"She is not to be found." He glanced at Blunder, hoping he would not speak of her. Apparently, the pup agreed, for he growled again at the stranger.

"I don't know who you really are, but there is nothing for you here," Gray said.

"Then I thank you, Prince of Stallions," Fetch said. "But keep my gift and use it. Then you will know I mean you well."

Gray looked down at the flask. When he looked up again, Fetch was gone, vanished into the mist. Blunder bounded to where he had stood, sniffed the earth, and pointed his nose to the right. "He went that way, Gray. Should I follow him?"

"Let him go." Gray stared into the mist. If not for Blunder and the flask, he might think the man a vision. What was he? Why had he come at this moment? Why was he looking for Joiwend? Could she really be in danger? He thrust the thought away. The creature was surely a liar and a scoundrel, appearing out of nowhere as if he were a portent. He frowned. A portent of what? Doubtless, nothing good.

He studied the flask and opened it, releasing the sweet odor of spring flowers. He replaced the stopper in disgust. He had suspected the duke of using enchantment on Tana, and here was but another form of manipulation. Whatever Fetch's motives, he was as vile as Nortallion.

The thought made him pause. Kings fought wars for many reasons—land, power, sometimes even for justice; but Nortallion would take away not only the republic's freedom, but its intelligence. Bad enough if the Ruheens practiced the crime of slavery; in Animonea they would enslave the inhabitants' minds. Gray's father and old Aristides would never countenance him giving his allegiance to such a ruler. He glanced at Blunder, who watched him in adoration. If Gray went to Ruheen, the pup would want to go with him. He couldn't bear to see those eyes grow dull, that lolling tongue lose its voice. The creatures of Animonea, filled with their idiosyncrasies, were too beautiful and precious to be turned back to unthinking beasts.

Beyond even that, Joiwend had placed her trust in him. She had already chosen her side; Gray could do no less.

He clutched the flask, intending to break it against the rocks, but shoved it into his pocket at the last instant, not knowing why he did so.

They returned to the cave. Another wolf, equally as thin as Loogth, must have brought kindling, for Vasps held a sputtering torch. The flames threw shadows on the walls of the grotto; the acrid smoke rose to the ceiling, whispering, *"Upward."* Blunder sneezed twice.

"I don't know how I can help defeat the duke, but I will do what I can," Gray said.

"You give your word?" Brythibain asked. "You promise to free me?"

"I give my word, the word of the Prince of Stallions of En, to aid you in whatever way possible."

A fluttering arose overhead. A crow landed on a jutting rock near the roof of the cave. "That is good. Good that is. That is helpful. Perhaps, perhaps it will do." His black eyes glistened in the torch-light.

"Quacaw!" Gray exclaimed. "Where did you come from?"

"I came from an egg," Quacaw said. "From an egg I came. The trees spoke, the wolves told me where you are. My murder flocks through the forest, flying everywhere. We find the soldiers. We bring them back to Oldbeard. To Oldbeard we bring them."

"The marshal lives?" Vasps asked.

"We thought him dead. Dead we said he was. That is what we said. Perhaps, perhaps. His wing was wounded. How could he live? He could not live with one wing. Now it heals. It heals so nice. Oldbeard lives. He lives again."

"Praise the fires of the fountain!" Vasps cried, bursting into tears.

Blunder padded over and bounced against the arbiter's leg. "Why are you crying, Vasps? The marshal is our friend. Why are you un-happy?"

"The duke flies back to his nest," Quacaw said. "He takes his soldiers with him. Oldbeard says everyone must come. Everyone must come, he says. Perhaps, perhaps we will break the duke's eggs and eat his young. That is what Oldbeard says. He says it can be so. So it can be, he says. Perhaps, perhaps."

"That is good," Brythibain said. "Raise your army and destroy my enemy! Then you must break the dam and let me flow free to the sea. I will no longer create the mist, so you can travel more quickly. Go now! Go! Make haste!"

"We will try to find a way," Gray said, but even as he spoke, he wondered how they could overcome the duke's iron men.

CHAPTER SIXTEEN

THE FORTRESS

Gray watched Master Thomas Tatters dance with the crows.

Brythibain was lifting the fog, and a shaft of the dawn's light shone on the clearing where the birds hopped along the ground, fluttering their wings while Tatters swept and swirled his cloak as if in flight. He moved in a slow circle, chanting, bobbing up and down, cawing, his worn face suffused with joy, his spirit lost in the dance. He seemed almost a crow himself, a barrel-chested bird arching and strutting, arcing his cloak like a cowl. Quacaw and the other crows cawed in answer, striding and hopping, lifting themselves a foot into the air, turning their heads, mouths open in laughter, their black eyes fixed on the old pioneer, following his steps, weaving about him, one bird turning wide circles around his head, another darting in and out between his legs. So Master Tatters danced with the Comanches; so he must have danced with his Jennie.

Gray gazed in wonder at the beauty of it. Only in the Back of the Beyond could such a sight occur, and it left him breathless.

The dance ended, Tatters fell chuckling to his knees, hands outstretched above his head. He dropped to his stomach and the crows mobbed him, perching on his head and back, squawking their delight, preening his cloak, Quacaw tugging at his turquoise bracelet, seeking to carry it away.

"No, no." Tatters laughed and rolled over. "None of that, old thief! Off, off and away, you rapscallions!"

The crows fluttered into the air. Quacaw landed on a branch above Gray's head. "Tatters is crow-friend. Crow-friend he is. He is friend to the murder. He is half-crow, perhaps, perhaps."

"Perhaps he is." Gray was glad to see the old pioneer, who varied between exaltation and utter despair, in one of his happier moods.

Russ, Vasps, and the Prince of Stallions had reached Dartmallow's camp two days before and found Jaunter and Tatters already there. If the Scythian had been at full strength, rather than ashen-faced and scarcely able to walk from loss of blood, his bone-jarring hug would surely have broken Gray's ribs. Nor had there been time for rest, for within an hour of their arrival the army had set out for Ironwood Station. Along the way, Gray told how Fetch had appeared seeking Joiwend; and Jaunter, struggling to remain on Ransom's back, had grown even more pale. Tatters and the Scythian related their own history with the creature.

"Is he truly a wizard, as he claimed?" Gray had asked.

"Vadispur was his people's shaman," Jaunter said. "His curse wouldn't have worked unless he possessed strong magic. You did well to say nothing about Joiwend."

In telling his story Gray hadn't mentioned the love potion. Jaunter's words made him think it might really be what Vadispur claimed, but he had thrust the idea from his mind, chilled under the morning sun at the thought of a dead man returned to life.

Topper approached Gray, his long face stoic as ever. "The marshal wishes a word."

Gray rose, Blunder at his heels, and followed Topper past a pair of sentries to where Dartmallow and Vasps sat side-by-side on a fallen oak. If the marshal's wound discomfited him, he showed no sign. Despite his setbacks, he appeared confident, even cheerful. Loogth rested on his haunches a few strides away, and Blunder's mother, Sniffdaisy, lay at the marshal's feet, her eyes fixed on the wolf. Here were hereditary enemies, and Gray recalled that the purpose of the dogs' spiked collars was to protect their throats from lupine jaws. Blunder wagged his tail at his mother and growled at Loogth.

"Insolent pup," the wolf snarled back.

Sniffdaisy rose to her feet. "He is mine."

Vasps stroked her back. "Remember the truce, girl."

"Yes, remember, slave of men." Loogth grinned—malicious, superior, taunting. Gray shuddered, wondering just how intelligent he might be. With her wide jaws and powerful frame, Sniffdaisy could match him in both size and strength, but not in cunning.

She growled, her hackles rising. Two other nearby dogs stood, preparing to join in battle.

"None of that!" Dartmallow ordered. "Perhaps you best go else-where."

Sniffdaisy did not look at her master. "I will not."

Dartmallow exchanged glances with Vasps, not without some pride. "No, I don't suppose you will. Behave yourself, then."

"I am being a good dog." She glared at the wolf. "I will watch you."

Loogth hunched one shoulder, as if giving a careless shrug. Imitating his mother, Blunder stood vigilant by Gray's side.

The marshal turned to the Prince of Stallions. "What your people and Joiwend have done creates a quandary. When we first met, you claimed none of your company were sorcerers, yet she has used magic. What do you say to that? Speak well and speak plain. Much depends upon it."

"Soonderkainen was a bard-enchanter," Gray said. "He could raise storms, calm the seas, create light and fire with his hands and his harp. Joiwend isn't anything like him. She can alter her form, but that is all. Perhaps it is magic; perhaps it's something else. She calls it a gift, one she always used wisely."

"Yet her powers are not unlike those of the enchanters of Ruheen," Vasps said.

Gray felt his anger rising. "I know nothing of that, but she has calmed the forest. I don't understand how she did it, but she may have given up her humanity to save your army from destruction."

The marshal chuckled. "And because of it I am looking for any excuse to ignore the laws of Animonea, of which I am a steward and Vasps, a judge." He met Gray's glare. "Four days ago Morlane grew calm, falling into deep reflection, bereaving the duke of its ears and eyes, forcing him to retreat to his fortress. Not only that, but your meeting with Loogth's pack has brought us unexpected allies. We have a chance again. So it is my judgment to overlook

Joiwend's use of magic, and to declare you and your followers' Service of Restitution complete. What do you say, Vasps?"

Vasps Geometer frowned. "It is within your power to end the Service of Restitution, but only the High Court at Ravenperch can decide concerning Joiwend. The matter must rest until such time as they make a ruling."

"Doesn't her sacrifice mean anything to you?" Gray asked.

"Do not misunderstand," Vasps said. "The Rule of Law is the heart of the republic, greater and more precious even than our own lives. Many have died to defend it. Our gratitude to Joiwend cannot supplant that."

"It is the best we can do; it is what we will do," Dartmallow said.

"You speak of laws while Morlane perishes," Loogth said.

"Quite right," the marshal said, "but it needed to be dealt with. Let us turn to other matters. Much of my army has already re-formed, though our numbers are nearly halved. Our greatest obstacle is a lack of supplies, most of which were lost in the battle. With so little game in the Wileywood, we must complete our mission quickly, before hunger drives us out. Thanks to the wolves, we are now within an hour's march of Ironwood Station. I want to see it for myself. We will take a small company. You will go with us, Gray, along with any of your people you choose. I'll need you too, Vasps. Some of Loogth's pack will join us." Clearly, Gray's status had risen in the marshal's eyes.

Dartmallow strode away, Sniffdaisy following close behind. Gray glanced toward Loogth, but the wolf was already gone, vanished into the foliage.

"Have you had breakfast?" Vasps asked.

"Only a bit of dried venison I found in my pocket," Gray said.

"Gray gave me half," Blunder said.

Vasps pointed toward the log where he sat. "There are some edible lichen here."

Gray looked at the growths, long strands like fine hair. Blunder sniffed them.

The lichen shouted in alarm, too softly to make the words clear.

"I can not eat that," the pup said.

"This kind is quite nutritious," Vasps said. "There is another variety that looks similar and is poisonous. Both grow in Morlane."

"You make a persuasive argument," Gray said, "but I'm not that desperate."

Vasps laughed. "I didn't present it in an appealing manner, but we may all be eating things we do not like before leaving the forest. You may find it interesting, however, that because the lichen does not wish to be eaten, as would an egg or a bowl of oatmeal, it is more akin to the case of a deer hunted in the forest. With the deer, the Mandate of Gratitude is given after it is slain, but because the lichen cannot flee, we give the Mandate beforehand as we would with more agreeable foods. A slight, but important distinction."

"Are you going to eat it?" Gray asked.

"I too am not that desperate. We do have a few rations, recovered after the fight." He gave a faint smile. "Besides, there is a small chance I could be mistaken about which kind are poisonous."

Gray and Blunder went to find the others.

"Gray?" the dog asked.

"Yes, Blunder?"

"I do not want you to eat poison."

"Vasps was only joking."

"Oh. I did not know."

"At least, I think he was," Gray muttered.

They soon found their three companions sitting on the ground eating cracked grain out of a sack.

"Have some," Jaunter said.

Gray took a handful. It was dry and tasteless, but he was hungry enough not to care. "At least it's better than lichen."

"Or raw meat," Jaunter said, "but not so filling." Despite being weak, the Scythian was in good spirits. The secret curse he carried had gnawed at him for years. Now free from the nightly hauntings, his eyes shone clear as a boy's.

Gray recounted his discussion with Dartmallow. "I want Russ and Tatters to come along. Jaunter stays. You're still weak."

"I'm yet strong enough to strangle an ox," Jaunter said. He glanced at Loogth's hunting pack, standing aloof at the edge of the camp. "Or a wolf."

"We will need your strength later," Gray said. "Rest now, my friend."

"As you say." His ready agreement told the prince he was not fully recovered.

"You've come up in the world," Russ said, as they walked to their horses. "I'm glad to see it. You deserve some recognition."

"We all have." Inwardly, Gray beamed at Russ' praise. For the first time, he felt himself the true leader of the company. Fox had been much of the problem; it was strange how one person could make such a difference.

Joining with Dartmallow, Topper, Vasps, a score of cavalry, and Sniffdaisy and three other dogs, they traveled toward Ironwood Station. Loogth's wolves kept to the fringes of the company, and fearing for Blunder's safety, Gray ordered the pup to remain close. Tatters drifted ahead and could sometimes be seen riding with the wolves, talking to them like schoolmates. They did not encounter any of the enemy, and within the hour Loogth reported they were nearing their destination.

"The horses will remain here," the marshal said.

"With the wolves?" Nutmeg rumbled, eyes wide. The steeds had been nervous throughout the ride.

"We have a truce," Dartmallow said.

"They do not have a truce with us," Dreamer said. "They look lean and hungry."

"I will protect you, small one," Flapjack said.

"Six of the men and two of the dogs will stay with you," Dartmallow said.

"Keep together and you will be safe," Vasps suggested. "The wolves have given their word."

"Wolf words!" Nutmeg blew in disgust. Gray suspected she would have spat on the ground if she could.

They left the horses, and Loogth drew near the men. Sniffdaisy kept herself between him and her master. Blunder drifted close to Gray's legs.

"Because we are clever, our prey fears us," Loogth growled. "We mislead in our hunts, but we do not lie. We do not break truce."

"We know that," Vasps said. But Gray wondered about the wolf's distinction between deception and lying. Perhaps they were little different than humans in that way.

Loogth vanished, but soon returned with Master Tatters.

"Tread softly now," the old pioneer warned. "The fortress is just over yonder rise, and there are sentries."

"Listen to him," Loogth added. "He is not clumsy like the rest of you. He walks silent as one of us."

The marshal raised his hand and the men halted. He spoke softly. "Topper, Vasps, Gray's people—with me. The rest wait here."

"I want to go," Blunder said.

"You mustn't bark or growl," Gray said.

"I will be quiet as sleeping. I will be quiet as a cat, but prettier."

"I envy your self-esteem," Vasps said.

As they approached the rise, Tatters dropped to the ground and climbed on hands and knees to its crest. He surveyed the area and beckoned the men to follow. Gray crawled up beside him and suppressed an exclamation. Dartmallow exhaled a shocked breath.

In a wide clearing stood a vast fortress, built of huge blocks of black granite, a citadel alive with watchfulness. Every massive stone looked out upon the land with etched eyes of swirled gray. Other eyes looked down from the ramparts above its iron gates. The duke's banner, a white whirlwind on a background of blue, sang his name as it wafted on the heights. Vigili surrounded it, stationed in groups outside its walls.

"How could they construct something of this magnitude?" Vasps whispered.

"The forest allowed it," Loogth said. "In summers past, lightning lit a fire that burned this part of Morlane, so no living trees had to be cleared. We watched them build it. It did not take long."

"But those walls, how did they make them?" Uncustomary despair tinged the marshal's voice. "We can never hope to storm such ramparts."

"Are your men cowards?" Loogth asked. "The pack is not afraid."

"Even if the Vigili weren't protecting it, a direct assault is impossible," Dartmallow said. "I told you we can't maintain a long siege without more supplies."

"It was difficult convincing the All-Council to authorize our incursion," Vasps said. "If we return in failure, there will be more delays, more time for the duke to reinforce his position."

"What good is it to make truce with humans if they lack courage?" Loogth asked. "What of you, Gray Darien? The Joy Wind said you could help."

Gray bit his lip. His Greek mentor had taught him the principles of siege warfare, but he had never experienced it. By any standard, the fortress appeared impregnable, yet something was wrong. Loogth said Ironwood Station had been built quickly, but its massive blocks must have been carried from a stone quarry, dragged through the forest, and shaped, a task requiring hundreds of hours and laborers.

Awareness dawned on him. "Blunder, when you look at the fortress what do you see?"

"There are not-men around it."

"Yes, but what else? Describe it. How tall is it?"

"It is taller than you, Gray," Blunder said. "It is made of wood."

Vasps chuckled. "Of course. An illusion. We should have guessed."

As if a veil had fallen from their eyes, the massive citadel vanished, leaving a fort of rough-hewn timber, its walls little more than twice a man's height. Instead of a majestic banner, a single flag flew atop a slender pole.

"Having seen its construction, the wolves could not be fooled," Vasps said.

Gray ruffled Blunder's head. "Nor were you. Good boy!" The pup wagged his tail and happily licked Gray's fingers. Gray wondered if it was the dog's simplicity that kept him from being deceived, or something in the way his eyes worked. Whatever the case, the duke's illusions could not stand once the duplicity was known.

"You're supposed to be my wise counselor, Vasps, but this young prince was leagues ahead of us both," Dartmallow said.

Vasps bowed at the neck, nonplussed. "My deepest apologies, Marshal."

But Dartmallow gave him an uncustomary grin. "Now we have a fighting chance."

"You are no longer frightened?" Loogth asked.

"We are not, but there is still the question of the iron warriors."

The company fell silent. Studying the identical, implacable faces of the Vigili, Gray nearly lost hope. No ordinary soldier could defeat one of them.

"It's like facing an armored division," Russ said. "How do they control them? I worked in communications in the war. We followed

General Patton's tanks for awhile. The duke has to have some way to coordinate them."

"I do not know this general you speak of, but your words make me think of the army elephants I saw in my native India as a child," Vasps said. "They are intelligent animals, but willful. They must be made to respond to specific commands, both individually and as a group."

"If we knew those commands, we could control them ourselves," Gray said.

"Notice that there is at least one human for approximately every twenty Vigili," Vasps said. "They are surely directing the creatures."

"Two for each," Tatters corrected. "A commander and a bugler. When I scouted for the U.S. cavalry, they used bugle calls to signal. We heard horns sounding the night these varmints ambushed us."

"I want to capture a commander, a bugler, and one of the Vigili," Dartmallow said. "We will win that prize; we will win this war."

* * *

Before dawn of the next morning the marshal's preparations were complete. A short distance into the treeline surrounding Ironwood Station, scores of deep pits had been dug and camouflaged with vegetation. The archers were in place, positioned behind the protection of the trees. Quacaw and his crows fluttered among the branches, but kept silent to avoid alerting their enemies to their presence. The wolves lurked nearby, their coats blending into the forest floor; the horses stayed at the rear. The forest remained quiescent.

The main body of the Animonean army had been brought within two furlongs of Ironwood Station, but only a small company, intended to give the impression of an harassing force, waited near the duke's stronghold. In any ordinary country, Nortallion would have cut down the trees within bowshot, but because the Wileywood had not allowed it, the Animoneans could utilize the protection of the foliage. The archers numbered less than twenty, Gray and the others, twenty more. Ropes had been salvaged from the Animonean supplies, and Russ had spent an hour teaching the men to use what he called a *lariat*. Gray had taken to it easily and found roping a delightful skill. Previously experienced, Master Tatters was adept enough to leap and dance through the spinning hoops he created. The other soldiers showed varying degrees of adroitness, and Russ had chosen five of the best.

At Dartmallow's signal, the archers released their shafts. Gray heard the twang of the bows and watched the arrows arc high into the cloudless sky, singing, *"Up, up!"* and then, *"Down, down!"* as they descended. They fell among the nearest Vigili, screaming, *"Strike!"* but bounced off their impenetrable shells, broken and defeated. The archers were instructed not to aim for the human overseers, and the shafts fell all around the nearest of these, while the commander and his bugler crouched behind their shields.

Dartmallow signaled again, and the archers left the safety of the trees and moved into the clearing to release another volley. Again, the arrows sang their death-song, this time falling beyond the Vigili, a few clattering against the palisade wall, most landing vainly in the ground. The enemy archers gave their reply, and Gray held his breath. Ordinary arrow assaults were terrifying. These—shrieking their eagerness to kill—were worse; but the Animonean archers stood their ground while the shafts, bitterly bewailing their failure, fell several spans short.

His cloak billowing around him, Master Tatters leapt from behind an oak and plunged forward as if preparing to lead a charge, shouting and shrieking, pumping the air with his fists. Reaching the front of the line, he bounded up and down, waving his arms, yelling in what was surely the Comanche language. But his purpose was to tempt rather than to command. He seemed to rush forward, raising his legs in high steps, but sliding his feet backward, creating an illusion of motion. The men too raised and lowered their feet as if marching, all the while maintaining their places.

Now we will see what they do, Gray thought.

From within the palisade, a single horn sounded a series of notes, answered at once by a shouted order from the enemy commander closest to Dartmallow's soldiers. In response, the score of Vigili under his command marched toward the archers.

"Hold your ground," Master Tatters told them. "Fire again at the loathly creatures."

The eager arrows took flight, only to splinter on iron skin. The return volley fell short once more.

"Stay, lads!" Tatters ordered. "We've time yet."

Gray gritted his teeth. He could see the expressionless faces, hear the creaking of metal limbs. The old pioneer was playing it close, his back to his foes, not turning his head to watch their approach, judging by sound alone. The enemy commander and his bugler trailed far behind the warriors. Perhaps too far. The plan would fail unless they followed their servants into the woods.

The Vigili marched on, raising their swords mere strides from where Tatters stood. He gestured madly and the archers took flight while he leapt after them, leaving a blade whiffling through the air where his head had been. He ran as if panicked, stumbling, shouting, limping. The archers too fled as if overcome with terror, putting distance between themselves and the enemy.

Once within the sheltering trees, the bowmen broke along paths marked by lines of stones, scrambling to get out of the way. No sooner had the Vigili entered the forest than the Animoneans began screaming, imitating men dying in combat. Gray watched, keeping an eye on the bugler and the commander. Hearing the noise, thinking their Vigili were causing utter panic, both men hurried toward the treeline.

The first Vigili reached one of the concealed pits and went crashing in. Others, unable to halt their momentum, followed after. Almost a dozen went down before those remaining began circumventing the traps. Crows streamed around the survivors, confusing their vision while the wolves attacked, striking with their forepaws from behind, pushing more of the Vigili into the pits. Less than a handful of the metal men made it past the obstructions.

Dartmallow shouted a command, and Gray twirled his lariat and cast it at a Vigili. To his delight, it dropped neatly over the creature's head. He pulled hard, tightening the rope before it fell past its arms, catching it when its sword hand was at the bottom of a downward stroke. It struggled against the bond, but three soldiers seized the rope, using their combined strength to pull it off its feet. Planting a pole between its thighs, one of the men used it as a lever against the creature's sword, pushing downward against its blade, tearing the weapon from its grasp. Two other soldiers bound its legs with more ropes.

"I must attack," the Vigili said, struggling against its bonds. Four men took hold of it and trotted away, carrying its heavy frame back to the main camp.

Gray glanced around. The remaining Vigili were vainly trying to climb out of the pits, the rock and earth crumbling beneath their weight.

The Ruheen commander and his bugler burst into the woods. Gaping at his defeated Vigili, the commander turned to run, pulling the bugler with him. A pair of wolves blocked their path.

Crows dove down, flying in the bugler's face, snatching the horn from his hand; but it was too heavy for them to carry and fell to the earth. More soldiers and wolves closed on the pair.

Seeing himself surrounded, the commander plunged his sword into his own throat. The bugler, eyes wide with terror, drew a knife to take his own life, but Master Tatters leapt upon him, knocking the blade from his hand and pinning him to the ground.

"Well done!" Dartmallow said. "I wanted them both, but the bugler will have to do. Tie him up, Topper. I wish we had time to fill in these pits, to see if a few pounds of dirt can stop the things from climbing out. They'd forget their purpose soon enough, I wager, and sleep like rocks in the ground. But never mind that."

Quacaw flapped down. "We took the shiny horn. The shiny horn we stole. It was taken by us. It is ours, but Tatters has it. Can I have it, perhaps, perhaps?"

Dartmallow gave a rough grin. "You can't even lift it, Quacaw."

"It shines in the sun. The sun shines out of it. It is nice. Nice is it."

"Do not try to steal the horn. Our plan fails without it."

"Perhaps, perhaps after?"

"When we drive the duke from Morlane, I'll have it chopped up, and you can split it among your murder."

"The leader should get the most," Quacaw said. "That is fair. Is it not fair? Fair it is."

"You'll have to defend that decision yourself, my friend. I haven't time to do it for you. Where's Topper? We need the bydord."

Following a Mandate of Gratitude, a bydord horn had been previously cut to pieces to fool the duke into believing someone had destroyed the Ruheen bugle with an axe. The metal looked similar, and only enough fragments were left scattered beside the dead commander to identify it as a musical instrument. So Dartmallow hoped to prevent the duke from retraining the Vigili to respond to different signals. That and speed were his best allies; they would need to assault Ironwood Station that very day.

The marshal's eyes fell on Gray. "Come with me. We've only a moment, but I want to see."

Gray and Blunder fell in beside Dartmallow, who brought them to the treeline. The rest of the duke's forces remained in place around Ironwood Station, unaware of their compatriots' defeat.

"They're in for a surprise," Dartmallow said. "They think their mechanical monsters invincible. Eventually, they'll come out and discover how wrong they are; they'll know for the first time that we can stop them."

"They won't be deceived by the trick of the pits again," Gray said.

"Perhaps they won't, but perhaps they will. The Vigili can scarcely think. Do you know why we're going to win?"

"Because we are good dogs," Blunder said.

"That doesn't hurt, but it's more complicated," Dartmallow said. "The duke came here and lied to the forest. Because of it, he's driven away everyone who could be his allies. He's isolated himself. He thinks he holds a fort; he actually owns a prison. We won today because we are united in our purpose. The duke scorns the foolish greed of the crows, the haughty independence of the wolves, the dashing inconstancy of the horses, the pondering deliberation of the trees." Dartmallow bent to pat Blunder's head. "He disdains this pup's fierce loyalty. But we are the Republic of Everything and it makes us strong. We fumble and bumble; with our hundreds of voices we disagree; but so long as the hearts of its inhabitants are good, so long as we choose what is wise and reject what is evil, we will prevail. I tell you this because I want you to understand us."

"In my country of En, my father and his noblemen reign," Gray said. "It is a good land, where my sire tries to rule wisely, but I've known wicked kings. Your republic gives me much to consider."

"Good," Dartmallow said. "You will grow from it."

"Why did the commander kill himself?"

"Part of it was to keep the duke's secrets, I suppose, but the people of Ruheen are taught that talking animals are an abomination to their gods. They tell their soldiers the beasts will torture them if they are taken prisoner, each according to its own ways. But animals never intentionally torture anything. A cat playing with a mouse does so only because that is her hunting nature. Only humans use torture, and the laws of the Omnifire, passed down from those who have entered its flames, forbid the people of Animonea from doing so."

"If you defeat the duke, what will become of him?" Gray asked.

"If he is taken prisoner, the All-Council will decide. Perhaps he will be returned to his people, perhaps he will be imprisoned or executed. That isn't my decision."

"Tanabel-Tunia may be inside the fortress."

"She is said to be the duke's daughter."

"How do you know that?" Gray asked, surprised.

"A little bird told me. One of the crows, actually. It's difficult to keep secrets when everything is listening. You're wondering what her fate will be once we take the fortress. If she is an enchantress, she can remain in Animonea only if she renounces her magic, but unless she commits some act against the Republic, I would hold her blameless. The All-Council will accept my judgment on this, I think; but I cannot guarantee her safety in the midst of a battle."

They hurried away, Gray considering Dartmallow's words and longing for Tana, hidden behind the fortress walls.

CHAPTER SEVENTEEN

BEFORE THE WALLS

When the company returned to camp, Vasps Geometer was given charge of the captured bugler and his horn. The arbiter sent the prisoner to an isolated part of the camp, then called Gray to him. "I believe you can be useful when I question that man."

"In what way?"

"That we will see. I have an idea."

"I will go too," Blunder said.

"I am sorry, little friend, but you must stay," Vasps said. "This fellow may find a talking dog disconcerting."

"I do not know what dis-con-ing means. I want to go. I will not talk."

Gray knelt and patted Blunder's head. "I need you to stay."

Blunder whined, turned a circle, and lay down on his front paws. "I will stay."

When they reached the prisoner, he had been stripped of his upper armor down to his blue tunic and made to sit on the ground. Two soldiers stood guard on either side of him. Like most Ruheens, he was shorter and lighter in color than the bronze-skinned Animoneans.

"You look uncomfortable," Vasps said. "See if you can find something for this fellow to sit on."

One of the soldiers brought a log and ordered the prisoner to sit.

"Is that better?" Vasps asked.

The man spat on the ground at the arbiter's feet.

"I see we are off to a wonderful beginning," Vasps said.

The man spat again, a stream that landed on Vasps' boot. "*Defend*!" the boot cried.

The arbiter looked at his foot and shrugged. "My name is Vasps Geometer. This is Gray Darien, Prince of Stallions from the land of En. He is one of our allies."

Gray kept silent, uncertain of Vasps' intent.

When the Ruheen remained mute, Vasps said. "I doubt one of Duke Nortallion's warriors fears to tell us his name."

"I am Geel. Do your worst. I am prepared to die for my duke."

"We have no worst, regardless of what you have heard," Vasps said. "We have a disagreement with your lord, that is all. We wish your people to return to Ruheen and respect our borders."

"Your country is a land of demons," Geel said. "Talking trees! Scheming wolves! Abominations! The gods will put an end to you."

"But they have not yet done so, which we take as a reassuring sign. We desire only peace. And many, such as Prince Darien, do not find fault with us. Are we less virtuous than your enchanters, who ally themselves with the Vigili?"

Geel's face clouded, but he said nothing.

"What city are you from?" Vasps asked. "Ganton? Lazdee?"

"Kholotara."

"The White City. I have never been, but I have heard tales of its twelve temples, its marble statues, its singing fountains. Perhaps if there is someday peace between Ruheen and Animonea, I could go see it."

Vasps spoke then of other places in the bugler's land, the great granite busts overlooking the wide harbor of Olf, the golden fields of grain stretching across the Plain of Jetoch, the thousands of butterflies covering the trees in spring in the Witalowin Forest of Setch. Gray noticed he avoided asking Geel questions about his country, lest he seem to be seeking information.

"How do you know all this?" Geel asked.

"From the migrating birds of Animonea. They cross your land and soon lose the power of speech, but they do not forget their instincts, and when they return to our country, those wise enough to be articulate tell us much."

"Spies!"

Vasps smiled. "Travelers. They remember no military secrets — they understand neither your armies' numbers and formations nor your weapons of war."

Then the arbiter spoke of Animonea, the myriad hawks thronging the hills in spring, the herds of horned antelope dotting the veldts of the south, the wild laughter of the dolphins surrounding Gelebar Reef. "Our cities are small, but our inhabitants many, and when the late rains come, you can stand on the tors of Roost Haven and hear the chanting of the stalks of grain, the sweet piping of the cardinals, the violin laughter of the evening crickets. There is nothing like it in all the worlds."

Geel curled his lip in disdain. "What is that to me?"

"I wanted to show you that there is beauty in both Ruheen and Animonea. Our countries have their faults, but each can be looked on with favor. You spoke of abomination. To us, the Vigili are an abomination, possessing a semblance of life, but made slaves to a single purpose. To defeat them, we need to know how you control them: the voice commands, the bugle calls."

"You would have me betray my duke."

"Perhaps, but not your city of Kholotara." Vasps drew a heavy sack from behind a tree.

"*Open me and see!*" the sack entreated. Vasps did so, revealing gold ingots. "There is enough here to make you a wealthy man."

Geel stared at the gold. "The duke would know."

"He would not. I have not yet questioned your bugle. It knows the commands and will soon tell us, anyway, but you can be more exact. If you help us, you can remain with us until the duke departs. In a few weeks, you could return to Ruheen a wealthy man. Or stay forever, should you decide our country is not as abominable as you suppose."

Geel looked at the sack and wet his lips. "The commanders order the Vigili directly when they are within earshot. The bugle calls are used when they are farther away."

Vasps nodded, smiling encouragement.

The Ruheen horn was brought. "*Play me,*" it begged, its voice a breathy whisper. Geel taught the bugle commands to two of Dartmallow's bydord players.

As Vasps and Gray walked away, the prince asked, "Why did you want me there?"

"A bit of theater. The idea of a foreign monarch allying himself with us disquieted him. Your presence suggested nations willing to accept Animonea's existence."

"Will you really give him the gold and let him live in the Back of the Beyond? He's a traitor to his own people."

"I gave him my word. He is unscrupulous, but not as much as you suppose. Ruheen's city-states form a loose affiliation without a national identity. They often war with one another. Even the name *Ruheen* simply means *The Land* in their language. Geel's loyalty is to his family and his city. The twelve gods they worship are portrayed with all the human faults. Bribery is a way of life, and alliances can shift in a moment.

"Every country, your land of En included, is shaped by the beliefs of its people. Those beliefs matter. The Omnifire has given us few laws, but they are engraved on the hearts of our inhabitants—or at least the human ones: loyalty, honesty, respect for one another. We love our little republic. Most of us would die for it. Geel's code is far different. Now let us go see what can be learned from the captured Vigili."

The iron warrior was tied standing upright to a tree. "Attack," it repeated over and over, the last command it was given. Russ and Jaunter had pried off one of its arms.

Vasps spoke a word of command and the Vigili ceased its struggles. The arbiter grinned. "Geel spoke the truth. Now we have knowledge we can use."

Russ held up the disconnected arm. "We've been looking for weaknesses. There aren't many, but if you look at the shoulder, leg, neck, and knee joints, whoever built it used wood and rubber in the gears, probably for flexibility. A solid hammer blow should shatter them."

"Vigili, do you hear me?" Vasps asked.

"I hear."

"Your master controls you. You obey his will. Have you any desire for freedom?"

The Vigili kept silent for several moments. "I . . . would like that. But I must obey."

"Why?"

"Because . . . I must."

"What would you do if you were free?"

"I would . . . be."

Vasps shook his head. "How is this possible? Everything in Animonea follows its own course. Even bowls and plates sometimes refuse to be of service. To design the Vigili without free choice—their creator is surely a genius. When there is time, I would like to perform geometric calculations on this creature's proportions. They might illuminate the matter. A shame such art is practiced for evil when it could do much good."

"Genius or not, it's only another form of slavery," Russ said.

Looking at the iron face of the Vigili, Gray weighed Russ' words.

* * *

The Prince of Stallions lowered his spyglass. It was the afternoon of the same day, and the army was ready, its preparations done with remarkable speed. Its eyes—Quacaw and his murder—were scattered among the trees surrounding Ironwood Station; the wolves roamed amid the infantry; the archers stood along the treeline, every arrow aimed at the commanders and buglers directing the Vigili. The bulk of the infantry and cavalry were stationed in the woods close to the sides of the palisade. Hidden by the forest, the marshal's men had dug more deep pits covered with dead limbs and vegetation. The trumpeters stood together, one holding the precious horn taken from the Ruheens. Their usual instruments, the bydords, had failed to command the captured Vigili, and there was neither time nor materials to fashion others.

Gray, Russ, and Dartmallow had conceived the plan together. Accompanied by Jaunter and Master Tatters, Gray commanded the left cavalry expedition, a group of less than thirty men, but crucial to its execution, while Topper led its counterpart on the right. Looking across the clearing at the rows of Vigili surrounding the palisade, the prince's stomach tightened. He told himself it was always so before combat—the anxiety, the fear, the suspension of thought, the marshaling of courage—but the cruel faces of their inhuman foes filled him with dread. He tried not to think about the unstoppable way they had marched through the Animonean lines before. He gripped his sword and stroked Nutmeg's neck. She blew but said nothing. The Scythian, stronger than the day before but still pale, had insisted on joining the battle, and he gave the prince a fierce grin. Blunder and Sniffdaisy kept close, ears up and alert. Gray had wanted the pup to stay safely in camp, but for the first time Blunder had refused his orders, and Sniffdaisy had agreed, both insisting the pack must fight together. There were codes among canines Gray had yet to understand.

Dartmallow gave the order and the men sounded their bydords. The archers released their shafts, the twang of their bowstrings a low hum, the arrows thrilling through the air, joyful in flight, keen for their targets. Gray watched the missiles fall among their foes, most bouncing harmlessly off the Vigili or plunging into the ground, but a few reached the commanders and buglers, and cries of pain rolled across the clearing.

In response to the earlier attack, Duke Nortallion had armed a score of the Vigili with bows, and their return fire, propelled by their iron limbs, reached all the way to the treeline. The Animonean archers had already stepped behind the protection of the boles, but a dozen shafts embedded themselves in the trunks, and though the trees shuddered, they did not break their silence.

Dartmallow's archers released two more volleys. Gray raised the spyglass to his eye. Several of the commanders and buglers were down. So far, the plan was working. He glanced back at the trumpeters. At Dartmallow's sign, one of them blew the captured horn. Everything depended on how the Vigili responded. If the duke had taught them new signals, the attack would fail.

For a moment nothing happened. Then the Vigili marched forward, moving straight ahead, holding their weapons flat against their sides. Through the spyglass Gray watched one of the surviving commanders. The officer looked around, confused by the bugle call. After some hesitation, he rushed toward his Vigili to order them back, but before he could reach them, an arrow took him in the throat. From positions high in the trees, the marshal's best archers placed careful shots.

Confusion momentarily reigned among the duke's forces. Counter signals arose, halting the Vigili. Dartmallow's bugler sounded again, ordering them forward. Tests on the captured Vigili had shown that spoken commands superseded the horns, and some remained motionless, but more than half continued toward the treeline.

The Animonean infantry facing the palisade gates marched out of the woods, a feint intended to draw fire, their shields held high to fend off the arrows.

"Get ready," Gray told Nutmeg. His pulse thrummed in his neck.

The bydords blared the command. With neither word nor cry, under the archers' covering fire, Gray's men charged from beneath the protection of the trees. Across the distance, Topper's company also broke into the open, both groups aiming for points where the Vigili had been lured away, leaving the Ruheen lines thin.

Only speed and the element of surprise could serve Gray's advance. Crossing the field filled him with a terrifying ecstasy, his senses heightened by the danger. He heard the thunder of hooves, the creak of armor, the growling of men; smelled the scent of dust and horse sweat. Lacking a saddle, he wrapped his legs around Nutmeg's withers, clutching her mane with one hand, maintaining his balance with his sword-arm. Blunder ran beside him, his body stretched long to cover the ground. To Gray's other side raced Loogth, lean and majestic.

They approached a formation of marching Vigili, whose commander and bugler lay dead. There was no time to avoid them, and just enough room between their lines for a horse to pass. Gray led straight ahead, taking a gasping breath as Nutmeg plunged into their midst, depending on the commands of the horns to keep the iron warriors moving mindlessly forward. He saw, with incredible clarity, their unwinking eyes, their identical noses, the uniform clefts of their chins. Not all were made of metal, but of fired clay and even white marble. If they simply raised their swords, they would butcher both horses and riders.

The Vigili did not turn their heads nor lift their blades. They marched, eyes forward, ignoring the passing foes. Gray heard himself laughing.

As he passed the last of them, the horse directly behind him stumbled, crashing into the Vigili ranks, knocking two of them down. The horse screamed; the rider went flying. Gray dared not look back to see how it ended.

They were behind the lines of Vigili, aiming toward the commanders. The enemy archers had targeted the infantry at first, but now arrows fell among Gray's company. A rider went down to his left. Struck in the breast, a horse tumbled to the earth.

The first of the commanders was before them, shouting orders to his Vigili, who turned to meet the charge. Wielding his bow, Jaunter fired arrow after arrow with almost inhuman rapidity, riddling the man's body, striking his face and the soft places between his armor. With a shout, Gray veered away from the Vigili, leaving them helplessly pursuing.

The cavalry tore in front of the palisade, targeting buglers and commanders, ignoring or avoiding the Vigili. Gray saw Loogth spring on a bugler, his teeth to his throat, ripping him open with the weight of his body. Without pausing, the wolf clenched the horn between his teeth and loped back toward the forest.

Some of the commanders, seeing their deaths before them, panicked and fled toward the palisade. Astride Jingles, Master Tatters ran a pair of officers down, his voice raised in a Comanche battle song.

Every commander on this side of the palisade had fallen, and the only notes which rang out were from the captured horn. Gray turned Nutmeg's head, seeking the fastest escape route, a path straight from the gates. Almost all the Vigili heeded the bugle calls now, and were tramping in every direction. Gray's cavalry passed groups of them shambling toward the treeline. Dartmallow's infantry had retreated into the forest, and when at last Nutmeg passed beneath the sheltering branches, Gray saw them, along with Russ, forcing the Vigili into the pits. A wave of exultation ran through him.

The Prince of Stallions ordered a halt and surveyed his followers. They had lost nearly half their men and horses, but Jaunter and Master Tatters were unharmed. The Scythian laughed, eyes wild with excitement. "*Tabitha*! That was a ride!"

"The bards will sing of it," Tatters said. "I thought we were done for, riding between those iron rascals!"

Gray laughed too, inflamed by their success. Remembering Blunder, he looked around, and his mirth died. The dog was nowhere to be seen. The prince searched the battlefield, hoping to see him trotting across the clearing, but it was difficult to tell anything through the dust and chaos. The other cavalry wing rode in, led by Topper, but Gray spied no sign of his friend.

He forced his mind back to his duty. The horses were covered in sweat and foaming at the mouth, too excited to speak. Three or four were riderless, their owners left wounded or dead on the battlefield. He ordered his men to dismount, to walk and rest the animals before the next phase.

From the flanks, the bydords sounded, and the main body of the Animonean infantry marched in from both sides of the palisade. In response, the gates of the keep flew wide.

Gray whooped. They had forced the duke into leaving his fortress to prevent his precious Vigili from being drawn away. Here was the moment. With his superior numbers, Dartmallow could win the field.

More horns sounded. Gray recognized the marching call. Apparently, the wolves had taken a number of the bugles. But new Ruheen commanders were rushing out of the palisade onto the field, accompanied by Vigili reserves.

The Animonean infantry poured toward the gates. More arrows flew from both sides, and the screams of the dead and dying filled the air. The struggle became a writhing mass. If the infantry could push through the gates, the duke would be lost. Gray raised his spyglass, but the field was covered with a haze of dust which kept forming into faces, leaving nothing clear.

"Hello, Gray," a garbled voice said behind him. Blunder stood there, a horn clenched between his teeth.

"Blunder!" Gray took the horn from his mouth and knelt, running his hands over the dog's flanks, feeling his rolling panting.

"I saw a man drop the horn, so I took it, but you had roded away. Do you like it, Gray? Do you like it?"

Gray choked, unable to reply. He cleared his throat and ordered a soldier to take the horn to a bugler. His hand still on Blunder's head, he turned back to the battle.

"What is that new horn sound, Gray?" Blunder asked. "I have not hearded it before. It is screechy."

"What horn?" Gray raised his spyglass to his eye. Amid the cacophony of battle, he wondered how the dog could pick out a single instrument. Through the glass, he saw the Vigili emerging from the dust clouds. One by one they turned, swinging their swords to clear their way, abandoning the battle, moving south.

Surprised exclamations sounded all around. The Vigili who had marched into the forest but not fallen into the pits also turned south, beating the air with their blades.

"What in tarnation is going on?" Tatters asked.

A bugler sounded the horn Blunder had captured, but the Vigili did not respond.

"This way!" Gray took Nutmeg by the mane, leading her and his men out of the path of the Vigili leaving the timber. Once safe, he used the spyglass again. The Vigili on the battlefield were cutting a swath through both armies, throwing everyone into confusion.

Gray became aware of a low, three-note tone coming from the direction the Vigili were headed, the signal Blunder had heard. Searching with his glass he saw an extraordinary man, long-faced and long-bodied, driving a tall coach drawn by twelve Vigili built with short legs for rapid movement and wide feet for traction. So narrow was the vehicle, it could pass easily between the trees. Curved panels like those in Greek chariots surrounded the coach-box, and the man, dressed in dark armor, an ash-gray cloak billowing behind him, his face a sigil of fury, rose from his seat, gripping the reins and urging his Vigili onward. At his back a soldier stood playing a large, oddly-shaped brass horn, a siren call for the iron warriors.

The entire Vigili army soon reached the edge of the battleground, where they turned, forming ranks, three hundred killing machines no longer under the command of either Dartmallow or Duke Nortallion. The Animoneans, thrown into retreat, took positions facing them across the field. Nortallion's men fled into Ironwood Station, closing the gates behind them.

Gray stood stunned. Their plan had been perfect, the execution, flawless. The battle was over and neither the marshal nor the duke had won. And if this new foe ordered the Vigili to attack, how could they hold against them?

CHAPTER EIGHTEEN

ENVOYS

A silence fell across the battlefield. Using a spyglass, Fox Lodan peered through an arrow-slit at the man riding the coach. The stranger descended from the vehicle, a peculiar figure with mottled skin that made him appear charred, like a burnt cinder in the shape of a man. Taking long strides, he hurried to the front of the Vigili ranks, accompanied by two human servants bearing a cumbersome instrument, a cross between a brass horn and a bellows. He spoke through a dangling nozzle, and the device amplified his voice, sending it booming across the field.

"*I* . . . am Tregor Rathus Nethodian Dumaud, the Sculptor of Treg Keep. My genius designed these carvings; my thoughts steered their making; my servants cast their molds; my hands approved and applauded each step of their construction. Magnificent as they are, they are the most trivial works of my high art. You—with your implausible politics and pathetic machinations—have used them as your toys. Because I am benevolent, I, who care nothing for your inconsequential wars, allowed it. But you have deceived Treg, with whom none dare trifle. Did you believe I could not control my own creations? You will send me representatives; you will make amends. Otherwise my Vigili will shatter your matchstick fortress, trampling the soldiers of both your armies into the earth. I am Tregor Rathus Nethodian Dumaud, and I have spoken."

With all eyes upon him, Treg stalked back to his coach.

Fox turned to Duke Nortallion. "The man hasn't any lack of

bluster. Who is he?"

The duke's face was livid. "That copper-coin mountebank! That insolent dauber! He's finally gone completely mad! How dare he interfere with me!" He fell into glowering silence, and when he spoke again, his voice held a deadly calm. "I shouldn't be surprised. Genius? An itinerant trifler of gyroscopes and geegaws, an egotistic blacksmith. I'll have him flayed alive. What did he say about deception? I've done more than enough to stroke his vanity, even visited him thrice and listened to his ravings."

The duke scowled and clapped his hands together, summoning a subordinate. "Rendan saw him last. I want the captain in my chambers."

Fox followed Nortallion down a ladder and across the grounds. He had been dismayed at his first sight of the fort's wooden buildings and timbered walls. Having occupied Morlane for years, the Ruheens should have constructed a proper stone fortification, but this was no ordinary country; nothing in the Wileywood was easy.

By the time they reached the house serving as the duke's headquarters, Captain Rendan was already there. To Fox's surprise, Tanabel-Tunia had come as well. The captain rose from his chair and bowed at the waist. Tana remained seated, her face unusually pale. Furniture and objects raised small voices, begging to be employed.

"Do you know anything about this, Captain? Can you illuminate it for me?" the duke asked.

Rendan looked his master in the face. "The fault is mine, Your Grace." In a few clipped words he told of Ninette's escape from Treg Keep.

The duke's eyes smoldered. "You have betrayed me!" The furnishings fell silent, startled by his anger.

"I am the one to blame," Tana said. "Chel didn't know."

"Duchess, you promised to let me deal with this," Rendan said.

"But you've mentioned nothing of my part, and I cannot be silent. Father, the plan was mine. We were on the road before the captain discovered her presence."

The duke paced back and forth, looking first at his daughter, then at Rendan. "Why would you risk everything for this woman? Who is she that you would bring ruin to a decade of planning? When you found she was there, why didn't you send her back? What is one more slave?"

Tana burst into tears. "I persuaded the captain to let her stay! I didn't know Treg would pursue her! I swear it! He's so strange a creature; I never thought he would come this far!"

If his daughter's tears moved Nortallion, Fox could not detect it.

"I should have you both executed," the duke finally said.

"Your Grace, the responsibility is—" Rendan began.

The duke swiped his hand through the air, cutting him off. "Speak not to me of responsibility! Without Treg's Vigili our cause is lost. I will be laughed at in Kholotara! I will be mocked in Noss!"

Nortallion turned his back, facing the wall. As a simple matter of discipline, Fox assumed Captain Rendan would be slain, imprisoned, or exiled. Despite her royal blood, his personal inclination was to treat Tana the same, but he doubted that would happen.

The enchanter faced them once more, his expression set, his eyes calm. "What is done is done. We must decide. How do we placate our mad engineer?"

"If I might, Your Grace," Fox said, "some good may come of this. The battle at the gates was precarious. Treg's interference kept Dartmallow from entering the fortress. For the price of a single woman, we might persuade him to give us the instrument that controls his creations. The advantage would be ours once more."

"Don't listen to him, Father," Tana said. "Ninette doesn't deserve—"

"Quiet, girl." The duke spoke softly, but in a voice not to be disobeyed. He pondered a moment. "We will send our representatives. I will not go myself. Treg is erratic and might decide to kill me. You will go in my place, Prince Lodan. You will offer the woman, and you will obtain the instrument."

"As you wish, Your Grace." Fox little liked the sound of it.

Nortallion tapped one hand against a chair. "Captain, you have erred in your judgment. You deserve to die."

"Yes, Your Grace." Beads of perspiration sprang onto Rendan's forehead, but he stood rigid, shoulders back, eyes steady. Fox admired his courage.

"You have been a steady hand by my side for seven years," the duke continued. "You have stood beside me in battle; there is none braver. Knowing my affection for my daughter, your loyalty to me hindered your judgment, blinding you to the obvious course. I cannot afford to lose a valiant officer when I need all my strength about me. However, I will not forget the lapse. From this moment you walk a line thin as a sword edge."

"Thank you, Your Grace." Even then, Rendan showed no sign of emotion.

"You will accompany the prince," Nortallion said. "Choose four men to go with you. Meet with Treg and recover my Vigili."

Rendan bowed and walked out. Fox followed, leaving the duke staring at his newfound daughter. He would like to have heard their conversation, but it didn't matter. Nor did the prince have to consider why he, a newcomer, had been chosen to deal with Treg. Nortallion had taken his measure and found him capable; and sending someone not from Ruheen created distance, perhaps blunting Treg's anger. Besides, Fox was expendable. The duke had made it clear that the erratic artist might execute the entire party. Rendan, of course, was intended to ensure Fox did not betray the duke. The prince felt momentary pity for the captain. Nortallion needed him for now, but once the campaign was won, Fox suspected the sword edge the duke mentioned would take the man's head from his shoulders.

"Captain," Fox said, catching up to him as they walked across the palisade grounds. "Tell me as much as you can about this Treg: his motives, his mannerisms, anything we can use to manipulate him."

Fox listened closely, knowing his life depended on it.

* * *

Having withdrawn his troops into the forest, Dartmallow assembled a council at the edge of the treeline consisting of Gray, Loogth, Topper, and several officers. In a few words, the marshal outlined a plan of retreat in case the Vigili attacked.

"I wish the trees would talk to us," Vasps said. "They might tell us about our new opponent."

"Let them sleep, I say, and be grateful they're not attacking us," Dartmallow replied. "Ah, here's Quacaw. Perhaps we'll find out something."

The crow landed on the ground before them. "You called me. I heard the call. The call I heard. I am here. Here am I."

"Can you tell us who this upstart is, where he comes from, what he wants?" Dartmallow asked.

"We know little. Little we know, "but we know something. A swallow told us once. She made her nest in the Great Cliffs by Eddy the River. By the river she made her nest, beneath high doors. She heard his name, his name of Treg. Treg is the name she heard. She says he digs shiny stones and glistening metal from the earth. Sunglisten bright gold. The murder remembers. We say someday we will go there, perhaps, perhaps. There we will go someday and steal the pretties."

"The canyons to the east?" Vasps asked.

"That is them. Them that is. The Great Cliffs, where the white flowers grow."

"The Yarrow, on the border of the Wileywood," Vasps said. "Decades ago, there was a considerable mining operation there. Treg has surely reopened the mines to build the Vigili."

"The pack remembers the mines from of old," Loogth rumbled. "We have witnessed the men of iron marching out of the east, but of Treg we know nothing."

Dartmallow scowled. "It's little enough information. Very well. We will take action to see reaction. Vasps, you will speak to him. Find out what he wants and try to convince him to side with us rather than the duke."

"Marshal," Topper said, "there is movement on the field."

Gray glanced across the way. Six men bearing the duke's blue standard were leaving the fort and walking toward Treg. The prince raised his spyglass. His heart went cold; he lowered it slowly. "Marshal, I must accompany Vasps. Fox is among the Ruheen emissaries."

The marshal lifted his eyebrows. "That's disappointing. He is a brave man. I suppose it is his affinity for royalty." He studied Gray, as if thinking: *You too are a prince. Will you turn on us as well?* But he only said, "Why do you wish to go?"

"I know him. He's shrewd. Perhaps I can counter that."

"So be it," Dartmallow said. "Take a number equal to those of the duke. You will ride your horses. It will make us appear stronger than Nortallion's men."

Gray climbed onto Nutmeg's back, wishing he had a saddle. Blunder padded up beside her.

"Not this time, boy," Gray said. "We're under a truce. There won't be any fighting."

"I want to go, Gray," Blunder said.

"You must remain in the camp," Dartmallow said. "This is a time for discussion. I don't want you biting anyone."

Blunder lowered his ears. His tail dropped to the dust. "I will stay, but I do not like it, Gray."

With Topper bearing the green Animonean standard, they rode across the battlefield under a sky grown heavy with enormous, staring cloud faces shot blue and gray with the promise of rain. Under the silent scrutiny of their ever-changing formations, Gray wondered if the trials and exploits of humans meant anything to them, if they possessed any curiosity concerning the tableau. One particularly large bank drew backward to either side, like the parting of a veil, revealing a visage whose eyes reminded Gray of Soonderkainen. He smiled sadly, remembering the bard-enchanter, wishing he were there to help. What wonders he could perform, if only he had lived! The clouds shifted, the semblance vanished. Gray shook himself, bringing his thoughts back to the task at hand. This was no time for vain fantasies.

They passed through the silent, unmoving ranks of the Vigili, their unwinking eyes sending a shiver up Gray's spine. The Ruheen party stood several yards from Treg, who had returned to his place atop the coach. As the Animoneans approached, Gray met Fox Lodan's gaze. Fox grinned. "Prince Darien! So, even in a country run by rabble, the nobility rises to the fore. Well met!"

Gray stared, surprised by so friendly a greeting. "So you've joined the duke?"

"I've seen enough yammering chattel. You should accompany me. I found Tana, but we're no longer engaged. Perhaps you could win her heart, after all."

That was the Fox Gray knew, the mocking eye, the stinging words. He bit back a reply.

Both embassies approached Treg. Gray had never seen a more

unusual, nor more repulsive being. Arrogance was common among the nobles of the courts of kings, but Treg's face was a portrait of pomposity: the goggling eyes, the lifted chin, the contemptuous curl of the upper lip. He radiated vanity as the sun radiates heat.

The sculptor's imperious gaze swept over them. He laughed triumphantly. "Treg calls and they come, all the little soldiers at my bidding, like the playthings I make. And Rendan among them. So good to see you, Captain. So good."

"Treg," Rendan said, bowing at the neck.

The sculptor beamed, the grin of a child getting his way. "Yes, it is good to see each of you awaiting the edicts of Treg."

Fox stepped forward. "Master Dumaud, I am—"

"My proper title is Lord Treg."

Fox blinked, hiding any irritation. "*Lord* Treg. I am Fox Lodan, a prince neither from Ruheen nor Animonea, though I represent Duke Nortallion. We have come to inquire. You say you have been betrayed, but if so, by whom? Has the duke failed to pay you for the work you have done?" He gestured broadly toward the Vigili. "Hasn't he given you precious gold for each of these? Yet now you reappropriate them to yourself."

"I take back what is mine," Treg said, "just as Captain Rendan stole Ninette Argilla from me. I was promised her, and she was spirited away by treachery. You have besmirched the desires of Treg, forced me to leave my work—my precious work!—to traipse through the woods in an odious cart." He ground his teeth together so violently Gray could hear it.

"I see you are offended, but surely we can set the matter right," Fox said. "We had nothing to do with taking the girl. She planned the whole thing. She resides in the duke's fortress and can easily be fetched, if that is your desire. Let us reach an agreement and be allies once more."

"Before you commit to anything Fox says, we ask you to consider your present situation," Gray interjected from Nutmeg's back, meeting Treg at eye level. "I too am from neither Animonea nor Ruheen, but you stand on soil belonging to the Republic of Everything, land falsely claimed by Duke Nortallion. I am told your mines also lie within the Republic. Your alliance with the duke puts your properties in the Yarrow under great risk."

"I am Treg. Borders and nations mean nothing to me. My work is everything."

"An understandable artistic perspective," Vasps said. "In Animonea we respect artists, but political and geometric realities affect even great men. Eventually, we will drive the duke from Morlane. If you choose to befriend the Republic, we will leave you to your work as we have always done, and could even provide additional materials, so long as you do not make any more weapons of war. We only ask that you withdraw the Vigili from the struggle, and let our disagreement with Ruheen remain between the two countries."

"Don't be fooled by empty promises," Fox said. "Will Animonea overthrow the duke with its talking birds and rabbits? Is there any strength in a land where every inhabitant has a say? Today, they choose to leave you alone; tomorrow they may change their minds. Only kings or men like kings can rule. Animonea is the squawking of magpies and crows. The duke will soon control all the country surrounding Morlane, and then who will pay you as lavishly as he?"

Treg snorted. "This discussion is inconsequential. My Vigili can defend my mines against your ludicrous armies. I want Ninette Argilla or I will destroy all of you."

"If we give her to you, will you restore your creations to the duke and give him the horn you use to control them?" Fox asked.

"I will, but first I want Ninette Argilla, and I want that one." Treg pointed to Rendan. "He is responsible for her escape from my keep. I will cut off his head and send it back to the duke."

"You are making a mistake," Gray said. "You need to ally yourself with Animonea—"

"I am Treg. I need not do anything."

"Lord Treg, there is no reason to punish Captain Rendan," Fox said. "The captain was tricked too, erring only in not recognizing Ninette's importance to you. We earnestly desire your friendship, but we hold the girl's life in our hands. Should you attack the fortress, she will not survive. Come! Let us both get what we want. We can have her brought to you at once."

"Prince, at your word, I will remain with Treg," Rendan said.

"No," Fox said. Gray wondered why he cared so much about the captain's life. Perhaps it was a matter of pride.

Treg fixed his gaze on Rendan. "Very well. He is an insignificant pawn and Treg is magnanimous. Produce the girl."

Fox turned to Rendan, who took two of his men to fetch Ninette.

"Lord Treg, I beg you not to act in haste," Gray said. "At least let us present our case for allying yourself with Animonea. The freedom of the Republic—"

"I grew up in the Fluted Hills of Animonea," Treg said. "I have often made use of its brightest creatures. Speak if you wish while we wait for the girl. Try to convince me."

Gray spoke, doubting it would do little more than salve Treg's endless ego.

* * *

Ninette would never have drawn her knife if Sergeant Cleaver hadn't struck the slave with a chain. Now she held it at the sergeant's throat while his shocked soldiers leapt to their feet.

"That was *so* mean!" Ninette cried, ignoring the stir around her. "Why would you do that? You hurt him!" They were outside one of the few buildings within the fort, and had been talking together like friends, even though Ninette was certain the men were there to see she didn't try to escape. The sergeant had told her stories, making her laugh, keeping her from fretting about what Treg would do; he had asked for a lock of her hair, saying it was fine as spun gold, and she had cut a few strands and given them to him. He had a nice smile and she thought she liked him, but when he ordered the slave to pour wine into a tin cup for her, the man had spilled it, and Cleaver had hit him with a chain.

Her blade hovered at Cleaver's jugular, and no one dared move. The sergeant kept his eyes on her face, not looking at the knife whispering its longing to cut. "Let's not do anything foolish, lass."

"But that was *so* cruel! Why did you hit him? He didn't spill it on purpose." Her voice shook in anger. Most of the few slaves in the fort served only the duke, and she hadn't seen any mistreated before.

"Things may be different where you come from, girly," Cleaver said, "but in Ruheen a slave does what his master says, and a master disciplines him as he likes. Gojjers there is a company servant, been with us for years. He understands the way of things. Isn't that right, Gojjers?"

Still stunned by the blow, the slave, a gray-haired ancient missing a front tooth, crept to his knees, his neck crimson where the chain had struck him. "It's as he says, my lady. If you kill him, it'll go hard on both of us."

Ninette furrowed her brow, uncertain, but finally sheathed her knife.

Cleaver smiled. "That's better, lass. If you want to stay with us, you best learn our ways."

Before she could reply, another servant appeared at her elbow, dressed in the livery of the duke's house, accompanied by six guards. "You must come with me."

Ninette looked around at Cleaver's men and the injured slave, suddenly bewildered. Everyone was looking at her as if she was the one who had done something wrong. Would everything always be a mystery to her?

Sergeant Cleaver grinned and wiped a daub of sweat from his brow. "Off with you, lady. You're a feisty one, and I won't take it personal. Maybe you and I can talk later. I can teach you the way of things, if you'd like."

Ninette followed the messenger while laughter rose at her back. Once beyond Cleaver's hearing, she turned to the servant and burst into tears. "I don't understand! Why am I trembling? I can't stop trembling." She grasped his shoulder, startling him, forcing him to halt. "I've fought plenty of battles. Why did it frighten me, the knife and the soldiers? Why am I shaking?" She fell to her knees, suddenly sick on the ground while the soldiers stood silently waiting. When she rose again, the servant eyed her warily.

"Stop staring at me!" Her tears turned to anger. "You should help someone when they feel bad. You should hug me or something. You should be nice!"

The servant kept his distance. "My lady, we must make haste."

"Oh, you're as bad as Treg!" Arms folded over her chest, she followed him to the palisade gate, where Tana and Chel Rendan waited for her. Tana hurried to her, her face rigid, clasping her two hands over Ninette's own. "I tried to convince him, Ninette, I really did, but father said this is the only way. If you don't go, Treg will turn the Vigili on us."

From the moment the sculptor arrived, Ninette had known what he wanted, yet when Tana spoke the words, a pall fell upon her. Her head swam; she thought she might faint, but this passed, leaving her furious. She felt betrayed by Tana, though part of her knew that was unfair. She wanted to cry or scream or fight. Yet, perhaps because of her previous outburst, for the first time in her short life she did none of these. Tana had been trying to teach her how to ignore the constant fusillade of warring emotions, and with the force of a revelation, she at last understood she could choose her response, as if she looked on a list of possible reactions and rejected them one by one. The result left her numb, her insides so cold she wondered why she didn't shiver.

Tana studied her, clearly puzzled by her seeming poise. "Are you all right?"

She understood the concept of courage, but had never had to be brave before. It had taken fortitude to climb into the trunk to escape Treg, but that had been breathless excitement too, the joy of tricking the sculptor, the fun of sneaking away. Now she decided she must be brave as in battle, courageous as a warlord.

"I can't let everyone die for my sake." She liked saying it; it made her feel noble, like an actress on a stage.

Tana hugged her fiercely, her eyes filling with tears. "If I can, I'll find a way to ransom you. I will. I promise!"

Ninette returned the hug, wanting to say something splendid and high-minded. "You've been *so* kind to me. I'll never forget it. But be careful with your father; be careful in a land that owns people like they were things. Serving a slaver in Ruheen may be as bad as being enslaved by Treg."

"On the duke's orders, I must ask for your weapons," a doleful Rendan said.

She handed over her protesting knife and sword and followed the soldiers to the gates.

"*Opening*," the gates said, as the sentries drew them wide.

"*Standing fast!*" the timbered fort wall responded, its voice resonating low and woody along its length.

Ninette walked between the soldiers across the bare ground,

solitary figures crossing the clearing. Gone was her momentary resolve. She felt small and shy with so many eyes upon her: the soldiers in the fortress, the Animoneans at the tree-line, the Vigili in their long rows, even the floating faces of the clouds. But more than anything, knowing Treg awaited her, she was afraid.

Such dread was new to her. Seeing the slave unjustly punished, she realized the sculptor might torment her for escaping him. Before she became fully aware, she had experienced pain in battle, but it had been injury without emotion. How could imagining what might happen fill her with such apprehension? She wanted to drop to the ground and cover her head. Nor did she comprehend why she failed to do so. What was inside her that made her act strong when she felt so weak?

She drew a deep breath and lifted her chin. Whatever it was, she would use it. She would give them a good show.

Perhaps, she thought, I'm learning how to grow up.

* * *

After Ninette left the fortress, Tana threw herself into Rendan's arms.

"I still have you, don't I?" she murmured. "You won't leave me too?"

"You know I won't," he whispered. "Please, Tana, you are the daughter of the duke, and I am but a soldier. You must be strong before the men."

She realized he was correct. She had a place now and a position; she had a father. She would be taken care of. She would miss Ninette, of course, but it would still be well. Releasing him, she brightened, speaking loud enough for the men to hear. "Forgive me, Captain Rendan. I fear my emotions overcame me."

He gave a bow. She turned and walked away as if it meant nothing.

I will be well, she repeated to herself. She is gone, but I will be well.

* * *

Ninette and her guards passed the Vigili and came into the presence of Treg. His smoldering gaze followed her as she approached. Dressed in his armor, his long face and long limbs made him appear like a god of war.

"Ah, my puppet, my little poppet! You return to the fold. Our drama nears its end."

Seeing Gray, Ninette broke from between the soldiers and rushed to Nutmeg's side, her hands on his leg. "Oh, Gray! I didn't know you'd be here. I'm *so* glad to see you again!"

Gray studied her, eyes veiled, until she grew embarrassed and looked away. "Oh, I keep doing this! You don't really know me, do you? I wasn't me when we rode together, but I'm me now; and if we weren't friends, we were comrades, weren't we? That night at Duskell Watch, Russ said we were the Company of the Far Riders."

His expression softened. "Yes, we were one fellowship, and you always fought with great courage. I'm sorry you have to do this."

She felt herself blush beneath his faint praise. "Are you here to help me? I don't want to go to Treg. I think he wants to take me apart and see what's inside."

The prince bit his lip, opened his mouth to reply, and shut it again.

"I see." Her eyes welled, but she didn't cry. "Tana is safe. She's like Joiwend; she can protect herself by changing her shape. And the duke loves her. She . . ." Her voice caught and failed.

He touched her hands, which clung to his knee. "Thank you for telling me."

"You know one another," Treg rumbled behind her. The sculptor had descended from his coach.

She backed away from Gray and turned. "We came to Animonea together."

Treg cast a suspicious glance at the Animonean party, then beckoned to Ninette with his long fingers. "Come here, my dear automaton."

Ninette raised her head high. If she had to surrender to him, she would do so with dignity. She walked to the sculptor and stood by his side.

Treg surveyed the envoys. "Treg has what he desires. Our audience is concluded."

Fox spoke, making Ninette realize for the first time that he was there. "And the Vigili?"

"I will send them and the horn to you shortly."

"Duke Nortallion will want to know how to use the instrument," Fox said. "Will you send a man to the duke's fortress to show us? Or perhaps I can remain here and receive those instructions."

"I will come there myself," Treg said. "You may depart with the others."

"As you wish."

"Lord Treg," Vasps said. "I beg you to reconsider. If you do this, this war will not end well for you. The Republic—"

"You have convinced me of nothing. Begone."

Treg made a hand-signal and six of the Vigili moved toward the envoys as if to drive them away. Ninette watched them depart, the Animoneans riding, the Ruheens on foot.

"You have wasted the precious time of Treg, but I am not dissatisfied," the sculptor told her. "Nortallion and the Animoneans require a lesson on the scope of my genius. When I am done, they will never again trifle with me."

"Isn't it over?" Ninette asked. "Aren't you going home?"

Treg laughed his ghastly laugh. "Do you believe the duke will allow this affront to pass? I have humiliated him before his army. No, he will find a way to punish me. Nor do I think it coincidence that you came to this country with someone who now rides in the ranks of the Animonean army. They speak of driving the duke from Morlane, but perhaps they desire a greater prize? They doubtless want you too, for reasons I do not yet comprehend. Maybe they hope to use my skills for their own ends. But Treg will show them."

"That isn't fair!" Ninette said. "You promised!"

"I vowed to send my creations to the duke and to go to his fortress myself. I will do both. My Vigili will indeed march there. They will dismantle it and hunt the duke and his followers down. As for the Animoneans, I will drive them from Morlane. They have treated Treg like a tinker, but I see now I must own this forest to protect my mines and my keep. Hereafter it shall be known as Tregland, for who can stand against my constructs? The timbers of Morlane I will use in my continuing art."

He chuckled. "No one treats me with impunity. Not these little soldiers, these common men. Nobles, they call themselves. But only Art is noble, and I am the greatest artist of all."

Striding to his strange amplifying horn, he spoke in a language of his own devising, sending the words echoing across the field.

The Vigili strode forth.

CHAPTER NINETEEN

CIRCLES AND RINGS

As the envoys departed Treg's camp, to Gray's surprise Fox drew near, keeping pace with Nutmeg by long strides. "Why do you ally yourself with these freaks and commoners, Prince?"

"I question your choice of friends as well," Gray replied. "Nortallion is a tyrant."

"I'm talking about you. We've had our differences, lad, but circumstances have changed. Tana no longer concerns me."

"Because you don't have a use for her anymore."

Fox grinned. "Always the romantic, eh? Try to be pragmatic for once. There's no place for princes and kings in Animonea. Leave these rabble behind and join the duke."

"Why do you care?"

"Because we're both royalty, and royals look out for one another."

Gray snorted. "Admirable if you had felt the same when we rode together."

"I was the Unjust Prince, a role thrust upon me by the Elf King. We were rivals then, but you've grown up since our quest began, and in the last few days my thinking has changed. I was wrong when I said we should return to Faerie. I'm never going back. I'm going to establish myself in Ruheen. You're headstrong, but that isn't a bad trait. True blood bleeds true; I want someone like you beside me, someone I can trust to handle himself in a fight."

He brought his eager, arrogant face closer, lowering his voice so Rendan's soldiers could not hear. "Tana will be there for you to woo; I have the duke's ear, and will do anything I can to promote you to him so you can win her. Doing so will further my own goals. I can see so many possibilities now, the whole world open before me. Once in Ruheen, I'll soon rise to power, don't doubt that. I'll not be answering to Nortallion for long. Come with me! Together, you and I can build an empire."

Gray's thoughts swirled. To be close to Tana again . . . his hand swept unconsciously to the vial Vadispur had given him. Even if he never used it, there was the chance she could learn to love him. Torn by the temptation, he glanced at Vasps, who was studying him intently.

He thought of Joiwend, a Golden Rain tree standing in Morlane, sacrificing herself to resist the duke's will. She would say this was a trap, that even if Fox, no longer the Unjust Prince, meant what he said, Gray should remember the man's innate cruelty. The instant he placed himself under Lodan's sway he would become the target of his malice.

Gray shook his head, annoyed at even having considered the proposition. He locked his eyes on Vasps'. "A prince's duty is to protect his subjects, great or small. I doubt Duke Nortallion shares that view. I've given my word to help the Animoneans. I prefer to commit my allegiance to men—and beings—of good will."

Fox scowled. "You're a dreamer, Prince. Once we regain command of the Vigili, we will annihilate Dartmallow's army."

"Perhaps, but I wouldn't place my trust in the sculptor."

Lodan turned and strode away to catch up to his men. For an instant Gray was tempted to call to him, to send his regards to Tana, but Fox would never deliver such a message.

"We must inform the marshal at once," Vasps said.

Topper gave the order and the horses broke into a rapid trot. When they were still halfway across the clearing, Treg's amplified voice blared, and the Vigili began marching.

"To the gallop!" Topper commanded. Nutmeg blew; Dreamer whinnied; the horses broke into a run. Glancing toward Fox's party, Gray saw them sprinting toward the fort.

The marshal was already moving his forces by the time the envoys reached him. If the setbacks had discouraged him, he gave no sign, speaking almost cheerfully. "Didn't convince them, eh Vasps?

We'll make a rapid retreat, put distance between ourselves and the monsters, and find our strength in strategy."

By the time the Vigili reached the fort, Fox Lodan's party had already entered, shutting the gates behind them. The metal warriors began hacking at its walls while its timbers roared their defiance, a massive shout reverberating through earth and air.

Watching from the clearing's edge, Vasps exclaimed, "The duke is betrayed!" He glanced at Gray. "Your words proved true. How did you know?"

"I didn't, but my old tutor taught me that arrogance breeds contempt for all things, beginning first with honor."

"They're coming for us too," the marshal said.

A second group of Vigili were marching straight toward the Animoneans.

"Have the men make haste," Dartmallow ordered, turning his horse to go.

Gray hesitated, putting his hand to his head in black despair. He should have gone with Fox to protect Tana. His only comfort lay in Ninette's words: if his beloved could change her shape, she could find a way to escape. But how he ached to stand beside her!

He took one last look before riding into the forest depths.

* * *

If the duke's stronghold wasn't as invincible as it first appeared, Spence had to admit it was well-provisioned against an assault. The hot pitch he and the other soldiers poured down on the Vigili gummed up their joints, leaving them helpless. The fort's timbered walls resisted their blows. Even the gate, the weakest link in any installation, was reinforced with iron, and within moments of the assault, a ditch was dug and heavy timbers set in line to brace it from inside.

Spence and his fellows were stationed on the ramparts directly above it. He wore a Ruheen uniform, but had discarded the headpiece for his old army helmet. He worked with the precision ingrained into him by his time in France and Germany, humming "The Boogie Woogie Bugle Boy of Company C" as he poured the pitch, his helmet droning along, slightly off-key.

From his position, he could see across the clearing, but it left his head and shoulders exposed, making him glad that few of the Vigili had bows. Half the creatures were attacking the fortress while the rest pursued the Animoneans. Treg sat atop his coach before the stronghold, surrounded by a score of his servants, Ninette standing on the ground beside him, her bronze armor reflecting the sunlight.

He scowled. Everything was falling apart because of her, and he couldn't see it ending well for the duke. Which meant it might be bad for him too. He never should have taken her along, the day he found her by the river; he should have dragged her into the stream and let her armor pull her to the bottom. It would have been better if he had stayed with Treg. He should look for a chance to get back into his favor.

He and another soldier poured more pitch on the Vigili, the tar rejoicing in a thick, indolent voice. Several iron warriors stood covered in it, and the sculptor spoke into his strange horn, ordering their withdrawal. Those covered in pitch tried to obey, futilely grinding their limbs. One toppled to the ground, its legs helplessly toiling in air. Spence pointed and he and his helmet laughed at it, the helmet's mirth a metallic echo.

"What's so funny?" the soldier beside him asked.

"It's a stalemate. If he loses too many, he knows we'll come out and get him. Maybe things won't be so bad after all." He looked around. "Let me see your bow. I left mine in the barracks."

"What are you going to do?"

Ignoring the question, he seized the weapon, strung it, and nocked an arrow. Tormented as a child for being short, he had developed his upper-body strength until anyone trying to pick on him did so only once. He tested the tension and drew it back to its full extension. The bow groaned in complaint; the string sighed along its length. His mind went blank, empty, judging distance and angle with an almost preternatural instinct. The released arrow sang its joy, speeding upward, hurtling down. It quivered in the wood of the coach an inch from where Treg sat.

Spence cursed and fitted a second shaft, but the sculptor had already leapt from his seat and fled, taking enormous strides, the soles of his boots broad as signposts.

"I didn't think anyone could shoot that far!" the soldier

exclaimed.

Spence danced up and down, his hands over his head, shaking his fists while his helmet growled. "Run, you coward! Or come back and get some more!" He clicked his heels until his shoes groaned in leathern complaint. "Run, you bully!"

"That was truly remarkable," a voice said. "A pity you missed."

Spence turned, ready to give an angry retort, but bit it back, for Duke Nortallion had ascended the ramparts.

"One more shot and I would have had him."

"I'm told you came with Ninette."

"We traveled together some."

"Do you too harbor secrets I should know about?"

"I'm just a soldier doing his duty, Your Grace."

The duke turned, surveying the battlefield, his thoughts unreadable. The Vigili drawing Treg's coach had swung around to where their master stood, fifty paces farther from the walls. The sculptor issued another command through his horn, sending his warriors marching, leaving a squadron to serve as a buffer between himself and the fort while the rest encircled the stronghold.

"That was bound to be his next move," the duke said. "What do you make of it, Spence?"

Spence thought of Bastogne. He and Sarge had left there two days before the Germans surrounded it. "It won't be easy breaking out of here once they close the circle. If we could kill Treg it would finish his army, but an assault would never reach him. If there's a side-gate, we should use it before it's too late."

"There is a way out," the duke said. "As I suspected when I climbed up here, our gates cannot long hold. But there is one thing I can try."

Looking across the battlefield, Nortallion lifted his hands, palms outward. Many paces behind Treg, a troop of Animonean soldiers appeared at the treeline, shields before them, forming skirmish lines. Treg did not see them at first, but soon turned. He issued a command through his instrument, and the Vigili ceased surrounding Ironwood Station and began returning to their master to meet this new threat.

"It is illusion," Nortallion said. "It will not deceive the sculptor for long, and the Vigili cannot even see it, but it will purchase us time." The duke turned from the field. "Come with me. A man of your skills might be useful. You can tell me more about your companion."

"Yes sir, Your Grace." Spence fell in line behind the duke, taking the bow and arrows with him. As Nortallion descended the ladder before him, Spence studied the sapphire on his right hand. Whoever or whatever Fetch was, he was right about the duke having a ring identical to Joiwend and Tana's. Was it his imagination, or had it glowed when the duke cast his spell? Spence had spent some time thinking about those jewels, and had soon realized that Tana had tricked Treg by making herself look like Ninette. If his hunch was right, the rings were the source of her and Joiwend's powers. If he could get his hands on one, it could be his ticket out if things went wrong. He could change into some kind of animal and slip away. He wondered how it worked. Joiwend never said any words or anything. Maybe you just thought what you wanted to be. He needed to figure it out. He wasn't about to die for Ruheen.

They left the ramparts, the duke calling commands to his subordinates, sending messengers scurrying across the compound, gathering portions of his troops. Nortallion strode toward the back of the fortress, his face a mask of serenity. He seemed to have forgotten Spence, but the corporal kept close behind.

Fox rode up on Dauntless. "Your Grace, my stallion is yours."

"I am my own," Dauntless huffed.

"Keep your Talker," the duke said. "I'll not trust him. Besides, where we go a man cannot ride. But bring him along."

More and more soldiers joined the company, their equipment and armor rattling and murmuring in curiosity. Tana appeared, escorted by a group of soldiers led by Captain Rendan. The duke took her hand.

"What are we doing, Father?"

"When fortresses fail, when defenses collapse, when fortunes fade, the cunning continue. This setback will not defeat me."

They entered a wooden granary near the rear wall of the fortress. The duke waded placidly over the piles of wheat, helping his daughter along while tiny, grain voices lifted in protest. Spence sunk into the wheat, grimacing as it spilled inside his boot-tops.

The duke pointed to shovels hanging on the walls. Spence

grabbed one and joined in moving some of the grain. When a space was cleared, the soldiers lifted a section of flooring, revealing an angling tunnel, wide enough for two men to walk abreast and high enough for the tallest soldier to travel without stooping. The duke was clearly nobody's fool.

"*Travel through us,*" the rock walls intoned.

"Only I knew of this," the duke said. "The slaves who dug it are no more. We must hurry. The men on the walls and the gate must hold until the rest escape, then follow after." He turned to Fox, who had led Dauntless into the room. "Fox Lodan and Lieutenant Lur will lead. Once outside, Prince, use your horse to scout the way for us."

Fox brought Dauntless over the grain and into the tunnel. The horse blew nervously, but did not complain. When the first group had passed inside, Captain Rendan said, "You and the duchess should go next, Your Grace, while there is time."

Nortallion shook his head. "There is time enough. Get my men out first."

The soldiers around the duke murmured their approval. If they survived, the whole company would celebrate the duke's courage. One by one, the soldiers filed into the darkness. Spence debated falling in line with them. The gates might go any minute. But the duke hadn't dismissed him, and if he looked the coward, it might go hard on him later.

Messengers came and went, keeping the duke apprised. At last, when most of the soldiers had passed through the opening, a frantic lad, no older than fourteen, burst into the room. "The gate has fallen! The men are in retreat. We can't hold!"

"Please, Your Grace, you must go." Rendan's eyes were on Tana. Her face was flushed. Even from where he stood, Spence could see her trembling.

The duke nodded and stepped into the tunnel, the captain before him, Tana by his side. Spence and several others brought up the rear. They marched quickly, but not as fast as Rick wanted. Close places reminded him too much of foxholes and bunkers. The passage whispered to them, a continuous hissing. "*Follow me and be safe. Hide in my depths,*" but instead of comfort, it gave him the creeps. The tunnel proved surprisingly long. He didn't like to think about how many slaves it must have taken to dig it; he didn't want to end up a slave in Ruheen.

They exited the tunnel inside the treeline, coming out from beneath a tall hillock. He drew a deep breath, relieved to be back in the open air. A few men were ordered to stay behind, to seal the opening with heavy boulders previously placed there for that purpose. Spence was glad he wasn't one of those picked to remain.

They headed east toward Ruheen, in what he hoped was a full retreat. He had no desire to face Treg's Vigili. One bazooka could turn the sculpture's army into scrap metal, but lacking that, battling them was like hitting a B-52 with a fly swatter. He moved closer to the duke, attempting to overhear his plans, but Nortallion wasn't talking.

Generals and dukes are all the same, he thought. Nortallion can afford to swagger away, looking noble, pretending he isn't as scared as the rest of us. His men will love him for it—they'll call it courage. I'd be brave too if I knew I could send two hundred soldiers to die for me while I sat back and watched. If I had that kind of power, I'd act just like that, smirking and collecting the glory.

His eyes ran to the duke's ring. Tana had hers on too. It was a stroke of luck, being this close to them. Opportunity was what you made of it.

He froze, his thoughts interrupted by shouts in front of them, the sound of metal on metal, the noise of battle. The duke raised his hand and the men halted. Spence pulled his helmet down tight. They waited, everyone listening. Sweat beaded his forehead.

A messenger bolted from between the trees. "Your Grace! It's a trap! The enemy was waiting for us! They attack from two sides."

Before the duke could reply, Spence heard the breaking of branches on the hill above them. The Vigili came shambling, stiff-legged, down the slope.

* * *

Spence sat with his back against a tree, eating cold rations. The sun was westering, an hour away from twilight. Whatever was left of the duke's forces was scattered across the Wileywood. Most of those in Nortallion's immediate party had died covering his escape, leaving Spence, Rendan, Tana, and three other survivors. One of the soldiers was wounded and would probably die before the night was over. They had spent most of the day running.

Altogether, it had been a crummy week.

On the other hand, there had been some good moments. During the retreat Spence had parried a Vigili sword, saving the duke's life. That might lead to a promotion.

Then again, Nortallion's failure might cause him to be overthrown back in Ruheen. Being connected to him could be bad for Rick's health.

He mentally shrugged, muttering, "You pays your money; you takes your chances." He tugged his helmet down. It sighed contentedly, echoing the words.

They were camped beneath tall birches. The eyes of the trees remained closed, unresponsive. Tana lay on a blanket Rendan had given her, the captain sitting beside her. The other soldiers rested on either side of their dying comrade. Duke Nortallion stood looking east, one hand on a tree trunk, his face haggard, his eyes those of a caged falcon — scarcely surprising, since in the last two hours Spence had seen him change into an enormous hawk and go flying to seek his scattered forces.

After seeing Joiwend, Tana, and now the duke alter their shapes, Spence was certain the rings were the source of their transformations. It would be a handy trick to have. You could go almost anywhere.

Duke Nortallion and Rendan were conferring. Spence strained to overhear.

"Your Grace," the captain said, "I don't see a path to victory so long as Treg commands the Vigili. We require more men and a way to counter his warriors. We lost most of our supplies and equipment. I would advise a return to Ruheen."

The duke gave him a long stare, then nodded. "Sound strategy, as always, My Captain, yet there is a chance, a hope, a second choice. If I could reach the traitor personally, strike him among his warriors with eagle claws or wolf fangs." He glowered. "I have tried. The last time I flew, I soared above his soldiers. He surrounds himself with a wall of Vigili. His armor protects his throat. He is no general, no tactician, no soldier, but he is no fool. I underestimated both his intelligence and his madness."

"What if you changed to something smaller?" Tana asked. "A viper or even a mosquito?"

"I still have much to teach you, Daughter. There are limits to how small we can become. It is easier to add weight than subtract it. I would become a serpent the size of a bear." The duke scowled. "We shall gather our forces and we shall see. One thing I tell you, Captain; if I must retreat from Morlane, I will burn it behind me. We will start a conflagration Treg cannot extinguish."

He turned away. "I'm going to seek more of the men. The soldiers I found earlier should be here within the hour, so expect them."

"Yes, Your Grace," Rendan said.

The duke stalked away. He usually put some distance between himself and his followers before changing, but Spence had kept his eyes open enough to witness his transformations. Tugging at his helmet, he glanced at the others. The captain and Tana were talking, their hands touching; the soldiers were too exhausted to notice anything. Spence slipped away, following Nortallion.

It took a minute to locate the duke, but he finally caught sight of his acorn hat. He kept his distance, avoiding breaking even the slightest twig while inwardly locked in a furious debate. The duke might be his meal ticket, or Nortallion might be finished. He'd seen enough war to know when things were on a downhill slide. He remembered what happened to General Patton after he slapped around a soldier suffering from combat fatigue.

And those rings were something else. Even if he couldn't use one of them, he could probably sell it, and not necessarily to Fetch. He didn't know anything about the man and didn't see any reason to trust him.

The duke halted just ahead. Spence bit his lip in indecision.

Nortallion changed, his back arching, his arms widening, his clothes vanishing beneath the gray and white feathers sprouting over his body. His feet became talons, clutching the earth. He turned his beak, his form majestic, studying the sky. Flapping his wings, he started to rise.

Spence acted on instinct. In a split second he had his bow bent in his hand. As the shaft flew, he sucked in a desperate breath, knowing this would be his only shot. If he missed, he would have to hide from the duke's vengeance, an exile again, everything he had worked for ruined.

The arrow pierced the hawk between the shoulder blades. Spence stifled a joyous shout and broke into a run. Everything depended on what he did next.

The bird had fallen out of sight. Spence didn't know if the duke would remain an animal or turn back into a man. If he was dead and didn't revert, the ring might be lost—it always vanished when Joiwend changed.

He halted, uncertain. The hawk was almost the same color as the background. He searched the woods until his eyes fastened on his prey. Then he gaped. The duke had indeed returned to his original form, but a figure knelt beside him. Spence nocked another arrow and rushed forward.

Fetch rose to his feet, holding a bloody knife and the ring.

"Crime in Italy!" Spence kept his bow aimed at the man's chest. "How did you get here?"

Fetch grinned. "Did you think I wouldn't be watching? Your skill with weaponry is a wonder, Richard."

"Skip the compliments. Tell me why I shouldn't use my wondrous skill to drill you?"

Fetch held the ring on his open palm. "You want to slay me for this? That would be a mistake. This is a tool. A powerful one. But I am the key to your success. You and I together will go to Ruheen, where we will seize wealth and power and glory beyond your fondest dreams. You want the respect of men? They will bow before you. You want your choice of women? They will clamor for your regard. This ring can give you certain abilities, but if you do not know how to use it, it will be in vain."

"Why me?" Spence asked.

"Because I know you. Because I have ridden and fought with you. Because you and I are much alike, and I believe I understand you."

"The devil you do! What kind of mumbo jumbo is that?"

"Jaunter and I are brothers in blood, in ways you cannot comprehend. What he knows, what he has seen, so too have I. The Company of the Far Riders who left from Faerie guided by the elf, Koothlin, who passed through Duskell Watch, who found the strange world of Animonea—each of these I love. Even

Soonderkainen who perished; even Thomas Tatters, who gave me my limp, though someday he will pay for that. I will chide him with my retribution, for I am Fetch Vadispur, who was slain, yet lives again. From the world of ghosts and specters I came, and there I learned many things of mind and spirit. I saw far. Then the blood of Jaunter made me whole. I will be a god in Ruheen, where they worship many gods; and if you come with me, you will become one too."

Spence lowered his bow, impressed and chilled. All the time Fetch spoke, he never blinked once, his wide-eyed stare that of a corpse. There was something supernatural about him for sure. In Faerie, magic made impossible things possible, maybe even ghosts coming back from the dead. Spence didn't trust him, but it never hurt to play the odds. "You talk a good fight, mister. If you have something behind it, I'm in. What do we do next?"

"I will hide the duke's body. Your camp is nearly empty, and there is a second ring there. Seize it for yourself if you can."

"You're asking me to take all the risks."

"I will be watching when you make your move. I will help you if I can."

Spence unstrung his bow and turned back toward the camp, unsure if he had done the right thing. Fetch had what he wanted; it might be a con. Spence might never see him again, but his gut-instinct said otherwise.

He hesitated, uncertain where the camp lay, then set out again, but had gone scarcely fifty yards through the underbrush when he met Captain Rendan.

"Where have you been?" the captain asked.

"I heard something and thought it might be our soldiers, but it wasn't anything." He repressed the urge to turn around and see if Nortallion and Fetch were visible. The trees probably hid them, but his pulse rose when Rendan's gaze hung over his shoulder for several seconds. Spence kept his expression level. Rendan had probably never trusted him—a typical officer always thinking the worst of a fellow. Why else had he followed him out here? If he suspected what had happened, he would either draw his sword, or play innocent and have the soldiers kill him once they were back at camp. Spence kept his hands still but ready, close to his long-knife.

"Let's return to the others," Rendan said.

They walked side-by-side. Gradually, Spence drifted slightly behind. If the captain was suspicious, he didn't show it.

Spence couldn't take the chance that Rendan hadn't seen anything. He had to act before they reached the camp. In one swift motion, he brought his knife out and up, catching Rendan in the side between the joints of his armor, getting his arm around the man's throat before he could make more than the barest cry of pain. He finished the job with expert precision, then laid Rendan down and watched the light fade from his eyes.

Now there was another body to hide. He threw dirt over the bleeding wounds to absorb some of the blood, then dragged the corpse several yards away, where he concealed it as best he could in a gully, behind a stand of brambles which whispered in outrage. Throwing some dead tree branches over it, he left, depending on luck that it wouldn't be found.

He checked himself carefully, making sure there were no blood stains on his hands or clothes. He couldn't check his face until he thought to ask his helmet. He held it facing him.

"Can you see me?" Spence asked. "Is there any blood?"

Dim bumps, the barest of eyes, appeared on the helmet's surface. "I see you. There is no blood."

"You know what blood looks like, right?"

"It is red. When it is dry, it is brown. I've seen lots of it."

"All right, thanks." Was it his imagination or was the helmet getting smarter?

He circled around the camp, making sure he came in from a different direction, wanting to slip in unseen, but as he approached he heard rising voices. Peering between the vegetation, he saw Fox Lodan astride Dauntless, leading a squad of about forty men. Riding point when the Vigili attacked, most likely to be the first killed, the prince had somehow managed to survive. Pence shook his head; the man was wily as his namesake.

Amid the confusion, Spence had no trouble blending in, but his chance to get the ring from Tana was gone. He'd probably killed Rendan for nothing. It was a shame; the captain had been an okay joe. He wondered if Fetch had deserted him.

CHAPTER TWENTY

THE RESERVOIR

For two days Dartmallow's army fled from Treg's Vigili, traveling ever north through a narrowing valley with mountains on either side. The iron warriors did not march swiftly, but with tireless tenacity, halting at night only long enough for their human overseers to snatch a few hours of rest. The crows told of the fall of Ironwood Station, but knew nothing of the fate of the duke and his daughter, leaving Gray miserable with worry, his slender hope lying in Tana's ability to change forms.

Having defeated Nortallion, Treg now commanded the pursuit himself. At first, Dartmallow successfully sent archers to kill the overseers, until the sculptor responded by ringing them with Vigili, making them almost impossible to target. With their diminishing rations, Vasps and some of the officers counseled abandoning the campaign, retreating east, escaping around the enemy flank, and leaving the forest. "We must live to fight again," the arbiter insisted.

The marshal refused, giving Gray a squinting glance. "I won't consider it yet. Whether for good or ill, Vasps and our young prince narrowed my options when they made a pact with Brythibain."

"They did so without your sanction," one staff member protested. "Our government would never hold you responsible."

"I spoke only for myself, not the army," Gray said.

"And I only stated our original intention to stop the duke, without making any specific promises," Vasps said. "Certainly we will free Morlane if we can find a way, but—"

Loogth growled, hackles rising. "Humans find ways when it suits them. If you abandon us, the pack will remember. Our night songs will rise to the moon, telling him of it, until every wolf in Animonea knows you betrayed us."

Dartmallow's face paled at Loogth's threat, but he spoke resolutely. "You have the right of it. Nortallion has broken our laws and violated our borders; Treg is a rebel and a traitor to our country. It must not stand. Failure will allow Treg to consolidate his forces; another year may pass before we can liberate the woods. What will the Wileywood become by then, influenced by the sculptor? Would it even allow us to enter it?" He swept his gaze over his officers. "This is not recklessness, gentlemen; it is a calculated risk. Our enemy's weakness is the mindlessness of his soldiers. We will exploit it if we can. We will march to the dam, the stronghold of Brythibain, and seize it from the Vigili. It will give us the advantage of height. If we can rouse the trees to fight for us, we will destroy Treg's army."

"But they haven't responded in any way," an officer retorted.

"No, but perhaps we can yet convince them. For now, it is enough that they are no longer attacking us. If they refuse to answer, we will explore other options." The marshal's demeanor darkened. "If the worst occurs, we can cross the mountains and work our way east, but only as a final resort. Our enemy is unpredictable. Once Treg consolidates his position, he could decide to form a pact with Ruheen. We must stop him here or risk an escalation of their forces and greater bloodshed later."

Gray kept silent. During their journey, both he and the marshal had tried communicating with the trees. He had invoked Joiwend's name without response and held little hope of their aid.

* * *

At mid-morning of the third day, Quacaw flapped by, cawing and circling the marshal twice before landing on his saddle horn. "Before Great-light stands highest, the highest it stands, you will reach the water. It is guarded as we said. We said it and it is so. It is the metal men. The men of metal. Not many, but some, and the mist is gone. Brythibain needs it no more, he says. He says it. It is said by him."

The wolves went scouting, and Loogth returned with glinting eyes to report that the Vigili guarding the earthen dam numbered less than sixty, each standing thirty paces apart, positioned in two lines, one along the top of the dike, the other at its foot. Grinning at the news, Dartmallow led a council of war to plan their destruction.

"Our forces must strike simultaneously at all points," the marshal said. "We will outmaneuver them, defeat them, and fortify our position."

Within the hour they were ready, the army lying hidden by the trees, strung along a narrow band fifty strides from the dam. Gray stood beside Nutmeg, his hand on her mane. To his right, Jaunter, Master Tatters, and Russ waited, several feet apart, beside their horses. At Gray's feet and those of the men lay a stone just light enough to carry. Behind the cavalry waited the archers, and behind them infantrymen wielded fallen tree trunks found by scouring the forest for dead timber. Though Morlane remained silent, no one dared put an axe to living trees.

Crows passed silently among the branches. Loogth's wolves prowled back and forth before the army, making the horses stamp in consternation; Blunder, lying at Gray's feet, gave a low growl whenever one passed. Gray reached down and stroked the pup's ears, wishing he could order him to stay behind, knowing the dog would refuse. But what good were teeth and paws—or human flesh—against iron?

He cast the thought away, steadying himself. When would the battle begin? It was taking a lifetime.

He leaned close to Nutmeg and whispered in her ear, "Do you remember what to do?" She bobbed her head, maintaining her silence.

Topper gave a hand signal, answered by a single caw; then every crow sounded the advance. Gray bent and lifted the heavy stone. The line jogged forward at a steady pace over the rough ground. No other battle cry was given; every creature moved in its place, the only sound the tramping of hooves, the padding of paws, the noise of booted feet on dead vegetation.

Gray scrutinized the forest, trying to catch sight of the enemy. A wall of brown rose before him, the foot of the dam seen through the vegetation, growing clearer as they approached. Gray spied a Vigili standing motionless, holding the hilt of its sword against its chest, unaware of its enemies.

The soldiers halted at the ragged edge of the treeline, but the horses bounded across the narrow, nearly-bare strip between the trees and the dam. Gray fastened his eyes on Nutmeg and time seemed to slow. To either side of him, he heard the twang of bows, the cries of the arrows streaming toward the enemy commanders, the screams telling that some had reached their targets.

The Vigili at the dam's base reacted, raising their swords above their heads. As one, the horses turned and kicked with their back legs. Nutmeg's blow, sent with all the weight of her body, caught a Vigili in the jaw, taking its head off and sending it bouncing against the earthen dike.

The Animoneans charged. A low growl erupted unbidden from Gray's throat, a noise echoed by every man, growing to a roar. Nutmeg struck again, hitting the beheaded Vigili in the chest, knocking it off its feet. Though blind, it sought to rise. Its lost head, rolling down beside it, shouted, "*Defend!*" Gray hurled his stone with all his strength, striking the creature's blade, breaking it off at the hilt. Before the Vigili could more than half-rise, Nutmeg sent it sprawling again. Gray picked up its head and cast it into the forest.

Her mission done, Nutmeg and the other horses trotted back into the treeline. Retrieving his stone, Gray hurried to help Master Tatters, whose target was down but still intact. The old pioneer had dropped to his knees to bash his stone against the hand and shoulder of the Vigili's sword-arm, driving it down, attempting to break the vulnerable shoulder gears. Gray went to work on its kneecap, hammering until he heard something give. Another soldier appeared and wedged a spear into the shoulder-joint, prying the arm away, leaving it dangling.

Gray looked around, seeking another opponent, but the Vigili had been taken by surprise all down the line. The wolves and dogs sprang up the dike, confronting the guardians there, not attacking, but howling and threatening. Marshal Dartmallow's strategy depended on keeping the enemy atop the dam and preventing them from uniting. Gray spied Blunder taunting a human overseer, darting in, barking, only to drop to his belly, ducking beneath the man's sword stroke, rising to harass him again. Seeing his friend fight with such courage, so small and fragile against his armored foe, sent a wave of pride and fear through the prince.

The infantrymen carrying the tree trunks charged up the dike, aiming them like battering rams, and Gray followed, breathless but eager to press the attack. The slope was steeper than he expected; stones rolled under his feet, sending him twice to his knees. One of the men carrying the trunk tripped, fell, and rolled down the dike. With an effort, Gray scrambled forward and took his place. Slipping, sliding, losing their balance and struggling to recover, the men gained the top.

A Vigili stood before them, sword aloft, trying to close on Blunder, who continued to harry the overseer, daring not one blade, but two. A snarl of rage broke from Gray's throat. Thrusting the battering ram with all his strength, he helped drive it into the Vigili's chest, pushing it backward, thrusting it into the reservoir. Brythibain's furious face rose high into the air, a waterspout eager to take his foe. The Vigili sank into his depths, helplessly thrashing, lost in the lake's muddy bottom.

Lungs burning, Gray and the other soldiers fell to their knees, exhausted by their efforts.

But in his struggle, Gray had lost track of the overseer, who loomed over him, blade flashing in the sunlight. Too late, the prince shifted his sword. In a moment of perfect clarity, he saw the man's eyes, wide and brown, his brow furrowed in concentration, his sweat beading his face, the sunlight reflecting off the pommel of his weapon.

Blunder attacked with a ferocity which surprised even Gray, hurling himself six feet in the air, catching the man's sword-arm, clamping his jaws onto his wrist. Shouting in pain, staggering against the pup's momentum, the overseer tried to shake him loose, flailing his arm helplessly against that unyielding grip. Balling his fist, he struck Blunder's side a terrible blow, but still the dog held on. He drew back to strike again.

Gray slid his sword into the overseer's side. Blood spurted; the man toppled to the ground. Gray struck again, finishing him. Still Blunder held on, growling. Gray threw his arms around the pup's neck. "You got him, boy!" Gray cried. "You can let go!"

Gradually, Blunder released his grip. The dog had broken the man's wrist. He abruptly dashed into Gray's arms and licked his face, his eyes furious. "We are winning, Gray! We are winning!"

For a short time, the fighting continued along the dike, but the Vigili were soon cast into Brythibain or left wandering, headless or without weapons.

* * *

The Animoneans now had plenty of water, and Brythibain provided abundant food by washing fish toward the shore, allowing the soldiers to catch them by hand. Gray learned the Animonean way of pronouncing the Mandate of Gratitude while holding a fish underwater before stunning it unconscious with a quick blow to the head and cutting a main artery to bleed it—the quickest, most humane death; but the fish's gasping, pathetic protests were unnerving, making the prince understand why meat was eaten less often in the Back of the Beyond. The soldiers soon had fires burning below the dike, cooking and devouring their first filling meal in days.

Their hunger satisfied, Gray, Russ, and Vasps accompanied Marshal Dartmallow and his officers to survey the dam, ascending on horseback where its east end met the mountains, Loogth keeping pace, Blunder and Sniffdaisy trotting ahead. Not far from the cave where Gray had spoken to Brythibain, a wide shelf met the crest of the dam, occupied by ancient oaks which had escaped destruction during the reservoir's creation. Gray ascended beneath their cool shadows and was glad the mist was gone, for the sunlight crept playfully through branches swayed by a whispering breeze. He studied the trunks. Their eyes remained closed and invisible, lidded with bark.

When he rode, no longer distracted by battle, from beneath the trees onto the dam, the sheer size of the lake wrung an involuntary gasp from his lips. Wide enough for six horses to ride abreast, the dike stretched four furlongs, imprisoning the waters of Brythibain in a valley running along the mountains' feet to the northern horizon. Brythibain's swirling, furious features glared up at him. "Free me, Gray Darien!" he chanted with every surge of his waters. "Free me as you vowed."

Marshal Dartmallow appraised the dam with a cold eye. "When we spoke of a lake, I never expected anything of this extent." His gaze swept the length of the dike. "I imagined rough earthworks and a shallow basin, not this . . . this engineering marvel. How did they do it? They must have worked from the moment Nortallion first entered Morlane. Little wonder Ironwood Station was undeveloped; they spent their resources here."

"They did not do it alone," Loogth said. "The manling Treg helped them. He planned it. It is built on bones of metal, brought by his creatures from the mines of the Yarrow."

"Reinforced with iron?" Dartmallow's face remained unruffled, only his voice betraying his disquietude. "If only we had known what they were doing. If Morlane had told us, if the wolves had brought word. If the rivers had warned us—"

"If we had, would you have listened?" Loogth asked. "We sang our mourning songs; the packs outside Morlane heard. You manlings must have known, but you did nothing."

"There were clues, things the moon said," Vasps admitted, "but he sometimes speaks lunacy. Nor do you wolves trust us enough to send representatives to the All-Council. The rivers think only of traveling to the sea, and if they spoke of the dam, we did not know. Our information came from the birds, who cannot describe size and measurements. It was Morlane's silence that proved our undoing; we would have known if the forest had spoken. Our stubborn independence is our greatest weakness."

"And our strength," the marshal said. "The past is past; we must look to today. Destroying the dam could take weeks. Even if we had the time, unless we defeat him, Treg can repair any damage we do to it."

"Nor is our position long defensible," Gray replied. "As you said, the dam gives us the high ground, but if the Vigili attack in full force, we lack the numbers to defeat them."

The marshal nodded, his expression grim.

Quacaw appeared, cawing excitedly, circling twice before landing on Dartmallow's saddle-horn. "Oldbeard! The news is bad. Bad it is. Bad is the news!"

"What now?" Dartmallow asked.

"The iron-maker, the maker of iron is clever. He is clever as the crows. The burrowing owls told us. It was told us by the owls. More of his iron ones have crossed the mountains. They block your way east. Perhaps, perhaps, there is no way out."

For the first time Gray saw Dartmallow visibly shaken, his face gone pallid. They were caught between the arms of the mountains. To retreat to the west in the early spring, bereft of supplies in a forest emptied of game, would be disastrous.

"Treg planned this carefully," Gray said. "He must have sent them days ago."

"From the time the woman was taken from him, I wager," Vasps said. "It leaves us in a poor position."

The company dismounted. The marshal paced beneath the trees, surveying his officers, Brythibain, Loogth, Quacaw, and the un-speaking oaks. He remained silent so long his men shifted uncomfortably. Finally he said, "Give me your thoughts."

"The geometry of the situation bodes ill," Vasps replied. "True, there is a certain symmetry to it—the reservoir, the mountains to either side, our people in the center, but the Vigili approach from two directions, a clear disequilibrium. We have a chance if we can replace it with a mathematical balance. This might be done by attacking one of their forces before the other arrives; or conversely, we could send ambassadors to try to negotiate. With the duke defeated, we might reach some agreement. It was not we who offended Treg by stealing the woman."

"Aw nuts!" Russ exclaimed.

"There are nuts?" Quacaw looked greedily around.

"It's an expression," Russ said. "What I mean is you can't trust anything Treg says. He's already proved it. Anyway, why should he negotiate when he has nothing to lose except some of his mechanical toys?"

"There are no nuts?" Quacaw asked.

"Russ is right," Dartmallow said. "We will not negotiate with a traitor, nor can we expect mercy if he overwhelms us."

The men looked away from one another, uneasy at the mention of defeat.

Loogth growled. "Humans! The pack never surrenders."

"But the pack knows when to flee," Vasps said.

"If you could fly it would be easy," Quacaw said. "Easy it would be. Over the mountains you could go."

Dartmallow gave a worried smile. "I'm too old to grow feathers, my friend."

Brythibain fountained up, an enraged waterspout. "Why do you waste time talking of treaties and retreat? Where can I run to? Destroy the dam. Free me!"

"A difficult task even if the enemy weren't breathing in our nostrils," Dartmallow said. "If the trees would help us, we would have a chance. If we could rouse these ancient oaks . . ." He paced again, then halted. "Prince Darien, Joiwend believed you were the one who could aid us. Why did she think so?"

Gray felt everyone's eyes upon him. "I don't know. I've asked myself that too."

"The Joy Wind said Gray Darien could be trusted, that he would keep his word," Loogth said. "So the trees told us. Morlane does not trust any human. Trust is a great thing—it is pack law and pack love. If the trees trust you, they will listen, but you must be pack true."

"Trees don't dwell in packs," Gray said. "Do they think in those terms?"

"I speak in the manner of wolves," Loogth said. "I do not know if it is the same with trees, but it is the only way I can say it."

"I've tried speaking to them," Gray said. "Why won't they answer?"

"They will not talk to the wolves anymore, either," Loogth said. "I do not know the cause of their silence."

Gray paused, pondering beside the towering oaks, staring through their gnarled branches at the blue waters of Brythibain surrounded by the fir-covered mountain peaks. A pair of ospreys glided, hunting above the lake's surface; competing thoughts drifted through Gray's mind. Animonea was marvelous beyond belief: delightful, miraculous, at times more perilous than any other country. What was his place in it? If they fought Treg's army at the dam, he might lose his life. But it wouldn't be for Tana. She was beyond his reach. Why didn't he abandon the army and go find her?

But what good would it do if she didn't love him? And there was this: he had made his decision to ally himself with the Republic; he didn't want to see Morlane struck dumb. The talking animals, so alien to him at first, were beautiful—Blunder, with his curiosity and joy, Nutmeg, stubborn and insistent, even the sly wolves and the unfathomable forest. He had come to Animonea thinking his love for Tana the greatest, most important ideal in the world. All the romances said it, the poetry and stories he had read as a youth. But they had spoken of higher matters as well: self-sacrifice, loyalty, fidelity, the precepts his old Greek tutor had taught him.

He had made a promise to Brythibain, given his sacred word, but he had not remained true to it; he had kept his thoughts divided, looking for a way out, journeying through Animonea but selfishly ignoring its wonder, never really *being* there. Heat flowered through his chest; his face burned in shame.

"Marshal Dartmallow," he said. "You've called your country the Republic of Everything, but that is a falsehood."

Dartmallow's face clouded. "What do you mean?"

"You say the Republic represents all creatures, but if Morlane and the wolves were humans, would we talk of deserting them?"

"If they were human, we would take them with us. We can't transport trees. I run an army; my men's blood must not be spilled needlessly."

"True enough, but not pack true." Gray glanced at Loogth. "There is other blood here. Marshal, if we expect the trees to help us, we must commit everything. I speak for myself as well as you. You came here to drive an enemy from your borders, but that isn't the mission. Boundaries change and governments shift. We must free Morlane. We must free the Red Wolves and the osprey, the squirrels and the blue jays, every member of your Republic. We must do so or perish trying. We must make our stand here, beside our allies, and they must know we won't abandon them."

Dartmallow stared at Gray, his face a mask. "That is a hard saying, lad."

"It is. How will you respond? Everything may depend on your answer."

The marshal bowed his head. He looked at his officers.

"The prince has a point," Vasps said. Topper nodded his agreement.

Dartmallow looked up. "That's the heart of it, isn't it? We are either a republic for every one of our citizens or no republic at all. Disunity is destruction; justice and mercy in equal measure are our guides. We have given our word; we will honor our word. We will make our stand, come what may."

"Do you hear, Brythibain?" Gray asked.

The lake erupted. "My waters have heard."

"Loogth?" Gray asked.

"It is pack-true. The Red Wolves will stand with you."

"We fight with our humans," Flapjack nickered.

"I will fight too, Gray," Blunder said.

Gray put his hand on an oak, raised his voice, raised his eyes to its branches. "Morlane! Do you hear us? I am Gray Darien, Joiwend's friend. Will you answer? I am told you do not decide matters quickly, but if you don't wake, if you don't act, you will lose your minds and your thoughts. We need your help to defend against the Vigili. If they defeat us, Brythibain will remain imprisoned, and without his waters your intelligence will continue to wane."

Seconds ticked away without a response. The trees remained sightless, seemingly unaware. He hesitated, uncertain what else to say. "Please!" His voice rang against the mountain slopes. "Your survival depends upon it. Why do you sleep? Speak to us!"

His words passed through the woods, died among the leaves. Joiwend had told the wolves he could help free the land. She had placed her confidence in him. But why? What could he, a stranger in Animonea, do? Why had she thought he could do anything? The heat rose on his face. "Don't you understand? Wake up! This isn't a game! Wake up, for Joiwend's sake!" In frustration, he kicked the trunk. "Wake up!"

"Gray!" Vasps warned.

His anger died, draining away to despair, leaving only an aching foot. He ran one hand over his face, embarrassed. "I'm sorry. I shouldn't have struck you, but you must listen before it is too late."

Blunder nudged Gray's knee with his nose. "They are still sleeping, Gray."

Gray lowered his voice. "I'm a fool for thinking otherwise. Why should they listen? I don't know their ways. Who do I think I am?"

"You tried, Gray," Blunder said. "Should I bark at them? Will that help?"

"No, we're wasting our time. Let's let sleeping trees stand." He turned back toward the others, shaking his head.

The barest whisper ran across the glade.

He hesitated, uncertain what he had heard. Nothing had changed. It had only been the breeze through the branches.

"*Gray Darien,*" the leaves soughed.

The horses lifted their ears, the men turned their heads.

"Where?" Gray asked.

Blunder trotted back to the tree and put his front legs against it. Gray studied the old oak. So slowly he could scarce detect the change, the bark shifted, eyelids appearing, closed at first, but gradually raising like a sleepy child's. Intelligence touched the expression, a mouth appeared, leaf-eyes opened.

"Morlane hears." The oak's words were slurred. "We do not slumber. We ponder. Joiwend told us much. She has shown us our error in trusting the duke."

"Will you help us fight Treg?" Gray asked.

"Humans are like wood ants, eating our limbs one moment, gone the next. The duke, our deceiver, is no more. Treg too shall pass."

At word of Nortallion's death, Gray's breath caught. What then of Tana? Before he could ask about her, Vasps said, "You may be stripped of your intelligence before that happens. Surely you don't want that?"

"We do not," the oak said. "Brythibain must flow once more. You must free him."

"How?" Gray asked.

"You have hands. Use them."

"To succeed, we must have your aid against the Vigili," Gray said. "It will take time to open the waterway, and they will soon overrun us."

"Release the waters first. Prove we can trust the words of a human."

"It would take an army of engineers with explosives to destroy the dam," Russ protested.

The oak did not reply.

Gray struggled to rally his thoughts. "If we could do it, release the reservoir all at once, what would happen?"

"This much water pouring through the valley would be a torrent," Vasps said. "It would flood the forest for leagues."

"And the Vigili as well," Dartmallow said.

"Again, there isn't time," Russ countered.

"Make an opening and I will pour through it," Brythibain said.

"There may be something in that," Vasps said. "Water from the mountains continues to enter the reservoir. There is doubtless a spillway somewhere to the east, funneling the excess away from the Wileywood, back into Animonea, but if we can create a sufficient opening in the dam, the exit pressure would be tremendous."

"There is another consideration," the marshal said. "If the water takes too long to subside, plants and insects will perish. Even trees might die. What would Morlane think of us then?"

They waited a long minute for the oak to reply. At last it said, "Water cuts a river bank and an ancient tree falls, carried downstream. Some must live and some die. That is the way of life."

"Trees always take the long view," Vasps said. "We could warn as many animals as possible, of course, though most have already left the forest. The crows could tell the birds. The lives of insects are ephemeral. Natural disasters often destroy them, maintaining the geometric equilibrium."

"We are not a natural disaster," Dartmallow said. "We are thinking creatures who must consider the consequences to the land. That is part of my responsibilities. The insects have no representatives; we must make the moral choice."

"The river must be freed, slowly or by flood," Loogth said. "That is the decision of the pack. The woods will perish without its waters and our prey will not return to Morlane. Where will the insects be then?"

"So too says Morlane," the oak said.

"Very well," Dartmallow replied, "though it makes me uneasy. I wish the Overcowls were present to have their say, but we will set our course and follow it."

"Fellas, this is all well and good, so long as we can break the dam before the Vigili get here," Russ said, "but if we can't, we need some help fighting them."

"Exactly right," Gray said. "If we show our good faith by

beginning work on the dam, will the forest join us in battle?"

The oak kept silent so long Gray thought it had not heard. He found himself holding his breath. Finally, it rumbled, "We must consider our answer. All of Morlane must decide. Joiwend too hears your words, carried branch to tree, tree to root, root to tree. We will seek her counsel. If all humans were trees like her, we would know their words were true, for we see her whole mind." Its eyes on leaf and bark closed.

"Wait!" Gray said. "You must give us more. We need a strategy!"

The mouth and lids vanished. Though the company waited several minutes, they did not return.

Gray turned unhappily to the others, uncertain what they had gained.

Vasps shook his head. "The ways of trees! Time is almost meaningless to them."

The marshal's expression was bleak. "If we spend our efforts trying to destroy the dam, and the forest doesn't fight with us, we will be caught before the Vigili. It will be a slaughter." He glanced up at the oak. "I have given my promise and I will keep it, but if you do not help us, Morlane, we will surely perish."

"The pack will fight beside you," Loogth said.

"To the death?" Dartmallow asked.

The wolf's eyes shone with a crafty light. "The pack will fight."

Gray took a deep breath. "Joiwend will convince them."

"If she can," Russ said.

"Very well," Dartmallow said. "A plan made is a plan begun. I will divide our force. Some will work on the dike; the others will prepare the defense. We can do no more."

Quacaw, strutting on a branch of the oak, said, "There will be battle?"

"There will," Dartmallow said.

"It is good. Good it is. If you die in battle, Oldbeard, we will feed on you and your army. You will nourish the murder."

Gray frowned, but Dartmallow gave a slight bow. "We are greatly honored by the crows."

"We would do this for you. For you we would do it." Quacaw preened, then cast one eye on Dartmallow's hand. "If you perish, I will take your gold ring from your finger, perhaps, perhaps.

Perhaps I will take it."

"Tremendously thoughtful of you," the marshal replied glumly, then brightened. "Old rascal, you help me win the battle and I'll give you this ring."

Quacaw fluttered his wings in excitement. "That is good, Oldbeard! Good that is! So I will have the ring. The ring I will have. I will win it or win it." He paced happily across the branch, then halted, head turning back and forth in thought. "It is better if you do not die, Oldbeard. I would like that better."

The marshal grinned. "Why, thank you, Quacaw."

"It is nothing. Nothing it is. It is because we are friends."

The marshal gave orders. Gray and Blunder went to help with the dam, leaving Nutmeg with the other horses.

"You talked good to the tree, Gray." Blunder brushed his head against his master's hand.

"I hope so." But a chill ran through him. Men would live or die because he had convinced Dartmallow to commit to the fight. And if the forest flooded, what would happen to Tana?

* * *

Fox Lodan arrived at the dam an hour later under a banner of truce. Escorted from the forward position by Animonean cavalry, he rode in on Dauntless, followed by two-score foot soldiers. At Dartmallow's bidding Gray and Vasps stood on the dike beside the marshal while the company waited below.

"Marshal Dartmallow," Fox called, "it's a relief to see you." Even from a distance, Lodan looked haggard, his usual arrogance subdued.

"State your business, plain and direct," the marshal said.

"We come to offer aid, Marshal. The duke's army is finished — scattered or slain. The duke himself has disappeared. The Vigili are behind us. We tried to escape to Ruheen, but kept running into Treg's warriors. We fight against a common enemy now. Old feuds should be forgotten. Surely you can use a few more men."

"Led by you?" Dartmallow said. "You broke your trust."

"I did not." Fox sat straighter on Dauntless. "I swore no fealty to Animonea. I complied in good faith until captured. Under the duke

I realized my allegiances align better with the royal houses of Ruheen than the Republic of Everything. I will not recant that. Will you accept our offer of aid?"

"I accept your surrender," Dartmallow said. "You will relinquish your weapons. Your men will work on the dam. You will work beside them."

"I am a prince in my own country," Fox said.

"You are a traitor in mine. Your argument has weight, or I would execute you at once. You will go where I send you, or your young head will go down to the grave."

Gray thought Fox truly weary, for he neither glowered nor demurred. His voice sounded resigned. "To what purpose shall we labor?"

"To the purpose I intend."

"If the Vigili come, we would prefer to be armed," Fox said.

"I will decide that when it occurs."

Fox dropped his gaze. "We will obey your orders. If we could get some rations, Marshal, the men would be grateful. Our supply wagons were destroyed in the attack. We haven't eaten in two days."

"I will see that you are fed." Dartmallow turned to Topper, speaking in an undertone. "I don't like it, but we can't afford to spurn their aid. Still, they'll have to be guarded. See to it."

Gray descended the dike and approached Fox.

"Hello, Gray," Dauntless neighed.

"Coming down to gloat?" Fox asked.

"Where is Tana?"

"By the Elf King! Is that girl all you ever think about? Turns out she's a witch like Joiwend; maybe she has you under a spell. She changed into a night heron and flew away. I haven't seen her since."

Gray drew a relieved breath. "You never cared anything for her, did you?"

"I never claimed I did. You have much to learn about politics, Prince. Didn't they teach you anything at court?"

"I was taught to be forthright," Gray said.

Fox chuckled, genuinely amused. "When I first met you, I thought you a spoiled brat sent to play with his betters. I was wrong, but unless you start viewing the world the way it really is, your noble notions will get you killed."

"You're wrong again, Fox. Ideals are what make people greater than they are. You would do well to learn *that*. You're here for only one reason: your men don't know you, they don't trust you, they haven't eaten, and they're ready to cut your throat."

Fox shrugged. "I won't deny it. Any soldier will turn if he gets hungry enough. I would have led them to Ruheen if I could have, but there's more to it. The duke is probably dead because of that pretentious sculptor. Under Nortallion's banner, I might have ridden triumphant into Ruheen; instead, if I get there at all, it will be with a remnant of the duke's soldiers, announcing his defeat. There's a chance I'll be executed as a spy. I don't forget a wrong. I'll have my vengeance on Treg, somehow, some way. He will learn what it means to thwart a prince of the royal house of Jenar."

Gray shook his head and turned away, not even angry. Tana was alive and Fox no longer mattered.

CHAPTER TWENTY-ONE

FORCES OF NATURE

Russ Rogers asked to be in charge of opening the dam. He didn't claim to know much about engineering, but he understood hard work and was good at digging. He only wished the men had real shovels instead of swords and helmets to break up and move the dirt. Wildflowers, weeds, even some saplings grew along the side of the dike, and the ground was full of stones, making the job even harder. The water level lay three feet below them. They had begun carving trenches a few yards apart, only to encounter the iron girders Treg had used in the dam's construction, forcing the workers to excavate around them. The rocks complained about being moved; Brythibain splashed against the barrier, his many voices urging haste; the implements chanted, "*Dig! We dig!*" in unison; the dike rumbled, "*I must hold!*" its voice undulating through the earth. Russ wondered how anybody got anything done quietly.

When Topper appeared with the Ruheens, Russ grinned and shook Fox Lodan's hand. "Glad to see you made it." The prince was cocky, but quick, clever, and courageous, a good man to have in battle. Seeing him raised the sergeant's spirits.

The prince returned Russ' handclasp. "Well met. Our quest has taken many turns."

"More like it's fallen apart, but at least it got us out of Faerie."

"It did indeed. You were right in the end; I was nothing more than a prisoner there."

"We all were."

"These men are to be put to work," Topper said. "They aren't to have any weapons. Marshal's orders."

Russ frowned. "The heck you say! I've got a waterway to cut. You in charge of these people, Fox?"

"I am. Their officers are dead."

"Do I have your word they won't try anything?"

"You have my solemn promise."

Russ turned to the Ruheens. "All right, you fellas. Listen up! You want to stay alive?"

The soldiers murmured their agreement.

"Good! If we don't open this dam, the Vigili are going to overrun us. I'm having Topper here give back your knives. Use them to dig and maybe we'll all survive. Understood?"

"Answer him," Fox commanded.

The Ruheens complied.

"But the marshal—" Topper began.

"Give them their weapons and tell the marshal what I said. I don't want them working in a group, Fox. Scatter them among our people and keep them in line. Maybe you can help us figure out how to get this job done before Treg arrives." Humiliating the prince by forcing him to dig would only make him resentful. Better to have him do what he did best.

"As you say," Fox said, obviously pleased.

Russ spotted Spence's olive army helmet among the gray Ruheen uniforms. "Well, I'll be! Over here, Corporal. They still let you wear that thing?"

Spence separated himself from the group, not meeting Russ' eyes. "They do, Sarge." He tugged the helmet down with one hand. "I don't fancy parting with it."

"Glad to see you among the living. How are you?"

"Had some interesting times."

"You'll have to tell me about it when you can. I see you've still got your trenching tool. I wish I had mine."

"You can use this one."

"No, I've seen you dig. Nobody has your body strength. Let's get some work done."

"Sure, Sarge."

The men fell to the task. The time remained impossibly short.

They needed a miracle.

* * *

There was little sleep that night. With the Vigili only a day's march away, the Animoneans camped on the crest of the dam, working in shifts to free Brythibain, resting only enough to maintain their strength for the enemy attack. Wolves, dogs, and men labored side-by-side, the canines digging with their front paws, throwing the dirt behind them, their coats glistening in the hungry light of bonfires. The men glistened too, stripped to the waist, their skin slick with sweat.

Gray straightened himself to relieve his aching shoulders and back. It disgusted him to have to use his sword to scrabble in the earth. Judging by the overhead stars, it was two hours past midnight, and he was nearly witless from fatigue. Blunder, lacking the stamina of the older dogs, had succumbed to weariness and lay slumbering beside him; Jaunter, fully recovered from his bloodletting, worked nearby with Master Tatters; Russ, long without sleep, labored without pause.

Traveling downward and breaking through the clouds, the waxing moon boomed across the land. "It is a hard thing to admit, but I have not been all I should, but proud, haughty, self-serving. Having passed through a season of terrible darkness, I am repentant. Though weaker than I once was, in gratitude for my survival I vow to dedicate the remainder of my life to serving others. Below me I see quaint little men—how hard they strive—yet I, night-eye of Animonea, feel their pain; I hear the cries of Brythibain, river calling cloud-river above, river to river, through mists of atmosphere, rising finally to me. Hearing them, I know we are all one family— tree to river, river to cloud, cloud to moon, moon to the world. I will shine my beams and bring them peace."

"Half-moon, half-wit, I reckon," Tatters muttered. "At least he shows a tad humility now."

Gray stooped to dig again, his weary mind drifting. What a strange world this was! The moon babbling about the rivers below and rivers above. His drowsy mind turned the words into a song. The rivers below and above. Below and above. He imagined a mist rising from a river, flowing upward to another stream coursing through the sky; and in the sky the moon's face different, scowling like the face of a storm. Scowling like—

He started so violently Blunder stirred beside him, eyes heavy with slumber. "What is it, Gray?"

"Sleep, my friend. I'll be back." He headed along the dike, away from the bonfires. There had been clouds in the north earlier that evening, and several days before that. Had he seen what he suspected, noticing but not noticing? Had he witnessed it more than once since entering the Back of the Beyond?

Blunder padded beside him. "Where are we going, Gray?"

"I told you to go back to sleep."

Blunder nudged the prince's leg. "I want to go with you, Gray."

Gray smiled, heartened by the pup's loyalty. Away from the fires, he could see the sky clearly. Moonlight against the mountains cast a shadow over part of the lake; clouds crowded the northern sky, perpetually forming and collapsing into figures and faces. So many faces. When he first came to Animonea, their constant, disquieting stares had made him uneasy. Over time he had learned to ignore them. Perhaps that had been a mistake.

The moon lit clouds eggshell white, deep blue, or nearly black, marbled in texture and locked in continuous battle, vapors snatching tufts from one another to fashion sentient faces, life seeking to become and to be, struggling for the right to exist though enduring for only the barest moments. Yet there was victory in those moments. For a fraction of eternity they lived, and that was something, after all.

Gray watched the clouds, hoping he was correct, hoping to see a particular face, one that formed and reformed, gone only to return, a persistence beyond reckoning, passing unnoticed unless one thought to look for it. Had he dreamed it? He wasn't sure. He was so tired.

His eyes grew strained; he rubbed them and looked again. A breeze wafted his hair. Blunder sat on his haunches beside him, looking over the water, scenting the air, contented in the way of dogs, asking no questions, probably not even wondering what they were doing, satisfied like the clouds just to be.

Gray gasped. For a moment he thought . . .

The vapors gently rolled. He raised his arm and pointed, his voice a whisper. "There!" He saw the face; the familiar eyes, the shape of the head and jaw, the line of the nose. He burst into a run, eager to get closer. Reacting to his excitement, Blunder scrambled beside him along the top of the dam.

He came to the end of the dike and climbed upward over the rough mountain slope. He tried to call, but his voice came in gasps. Before ascending fifty strides, he had to stop to catch his breath.

The clouds rolled over; the face vanished, lost among the fray. Gray fell to his knees, one arm over Blunder's shoulder, staring, desperate to see it reform.

Long minutes passed without result. Finally, he rose, brain whirling, excited despite his exhaustion, and trudged back down the mountainside. When he reached the dike, he heard one of the many voices of Brythibain. "Why are you fleeing, Gray Darien? You promised to help me."

Gray was too tired to answer the insult. He stared at the face in the water, considering. "You are the river that flows from the mountains through the Omnifire?"

"I am a branch of that river. I have many names in many places. Here I am Brythibain, for I am always angry."

"A river is in contact with the air above it, isn't it?"

"I feel the wind upon my surface. Sometimes we speak together when her voice is strong."

"Can you talk to the clouds?"

"My riverbed stirs the wind, the wind stirs the clouds. I have spoken to the high-risers, but their lives are brief and they are stupid."

"There is someone up there who might help us, one who forms and reforms as a cloud. Could you try to contact him?"

"I could, but how could he help? Will he fight for us?"

"I don't know. Will you try?"

Brythibain and Gray talked for some time before the prince finally returned to his digging.

* * *

Ninette walked beside Treg late the following evening, tramping between scattered pines up the foothills of the mountains toward the dam, the sculptor marching resolutely forward, taking his long strides while she and his men struggled to keep pace. Leather cords bound her hands before her, making it difficult to catch herself if she fell. One of the soldiers, taking pity on her, helped her along. For a time, she had ridden beside Treg in his narrow carriage, but he had been forced to abandon the vehicle when they began their ascent. Throughout the journey, he remained in a high state of excitement, laughing in pleasure as he gave orders or received messages from his minions. He told her stories of growing up in the North Rond, where he had been ridiculed for his appearance, of the vengeance taken on the many who had wronged him, and of his work.

"The great artist is always misunderstood," he said, "especially a genius of consummate skill and imagination such as myself. My aspirations are so far above those of plebeian humankind, they cannot even conceive them." With his long face, thin waist, and high-crested plumed helmet, Ninette thought he looked like a starved chicken. That made her laugh, and she was glad, for when she first surrendered to him, she had wept.

"What do you find amusing?" he demanded.

Before she could reply, a messenger hurried toward them.

"Lord Treg, the commanders report the Vigili should all be in place by tomorrow afternoon."

"Excellent!" He pulled a folding telescope from his pocket and studied the dam, his face alight with pleasure. "You should see this, my puppet, the entire Animonean army trapped by the brilliance of Treg, lined up on the levee as if facing an execution squad. How easily my Vigili shall overwhelm them." He offered her the telescope, but she pushed it away. "I can see well enough without it."

"You are piqued, my dear. It ill becomes your beauty. When these are swept away, it will signal a new ascendancy for me. You will become a lovely side note when history records my majesty."

She thrust her lip forward. "I don't want to be a side note! I'm a person, and those are my friends down there."

"Friends, like family, are for weaklings and commoners," Treg said. "Forget them! Bask! Bask in the wonder of Treg! Take joy in him, and perhaps when he has dismantled you and learned the secret of your making, he will reassemble you as his consort. You should exalt! What honor I give you! Imagine yourself, the Lady of Morlane, Mistress of the Wileywood." He boomed in laughter while she paled in terror of being dissected. "Treg shall build a palace where the duke's insignificant fortress now stands. I see it in my mind, a mansion of ivory and iron, marble and timber of every hue and color, with statues of Treg twenty, no!—thirty feet high, guarding its gates. Flames burn on its ramparts, illuminating the carved Tregs gazing down like beatific angels. A thousand lanterns light its halls, the furs of Animonea's most exotic beasts carpet its floors. It is glorious! Glorious!"

Ninette grew pensive, not only frightened for herself and her comrades, but disquieted in seeing a fraction of herself in Treg's behavior. In Faerie she had witnessed the conduct of children. Though they had made little impression on her at the time, the sculptor acted the same, a little boy enamored of his toys. Had her own emotional reactions been so sweeping, so self-centered? Joiwend had once used a phrase in the language of her own country to describe an outrageous, unruly child: *l'enfant terrible*. That was Treg, a preening, sulking baby. Was she like that? Were the two of them spoiled toddlers thrown together by circumstances? If she survived, she swore she wouldn't be such a creature. And she wondered with some amazement if Treg were not more a puppet than she, dangling and motivated by strings of which he was unaware.

* * *

By late afternoon of the next day the crows and wolves brought the news of the Vigili's arrival.

"The iron manlings from the heights have spread themselves across the mountain," Loogth told Dartmallow while Gray and his companions stood by. "And on the other side too."

"Completely surrounded," Dartmallow said. "We're in for it now, wouldn't you say, Topper?" They were standing on the dike. Russ' brigade had the barest stream flowing down the dam, scarcely a trickle compared to what was needed. As it ran it sang a sparkling song so soft it could scarcely be heard. *To the sea, to the sea!*" The work was wearing the men down, forcing the marshal to give them more time to rest. The bulk of many-voiced Brythibain raged to no avail, swirling against the dam, pressing toward the opening. The trees remained silent. A storm roiled to the north, casting distant lightning across the horizon.

The army was arrayed along the top of the dam, the archers in front, the horses and other soldiers immediately behind. The men had collected heavy stones from the mountainside and dead tree limbs trimmed to use as poles to push the enemy away. If Treg's creations mounted the dike, the plan was to drive them into the water.

A breeze began to blow, the storm rising behind the lake. Faces lifted and fell within the clouds. Overhead, the sky remained clear. Gray licked his lips and studied the approaching tempest.

Master Tatters followed his gaze. "If that thunderhead gets here, we're plumb easy targets."

"If it does, the Vigili should make dandy lightning rods," Russ said.

Jaunter laughed. "That would make for a merry melee."

The moments passed. The army stood ready. The breeze blew cool, refreshing Gray's brow. He grimaced, gripping a pole shod with iron, keeping his sword—mostly useless against the Vigili— sheathed, wondering what chance they had. Unless help came, they could do little more than a holding action.

As if perceiving his thoughts, Blunder whined at his feet. He reached down and ruffled the pup's ears. "Are you afraid, Blunder?"

"I am ready to fight," the dog said. "I am not afraid to die, Gray. I have seen death, but I do not understand what it is."

"Nor I." Their mismatched eyes met, blue and brown. Gray laughed.

"What is funny, Gray?"

"We are two of a kind, little friend. Two odd creatures in a world filled with those whose eyes are both the same color."

"Is that funny, Gray? We are a pack."

"It isn't funny. It's good. Your courage comforts me. We are a pack."

The dog wagged his tail, happy beneath his master's hand.

The crows came flying, cawing, *They are there! They are there!* The Vigili had reached a predetermined position. Topper bawled an order. The archers strung their bows, nocked their arrows, and let fly. The familiar cries of the shafts dwindled into the woods, dropping in pitch as they sailed. The hope was to kill or wound some of the overseers. Even a handful could make a difference.

Three times the archers fired, then waited, shafts nocked, for the first Vigili to crash through the treeline.

Despite the breeze, sweat beaded Gray's brow. He wiped it away with the back of his hand. The noise of cracking branches rose from the forest. Shadows moved among the foliage. His pulse quickened.

The sounds stopped. Gray held his breath. They must be massing for the assault. The wind whispered around his ears. Despair tore at him. Why hadn't the trees awakened? Had they decided not to help? Or had they simply been unable to make up their minds?

Time slowed. The seconds stretched to minutes. Still the Vigili did not appear. Gray's hopes rose. Perhaps the forest was doing something silent but lethal; perhaps they had a chance.

A shout came from the woods, a command echoed by other voices. As one, the Vigili stepped into view, a solid line of inhuman soldiers, marching without hesitation toward the dike, covering the distance in twenty stiff strides. Gray gaped at their numbers. How could there be so many? Had Treg brought more from his caverns? Once more, they had underestimated the sculptor's guile.

Nutmeg nickered uneasily. Blunder growled. A wolf gave a long howl. The Prince of Stallions set aside his pole and lifted one of the heavy stones lying at his feet.

From the Animonean side, a trumpeter sounded retreat on the captured Vigili horn, a desperate attempt by Dartmallow to confuse the enemy. Disregarding it, the Vigili climbed the dike, clumsy but implacable, their emotionless faces more terrible than any expression of fury. Topper's voice rang out, a command passed down the line. The archers stepped back, watching for Treg's human overseers, but their quarry remained concealed in the woods. The horses turned, preparing to kick. Gray gripped the stone.

To his left, Master Tatters sang, but whether Comanche battle-hymn or death knell, Gray did not know. Both Russ and the old pioneer twirled their lariats, each hoping to pin at least one Vigili's arms against its body and drag it off its feet. To Gray's right, Jaunter lifted his sagaris above his shoulder, eager to strike.

The enemy ascended the slope in an uneven line. Gray lifted the heavy stone with both hands, aiming for the creature directly in front of him, heaving it when his target was halfway up the bank. It flew true, striking the warrior on the forehead, breaking its neck joints, leaving its head dangling down its back. No longer able to see before it, it collided with another Vigili, sending both rolling downhill. Nutmeg caught a foe at the kneecap, breaking the joint and sending it sprawling.

Gray seized another stone and cast it, but missed his mark, striking the warrior's chest. It toppled backward, unharmed, and returned to its feet.

A roar sounded behind Gray, and a wave cascaded over the dam, missing the Animoneans, but washing several Vigili off the slope. By gradually building momentum, Brythibain could create such a surge, but it was slow work, taking time to form in the depths of the lake.

Gray cast his final stone and seized his pole. The Vigili were within striking distance, and he swung with all his strength, sweeping under his enemy's sword, smashing at its arm socket. The arm dropped useless to the creature's side, but it still advanced, and another marched beside it.

Blunder dove in, biting at the second Vigili's legs. The iron warrior swept its sword down, straight at the pup's neck.

Gray thrust his pole forward, awkwardly parrying the stroke. Blunder ducked and drew back.

Russ' lariat fell over the Vigili, tightening, pulling its arms against its sides. Gray rammed his pole against the creature, knocking it down the dike, but the other warrior lurched forward, flailing at Gray with its good arm. The prince ducked beneath the killing blow, its wind whipping past his head. He fled backward, off balance, to avoid the follow-through, giving the Vigili time to reach the top of the dike. Holding his pole in both hands, the prince parried the next stroke, a blow jolting him to his shoulders. Driven back by its force, he stumbled, but caught himself on one hand and leapt up.

By the time he regained his footing, he stood at the water's edge. Brythibain roared behind him; the Vigili loomed before him.

Blunder attacked the creature from the side, teeth and paws

against unyielding iron. The warrior swiveled its head toward the pup.

As the Vigili's attention wavered, Gray wedged his pole between its ankles and pushed to the side, leveraging it off-balance. Carried forward by its momentum, it fell off the dike and vanished beneath Brythibain's waters.

Gray's efforts threw him to the ground. Blunder bounded to his side and turned protectively toward the advancing army. The Prince of Stallions stood. For an instant the whole battle lay before him, and he groaned in despair.

The Vigili covered the entire length of the slope. Several were crossing onto the top, relentless as marching ants. It would have been difficult enough facing the Vigili they had seen before Ironwood Station, but the additional ones, brought from unknown caches, made victory impossible. As the sunlight shone on the desperate visages of the defenders and the pitiless features of the enemy, Gray realized Treg had always intended to create his own kingdom.

Master Tatters lay on the ground—alive or dead, Gray did not know. Jaunter stood over him, chanting in his native tongue, swinging his sagaris like a hammer, striking with its side. Russ and several other Animonean soldiers fought furiously, a half-circle of resistance against the foe. On the other side of the channel carved by the Animoneans, Fox Lodan rode Dauntless back and forth across the top of the dam, rallying his men and battering the Vigili with a heavy mace. But none of them could last long. Gray would die here, defending neither his father's kingdom nor Tana, perishing for a land he had never truly understood.

Brythibain fell silent, his waves diminishing. Even the river knows we've lost, Gray thought.

Four Vigili crowded toward him at once. He raised his pole, bracing himself for the onslaught, determined to take as many of them with him as he could. Nutmeg appeared by his side, her flank bleeding from a cut. She turned, preparing to lash out with her back hooves.

A lightning bolt struck the four foes, a blast of electricity so deafening Gray lurched backward, tumbling into the reservoir. Nutmeg, instinctively fleeing, splashed down heavily beside him.

The water closed over him, mare and man entangled, hooves scarcely missing his head. He pushed against her belly with his feet, trying to get clear, struggling to return to the surface. In his ears, the voice of the lake sounded clear and deep. "He has heard and he has come! Now we strike!"

Gray and Nutmeg broke the surface at the same time. The mare floundered in the water, rumbling in fear, vainly trying to reach the top of the dike.

"Hold steady, girl!" Gray commanded, sputtering water from his mouth. "Rear up and push with your hindquarters!" He had to repeat the command twice before she mastered her fright, and with an effort, got her front hooves onto the edge and scrambled over the embankment. Once he knew she would make it, he grasped her tail, using it to help him ascend.

Crawling over the edge, he froze, astonished at the sizzling cacophony of lightning striking the Vigili all along the apex of the dike. Brythibain roared, twice as loud as before, surging against the dam, bringing all his weight against the channel carved by the soldiers. At the bottom of the long slope, the branches of the trees writhed in fury. Morlane had awakened. The earth itself quaked in concert.

A hoarse shout rose from Gray's lips. He leapt up with renewed strength. Near the treeline, several Vigili hung suspended by their necks between flailing branches. Human overseers broke from the woods to escape the grasping limbs.

Yet Treg's army was far from defeated, for the Vigili had no fear, and would follow their last orders to the end.

Dripping with water, Gray looked for his pole. Blunder, holding it in his jaws, dragged it to him.

A crash of thunder sounded, a voice within it so loud Gray could not comprehend its words at first. *"Stand away from the channel, all of you! Stand away!"*

Despite its booming pitch, Gray recognized that voice. He dared a look behind him, knowing what he would see, what he had hoped to see, what he had never truly expected to see, for the face of the tempest was that of their lost comrade, the bard-enchanter Soonderkainen. The visage hung gigantic in the sky, rain-swept but clear, formed of clouds dark and light, like a god of the storm, the features unmistakable even down to the flowing golden hair, its color created by coruscations of streaming electricity. When he had fought the gale on their first day in the Back of the Beyond, he had not been destroyed. His magic and the life-force of Animonea had saved and transformed him.

Soonderkainen's voice blared again in crackling thunder. "*Away from the stream!*" For an instant Gray did not understand the meaning, then he started shouting at Russ and the others, ordering them to get back from the channel. Even after they understood, they struggled to obey against the Vigili pressing around them.

Before they were scarcely thirty paces from the stream, the storm that was Soonderkainen released a wind that blew with hurricane force, blasts of air aimed at the cleft in the dike, but sending men and Vigili alike tumbling to the earth. Powered by the squall, Brythibain redoubled his efforts, smashing wave after wave against the dam.

There came a blast that was more than a bolt of lightning, a funnel of energy cackling down like all the world's witches laughing at once, striking the channel with an irresistible, unbelievable detonation, unearthing and melting the iron girders, boiling the water in the sedimentary rocks until they exploded. Gray buried his head against the ground, only to be sent rolling down the dike by the wind and the sheer force of the sound wave. He blacked out, but revived at the bottom in time to feel the earth give a final, tremendous shake and see the dam part, an enormous gash releasing the flood of Brythibain. Clambering to his feet, he sprinted back up the slope to escape the waters. Halfway to the top he saw Blunder sitting on his belly, ears down, either dazed or frozen in fear, the waves nearly upon him.

Gray leapt to his side, scooping him up an instant before the torrent slammed into the place where he had been. Then Gray ran as he had never run before, nearly straight to the side to avoid the deluge, then upward toward the levee's summit. He reached the top and threw himself to the ground, the pup in his arms. He gaped at the sight of Brythibain surging between the widening rift, pouring between the arms of the mountains, filling the valley, carrying away both Vigili and ancient trees.

The dam crumbled with terrible speed. The Vigili, knowing only to avoid obstacles, could not apprehend their danger. The collapsing earth sent them sprawling. The waters gleefully took them, Brythibain shouting, triumphant at his freedom.

Gray caught sight of Jaunter and Russ lifting a dazed Tatters to his feet. Spence was nowhere in sight. If Fox and his men had survived, they were on the other side of the rift. Joining his three friends, they soon found Dartmallow and Vasps.

The marshal led the army along the dike, heading east, barely keeping pace with the dam's deterioration. At last they reached the mountainside, but continued climbing to escape the rising waters.

When Dartmallow finally called a halt, they looked out over complete devastation. The dam was destroyed; the waters roared past it, endless, implacable, flooding Morlane, dragging the Vigili down to its depths.

* * *

Treg had camped the night before on the mountain slope and had spent the day giving orders and basking in his coming victory. Now, as the storm assaulted his Vigili, he screeched incoherently, his hands to his head.

Ninette watched in awe, uncertain whether to dance and clap her hands or cry in terror for her friends. At first, the sight of Soonderkainen's face billowing in the storm had filled her with delight. She *had* danced then, excited to see her old mentor and comrade; but when he struck the dam with his lightnings, it was as if he had forgotten his former allies, intending to destroy them all.

With her bound hands, she took the telescope from Treg's limp grasp, and if the sculptor noticed, he did not react. Through its lens, she watched the marshal's army retreating along the dike, fleeing in both directions from the sundering flood. She saw the Vigili swept away, leaving few to pursue the Animoneans.

"My creations!" Treg stood rooted, fixed on the scene of his disaster. "My beautiful creations!"

The dike crumbled, torn asunder by storm and trembling earth, shouting a long wail of despair as it fell. Boulders rolled down the mountainside, growling as they tumbled. Within moments, the water had risen nearly to where the sculptor stood. Treg looked upon it, uncomprehending.

"How?" he cried against the buffeting wind shrieking, "*Onward!*" in his face.

Soonderkainen rolled toward them, his visage blue with rain, his eyes calm but set. For an instant, Ninette thought perhaps he recognized her, but she couldn't be certain. He might target the Vigili guarding the sculptor. She looked desperately around at the rising water, seeking an avenue of escape, but there was nowhere to go and she was surrounded by the soldiers.

She tugged at Treg's arm. "We have to leave!"

The sculptor awakened to his own danger. "This way!" They hurried up the mountain's feet.

"I have more soldiers in the heights," Treg said. "Dartmallow may have turned me a nasty trick, but we will destroy him yet."

They had to move at an angle, and the way steepened the farther they went. The flood rose with incredible speed, and they were still below the level of the dam. They reached a long escarpment and followed it upward. In the confusion Ninette slipped a knife from the scabbard of the man beside her and cut her bonds.

The water rose to only a few feet below them, a rushing triumph of river, nature unleashed without mercy, jubilant in *being*, its mirth filling the valley, the laughter of victory and freedom and the end of bondage; and the thunder answered its glorious reply. The nearby pines, eyes wide, boomed their exultation even while their comrades vanished beneath the flood.

The escarpment under Ninette's feet began to slide. She shrieked and leapt forward to firmer ground. Turning, she saw the Vigili and their overseers had vanished, swept away in the stone deluge. Only Treg remained, hanging precariously onto the mountainside, one long hand gripping a broken tree root, the other forearm braced on the ledge.

"Help me!" he shouted. "Help Treg!"

Without hesitation, Ninette dropped to her knees, no longer seeing an enemy, but only someone in danger. The ledge lay below her, and she cast herself on her stomach, reaching for him.

"I will not end like this!" He grasped her hands, pulling himself up by the tree root. "I am Treg and I will not end like this!"

They were nearly face to face, his eyes wide with fright. She pulled with all her might.

The ghost of a smile touched his face, a whisper of triumph. He pulled one knee over the ledge. "Treg will prevail as he always does. I will destroy Dartmallow's little army with my Vigili. I will smash them like insects. I am—"

"Ooh!" Ninette pulled her hands free and gave him a shove.

"Treeeeeg!" he screamed. He hit the water hard. For an instant, she thought he would swim, but his magnificent armor dragged him down. He vanished beneath the flood, his own name upon his lips.

Ninette pulled herself to her feet. There was no time to think or feel. She hurried along the escarpment, running with desperate urgency on a crumbling edge scarcely a foot wide, struggling to keep her balance against the trembling earth.

By the time she reached solid ground and climbed above the surging waters, she was gasping for breath. The flood had reached the level of the dam. She was safe.

She looked over the devastation and wept in sorrow and joy. If Treg had kept his mouth shut, if he hadn't boasted about killing her friends, her pity wouldn't have turned to fury. She couldn't help it if she was an emotional person.

* * *

When Soonderkainen unleashed his lightnings, Rick Spence— fighting alongside Fox Lodan and the Ruheen soldiers—was thrown, deafened and dazed, halfway down the dike. He stumbled to his feet and turned just as a wall of water hit him, tossing him back down, then lifting him, helpless amid the deluge. He shot downward, twisting and turning, struggling to stay above the waves, powerless as driftwood. Swallowing water, choking, he was pushed deep, but thrusting with his upper body, regained the surface, coughing, sputtering, the surging flood turning him in circles. He collided with an Animonean soldier and pushed off the man's shoulders, plunging the warrior beneath the waves and raising Spence high enough to draw a deep breath. He never saw the man come up again.

Swept through the forest, his shoulder struck a trunk, and for the barest instant, his eyes met the tree's resolute gaze. In his desperate struggle, he scarcely felt the blow.

A log bobbed beside him, and he clutched it to his chest. He tried to face forward to see where he was going but—flotsam on the waves—was powerless to keep from spinning.

So rapidly did the water rise, he soon rode among Morlane's highest branches, and before he could catch hold of one, even they were engulfed. He careened onward, struggling to breathe, fighting to keep above the torrent while Brythibain's laughter roared all around him. The walls of the canyon were distant. He couldn't do anything but hold on, even as his strength began to falter.

He bit his lip, snarling. Never one to surrender, he had fought long odds his whole life. His childhood enemies had failed to kill him; the Nazis had failed to kill him; the dangers of Faerie he had overcome. His helmet, held in place by its chin strap, yelled for him to keep fighting. He thrust with his legs. If there was high ground, a plateau or a hillock, he would find it.

Still, he could make no progress. A leaf on the waves, he was swept along.

His legs grew weak, numb, until he could no longer kick them. He scarcely had enough strength to hold onto the log.

Something grasped his collar, a sharp edge cutting into his neck. There was movement above him, the beating of great wings. He was lifted out of the deluge, still clutching the log. A sharp beak came down, the head of an eagle, pecking his hand, impaling it like a spear. Gasping in pain, he let the log fall. The eagle pulled him up, his feet dangling a foot above the waves.

He reached up, grasping the rough talons. The bird was impossibly huge, as large as Spence himself. Even so, it struggled to stay aloft, and Rick's feet dipped in and out of the water. Slowly, heavily, they made their way across the flood, until at last the bird deposited him on a rough outcropping a few feet above the torrent. He fell to his knees; the eagle dropped exhausted to the ground.

"Who are you?" Spence gasped.

The bird changed, its wings and beak shortening, its head widening, its talons turning to booted feet. Fetch sat gasping for breath.

"Why?" Spence asked.

Fetch lifted his head, peering at Spence with his dead eyes. "I told you; I am bonded to Jaunter's friends, my companions in battle. Besides, you and I have an agreement. Now come! The water still rises."

Supporting one another, they made their way up the mountain-side.

CHAPTER TWENTY-TWO

THE PARTING WATERS

Gray stood alone on a wide ledge overlooking the flood far below. In the last shards of twilight the waters ran silver, less violent now, but still a rushing tide. The storm clouds had passed, leaving serrated wisps with squinting eyes that might or might not be those of Soonderkainen. The breeze was cool and sweet, the sunset, golden. Blunder dozed on his forepaws beside Gray, his body rising and falling with his breath.

After the breaking of the dam, most of the Animonean soldiers had reached high ground. From there the marshal led them farther up the slopes, a journey made more arduous by transporting the wounded, including Master Tatters, who had taken a blow to the head and a cut to the shoulder. With uncharacteristic tenderness, Jaunter carried him in his arms until he revived enough to ride on Ransom's back. Though dazed and weak, he would survive.

At the crest, they had encountered the rest of the Vigili army, silent and unmoving, their overseers fled. Lacking orders, they ignored the Animoneans passing through their midst, strange idols keeping futile watch; but Dartmallow prudently led his exhausted men a safe distance beyond their ranks before making camp.

Gray glanced back at the Animonean fires in the heights, but remained where he was, looking west. A sudden chill ran through him, a longing for heat. Despite his fatigue, he could not rest, thinking with a dull ache of Joiwend lying under the deep waters and Tana somewhere in Morlane, wondering if either still lived.

The moon, riding high in the sky, rumbled from the heavens. "Oh, Widfroth, Great River of the East, your dreadful fetters you have sundered! How wondrous, how marvelous! No more diminished your raging streams, no more the longing of your troubled waters for liberty. What a fight it was! What victory! I sing your freedom, Widfroth!"

Blunder raised his head. Gray smiled, reached down, and ruffled the pup's beautiful white coat, his sorrow turning to unexpected joy. He too was glad the river was free. Animonea had seeped into him without his knowing. Remembering he had not wanted the pup at first, he murmured, "The debt is canceled."

Blunder lifted his ears. "What does that mean, Gray?"

"Do you remember how I saved your life at the bridge?"

"I remember, Gray. The water was too strong because I was small."

"You saved my life at the dam by distracting the Vigili. If you hadn't been there, I would have died."

The dog looked up at him. "That is true, Gray, but I do not understand."

"I saved your life and you saved mine."

Blunder wagged his tail. "We are a pack."

"Yes, but—" Gray fell silent, realizing Blunder could never understand. Equity, either in favor or revenge, was incomprehensible to his mind.

Across the deluge birds flew, the fading sunlight on their wings, a flock of seven too distant to identify. Gray watched the slow beating of their flight across the flood. They came close, lifting to rise above the mountains, passing gradually to his left, and he realized they were blue herons. He started to turn toward camp, when one bird, larger than the rest, left the flock. He studied its faltering flight, thinking it injured. It drifted downward, ever nearer, gliding at the last before landing nearly at his feet.

Blunder stood, interested. Enormous for one of its kind, the heron cocked its head toward Gray, then fluttered and changed into Tanabel-Tunia, her eyes wide with relief. "Gray! Oh, Gray! I knew you'd wait for me!" She rushed into his arms. "My father is gone, the army lost! I've nowhere left to go! You're the only one who can help me!"

He dissolved into her desperate embrace.

* * *

A week passed and still the marshal's army lingered. Because of the slope of the land, Brythibain receded rapidly, though it remained a rushing flood. Helped by a flock of ravens, Quacaw's murder located those Animonean soldiers stranded on the far shore and guided them upriver to a passable crossing.

For Gray, the time with Tana was sheer joy. He refused to dwell on the way she had rejected him. In the confusion of battle and her need to find her father, she obviously hadn't been thinking clearly. Now he had a second chance. They spent time together, renewing their friendship without his pressing her for anything more. Having come so far to find the duke, she grieved terribly at Nortallion's absence, refusing to brook any criticism or suggestion of wrongdoing on his part, and Gray learned to measure his words carefully. He could not bring himself to tell her of the forest's claim that her father had perished, but did his best to cheer her, getting her to smile or laugh at his jests, though he learned she could not bear even the gentlest teasing.

When he asked her how it felt to change into another form, she became aloof, not looking at him at all, as she often did when dealing with a disagreeable subject. "It was pleasant enough when I took Ninette's likeness. I enjoyed that, but I hated being a bird. It was awful, thinking its thoughts." She scowled in disgust. "I never want to be an animal again."

Watching her in profile, he realized there was something different about her, a slight sharpening of her features, a touch of rose on her cheekbones.

"You've lost your freckles," he said.

"Have I?" Her gaze remained distant. "Perhaps the air of this strange country affects them. If so, I'm grateful; I never liked them."

"I think they're adorable."

"Do you?" She abruptly changed the subject, and they spoke no more concerning it, leaving him feeling he had given offense. He did not remember her being so fragile before, so vulnerable, but decided he was being unfair after her many hardships.

Ninette Argilla appeared the day after Tana arrived, hungry and limping from a fall. Gray scarcely knew what to make of her, this woman who burst into tears at sight of her former companions, hugging them with such fervor that Russ turned scarlet, and Master Tatters, still recovering from his wounds, chuckled with delight. But seeing her face for the first time, Jaunter stared wide-eyed and speechless, abashed as a boy, all boisterousness gone.

She and Tana became nearly inseparable. This vexed Gray, who wished to share his beloved with no one, but so sweet was Ninette's nature, so childlike her demeanor, he could scarcely stay annoyed with her for long.

* * *

One morning, at Marshal Dartmallow's behest, Vasps, Gray, and Loogth descended into Morlane, wading across scattered pools, sinking to their ankles in mud. The forest was a disaster, trees felled, vegetation uprooted, timber piled against the tallest boles. All the surviving trees were awake, their eyes peering from trunk and leaf, their gazes sharp, thoughtful, solemn.

Vasps addressed a pair of great oaks. "We have done as we promised. We hope this portends a stronger bond between Morlane and the Republic of Everything."

The oaks looked down, their expressions gentle. The largest spoke, his voice deep and ancient. "From Joiwend came the call. She woke us when we slept, we who did not know how drowsy we had become. He who was Brythibain and is now Widfroth flows to our roots again, bringing nourishment and knowledge. Our thoughts are no longer dulled. Joiwend's friend, Gray Darien, spoke to us; he spoke to the lake who spoke to the sky and brought Soonderkainen Stormlord down. Morlane is pleased. No more will we be the Wileywood to the children of the Republic, but Gladglade, where humans may walk so long as they do not cut us. Only the duke's men will be barred from the forest. Nortallion deceived us. We will not forget his face. If we see him again, we will tear him up by the roots."

Vasps flourished a bow. "That is excellent news! The All-Council will be elated. All of Animonea will rejoice."

A lump came into Gray's throat. "Is Joiwend still alive?"

"She lives," the oak said. "The waters flow around her, but she survived the flood."

"She remains a tree?"

The oak furrowed his bark. "Why would she wish to be otherwise? Surely being an unrooted human—running here and there to find nourishment, hiding in shelters from the snow and the rain—cannot be better than feeling the wind on her leaves, the sunshine on her boughs, the earth enveloping her burrowing roots. She dreams now, lost in the wonder of wood and leaf. When she has dreamed enough, she will speak again."

Gray hung his head, relieved to know she had survived, but fearful she would never be human again.

"The wolves fought for the forest," Loogth said. "Will the forest bring back the animals? Will there be prey again?"

"We will no longer drive them out," the oak said. "We will spread the word and they will return."

"That is well," Loogth said.

With low bows, the men and Loogth departed.

* * *

The next day Marshal Dartmallow ordered the breaking of the camp.

The red wolves had vanished into the depths of the forest, but the crows remained, sometimes slipping from the trees to snatch scraps of fish, or brass rivets or coins, making it unwise to leave anything shiny about. Quacaw, who strutted and preened as if his murder had defeated Treg single-clawedly, came circling the marshal three times before fluttering to the closest branch. Grinning, Gray pointed him out to Tana, but she only gave the bird a sulking glance.

"I have been patient, Oldbeard. Patient I have been," Quacaw said. "The gold ring sits on your finger. There on your finger it sits. Promises were made. Made were promises."

The pressure of battle over, Dartmallow threw back his head and laughed. "I am glad, old friend, that we are both here to recall those promises. But we are a long way from home. If I give you the ring now, will you carry it all the leagues to your nest? Better I should hold it for you a time."

Quacaw cawed and flapped his wings indignantly. "No, no! Oldbeard is clever, perhaps, perhaps. Wiley as the woods is Oldbeard. You said you would give it. It was said by you."

"Don't get your feathers in a flurry, though I must say I'm disappointed by your lack of trust." Dartmallow looked at the ring fondly. "I suppose Mother will understand." He handed it to the crow.

Clutching the treasure, Quacaw soared through the woods, cawing in triumph. "It is mine! Mine it is!" After several loops, he landed on another branch and held the ring in one claw to admire it. Immediately three other crows swooped down beside him, inciting a pecking and flapping altercation. Breaking free, Quacaw flew to the sanctuary of Dartmallow's shoulder.

"I have been thinking, Oldbeard. Thinking I have been. Perhaps, perhaps, you should keep the ring until we are closer to my nest, perhaps, perhaps."

"That is an excellent suggestion," Dartmallow said. "Very wise of you. Happy to do it. I'll give it back whenever you like."

All the horses had escaped the flood, including Joiwend's mare, Maravilla, whom Ninette rode. Gray led Tana on Nutmeg; Master Tatters and Russ traveled side-by-side. After losing his initial bashfulness, Jaunter kept close to Ninette, and the two were soon talking and laughing like old friends.

Before they had gone half a league, Quacaw returned. "There is news. News there is. News is there. The trees have told us. It is true. The fox who is Lodan asked the trees. The trees told him of the woman. They told him. He wishes to speak. To speak he wishes. To her. Her to. He asks."

"Fox is still alive?" Tana exclaimed. "I thought he was lost in Treg's ambush."

"How did he convince the forest to pass this message?" Vasps asked.

"He rode with Gray," Quacaw answered. "With Gray he rode. Gray is forest friend. He fought with us on the dam. The trees did not know what to do. To do they did not know. Perhaps, perhaps they did wrong."

Tana turned to Gray. "He was at the dam? Why didn't you tell me?"

"I assumed he perished in the flood." Though he spoke truthfully enough, he had been disinclined to entertain the possibility of Fox's survival. His face burned; his reply came biting and angry. "He's an enemy of the Republic."

"Oh, Gray, we have to see him! He must have news of my father! Why else would he come?"

"He wants to meet where the waters narrow," Quacaw said. "Where the waters narrow he wants to meet."

"I too would like to know if Duke Nortallion lives," Dartmallow said. "Tell him we will speak with him, but it must be at once. A journey interrupted is a poor beginning."

Quacaw took wing. "I will say it. I will go and say it."

Gray turned to Tana. "You should remain here. It could be a trick."

"I have to go. Fox wouldn't harm me. My father certainly wouldn't, either. I have to know."

An emptiness filled Gray's chest. "Very well."

Tana reached across, grasping Ninette's hand. "Oh, my friend, come with me. If the news is bad, you must stand at my side."

"Of course I will."

Led by a pair of Quacaw's murder, accompanied by a score of cavalry, Gray, Tana, Ninette, Vasps, and the marshal rode to the appointed place. Nutmeg and Maravilla bickered as they went, that being the way they loved each other best. They sloshed through puddles, Blunder sometimes wading up to his flanks. "Come in, come in," the water sang; the forest hummed around them; dragonflies drifted in every direction, murmuring indistinctly. A presentiment of disaster filled the Prince of Stallions, a fear of Tana being torn from him again. He fingered the vial Fetch Vadispur had given him.

The place where the river narrowed ran two hundred paces wide. On the far shore, half a furlong upstream, stood a single figure, his hair flaming red in the morning sun.

"To the sea!" the river sang in a multitude of voices. "To the sea for now I am free!"

"Great River Widfroth, we ask your aid," Vasps called. "The man on the far bank needs to cross."

A face appeared in the swirling waters, vanishing and reforming. "I am Widfroth and I must make haste. I go to the sea and cannot slow even if I tried. Perhaps I will embrace him if he tries to cross, carrying him with me."

Vasps gave the marshal a helpless shrug.

"Look," Dartmallow said, pointing toward Fox, who struggled to push a rough-timbered raft into the water. Once in, it nearly escaped him, and he fell, vanishing beneath the current. For an instant, it seemed he would be swept away, but he broke the surface and pulled himself onto the raft. It turned a rapid circle, hurrying along while he climbed to his feet, a pole in hand.

A desperate struggle ensued. Fox fought his way across, thrusting with all his strength while Tana bit her knuckles and Ninette bounced up and down shouting encouragement. When at last he neared the shore, Dartmallow's men waded out as far as they dared and dragged the craft to safety.

"*I am here,*" the raft said. Fox stumbled to land, drenched, hair matted to his shoulders, gasping and grinning. Despite Gray's dislike for the fellow, he couldn't help admiring his courage, but grimaced when Tana rushed to his side, her face flushed with excitement.

For several minutes, the prince could do nothing but catch his breath. At last, he straightened. "Duchess, we are well met."

"You've seen Father, haven't you? You've seen him! Is he well?"

His smile faded. "We've found no trace of him."

She turned, covering her face with her hands. "I thought . . ." Tears streamed down her cheeks. Gray stepped toward her, but Ninette reached her first. The two friends stood clutching hands.

"You risked your life to tell me this?" Tana cried. "Why did you come?"

"Perhaps we will find the duke, but whether we do or not, you are his only legitimate successor. If he has passed, you are heir to his extensive holdings. I came to tell you there is a place in Ruheen for you."

Her eyes widened. "I hadn't thought. I assumed . . ."

"You must come back with me. I have some of the duke's men waiting farther west. Morlane let me pass, but threatened to slay them if they journeyed deeper into the woods again. We will escort you."

Gray placed his hand on his sword, his voice cold with fury. "You won't take her."

Fox gave Gray a smug look. "I'm not here to duel. I once offered you a place in Ruheen. That still stands. Come with us, see her safely there. Ruheen will give us sanctuary, I'm certain of it. It's an honorable proposal, Prince, but it's the last time I'll make it."

"Do come, Gray, for I must surely go!" Tana said. "If my father lives, he will return to Ruheen. And if he doesn't . . . If he doesn't, I must keep his legacy."

Their eyes met. Gray's anger sputtered and died, leaving him speechless.

"My part in this matter is small, and that is to give warning," Marshal Dartmallow said. "Prince Lodan, you have chosen to side with the enemy. I regret that. You are a fine soldier. If you two accompany him, you will be our foes as well, barred from entering Animonea on pain of trial and swift justice. You can stay and become members of the Republic of Everything, or you can go, but the consequences are precise. We leave within the hour. I hope you will both be back at our camp before then." The marshal nodded at Fox. "Good fortune to you, Prince, so long as it does not involve my country."

Fox gave a slight bow of his head, and Dartmallow led his company back toward the camp, leaving only Topper and three cavalrymen to ensure that Fox recrossed the river.

"Give me a moment, Fox," Tana said.

"Very well." He strolled a short distance down the shoreline.

"Oh, Tana, must you leave?" Ninette cried, tears in her eyes. "Please don't go!"

Tana took her hands. "You can come with us. We can all be together!"

Ninette looked stricken. "I'm sorry, but I can't go there. I've been a puppet all my life. I can't live in a country where they enslave people."

"Can *you*, Tana?" Gray asked.

"Ninette, leave us please," Tana said. "If you ever change your mind, come to me in Ruheen. You've been a great friend in a time when I was dreadfully lonely."

The women hugged and Ninette rushed away, sobbing.

Tana wiped at her tears. Gray took her hands. "Don't do this. Don't place yourself under Fox's control. You don't know how cruel he can be."

She looked away. "Don't force me to make a choice. If my father is alive, Ruheen is where I will find him. Come with me."

Blunder put a muddy forepaw on his master's leg. "If you go, I will go too, Gray."

Gray stroked the pup's head. "You couldn't go there. In Ruheen you would lose the ability to speak."

"I will go anyway, Gray. We are a pack."

Gray bowed his head for a long moment, his whole world tumbling down. He lifted his eyes to Tana. "I've been a fool, haven't I, thinking you might love me?"

"Oh, Gray, I don't know! You've been such a good friend. You sought me and sheltered me when I needed it. That's why we should go together. Perhaps I could learn to love you then."

He shook his head, smiling bitterly. He had been a simpleton indeed, blinded by love. All Tana wanted was security. Sanctuary. "No, my lady. If you go to Ruheen, you won't ever learn to love me, for I won't leave Animonea. If nothing else, I won't desert this pup, who would give his life for me."

She looked at Blunder, her lip curling in contempt. "You speak of love and choose a *dog* over me? Father was right. This land is an abomination! I've hated it ever since I first crossed its borders. Why would you want to stay when you can be with real people?"

Her passion surprised him; his anger rose in return. "I'm not choosing Blunder over you. It's what he represents: unswerving loyalty, utter bravery. Look around you! Haven't you seen *anything* here? The majesty of it? The talking crows, the singing flowers, even the wolves. Was there ever such a country?"

She crossed her arms. "It's terrifying, all of it. I wish it had never been. I want somewhere safe and normal like En."

"En was never barbarous as Ruheen. You're going to a land whose gods require slavery and human sacrifice. It's worse than Faerie."

"Only the commoners are used thus. Even in En they served our purposes."

"Then I'm glad I'm here."

They glared at one another. Blunder whined at their feet. Tana turned away. "I don't want us to part in anger."

His chest felt hollow. How could she not love him, when he loved her so much? What could he say to make her stay?

He thought of the love potion Vadispur had given him. If he was going to use it, it must be now. A rapid, inner debate ran through him. He knew little of this Fetch, who looked so much like Jaunter. The Scythian said he was evil, the ghost of a dead man, but Tatters had spoken of his bizarre tenderness toward Jaunter, as if the transfusion of the warrior's blood had changed him. Vadispur himself claimed Jaunter had saved his life, making the Scythian's friends dear to him. In Faerie, magic potions were a reality, and if there was a chance that Tana could love him . . .

He made up his mind. "Let us at least drink a toast before you go."

She sighed. "If that's the way it must be."

"I have a water flask we can share. It will have to do."

He turned his back on her and petted Blunder. "Go to Ninette now, boy."

Blunder wagged his tail and trotted to where Ninette waited beside the cavalrymen. Still facing away from Tana, he slipped the vial from his pocket. The liquid shone golden in the sun. He unstoppered it carefully, poised to pour its contents into his open flask. It smelled sweet like sugar and roses. As he held the containers in his hands, his eyes fell on Ninette and Blunder, standing innocently together, too far away to see what he did.

He hesitated. Ninette had spoken of being a slave. Treg had tried to enslave her again. The duke wished to enslave the forest, to bend it to his will. The Elf King had enslaved his people through magic. If Gray used the potion to compel Tana to love him, wasn't he subjugating her? If he did, what was the difference between him and the duke? Or the sculptor?

He released the potion, letting it drop to the ground. The vial broke, its contents spilling onto the earth.

Gray turned and gave Tana the water flask. She took a sip. He did the same, tears stinging his eyes. Without another word, without looking back, she hurried to Fox Lodan. They conferred a moment and she transformed, her arms becoming wings, her feet, claws. A heron once more, she lifted in flight, gliding over the Widfroth. Gray watched until she landed on the other shore.

Fox approached him. "You're making a mistake, giving your allegiance to this rabble."

"The oaks told us Nortallion is dead."

Fox scowled. "I hope not. His being alive would make our return to Ruheen much easier."

"If he lives, you should beware. Once he no longer needs you, he may find an ambitious foreign prince a needless burden."

Fox smirked. "It's a chance worth taking. The duke understands the way of kings. I think I'll do well in his country." His eyes grew grim. "You and I have fought together, Gray. We've been allies, but if we meet again, it will be as enemies."

"Go back across the river," Gray said bitterly. "Get out of Animonea. Leave Morlane today or the trees will hang your carcass in the wind."

Fox laughed and strode to his raft. Gray turned toward Ninette and Blunder, not bothering to see if the prince survived the crossing.

Flies buzzed around the spot where the vial had broken. Walking past it, Gray heard a faint keening. He looked more closely. The flies who had drunk the potion lay whimpering on their backs, stricken and dying.

He shuddered. Sweat broke across his brow. Whoever Fetch Vadispur was, Gray hoped he had perished in the flood.

* * *

Fox and Tana rode beneath the mountains' feet, traveling west until they joined with the twenty-two survivors of the duke's army. The flood had failed to reach this part of Morlane, and the company traveled warily beneath the scowling faces of the great oaks, elms, and beeches. "*Get out!*" the trees rumbled as they passed. "*Never return!*" Spurred by such rancor they journeyed quickly, not daring to camp, resting only when they must.

Fox walked before the men, leading Dauntless, Tana astride the stallion's back. He regretted the horse would lose the power of speech in Ruheen, for he had always loved the animal, but that was the price of escaping this mad country, and he wouldn't part with it just so it could ramble on about grain, grass, and its love of running.

At twilight they struck a deer trail and followed it until they reached the Shadowshaw Pass. Stumbling with weariness, they crossed into Ruheen, where the forest abruptly thinned. Though the woods behind them continued its imprecations until they were out of earshot, the sparse trees before them neither spoke nor had faces. Eager to make camp, they marched around a foothill and found Duke Nortallion and Rick Spence awaiting them.

Fox grinned and raised a hand in greeting. "Your Grace! We thought you lost to us."

"The duke!" the soldiers cheered wearily.

"Father?" Tana slid from the horse's back, and nearly tripping on the uneven ground, rushed into his arms. "Oh, Father!" He gave her a perfunctory hug before taking her by the shoulders and moving her aside.

"I survived by the grace of the gods and the help of this man." The duke clapped a hand on Spence's arm and gave Fox a penetrating stare, wry amusement in eyes that appeared somehow different to the prince: colder, corpse-dead. Was their hue changed, or was it a trick of the fading light?

"Tell me everything that has happened, though I've guessed most of it," the duke commanded.

Fox did so, and Nortallion laughed heartily, strangely cheerful in the aftermath of a crushing defeat. "I could not have done better myself, Prince, siding with Dartmallow long enough to defeat Treg. You will be greatly rewarded for bringing my daughter home. Now Richard and I are famished."

Though they only had dried fish, two of the soldiers hurried forward to serve their lord. Despite Nortallion's odd demeanor, Fox was pleased. With the duke to vouch for him, his reception in Ruheen would be far better than hoped. He would need to be careful with Spence though, who had clearly saved Nortallion's life. Fox had never trusted the man; he would have to measure how far the duke's gratitude went toward the apish soldier.

* * *

They camped that night and set out again the following morning, the duke insisting Tana continue riding Dauntless.

"But Father," she said, "you should ride. You're limping."

"It's nothing, only the result of a minor wound. Lead the men, Fox. You've earned the right."

"Thank you, Your Grace." The prince moved ahead.

When Tana and Fox Lodan were beyond hearing, Spence spoke in the duke's ear. "What about the dame, Fetch?"

"Hsst!" Nortallion warned. "Use not that name again."

"Sorry. But what's the deal? I thought you wanted Tana poisoned."

"Only so Gray could revenge himself on her scorning him. It was a favor to him. For some reason he chose not to give her the potion. Surely he had the opportunity."

Spence bit his lip. "You thought Gray wanted her killed?"

Vadispur's dead eyes locked onto Spence's. "Of course he did, deep inside himself. She spurned him. What else could he want?"

"Why do you care what happens to Gray?"

"I told you I was connected to Jaunter's friends by the taking of his blood. I love those he loves; I hate those he hates. That includes you, Richard."

Spence suppressed an involuntary shiver, wondering if being Fetch's friend was any better than being his enemy. The guy acted half-crazy. "You said I could have her ring."

"Circumstances have changed. Eventually you will, but for now she might prove useful. Do not fear, my friend. We are on the road to glory. In Ruheen, I will accumulate power, and you will be by my side at every step."

Grinning triumphantly, Vadispur raised his voice to the men. "Have no fear, my valiant warriors! When we reach my holdings you will be rewarded in coins of silver for your unswerving service. We are defeated today. Tomorrow we will rise in victory."

They walked west toward Duke Nortallion's demesne.

* * *

For Dartmallow's army, the way out of Morlane proved arduous. With so much of the forest flooded, the company was forced to make their way along the slopes. When the mountains turned first to low hills, then to rolling woodlands, they traipsed through muddy ground for leagues, their only comfort the attitude of the woods, for the great trees watched them with obvious approval, their eyes half-lidded in contentment. Bumblebees and honeybees buzzed happily beside them; robins hopped and chirruped under the trees. A pair of squirrels screeched their raucous warnings from the branches. *"Who's this? Beware!"* The animals who had sheltered around Brythibain were already returning to their old abodes.

At last the warriors reached the Neprian Vale, exiting Morlane where they had first entered it. As they departed, Gray thought he glimpsed wolfish eyes watching from behind a row of thorns. He lifted his hand in farewell.

The way grew easier, and they were soon heading east on the Meadowlark Road. The horses picked up their pace, bickering happily with one another. Mockingbirds and swallows called down in irritation or curiosity. Deer ran from them, giving huffing cries of: *"Menflee, menflee."* The road encouraged them to follow it onward; the rocks and boulders watched them, stoic and unspeaking. Spring had passed while they were in the woods; full summer lay upon the land. Near the villages young crops grew in the fields, every stalk singing a song of growth and sunshine and the glory of rain.

To his surprise, Gray found the days pleasant. He and Ninette consoled one another on Tana's loss, but to his wonder it seemed Ninette missed her more than he did. Instead, he found bittersweet joy in his sorrow, perhaps because in the end it had been he, and not Tana, who had made the decision to part. Despite the failure of his desperate quest, it was a relief to finally reach its end. He wondered if he could turn it into a song or a poem. But it made him question himself. How much of his love had been for the woman he imagined rather than the real Tana, who hadn't been as strong as he thought her? The traits he had attributed to her seemed more those of someone like Joiwend. He tried not to think of his friend standing in the forest. He wondered if he would ever see her again.

He found Ninette both a joy and frustration. She was sweet as a child, unpretentious and naive, but temperamental. She said the most outrageous things and could cry at the song of a bird or the death of a beetle. She pouted at any slight, real or imagined, yet when she laughed, her joy brought smiles to everyone around her. She asked Vasps hundreds of questions, and the arbiter—clearly flattered by the wide-eyed attention of a beautiful young woman— answered her at great length. But Jaunter remained always close beside her.

One night, when they camped in a hollow a short distance from the road, and the companions sat around an impish fire, weary from the day's travel, their bellies full, Vasps Geometer voiced the question they had avoided. "What will each of you do now? You must decide soon, you see. The mission is over, and you are free to go where you will with the gratitude of our country. Will you stay in Animonea?"

"I won't go to Ruheen or back to Faerie," Russ said.

"Nor I," Ninette agreed.

Jaunter laughed. "There is no better country than this, where everything is a mostly friendly god. I too will stay if there is a place for my sagaris and a strong arm."

"Is there a need for scouts?" Master Tatters asked. "I reckon you can't always ask a tree where somebody went?"

"Our army is small. Good soldiers—and scouts—are needed," Dartmallow said. "Any of you would be welcomed."

"Fighting is all I know, but I'd like to try something else," Ninette said, "except I don't know what I would do."

Vasps raised an eyebrow. "You should go to the capitol at Raven-perch. I can give you names of tutors there. Preferably female ones; wherever you go, you will need your sword to fend off armies of suitors."

Ninette beamed and blushed, putting her hands over her face.

"I'm done with fighting," Russ said. "Animonea is a swell place, but I want to go home. I thought maybe I'd see the Omnifire. From what you say, maybe it can tell me what to do."

"The Omnifire is neither an oracle nor a god," Vasps said. "It does not speak to any save those who enter its flames. Those who have done so have always insisted on that point. It has no priests, no temples, but there are Caretakers. Perhaps they might offer guidance."

"I want to see," Russ said.

Vasps turned to Gray. "What about you, Prince of Stallions? What will you do?"

Gray furrowed his brow. "I don't know. I want to remain, but a prince is little use in a republic."

"Statecraft is valued in any government, especially a republic. A man willing to do the right thing, even at personal cost, has great worth."

Gray reddened, glad for the shadows, wondering if Vasps somehow knew about Tana and the love potion. "I'll do what I can."

They sat listening to the thrumming of the crickets, some calling for mates, some singing of the night. The moon rose, full and golden, his light shining down into the hollow, his voice booming across the land. "Good night, oh Animonea! Oh, beautiful night, oh lovely country. And I, its master, looming over all, tremendous in my glory, respected and cherished. Oh how you love me! How wondrous I am, your ruler and lord! Oh, give me adoration!"

From out of the darkness, Quacaw cawed, "Aww, nuts! Quiet be."

* * *

Two months later, when the waters had fully dried, Gray returned to Morlane, a Prince of Stallions riding a mare; but his title meant little to him now, and despite her stubbornness he was fond of Nutmeg. Blunder trotted beside him, bearing the spiked collar used to protect his throat from the fangs of wolves, still only half-grown, but now too large to ride in the saddle with Gray.

The forest was much changed; countless flocks of birds filled the woods with their cries; rabbits and deer roamed beneath the dense canopy; scattered patches of wildflowers bloomed in the clearings; moss grew on the trunks. The wind whispered its joy, and the branches curled upward, seeking the sunlight. Each morning Gray asked permission to travel, and the trees, remembering him, bowed their limbs in assent.

Following the direction given by a young ash, after some searching he finally dismounted in the glade.

She stood, stately, verdant, reaching toward the sky, her yellow blossoms fallen, replaced by graceful seed pods like lanterns.

"Hello, Joiwend. It's Gray. Can you hear me? The trees warned me you were still lost in reverie, but I had to find out for myself, to see if you wanted to be human again."

He waited, but she neither stirred nor spoke. No eyes looked out from her trunk; her branches drifted with the breeze.

He cleared his throat. "I'll tell you what happened after we left you, though I think you already know most of it."

He spoke to her as if she were a woman, his friend facing him with her compassionate heart and kindly gaze. He told of the battle and the appearance of Soonderkainen.

"We still don't know how he became what he is. We suspect you helped rouse him, but he never spoke. We know you woke the woods. If you hadn't, Treg would have won and Morlane would be mindless." His voice choked. "Thank you, my dear friend." He wiped his eyes with the back of his hand.

He told her what he had dared tell no one else: Fetch's potion, the temptation, the realization that his selfish desires had nearly killed Tana. He still didn't understand what the creature had wanted, only that it was evil.

He spent the night beneath her boughs, sleeping with his back against her trunk, hoping she would respond. With the morning light he woke, stiff and awkward, but filled with a strange sense of peace. She had not spoken; he hadn't dreamed any dreams he could recall, yet he felt she was safe and content, and that all would be well. He recognized it for what it was, the beauty of the spirit that was Joiwend—her loving kindness, her practical wisdom, her constant seeking after good. There were never enough people in the world like her.

He talked to her while he ate breakfast, then packed his gear and swung onto Nutmeg's saddle.

"I'll come back when I can, in the spring when the rivers thaw. I promise I will. I won't forget you."

Turning Nutmeg, he rode away.

"I am sorry Joiwend did not wake up, Gray," Blunder said. "I barked, but she did not listen."

"It was good of you to try."

"Where will we go now?"

"Home to Ravenperch. Marshal Dartmallow wants me to meet with the All-Council, something about troubles with willful geysers in the Southwest Rond."

"That is good, Gray. I like home. Everyone is kind there." The dog raised his head, sniffing the air. His ears perked. His eyes lit with excitement. "I smell a rabbit, Gray. I will hunt him. If I catch him we will eat well."

"Watch yourself," Gray said. "Beware the wolves."

But the pup had already vanished into the woods, following the scent.

ACKNOWLEDGEMENTS

As always, I must thank my wife, Kathryn, for her love and encouragement. Also, to Lon Mirll, Kreg Robertson, and Joe Trent, who provided priceless critiques that made this a much better book than it would otherwise have been. The friendship and insights of fellow writer, Dr. Robert Finegold, have impacted my life and my writing in ways beyond my own understanding. Scott Faris, skilled musician, brilliant record producer, and graphic artist, a friend and a light in this world, designed the beautiful cover along with artist extraordinaire, Bryan Burke.

The longer I work with Betsy Mitchell, the more I appreciate not only her amazing editorial skills, but her wonderful spirit and generosity. Thank you, Betsy, for helping me work through the book, most especially for advice that greatly improved the first chapter.

Unlike doctors, software designers, and engineers, there are no companies showing up at colleges to recruit people to write fantasy novels. This business requires a certain level of ego to believe that anyone, anywhere, would want to read what one has written. Mother always told me I was special, but in my humbler moments I am amazed that anyone is willing to spend the time reading my work. It is an honor beyond comprehension. So thank you to those who buy my books.

ABOUT THE AUTHOR

James Stoddard's short fiction and articles have appeared in publications such as *Amazing Stories* and *The Magazine of Fantasy and Science Fiction*. His short stories, *The Battle of York*, and *The First Editions*, appeared respectively in *The Year's Best SF 10*, published by Eos Books, and *The Year's Best Fantasy 9* from Tor. His novel, *The High House*, won the Compton Crook Award for best fantasy by a new novelist and was nominated for several other awards. He taught Sound Recording at the college level for many years before leaving to write fulltime. He and his wife live in West Texas.